THE KING'S RANGER

The King's Ranger Book 1

AC COBBLE

Cobble Publishing LLC

THE KING'S RANGER text copyright
© 2020 AC Cobble
ALL RIGHTS RESERVED
ISBN: 9781947683242
ASIN: B08BSWWVM5
Cobble Publishing LLC
Sugar Land, TX

FALVAR

EASTWATCH

YARROW

SPINESEND

THE DUCHY OF
·:· EERON ·:·
EASTERN
PROVINCE

Keep in Touch and Extra Content

※

You can find larger versions of the maps, series artwork, my newsletter, and other goodies at accobble.com.

I hope you enjoy the story, and when you're ready for more, **The Ranger's Path: The King's Ranger Book 2** out! Keep reading at the end of this book for a sneak peek.

Happy reading!
AC

Chapter One

Rew moved through the forest as quiet as a falling feather. He instinctively avoided the slender sticks and the first dry leaves of autumn that scattered across his path. His tall, leather boots padded across the soil without making a mark. He passed between the branches and boughs of the trees as effortlessly as the wind. In the coming months, brittle leaves would blanket the forest floor, and such silent stalking would be impossible even for him, but he did it now without thought.

He paused. Ten yards in front of him, a small brown- and gray-furred body leapt off a tree and scurried across the forest floor. A squirrel collecting acorns. Rew watched it, noting its unworried movement, and waited for it to gather its nut and vanish back up the trunk of a towering oak. When the squirrel climbed out of view, he moved again, passing unnoticed through the forest, his boots leaving no disturbance, no sign that the ranger had been there.

For another two hours, he trotted beneath the autumn canopy, the dapple light that reached the forest floor reflecting the brilliant reds, oranges, and yellows that burst amongst the green leaves like fireworks at the new year. Periodic stands of stoic pines held firm, their boughs the same green they were in the spring, the same green that they would be in the heart of winter. They were unchanging, like him, while the forest changed around them.

He stopped and knelt. A nearly invisible track passed through the forest, a deer trail going from the stream that cut along the base of the ridge into the deeper reaches of the woods. Gently, he moved aside leaves and sticks, placing them carefully out of the way as he studied the soft dirt. In a half-crouch, he moved along, following the tracks.

Impressions from hooves dotted the forest floor. Some were old. Some were recent. They showed the regular passage of large animals. There were other tracks intermixed from smaller animals, taking advantage of the work the deer did keeping the pathway through the forest clear.

And there, Rew found what he was looking for. An impression of four curled toes. He crab-walked along, confirming his hunch that the four-toed creature, with its curious, loping gait, followed the path of the deer. The ranger touched the ground, feeling the moisture and the depth of the tracks. They were recent, left two or three hours prior, no more.

Rew moved off the trail the forest creatures had left and, a dozen yards away, found another set of tracks. More impressions from toes and the balls of the feet, no heels. His quarry was moving quickly, jogging along the front halves of their feet. They weren't just following the deer's trail. They had a scent. He moved another dozen yards off the forest trail and found a third set of the four-toed impressions. A pack on the hunt.

He glanced up at the brightly colored canopy above him, checking the progression of the sun. It was mid-afternoon with another three hours of sunlight left. His quarry would pause to feast if they caught their prey, but otherwise, there was not enough time for him to catch up before nightfall. He had the tracks, though. The ranger was on the hunt.

Rew reached over his shoulder and checked the plain, wooden hilt of his longsword, rattling it to make sure he could draw it cleanly. He shifted the pack on his back, moving the cloak he'd bundled and tied to the bottom so it was clear of the bone-handled hunting knife hanging from his belt. He bent and felt the two daggers that stuck up from the sides of his calf-high leather boots.

Weapons in place, secure but ready to draw, he moved back to the deer trail and started along it, walking briskly, but not so fast that he couldn't maintain stealth. He covered ground quickly, untiring. He was at home in the forest and spent nearly every day moving through the citadel of oak and pine. He could maintain the ground-eating pace from dawn to dusk if he needed to, but after an hour, he stopped.

He'd found the corpse of a buck, or what was left of it. Its skin, torn and discarded, lay in stomach-churning piles. Bones, stripped of meat and then cracked and sucked clean of marrow, were tossed on top. The skull had been shattered like the shell of a nut and the brains had been scooped out. One antler was still attached, the other was missing. Rew saw dark blood on the tip of the antler, and despite the grim scene, his lips curled upward. The animal had died messily but not without a fight.

Walking in expanding circles, he spent several minutes searching the rest of the site then moved on, forcing down the uncomfortable feeling that in the chaotic swirl of tracks, there were impressions for more feet than he would have guessed. It was difficult to count, not knowing how long the creatures had been at the kill site, but he'd seen such scenes before. Something felt off about this one.

Narjags, bestial creatures that they were, had feasted upon the raw flesh and then moved on. It was unusual behavior for them. They'd eat anything that had a beating heart—deer, squirrel, or man—and preferred their supper while that heart still beat. They were naturally lazy, though, and it was surprising they hadn't paused to rest, bellies filled with fresh meat and perhaps some of the foul liquor they were known to distill.

Rew ranged back and forth across the trail as he left the kill site. He tallied the number of narjags that had departed and found there were too many. Too many to be traveling in a pack together. He hurried his pace, overcoming his trepidation with determination to catch up, to find his quarry.

The group he tracked was in a rush, but to where and why? He couldn't imagine the narjags had somewhere to be. That meant they were running from something, but it wasn't him. He hadn't yet encountered this party, and he'd seen no other tracks on their trail. The wind was from the west, so there was no chance the awful creatures would have caught his scent, or that of any other pursuer. Narjags were full of bluster as long as they thought they had the advantage, so why run unless they knew what was behind them?

His face twisting in a grimace, Rew glanced back the way he'd come, but he sensed nothing. The forest was calm, filled with the sounds of small life and an autumn breeze that was just enough to cut the heat from the bright, sunny day. He shook his head and kept going. What answers he would find, he would find ahead.

Rew stripped the bark off a long, straight stick. With his hunting knife, he'd already whittled the end into a sharp point. He knelt by the brace of skinned rabbits he'd set on the dirt beside his campfire. They were plump ones, fat from eating the summer's bounty. It was more meat than he could eat, and he hated to take more from the forest than he needed, but if he still had meat in the morning, he could break his fast with it.

If he had meat left in the morning.

He glanced around the forest. It was two hours past sunset now and dark. Dark and quiet. Most of the animals that lived beneath the trees had retired for the day, and their nocturnal brethren had not yet emerged. Somewhere out there was a party of narjags, but it seemed they were not disturbing the life around him. Incredulously, even after they'd been delayed feasting on the buck and after he continued hunting after the sun set, he had not caught them.

Narjags could be fast in short bursts, their muscular but squat legs propelling them in lopping leaps, but they tended to have low stamina and couldn't cover long distances quickly. The behavior of this party was unsettling. They hadn't paused after their kill, and they'd kept moving even after dark. Rew had no idea what could be motivating them.

Grunting, the ranger picked up his newly fashioned skewer and worked it through the two skinned rabbits, sticking them head-to-tail on the slender wood and then setting the skewer over his fire, suspending it in the joints of thicker branches that he'd knocked down into the dirt.

The rabbits would cook there, their flesh warming, getting crispy on the outside, tender in the middle. Their fat would heat and drip, igniting in the fire. The scent would make his stomach rumble, and he hoped, spread on the air like a banner to the narjags he pursued.

The creatures were slow-witted and lazy, but they had excellent noses. From leagues away, if the wind blew toward them, they could detect the scent of cooking meat. They were apt to eat flesh raw when left to their own devices, but they wouldn't turn down a cooked meal. And by cooking it, he could spread the scent across several leagues of forest. The narjags would come to him if they smelled it. They would come, for the rabbit and for him, unless they were frightened or too far away.

He stood and drew his longsword from where he'd sat it beside his pack. He stuck the blade into the dirt a pace away and, with his hunting knife, began to slice off bites from a fist-sized apple. He ate the apple and waited, occasionally turning his skewer so the rabbits cooked evenly, watching as their juices dripped into the fire, popping, burning, and rising on the smoke.

Rew waited until he began to worry that his rabbits were going to burn, and he began wondering if he should pull them off the fire before they were overcooked. Maybe, even though the narjags had been headed northeast for hours, the creatures had turned. He'd estimated they would be downwind from his campsite, but he could have been wrong.

Then, moments before he gave up, he heard a muffled snort and the crunch of bare feet stepping on fallen leaves. Rew sliced another hunk from his apple and popped it into his mouth, chewing loudly.

His eyes were on his fire, but his focus was on what was happening outside the circle of light it provided. In a normal party of narjags, there would only be four or five of them. That was as many as could travel together without their cantankerous natures getting the best of them and the group fracturing into violence. In years past, when the Dark Kind were more common in the forest, it wasn't unusual to find bodies of narjags killed by their companions and left to rot.

Rew's heart began to beat faster as he heard their movement around him. As he'd estimated from their tracks, there were more than four or five. Too many to identify with certainty just from their sounds. As they spread around him, he cursed his sloppiness. He'd hoped he was wrong, that he'd somehow over-counted the footprints he'd seen, but he'd known that wasn't the case. Known, yes, but that wasn't the same as hearing the creatures work to slowly surround him. A sliver of worry crept down his spine, and he chastised himself for not returning to town to gather another ranger. He'd been more concerned with the narjags escaping, but that may have been a mistake. He carved another slice from the apple and tossed the core into the fire. Blessed Mother, why were so many of them traveling together?

Shuffling quietly, they surrounded him. His night vision was weakened from his fire, so he couldn't risk rushing into the forest to seek them out or trying to break through the circle they'd formed. He had to let them come to him, to come into the light. Steeling himself, he waited.

When they finally did come, they came in a wave, a muffled growl his only warning.

Rew reached out with his open hand, grasped the wooden hilt of his longsword, and pulled it free of the dirt, spinning as he did and meeting a rushing narjag with his steel.

Squat, muscular, and only as tall as the middle of his chest, the narjag was clothed in a filthy loincloth and a tattered cape it must have looted from some long-dead traveler. It carried a short spear that wasn't more than a sharpened stake.

Rew thrust with his longsword, taking the narjag directly in the throat. Then, he pivoted, using his hunting knife to catch and deflect a blow from a second one of the creatures. He turned its rusty shortsword aside and ripped his longsword free of the first. He bashed the second narjag with the hilt of his blade, the heavy, steel pommel crunching bone as it crashed against the small monster's forehead. Wailing in pain, the narjag backpedaled, and Rew stepped forward to pursue.

He was knocked to his knees when a heavy body slammed into his back, clutching fingers grasping at him, foul breath blowing against the side of his face as he turned his head. Rotten teeth clacked shut beside his ear, barely missing his neck. Stabbing back with his hunting knife, Rew blindly caught flesh and bone. Dark, ichorous blood spilled onto his shoulder from the wounded narjag.

He let go of the bone hilt of his knife and grabbed at the narjag, snatching it by the arm. He threw it forward, grunting in exertion as he flung the heavy body into the path of two others that were charging at him.

One tried to leap its Dark Kind brethren but tripped as the thrown narjag flailed its arms and legs wildly. The second creature veered around, and Rew surged off his knees, lashing at it with his longsword and buying himself space to glance behind where three more narjags were circling his fire.

Rew attacked furiously, forcing the narjags away, and then bent to rip his hunting knife free of the injured one that had jumped onto his back. In the same motion, he slashed the blade across the neck of the narjag that had tripped coming at him, then turning and swinging wildly, he clipped the second one in front of him, cracking its skull and felling it. He skipped to the side, shifting to adjust to the three that had now circled the fire. His breath was coming fast, but he was uninjured, and he'd made some progress.

Four narjags dead, one injured, three hale. He heard a rush of feet in the forest still outside of the light of his fire. Not three uninjured. There were more of them.

He charged.

One narjag flung a rock-bladed hatchet at him, but Rew knocked it aside with his longsword. He smashed the heel of his boot into the face of the hatchet-thrower. He caught a spear on the edge of his hunting knife. Then, with an overhand chop, he brought his longsword down on the skull of the spear-wielder. He reversed his grip on his hunting knife and stabbed it into the neck of another narjag that was attempting to sneak up on him. It squealed in surprise and pain, and he yanked the blade free in a shower of dark blood. Whipping his longsword free from the narjag's skull, he swung backhanded and hacked into the creature he'd kicked.

Three more down. He turned, seeing the wounded narjag now flanked by two more.

Rew paused. Behind the three warriors, stood another narjag. It was taller by a head than its companions, and instead of crude weapons, it hefted an amber-tipped staff.

Rew blinked. A shaman? He'd never seen one before, but he'd heard stories about narjags being taught rudimentary magic by the spellcasters who conjured them. Notes scrawled in unofficial histories said it was common two hundred years ago, when the Dark Kind had flooded into the land, but it had been two hundred years since any spellcaster had allied with the Dark Kind. Could a feral species like the narjags truly wield magic? Could they teach themselves?

Rew waited, wondering, but if the creature had spells to cast, it did not. Instead, it aimed its staff at him and shouted in the guttural language of the Dark Kind. The three surviving warriors attacked.

Rew stepped forward and wheeled his longsword above his head, lashing it in front of him like he was scything wheat. Two of the narjags couldn't avoid the powerful blow, and the hard edge of the steel longsword burst through the body of the first and into the second, taking it in the head and crushing bone and cutting flesh. The third narjag, the one that was already injured, lurched out of the way, falling onto the ground and clutching at the black blood that poured from its wounds.

Rew left it and charged the shaman. The big narjag raised its staff above its head, howling, eyes bright with madness. He kicked his boot into its chest, knocking the narjag onto its back.

Screeching, the creature kept its gaze on him, screaming what he thought were most likely obscenities, because they certainly weren't a spell. Nothing happened. The creature's staff did not blaze with infernal power. No boiling liquid fire came shooting at him. No creatures were summoned. Nothing at all.

Rew waited for half a dozen heartbeats to make sure no slow-building spell was forming, and when still nothing happened, he stepped forward and plunged his longsword into the narjag's chest, silencing it. Turning, he was prepared to meet the last one, the one that had dodged his blow, but it was gone.

Looking around the clearing he'd chosen as his campsite, Rew felt a surge of uneasy confusion. Narjags didn't travel in large groups, and they didn't run. They didn't have shamans. At least, they hadn't in his lifetime.

Blessed Mother, what was going on?

Chapter Two

"Senior Ranger," greeted a man, glancing up from where he was repairing a tear in a patchwork woolen cloak. "You think the commandant will free up some extra funds this year? I've been wearing the same cloak since I began this posting."

"Aye, and it's kept you warm. Must be a nice cloak, too, if it's almost as old as I am," said Rew with a wink. "We do have some spares in the storage room, but I'm not sure they match your mature sense of style."

The ranger at the table snorted. "They don't make them like they used to, you mean?"

Rew shrugged. "You're the best judge of that, though, I've heard that past a certain age the memory gets a little foggy. When I look at that thing, I see more patch than I do cloak. Could it be that in all of those years you've forgotten your old cloak isn't any better crafted than my new one? Yours certainly seems to need repair often enough."

The other man grinned, placed one hand on his cloak and raised his needle and thread in the other. "Some things have aged well since this was first sewn, improved even. Maybe you'd like me to give you a little stitch, and see what I can do for you?"

Rew rolled his eyes and walked to the other side of the table from the man. He laid out the amber-capped staff he'd taken from the narjag shaman, a crudely constructed pack he'd found dropped in the woods outside his campsite, and a necklace made of shriveled bits of flesh he'd taken from the shaman's neck. "What do you make of these, Tate?"

Tate pushed his cloak and needle aside and leaned over the items. "Unusual. These are from the narjag party, the one Farmer Bartrim reported?"

"They are," confirmed Rew.

Tate stood, rubbing at the white stubble on his chin. "Quite strange to see narjags with something other than rudimentary weapons and clothing, unless they've been looted from their victims. Is that human or narjag flesh on the necklace?"

"Narjag ears, I think," answered Rew, "though, in their condition, they could be anything."

"I've never seen the like, and the only time I've heard of a narjag with artifacts like this it was a shaman," said Tate, looking up to meet Rew's gaze. "You chased down a narjag shaman? It's been years since anyone has seen one. Before my time, even."

Rew shrugged. "I don't know. It had the look of a shaman, but it didn't cast a spell against me. I gave it the opportunity. It yelled at me a bit in the Dark Kind tongue, and then I killed it. I don't know the nature of Dark Kind spellcasting, but a human would have had time to get a spell off."

Tate blinked at him, shaking his head.

"I would have struck before it actually cast its spell," assured Rew. "I had to wait to see if it had the capability."

The other ranger grunted. "But it did nothing except curse at you?"

"Nothing," agreed Rew.

Tate brushed back a lock of silver-white hair then hesitantly opened the pack. He peered inside, shuffled through the contents, and brought out a half-empty gourd. He sniffed it and scowled, shoving the gourd back into the pack.

He said, "Nothing remarkable in here. A container for that

awful liquor they drink. Some tools they crafted themselves, a couple of rocks. No food, which isn't surprising. Narjags feast or famine. A needle but no thread. Stolen, I imagine. Looks a bit rusty. Maybe it's been some time since they took it. A whetstone, probably stolen too, along with this little hand mirror. Doesn't look like they found that too long ago, but we've had no recent reports of attacks, have we? I suppose this is what a pack of narjags think is their valuables. It was in the woods, you said?"

"They dropped it before attacking me," said Rew.

"Well, the pack doesn't seem unusual, though it's odd one of the party was able to hold onto this stuff without the rest of them fighting over it," said Tate, fiddling with the items. "The necklace and the staff do sound like what the shamans were purported to carry, but if it was a true shaman, I agree it ought to have tried something on you. Maybe it's a sign of leadership rather than magical might?"

"There's something I'm missing here," replied Rew. "It was a large party. Nearly a dozen of them, counting the shaman, or whatever it was. That's twice the size we were seeing two years ago when the Dark Kind last passed through the forest, and these narjags were going somewhere as if they were in a hurry. That's the thing, Tate. They were in a hurry, but I still managed to catch up to them after getting Bartrim's report two days ago. Why were they moving so quickly now, and where have they been the last two days?"

"Narjags in a hurry?" asked Tate skeptically. "There have been rumors that the conjurers trained some of the Dark Kind as shamans years ago, but I don't think I've ever heard of narjags going somewhere in a hurry. Not unless there's a bloody piece of meat at the end of the journey."

"I'll walk you through from the beginning, from when I first found the tracks," said Rew. "I want to hear what you think in case I missed something. You've been out in this wilderness three times as long as the rest of us. In over three decades of service, have you ever seen anything like it?"

"Narjags traveling in larger groups than usual, sure, I've seen that," replied Tate, sitting back down at the table, his eyes still on the artifacts. "Narjags acting unusual or carrying odd items, of course. They pick up things, as you know, items from people they've encountered and killed, rubbish they've stumbled across. I've seen them adorned with plenty of strange trinkets. A shaman, though, nah, I've never seen one. Never heard of anyone else seeing one, either. Not even the old rangers when I first started had seen that. They spoke about it, though, like there had been shamans on the field during the last war against the Dark Kind. That's, ah, fifty years back, Rew. The wilderness has been clean of such since then. I will say it appears that whatever these talismans are meant to be, the narjags made them themselves. The staff is crude like the weapons they use, and I can't imagine any person going and collecting narjag ears."

Rew rubbed his chin while both men looked at the artifacts on the table. "Could it be, ah, narjag fashion? Some chieftain of theirs trying to set himself apart?"

Tate shrugged. "Could be."

Sighing, Rew said, "Pack them up and put them in the post to Yarrow, will you? I'd like to see what the baron's arcanist has to say about these. Maybe they're junk, but…"

"You never know," finished Tate, nodding. "I agree, Senior Ranger, it's best to get another opinion. If the Dark Kind have regained the ability to cast spells… I don't suppose you followed their tracks back and saw what they've been up to between Bartrim's farm and where you caught them?"

"Not yet," replied Rew. "With a larger party than normal, I figured I would bring someone with me in case we stumble across more of them. If it's the beginning of another migration, we'll need to start going out in pairs, me included. You fancy a quick jaunt into the wilderness tomorrow morning?"

Tate shook his head. He put a hand on his half-repaired cloak. "I've got a bit of work to finish here."

Rew raised a hand, thinking of reaching across to the older

man, but he dropped it. "Of course. You finish what you need to. Who else is in at the moment?"

"Just you and me," replied Tate. "Ang and Vurcell haven't returned from Yarrow, but they should be back within a day or two unless Vurcell got lost in the taverns again. Blythe took the new kid out to the southern range, trying to teach him a few things, I suppose."

"Jon has been here a year," remarked Rew dryly. "He's not new any longer, and he's two or three winters past twenty. Just because you're old doesn't mean everyone else is a kid."

"When he stops acting new, I'll stop calling him new," responded Tate, grinning.

"You could help train him," suggested Rew.

"Blythe'll sort him out," claimed Tate. "I trained her the best I can train anyone. What I know, she knows. Besides, you're the man in charge. You oughta be the one holding the kid's hand."

Rew snorted and rubbed his chin, feeling his beard and the rough stubble on his neck. "Time for me to see the barber, I think, and perhaps take a good long soak in the baths. You'll get these artifacts posted? Put in a note for the arcanist about what we're after. That daft bastard'll never send a response if we don't tell him we're waiting on one. If you need me—"

"I've sent a post before, Senior Ranger, and I know you'll be at the baths and then the Oak & Ash Inn for an ale," interrupted Tate. The older ranger stood, stretched, and stopped short of his full height, a grimace on his face. He held his side uncomfortably. "All this talk of narjag shamans got me distracted. Before you go, there's something I need to show you."

The two rangers peered at three youths locked on the other side of a wall of thick, iron bars.

"Theft?" asked Rew.

"Aye," said Tate. "Down at the Oak & Ash. Anne found them

behind the bar dipping their fingers into her coin jars. She started shouting and the patrons at the inn rushed these three and held them until Blythe and I got there. We locked them up yesterday, and they're still not talking. They're not saying anything I want to hear about, at least. I haven't been able to figure out who they are or where they came from."

Frowning, Rew studied the three younglings. A boy and two girls. They looked back sullenly as the senior ranger observed them. It went without saying that they weren't local. Both Rew and Tate knew every man, woman, and child in the territory. It wasn't often that Eastwatch, on the far fringe of the kingdom, drew strangers. No one passed through Eastwatch. There was nowhere to go, only wilderness behind the boundaries of the village. When someone came to Eastwatch, they had a reason for doing so.

"When are we going to be let out of here?" demanded the boy.

Or a man, supposed Rew. The boy certainly had the size of a man, though the ranger guessed the boy only had seventeen or eighteen winters under his belt. The two girls had one or two less, he figured.

"Are you both deaf?" asked the boy, rising to his feet, unconsciously dusting a bit of straw from his trousers. He stared directly at Rew, taking an aggressive stance. "I'll tell you like I told the other. On the authority of Baron Fedgley, release us immediately!"

"We report to the king, lad, not the baron," replied Rew, watching the boy. "Besides, it's Yarrow, Baron Worgon's town, that is closest to us. Not even peddlers make their way to the territory from Fedgley's Falvar. Where are you from, lad? How did you get here?"

"Contact Baron Fedgley," said the youth, stepping toward the bars. "He'll explain all, and he'll demand our release. Eastwatch may not fall under his jurisdiction, but he's a nobleman—a baron."

The boy was a big lad, eleven, twelve stone of what looked to be solid muscle and bone. He had a shock of shoulder-length, dark brown hair that he brushed from his eyes when he saw Rew studying him. His arms were thick, like that of a laborer, but he held himself with a confidence unusual for one on the wrong side of the bars of a jail cell. A soldier, perhaps, but the boy's hands bore no scars that would have been earned in work or battle. Rew couldn't see well enough in the low light of the jail to tell if there were callouses from the hilt of a sword on the boy's palms.

"Why should I ask Baron Fedgley about you when I've got you right here?" questioned Rew. "This is no time to be stubborn, lad. Answer our questions, and we can get this sorted."

The youth shifted, and one of the girls moved to stand beside him. She was dark haired as well. The boy's sister, suspected Rew. She was pretty and wearing a dress cut for travel that certainly wasn't bought with a mean laborer's wage. Were they nobles? They had the look and the attitude, but Rew couldn't fathom what they would be doing in Eastwatch alone. A noble in the eastern territory without an escort was even more unusual than a party of narjags led by a shaman. Rew drew a deep breath and let it out slowly, glancing at Tate out of the corner of his eye. The white-haired ranger nodded understanding. The younglings were hiding something.

"We're in the employ of Baron Fedgley," murmured the brown-haired girl. "Allow us to write him a letter, and I'm certain he'll send a man to explain all. It is true, we… we were attempting to secure some funds from the inn, but restitution can be made. Baron Fedgley will pay whatever is owed. We just need to reach him. It's important. There are… We have a mission, and we cannot be delayed."

"It would take two weeks to get a letter to Fedgley," drawled Rew, leaning forward against the bars of the cell. "That's two weeks to get it there and two weeks to get a response back. If you cannot be delayed, then let's clear this up right now. Who are you, and what are you doing in Eastwatch?"

"Two weeks…" muttered the dark-haired girl. She shot a look

behind her at the second girl, a slender blonde who glanced away uncomfortably. "We thought... we thought we were closer to Falvar. You are certain it is two weeks?"

Rew put his hands on his hips. "Look, I've been out on patrol the last few days and I want nothing more than a hot bath and a cold ale. Yes, I am certain it is a two-week journey to Falvar. We can talk now, or we can talk in the morning. It's up to you, but if we're to talk now, you'd best get started."

"If it's... if it's two weeks to Falvar, then let us serve our punishment," said the boy. "We didn't actually take anything, and it's foolish to hold us here any longer than necessary. Petty theft is what, a single lash? I'll take it for the group, and I swear to you, we'll leave Eastwatch the moment you allow us. We wanted funds for our travel, but we can make do without them. We will not cause any further trouble for you or the people of Eastwatch. Let us go, Ranger, and you'll never see us again."

Rew shook his head. "You're on the king's land, lad. Punishment for petty theft is a finger, and you're lucky you didn't get much of that coin, or we'd be talking about taking off a hand."

The boy blanched, and his sister clutched his arm. She stammered, "But-but we didn't even take anything!"

"You tried, lass, and the king's law is based on intent," explained Rew.

"Punishment is a finger or restitution," said the blonde from where she was still sitting in the corner. "A letter to Baron Fedgley, and he'll make it square. What is required, two, three times the value of the items we attempted to steal? There is no need to start chopping fingers off. Look, maybe you can send us to the baron and one of your rangers can accompany us so you're assured we won't slip away. I'm certain the baron will compensate you for the trouble, and it'd make you look good in the eyes of a prominent nobleman. I imagine that'd be nice, being owed a favor by such a man. I've no doubt that he'll grant you any boon you ask of him."

The blonde glanced at the backs of the brother and sister, if unsure whether what she said was true, but the siblings nodded emphatically.

Rew shrugged. "We're not releasing you that easy, I'm afraid. We can send Fedgley a note and see what he says. Restitution will include the bill for keeping you here, you understand? A month's worth of room and board isn't in my budget."

"He'll pay," said the boy.

At the same time his sister insisted, "We cannot wait a month."

The boy's fists clenched, and Rew saw a tremor in the young man's jaw, but the youth didn't argue.

"We cannot wait a month," repeated the girl. "It is imperative you release us tomorrow, if not today. We have critical information the baron needs to hear. Lives are at stake, Ranger."

"You've already admitted to the attempted theft," remarked Rew. "There's no doubt you're guilty. You want me to take a finger and let you go? If you don't want to talk, that's the quickest way to resolve this."

The girl swallowed uncomfortably, but she didn't say no. She met Rew's gaze, her hands clasped at her waist, fidgeting, as if she was counting her fingers. Beside Rew, Tate's breathing quickened.

In the back corner, the blonde spoke up again, "We'll ask the innkeeper for leniency. That's allowed under the law, is it not?"

Rew leaned to the side to look around the other two at the girl in the back. "No, lass. There's no provision under the king's law for leniency to be granted by a victim."

"But you are the King's Ranger, yes?" she asked.

Rew nodded, crossing his arms over his chest.

"Then it is your law that applies in Eastwatch," she argued. "Rangers are empowered to adjust to the circumstances, are they not? I was told that the King's Rangers were a law unto themselves."

"There's a little truth to that, but the allowance only exists because we're so remote," Rew told the younglings. "The king understands there are times rangers must act to protect the realm, and sometimes those decisions must be made rapidly. The allowance is in place for emergencies, not to avoid enforcing the established law."

"The allowance may be in place for other circumstances, but it is in place," insisted the blonde. "We shall ask the innkeeper for leniency, unless you refuse to show that small bit of mercy for an attempted petty theft. Ranger, we have no more desire to stay in the territory than you have for us to be here. You don't seem a cruel man, and I can't imagine you relish the idea of chopping a young girl's finger off. The easiest way for all parties to be satisfied is to ask the innkeeper for leniency. If she requires more than our words, the baron will pay whatever she asks."

Rew could feel Tate beside him. The older man was tense, uncomfortable with the idea of taking a finger from any of these three. It was the law, and the punishment was clear, but the blonde had it right as well. Rew was the King's Ranger. He'd been granted authority to make his own decisions about when the letter of the law ought to be applied, and that authority existed regardless of the circumstances. Rew knew the king wouldn't give a fig about how he applied the law in the case of an attempted theft by a few youths.

"I'll ask the innkeeper if she'll grant leniency," allowed Rew after a long pause. The three in the cell suddenly relaxed, obviously relieved that there may be a solution to their predicament. "Tell me who you are, and what you're doing here, and perhaps that will help her come to a decision."

"We… we cannot," said the dark-haired girl. "We are at risk, and you will be as well if you do not release us. There are bad men looking for us, and there could be trouble for anyone who has seen us and knows the truth."

"Are you threatening me, lass?" wondered Rew.

"No, not at all," said the girl. "There are people after us, and they will stop at nothing, including violence. It's not a threat, Ranger. We only want to leave, but these others…"

Rew scratched at his neck, muttering about the itchy prickles there and wondering if it was getting too late to see the barber. He let his hand drop. "I will ask for leniency, and I will let you know what the innkeeper says in the morning."

He and Tate left the three in the cell. The two men walked back out into the common room of the ranger station. Tate showed Rew three packs which had been seized from the younglings. They contained changes of clothes, a few items for travel, and not much else. They had only common provisions that could be purchased anywhere. There was nothing that would identify the youths. After checking the third pack, Rew grunted. Their supply of rations was shockingly low.

"Well, we know why they were trying to steal," remarked Rew, shaking a nearly empty bag of dried beans before stuffing it back into the pack.

"You know Anne will grant leniency if you tell her you're going to chop off one of their fingers," responded the white-haired ranger. "What are you playing at, Rew?"

Rew grinned. "Anne would grant leniency and loan them the contents of her coin purse if she thought it'd help someone in need. I have no intention of hacking off one of their fingers, Tate. I just wanted to pressure them a little to see what they'd say."

Tate snorted. "Which was nothing."

"Three youths not from Eastwatch and if I had to guess, not here on purpose either," Rew mused. "They certainly did not come from Falvar, which means they must have arrived on the road from Yarrow. The theft doesn't surprise me, and I can hardly blame them," he said, tossing the pack down on the table. "They're out of coin and food. They probably planned to spend what they stole on fresh supplies and then leave just as they told us. A crime of necessity, you could say. But why? Why are they here, coinless and with nothing to eat, at the edge of the realm? You saw them. They're not urchins. No one comes to Eastwatch without a reason. I worry they are…"

"They could be," replied Tate with a shrug. "But why no entourage? Go on, now. Get your bath and your ale. I've got my mending to finish, and I can watch things here until you return. If anyone comes for them, they'll have to go through me. Maybe another night in the cell will soften them up, and they'll be ready to talk in the morning. Or if we let them out and give them a few supplies, we'll gain their trust, and they'll tell us what they've gotten into. One thing I did believe, Rew, they spoke the truth when they said they were scared."

"Scared, aye, but of what?" asked Rew, scratching at the stubble on his neck again.

Chapter Three

Anne, the proprietor of the Oak & Ash Inn, filled a tankard full of ale for him the moment she saw him enter the common room. She sat it on the table and said, "I've got a shank of goat on the spit and vegetable soup in the pot."

"Vegetable soup," Rew replied, cringing at the memory of the scene the night before.

His two rabbits had been knocked from their rack by the falling body of a dead narjag. The foul creature had landed half in the fire, and the stench of burnt narjag was exactly as horrible as he would have guessed. The narjag's black blood had splattered across the singed flesh of the rabbits, and Rew hadn't been able to eat since then. Even after scrubbing himself with the pungent soap at the ranger station and letting the village barber lather his neck and scalp, Rew still had the awful scent of roasted Dark Kind stuck in his nostrils.

The innkeeper, seeing his expression, smacked him on the shoulder. "It's fresh goat. It's not as bad as that."

He grinned apologetically, "Sorry, Anne, I was thinking of last night. There was a bit of rough business out in the wilderness. There was a terrible… Ah, I can't stomach any meat just yet."

"I suppose you heard about our own rough business here?" she asked him.

"The thieves?"

She nodded.

"I saw them at the ranger station before I came here," he said, "and they didn't answer a single one of my questions. Tate's watching them, and I'll take over when I'm done here. There's something not right with those three, but I hate to hold them for an attempted petty theft. They've asked for your leniency. What do you think?"

"What's the punishment if I don't grant leniency?" wondered Anne.

Rew held up a single finger and wiggled it.

She shook her head, scowling. "Let them go."

"I figured you'd say as much." He picked up his ale and sipped it.

"You've already released them?" she asked.

"Not yet," he admitted. "They're lying, trying to hide why they're here, what they're doing, and who they are. I can't fathom a reason for it. They're not professional thieves. They're not assassins. What could they be involved in they wouldn't tell a ranger in the territory? No one passes through Eastwatch. You only come here for a reason, and I can't figure what theirs is."

"You sure they're not career thieves?" asked Anne, pulling out a chair and settling down across from him. "Wouldn't be the first time an innocent-looking face hid a darkness in the soul. Mayhaps they thought there would be easy pickings here in the territory. No baron's men, no city watch, that sort of thing. I'll admit I've never been careful with my coin. Everyone knows it's there, but in ten years, no local has stolen from me. King's Sake, half of my customers dig in those jars themselves to make change when I'm busy."

Rew sipped his ale and thought. "These younglings don't look the part of career criminals, and the thieves' guilds know to avoid the territories. It's true we don't have proper guards like the cities, but professionals are savvy enough to not risk a hanging. The king's law is stricter than elsewhere, and the risk and reward doesn't make any sense for someone trying to make a career of it. In a community this small, sooner or later, people will figure out who's stealing. Passing through? I supposed it could be, but it'd be the first time someone thought there was enough coin in Eastwatch to make it worth their while to come here. I don't think that's it, Anne."

She nodded. "For career thieves, that coin jar wasn't much of a score, and they did it right where the folks could see them. If they're that sloppy, they wouldn't last long."

"Not thieves, but what?" Rew asked, fiddling with his ale. "They don't have the look of laborers. Could be merchants, but that doesn't feel right. They're not old enough, for one, and even a down on their luck merchant wouldn't stoop to thieving such a small amount. If they were tradespeople and had fallen on hard times, there'd be no reason to lie. No, I don't think they meant to end up in Eastwatch, at least not for the long-term, and there's nowhere to go from here 'cept into the wilderness. They don't look like the type for that, either."

"They're running from something, then," suggested Anne, tugging down the sleeves of her blouse and then crossing her arms over her chest. "They have to be."

"Yes, they must be," he agreed, "but running from what?"

She didn't answer, but he knew she must be thinking the same thing he was.

"Nobles," said Rew, grimacing and making to spit but stopping himself with a glance at Anne.

She glared at him and raised a hand as if to cuff him for spitting on her floor. She repeated, "Nobles. They have to be."

They sat there for a moment, him sipping his ale, her glancing around the common room of her inn. There were a dozen customers in the room, all locals. It was almost always that way. Few travelers had any reason to come to Eastwatch, but when they did the Oak & Ash Inn was the only place they could stay.

Anne did a little business with truffle hunters looking for the delectable fungi in the forest, the occasional hunting party from the cities looking for something more thrilling than deer, and the handful of peddlers who made an adequate living freighting goods out to the frontier, but most of her customers were locals who preferred her cooking to their own or who had a hankering for some company along with their ale or cider.

Years ago, the Oak & Ash Inn would have had trappers coming in and out, looking for exotic furs in the wilderness, but the migration of the Dark Kind two years prior had ended most of that. Now, it was only with a ranger as escort that people ventured into the deep forest. And two years prior was also the last time they'd had a visit from the king's administration out of the capital. In theory, a governor ought to have been appointed to manage the territory, but the eastern front was small and quiet enough it seemed the king had forgotten, or no one wanted the job.

With the village under the king's direct authority, there was no writ for a mayor or even a burgher council. Without a governor, it left the village of Eastwatch rather leaderless. The denizens of the place had learned to fend for themselves, though, and when they needed help, they turned toward Rew and his rangers. He was the only official actually appointed by the king, and the rangers were the only people he'd hired. Rew, having come out to the frontier to avoid exactly that type of expectation and responsibility, had reluctantly assumed the mantle as a sort of unofficial governor.

Blessed Mother. Nobles. He sipped his ale.

"Another?" asked Anne.

He nodded, and she stood.

Several other customers, taking advantage of her break from sitting with him, ordered drinks and food as well, and it was a quarter hour before she returned with a fresh tankard and his vegetable soup. She sat down opposite of him again.

He raised an eyebrow.

"Did Tate talk to you?" she asked.

"About the thieves?"

"About him."

Rew shook his head, picking up his spoon and digging into his soup.

Anne leaned forward. "I've been offering him what empathy I can once a week, taking his pain and lessening the pressure, but I'm afraid his illness has progressed past the point I can help him."

"He seemed fine," muttered Rew, looking away from the innkeeper.

"He's not," she said. She reached across the table and put a hand on his. "Even you must have noticed it's been months since he's been out in the wilderness. It's because he's worried that if he goes, he won't make it back. The man isn't well, Rew. You should know that."

"He hasn't said anything to me," protested the ranger.

"That's why I'm telling you," replied Anne. "He won't say it, and you won't see what's as obvious as a spring storm. For two men so perceptive out in the forest…"

"I've been watching him," argued Rew, still unable to meet the innkeeper's eyes. "Do you think an empath in Yarrow may have more luck?"

Anne scowled at him, taking her hand back. "No, I don't think they would. Neither Yarrow nor Falvar have a more talented healer than I. Perhaps there is one in Spinesend, but Tate's not going to make the journey to Spinesend."

Rew picked up his tankard, frowning at her.

"I know my art, Rew," she told him. "I know what I'm capable of, and I know what's beyond the skill of any empath. You've seen me treating him. You've known he's sick, but it's progressed beyond what anyone can do. That's what I'm telling you, Rew. Tate doesn't have much time left."

"What do you suggest, then?" he asked her.

"Be ready to settle his affairs," she said. "You've got a week, I'd say, but Tate's a strong man, always has been, so maybe it will be two weeks. He's your friend, Rew. You should talk to him. Is there anything you've been meaning to share with him, any questions you've been meaning to ask him? If so, now is the time."

"Tate and I have said what needs to be said," claimed the ranger.

"Have you now?" questioned Anne, sitting up and jabbing a finger toward him. "A moment ago you told me you hadn't spoken to him about this at all!"

Rew looked down at his bowl of cooling soup. Meat or no, he found he'd lost his appetite. "He knows... We've said what we need to say to each other."

Anne snorted.

"I'll talk to him. I'll talk to him," mumbled Rew. "All he's going to say is that I should keep the ranger station in order and that Blythe'll sort out the new kid. We've... we've said our piece, Anne."

"You've known him ten years, Rew," barked Anne. "Surely you men have more to discuss than tidying up the ranger station. Tate's been a mentor to you. You don't think he'd like to hear you say it, how much he's meant to you?"

"He knows," grumbled Rew.

Anne threw up her hands. When Rew did not continue, she asked, "Another ale?"

"Yes, I think so."

Rew was on his fourth ale and the first third of a bowl of cold vegetable soup when a lumberman from the village burst into the room.

"Senior Ranger! You need to come quick. There's been an attack!"

Rew blinked at the man and then scrambled up from the table, reaching for his longsword, but he'd left it back at the station. Blessed Mother. Judging from the lumberman's panicked expression, there was no time, so Rew rushed out after the man, racing into the dirt street that ran down the center of Eastwatch.

The lumberman shuffled along at the quickest pace he could manage. Rew, trailing behind him, kept up easily. Night had fallen, but there was plenty of light from the shops and homes of the villagers. Those who could afford candles had lit them, and those who could not still had fires on their hearths and were finishing their suppers before tucking into their beds. It was quiet, and no one was acting with the panic Rew felt roiling off the lumberman.

Rew's heart sank as he realized where the other man was taking him. They were headed to the western edge of the village, where the only building close to the wilderness was the ranger station.

Rew asked tersely, "Narjags?"

"No, I... Ah, I don't know," replied the lumberman. "We heard the noise from the mill and came to investigate, but no one saw who did it."

"Wait outside. Go for help if I call out," instructed Rew. He jogged easily around the lumberman, hurrying toward the station.

The door was left open, and from the entryway, he could see the boots of Tate. Rew dashed in and stopped. The white-haired ranger was lying on his back, open eyes staring sightlessly at the ceiling. There was a gaping puncture wound in his chest. In one hand, he held his oft-repaired cloak. In the other, he held a sewing needle.

His throat was tight, and he felt bile rising in his gullet. It felt like he was falling, but his boots were rooted on the floor. He couldn't move. Tate was dead. How? Why?

Darting to the back of the building, Rew went looking for the only other people in the building. The rangers had two cells, and both were empty. One was clean and unused. The other was destroyed. Twisted iron was blown open, the ends of the bars still glowing from the heat of the force that had struck them. The bars were bent and shoved inside, making it obvious that the attack had come from outside of the cell. Blood speckled the ruined iron bars of the cell and streaked along the floor as if one of the prisoners had been dragged violently across the broken metal and then hauled away. At least one of the youths hadn't gone quietly, guessed Rew. Frowning, he assessed the pooled blood, and decided that whoever had been injured hadn't lost enough blood to kill them. They'd live, for a time.

Rew stopped by his room to collect his wooden-hilted longsword, his hunting knife, his boot knives, and his cloak. When he came back into the common room, he found the lumberman and Anne standing there. The innkeeper was at the feet of Tate, looking down at his motionless body.

"What happened?" she rasped.

Rew shook his head. "I don't know, but I'm going to find out."

Rew hung his hunting knife onto his belt and slung the strap that held his longsword over his shoulder. The leather sheath bounced against his back as he cinched it tight. He made sure the weapons were secure then told Anne, "I expect I'll be back by dawn, but if not, send an urgent post to Yarrow. Tell them what happened and request a company of the baron's men. Thieving nobles, jail breaks… There's more going on here than we understand."

"I'll come with you," she said. "You might need me."

Rew shook his head. "If I'm to catch them, I need to move quickly."

"You cannot do this alone," insisted Anne.

"I'm the King's Ranger," replied Rew. "It's my responsibility."

Chapter Four

❧

Rew ran out the back of the ranger station and looked at the moonlit ground. Whoever had attacked, whoever killed Tate and broke out the younglings, must have gone that way. Eastwatch was quiet at night, but people had not yet found their beds. A raiding party wouldn't be so foolish as to stroll down the one road that passed through the village, and he'd seen nothing amiss on the way there from the Oak & Ash. The only way the raiders could have gone was around the back.

The moon was a slender crescent, and the stars sparkled sporadically, half of them covered by thin clouds, but Rew would avoid artificial light if he could. Whoever he was tracking, if he brought a lantern or a torch, he'd give himself away as soon as he was in sight of them.

Besides, it seemed he didn't need the additional light. They kept one hundred paces behind the ranger station clear of forest, but knee-high grass grew wild there. In the moonlight, he saw the narrow trail the rangers used leading from the station to the forest, and a wide, trampled path where someone had stomped through going the other direction. Careless footfalls and the telltale marks of something heavy being dragged. Rew winced. Not something, someone. Someone large and bleeding. In the silver light from above, he could see fat drops of blood, black at night, scattered across the broken blades of grass.

Rew guessed the big youth had not gone peacefully. Whoever had broken into the station and killed Tate was no more a friend of the thieves than they were of Rew. Blessed Mother, what were those three running from?

The ranger trotted along the trampled path, not pausing to study the tracks, knowing that for now, speed was more important than any information he could discern studying the marks that had been left. Rew had felt Tate's body before he'd departed and estimated the man had been killed two hours prior. That meant whoever had attacked the station had close to a two-hour head start. Once Rew caught up, he would slow and proceed cautiously. He trusted his instincts and his own stealth to alert him when it was time. He would catch up and then figure out what he was facing.

Midnight had come and passed when Rew finally sensed something ahead. He slowed, taking his time and pausing when he saw the flickering of a campfire. He waited, listening, then began to stalk in a wide circle around the site.

His quarry had passed a league outside of Eastwatch before returning to the road. They made it two more leagues before settling down to rest. They weren't taking pains to hide, though he admitted this far from the baronies, the chances of them seeing another traveler at night were near zero. That left him with little question this group was the one he pursued. They were camped off the road, halfway to the tree line.

Getting low, moving cautiously on his hands and feet, Rew stayed below the height of the grasses and small bushes that lined the highway. He saw half a dozen figures standing and several more lying prone. The younglings, presumably.

He circled to the opposite side of the road, staying hidden in the low foliage, and when he'd come around the camp, he moved into the trees, standing slightly to get a better angle to observe his prey. Glacially slow, he stepped in the dark beneath the branches, avoiding putting his boots down on anything that could make a sound, studying the people around the fire.

There were half a dozen men with a motley of armaments, two more seated, and three figures lying down. Rew frowned. Eight opponents, all armed, and judging from the damage to the iron bars of the jail cell back at the ranger station, at least one of them was a spellcaster.

Eight against one were terrible odds, but at least he would have the advantage of surprise. If he waited until daylight, not even his skills in the forest would get him close enough to ambush the party. Around their camp, he saw that no one had laid out a bedroll. They were not preparing to sleep there. They'd started the fire for a little warmth and to boil some water for coffee. He could smell the brew steeping. The group was eating cold food from their packs, and he guessed that as soon as they'd quaffed the coffee, they would continue on, making it several more leagues away from Eastwatch before dawn.

Rew wasn't going to get a better opportunity unless he followed them all of the way to Yarrow. Muttering under his breath, the ranger moved to the edge of the trees and drew the two daggers from his boots. He studied the group, trying to identify the spellcaster, but none of them were wearing any of the usual high-collared, flowing robes of the profession. To a man, they looked like common thugs. One of them had to be a spellcaster, though, because there was no other way they could have melted the iron bars of the jail cell.

On the ground, Rew saw one of the youths stirring. The girl, the sister. She was craning her neck, checking on her brother.

"This cut needs binding," she called to her captors. Her plea was met with derisive laughter. Rew waited. She insisted, "If you do not help him, he will die."

A man broke away from the others and came to stand over the

captives, gesturing at the prone trio with a bit of dried meat he'd been chewing on. "Aye, and what makes you think that would bother me?"

"If you wanted to kill us, you already would have," snapped the girl.

"I'll be paid more if you're all alive, but I get paid even if you're dead," said the man.

"Who hired you, Worgon?" demanded the girl.

The man smirked down at her but did not answer.

Bandits, realized Rew, thugs hired by Baron Worgon of Yarrow and tasked with capturing the three younglings. At least he knew what they were running from now, but he still didn't know why. Was the speaker the spellcaster or simply the leader of the bandits? It would be unusual for such a small group of bandits to be able to afford a competent spellcaster, but Rew was beginning to accept that unusual was becoming normal.

"You're throwing away good coin by not treating him," said the girl. "Why accept less pay when you get it all? Unbind me, and I'll tend to him myself."

"Lass, do you think I'm stupid?" asked the bandit. "We know what you're capable of with free hands."

She was silent, but one of the seated men spoke. "She has a point about not letting the lad die."

"She's the one the baron wants," barked the leader. "Besides, you're the one who warned me not to let her free. She's an invoker, isn't she? If we let her go—"

The seated man shook his head and interrupted his companion. "I'm not saying let her go. Keep her tied, but we ought to bind the boy's wounds. Dead or alive, we've got to cart the body to our employer, right? He's paying for her, but he wanted to see them all. I'd rather the boy walk than me have to carry him. It's a long way to Yarrow, mate."

The leader kicked at the grasses around his feet, evidently thinking it over.

"Baron Fedgley will pay twice what Worgon's offered you," claimed the dark-haired girl.

The leader snickered and took a bite of his strip of dried meat. He made no move to free the girl or to tend to the boy.

"It's true," said the second girl, speaking up suddenly.

Rew waited, listening, his daggers held loosely in his hands.

The blonde continued, shifting on the ground so she faced the leader of the bandits, "I promise you. Whatever price Worgon offered, Fedgley will double. I'm granting assurances from the guild in Spinesend."

"Assurances of the guild, eh?" asked the leader. "And how is that?"

The blonde was silent for a long moment. Then, she answered, "I'm a member in good standing. Take off my boot. You can see my marking."

"Thieves' guild in Spinesend, is it?" asked the bandit leader, looking down at the girl's feet. "Why didn't you say so before, lass?"

"I-I didn't know if you were guild members as well," she stammered, "or if you were simple thugs."

The seated man who'd spoken cackled, and the leader turned and grinned at him. The leader stuck his thumbs behind his belt and addressed the captives again. "We're not simple thugs, no, but we ain't beholden to the thieves' guild, either. Not in Spinesend, not anywhere."

"I'm offering you more coin," hissed the girl.

The bandit leader shook his head. "Sorry, lass, in other times you may very well have appealed to my natural greed, but these aren't other times. Thieves' guild or not, promises of more coin or not, we're taking you to our employer."

The girl hissed in frustration, but Rew could see the bandit leader wouldn't budge. Was the seated speaker the spellcaster? Rew could only hope. He flipped the daggers in his hands and caught them by the blades. He raised both at once, one in each hand, and then flung them at the leader and the seated man who had been speaking.

Before the daggers struck their targets, Rew snatched his longsword from the sheath on his back and his hunting knife from his belt. He charged. The sharp steel of the thrown dagger caught the bandit leader in the shoulder, spinning him, while the other blade thunked into the seated man's throat. Rew was amongst them before any of the other bandits had time to react. He stabbed his hunting knife into one man's back and thrust his longsword over his victim's shoulder to take the next bandit in the eye.

Startled cries exploded in the camp, but Rew was already spinning and slashing his longsword into the face of a third man. Then, he whipped around and parried the swing of an axe from another of the bandits with his knife.

Four down, four to go, and one of those injured. Not great odds, but if he'd guessed correctly on the spellcaster, they were better than they had been.

He scraped his hunting knife along the wooden haft of the axe, taking off a few of the bandit's fingers in the process. Then, he smashed his fist into the axe-wielder's face, knocking the screaming man back. Sensing movement from behind, Rew ducked and felt the whistle of a blow sail overhead. He spun in a crouch, bringing his longsword around and disemboweling his assailant.

"Spellcaster!" shouted one of the girls.

Rew cursed and threw himself into a diving roll. A blaze of heat followed him from a glob of liquid fire. It splashed two-dozen yards past him and burst into a scattering of grape-sized puddles of searing flame. Rew rolled to his feet and was forced to dodge as a bandit came after him, swinging two heavy cleavers like a mad butcher. Wheeling back, Rew deflected a blow, slipped away from another, and almost ran into the bandit leader who'd attempted to circle him.

The man, one arm hanging limply at his side, was using the other to slash at Rew with a wide-bladed broadsword.

Rew scrambled away, the injured bandit leader, the butcher, and the fingerless axe man coming in a pack after him, forcing him back toward the camp.

"Behind you!" cried the girl again.

Rew flopped to the ground, and another melon-sized ball of liquid fire streaked overhead, catching the butcher square in the chest. The man screamed in agony as the fire consumed him, burning through his clothing, melting his flesh, and stripping him down to his rib bones. Rew jumped to his feet, turned from the wounded bandit leader and the fingerless axe man, and charged the spellcaster.

It was the second seated man, now standing, his hands held in front of him as he built a third ball of bubbling, liquid fire. Without pause, Rew ran straight at him and then dodged at the last second as the caster threw up what fire he had available. It sputtered by the ranger, improperly formed, two hand-lengths from his face. Not slowing, Rew swung his longsword at the spellcaster as he ran by, catching the man in the neck, chopping through flesh to the bone. The spellcaster was thrown back, an arc of blood following him as he fell to the dirt, dead before he landed.

Rew spun, finding the bandit leader and the axe man ten paces behind him. The two of them slowed, nervous eyes glancing at the carnage around their camp. Rew shifted, adjusting his grip on his longsword and hunting knife, and waited. Just the two of them now, both injured. The odds were getting considerably better.

The axe man must have thought the same because he flung his axe aside and ran, pelting down the road away from Eastwatch, headed toward Yarrow. Instead of following, the bandit leader darted toward the bound captives, raising his broadsword.

Rew leapt after the man. His hunting knife was heavy and curved, useless for throwing, so he dropped it. He lunged, thrusting his longsword out to the extent of his reach, diving at the bandit leader, stabbing into the man as he swung down with his broadsword.

Rew's longsword skewered the bandit, and the momentum from his jump brought him crashing into the other man's side. He and the corpse of the bandit tumbled to the ground, landing on the blonde, while the bandit leader's broadsword bounced to the turf next to her head.

Rew rolled away. The girl shrieked, thrashing impotently with her bound hands and feet. After scrambling back up, Rew grabbed the dead bandit and hauled the body off of the girl. Using his bloody longsword, he sawed through the ropes that were tied around her limbs, mumbling assurances to her that she didn't seem to hear.

By the time he finished cutting the girl loose, Rew looked up and saw the axe man was well down the road, moving surprisingly quick for someone rapidly losing blood from several severed fingers. Briefly, Rew thought about chasing him, but the dark-haired girl demanded his attention.

"No, not me, you oaf!" she protested when he knelt beside her. "My brother, Raif, he needs assistance. He was fighting as they dragged us from the jail, and one of those bars scored him deeply. They smashed him on the head after to keep him quiet. I can't... He's lost a lot of blood, and he hasn't been conscious since they took us."

Rew gestured for the blonde to take his hunting knife to free her companion. He moved to the big youth and saw he was breathing still, but slow and weak. There was a sizable lump on the side of his head where they must have struck him. Rew pressed his fingers against the lump and breathed a sigh of relief when he didn't feel the bone shift beneath the pressure. He thought the boy's skull was probably intact.

But as he moved along the youth's ribcage down to his hip, the ranger found a different situation. The skin had not just been torn but flesh and muscle as well, ripped in ragged tears down to the hipbone by the sharp iron bar of the broken cell door. Only the heat from the iron, apparently hot enough to cauterize some of the wound, had saved the youth. Still, blood soaked half the boy's clothing, and distressingly, it was no longer pouring from the gaping wound.

Working quickly, Rew cut the youth free of his bindings, then tore off his own tunic and pressed it against the deepest part of the laceration. He wadded it there and grabbed several lengths of the cut rope, using them to tie his shirt in place, cinching it tight onto the leaking gash. Rew sat back on his haunches, looking at the makeshift bandage. He shook his head. It was ugly. It would help but not for long. Unfortunately, three leagues from Eastwatch, without his pack with him, there wasn't much he could do except staunch the bleeding. Searching the surrounding woods for herbs to make a poultice at night would take longer than they had. Rew stood, glaring down the road where the axe man had vanished.

"Should we give him some stitches or something?" questioned the blonde, staring at the rough bandage bound across the boy's grisly injury. Already, Rew's shirt was turning bright crimson. "That doesn't look good."

"You have a needle and some thread?" Rew asked her. "Besides, that wound is extensive. Even if we had an entire physician's kit, I don't have the skill to patch him up. With my pack, I keep some ointments. We could slow the... It doesn't matter. If we're to save his life, we need to move. Are you both able to travel?"

"W-Will he..." stammered the boy's sister.

"Maybe," said Rew. "The innkeeper, the one you stole from, if we can get him to her alive there's a chance."

"I can run," said the dark-haired girl, looking at her brother with dismay. "I can—"

Not waiting for her to finish, Rew rolled the motionless boy over and wrapped his arms beneath the big body. The ranger stood, struggling to lift the twelve-stone, dead weight of the boy onto his shoulder.

"Come on," he grunted. "He's heavier than he looks, and we don't have much time."

Staggering under the weight of the youth, Rew trudged into Eastwatch in the pre-dawn gloom. Birds, just waking, trilled their happy songs, ignoring the tragedy playing out beneath them. Dim glows beckoned as a few early risers stirred their fires, but no one was yet on the street. It was eerily quiet except for Rew's and the two girls' heavy breathing. For the last league and a half, Rew hadn't been able to hear the boy's.

"Run ahead," gasped Rew, forcing his legs to move, thinking of little other than putting one foot in front of the other. Silently, Rew cursed whatever sick turn of fate had sent the younglings to Eastwatch and whatever demented cook had been feeding the giant youth for the last several years. It was as if the lad's trousers were lined with lead bars. Rew instructed, "Go to the inn. Tell Anne we're coming."

Nodding, the two girls started ahead, barely moving faster than he was. Their steps were sluggish, but he reminded himself they'd been stuck in a cell following whatever calamity had sent them to Eastwatch. Then they'd been taken captive, and now, they were hiking through the night. The two girls clearly weren't used to such exertion, but to their credit, neither one had voiced a word of complaint.

Watching the girls hurry down the street and then climb the steps to the inn, Rew hoped they'd been quick enough. The boy hadn't stirred since Rew had hefted him onto his shoulder. The boy's sister had walked beside them, constantly checking on her brother, but aside from confirming the youth still lived, she had little to offer.

Rew could feel the blood leaking down his bare shoulder, his side, and soaking his trousers. A tremendous amount of blood had drained from the boy even before he'd gotten there. So much blood… Rew had been shocked every time the girl had claimed that her brother was still alive. The ranger had doubted it more than once, but the body was still warm. Somehow, the boy's heart kept beating, kept fighting.

The inn, one of the few buildings that was fully lit so early in the morning, shone like a beacon. Lights were on in the common room, and silhouetted in the doorway, Rew saw Anne flanked by the two girls. Her sleeves were rolled up and her hair was bound behind her head. She must have been up all night, waiting on him to return.

"Blessed Mother," whispered the innkeeper as Rew staggered into the light of the open door.

"It's not mine," said the ranger as he lurched up the two stairs to the porch of the inn.

"Inside. Inside," Anne insisted, a hand raised tentatively toward the rough bandage Rew had made with his shirt and the ropes.

Rew stumbled in, and as gently as he could, he laid the giant youth down on one of Anne's tables. He fell back into a chair, exhaustion rolling over him like an avalanche.

Anne, ignoring Rew, began directing the girls like a general in the field, instructing them to gather water from the well, a kettle to boil it, linens, alcohol for sterilization, herbs, incense, and the other apparatus of her art. She removed the makeshift bandages Rew had made then leaned close, listening to the boy's faltering breath. She prodded at the wound, her mouth pinched with concern.

She turned to Rew. "I'll do what I can, but I'll need your help to finish this."

"Don't push it too far," Rew warned her. "If he's beyond saving, do not expend yourself."

"I know my art," she said, grim-faced. "I'll push as far as I have to. If it's possible, we will save him."

Rew winced. He forced himself to stand. He moved beside Anne for when she needed him. He mumbled, "I'm ready."

"What is she doing?" questioned the blonde, glancing down at the supplies they'd assembled, apparently realizing there were no potions, no threads for stitches, no sharp blades to clean the flesh, none of the normal tools of a physician.

"She's an empath," guessed the dark-haired girl. "This wound needs more than a simple transference, Ranger. Why did you bring us here? We need to find a physician. My brother needs—"

"Anne knows what she's doing," declared Rew. "Watch, wait, and be ready to help if she asks it. There are no physicians in Eastwatch, but even if there were, this is beyond their skill. Anne is the only chance your brother has of surviving the day."

Grim-faced, the two girls took the opposite side of the table and, at Anne's direction, helped strip the boy's clothes away, exposing the brutal, jagged tear in his stark white flesh. They wiped blood from it, cleaning him with hot water and alcohol, and watched as Anne began to work.

She placed her hands on the boy, unconcerned for the wet blood that had not been entirely cleaned away, and closed her eyes. She began to pray to the Mother, lips barely moving, the words hardly audible.

Rew couldn't hear her words clearly, but he knew them well. He'd heard them often enough before, dozens of times as he'd stood beside her over the injured body of one of his rangers, and occasionally, he himself had been the one laying on the table. Eastwatch had no physicians, just the barber and Anne.

Rew and his rangers had plenty of experience with the work of both, but the girls across the table stared, astonished. Empathy was low magic, the province of hedge witches and charlatans. It offered some relief, true, but what pain it took from the patient, it visited upon the healer. There were few practitioners who had the strength to take on the pain from a wound like what the boy suffered, and amongst those, there were even fewer who could be convinced to actually do it. But even that, transferring the pain, was a mere shadow of what Anne attempted. Taking on the pain of a wound was one thing. Bringing rapid healing was another. It was the type of low magic people had only heard of, the kind done in storybooks in the time before the kingdom had been formed. Few people would believe the miracle that Anne was working.

Before their eyes, the boy's wound began to heal. Flesh, pale where blood had been drained, gained a rosy hue. His torn skin crept back together, knitting deep inside of his body, covering the white of his bone in pale pink. In a manner that Rew knew tricked the eye and the mind, the skin began to crawl. It was impossible to see it happening but also impossible not to notice.

Shaking her head, the boy's sister stared with her mouth hanging open.

Anne put her hand on Rew's, and he closed his eyes, gritting his teeth.

The act of healing brought incredible pain to the empath. With a wound like the boy's, it was a deep, indescribable torment. It was more than a mortal soul was meant to handle, more than many could survive. It was more than Anne could do alone.

Eyes and jaw locked shut, Rew waited until the waves of agony rolled over him, scouring his bones, spiking lances of pure hurt through him. Later, he knew Anne would apologize, would cry at the pain she transferred into him, and he would forgive her, beg her not to worry, tell her it wasn't so bad, and secretly wish that it would never happen again. He wasn't trained for this type of pain, wasn't used to it, and the few times over the years he'd been forced to support her, Rew had always been surprised at the violence of the misery.

Was it the same for her when she drew the pain to herself? He didn't know, and she didn't say. In truth, it was a level of suffering neither of them could describe. He could not mark it against the physical hurt he'd experienced in life because it was magnitudes worse. It consumed everything, chased every thought from his mind except for the terrible pain.

Fleetingly, before he was overwhelmed, before his conscious curled into a trembling ball of unawareness, he thought Anne would regret using him, that the emotional toll it would put on her was nearly the equal to the psychological hurt he felt, but it had to be done. She couldn't do it alone, and without her, without him, the boy would die.

Minutes, hours, Rew didn't know, but eventually, the throb that enveloped him faded, and he was able to open his eyes. Slowly, fighting trembling muscles in his neck, he turned his head. Anne was sitting in the chair he'd slumped down in when he'd first arrived. Her head was in her hands, and she was weeping. He moved his head back, the muscles in his neck spasming in minor jolts of protest at the motion, and he saw the boy was breathing evenly, his skin bare and smooth, just a long, pale line where he'd been torn open. His sister stood on the other side of the boy, her hand clutching his, her gaze on her brother's sweat-streaked face.

"How long?" croaked Rew.

"An hour," offered the blonde, rising from where she'd been seated behind the dark-haired girl. "It took an hour. It's almost dawn."

Straightening, fighting twitching muscles, Rew stood his full height.

"How did she do that?" asked the dark-haired girl. "That... that's not possible. I've studied... What she did is not possible."

"Anne's staff should be coming in soon. We'll get him up to a bed," said Rew, ignoring the girl's disbelief. "Anne as well. They'll both need rest—days of it. Her people know what to do, but I'm certain they'll need your help moving the lad."

"One of them is here already," mentioned the blonde. "She's back opening the kitchen, stoking the fires. She said to call when we are ready for her. She... she said you and Anne needed time."

"This isn't the first occasion they've..." mumbled Rew. He breathed deep, trying to steady himself. "Anne's staff knows what to do. You two, we're going to talk. We're going to talk, and you're going to tell me what is going on, but first, I have to see to my man at the ranger station. Stay here, and I'll be back in an hour or two."

He looked at Anne, knowing soon she'd recover and that she'd be all right, but for now she was unreachable, trapped in a well of agony. Until she'd had time to let it settle, to dissipate, she'd sit there unspeaking. Gritting his teeth, Rew pushed his hands away from the table where they'd been grasping the edge. Forcing stiff fingers to move, he winced as spikes of discomfort stabbed up his arms with the small movement. He breathed in and out, trying to gather the courage to move his legs. Movement, painful at first, would help. It would help, if he could force himself to do it.

"She transferred the pain into you," surmised the dark-haired girl.

Rew returned the girl's look but did not reply.

"You need to rest as well, then," insisted the girl. "You were up all of last night. You tracked us and you fought those men. You carried my brother three leagues on your shoulder. You need rest as much as any of us. More, I'd think."

Rew nodded. "You're right, but not yet. I still have work to do."

Chapter Five

It was midmorning by the time Rew shuffled back up the two plank steps to the front door of the Oak & Ash Inn. Weariness hung on him like a cloak, and a sharp knife of sorrow twisted in his gut. Tate had been the most experienced ranger ten years ago when Rew had first arrived in Eastwatch. Rew had known some woodcraft, but Tate had shown him more. Rew had known how to swing his sword, but Tate had taught him when to do it. Tate was the one who'd guided the angry young man to shoulder his responsibility, had lived as an example of how to be a leader. The old ranger had demonstrated how to stand for something instead of running away. Tate had been a steady presence at Rew's side, no matter what difficulties they faced.

The old ranger had been popular in the village, as well. He'd been the kind of man people stopped and waved to on their morning chores, and the kind of man people listened to when he spoke. Tate was the kind of man that when you were in trouble, you invited him over late in the evening for a drink, and you spilled your problems to him. When he spoke his advice, you listened, and you did what he said. He hadn't been born in Eastwatch, which might have surprised many younger people who had been. Tate had become a part of the place and a part of the people.

In recent years, Tate had been sick. In recent months, it'd gotten worse. Despite what Anne thought, Rew had been watching, and he'd known it was near the end. He and Tate may not have held hands, gazed into each other's eyes and spilled their souls out, but they'd both known. Tate had accepted it, and Rew had gotten as close as he could to accepting it.

He had come to terms with the older ranger dying, but not like this. Tate had earned an evening with too much mulled wine before the fire, having his friends surround him with love, and then a quiet passing in the night. The old ranger didn't deserve to be cut down in the common room of the building that had been his home for the last three decades. He didn't deserve to die in pain with no idea why.

Tate had survived the migration of the Dark Kind two years prior. He'd lived through countless scuffles with narjags, ayres, valaan, ogres, simians, and trolls. There were stories of an encounter before Rew's time with a drake. There had been fires, famines, years where the tax collectors showed twice, and years where the king's bursar forgot to send the ranger's stipend. Through it all, Tate had been someone that the village had leaned on.

There had been plenty of good as well, and that was what Rew had tried to keep in his thoughts as he'd buried the man. The old ranger had an infectious smile and a jolly laugh. There had always been a sly quip waiting on his lips. He'd been the first in the circle to dance at a marriage feast and the last to leave the party. But now, Tate was gone, and Rew didn't know why.

He knew who might, though.

Rew strode into the common room of the Oak & Ash Inn with purpose. Anne's staff had been hard at work, it seemed. The innkeeper and her charge had been moved upstairs. The tables had been rearranged, and the bloodstained one had been taken away, either to be cleaned or fed into a fire somewhere. A scattering of locals sat around tables over bowls of lumpy porridge. There were none of the fluffy eggs, hunks of fried ham, or pastries that drew Eastwatch's denizens from their own hearths to Anne's, but with such a commotion that morning, everyone would understand. The people of Eastwatch had been through worse, and they knew when it was best to simply lower your head and eat your porridge.

Rew frowned. The boy would be upstairs, asleep for at least another day, but the two girls?

Jacqueline, one of Anne's serving staff, caught his eye and nodded toward the corner of the room. Rew walked over to find the two girls curled up on a short couch Anne kept in front of one of the fireplaces. It was there for the old men to gather during cool nights, sipping their brandy or their cider, smoking their pipes. The girls were sound asleep on it.

They were not cuddled together like sisters after a trauma. Their legs were tucked under their own bodies, half a pace of open space between them. They slept under separate blankets, facing away from each other. Not sisters, not friends. These two only knew each other because of their journey.

Rew thought to wake them but sat down to give his legs a bit of a rest first. He'd just spent the last two hours straightening up the ranger station and burying Tate. He'd been up the entire night before, he'd fought the bandits, had carried the boy several leagues on his shoulder, and been through the torment of the youth's healing. Rew could feel the weariness in his bones, like the marrow had been replaced by dead iron. Just a few moments of quiet, then he would wake them.

Rew drew a deep breath and opened his eyes. Confused, he saw he was not looking at the wall of his room in the ranger station but at an empty couch. He was tired and dreadfully sore. An empty couch?

He raised a hand to his face, rubbing at his eyes with a balled fist. It was warm, but he had no blanket on. He was dressed. What — He bolted out of the chair in the Oak & Ash's common room, his hand going for his sword.

"Calm down, Senior Ranger," suggested Ranger Blythe from a nearby table. "You fell asleep."

Rew looked at her, blinking to clear his vision from the slumber that still crowded his eyes. Blythe was sitting at a table a dozen paces away with Jon, the new ranger, and the two girls from the cell. The girls were hunched over bowls of soup and looked at him with a mixture of concern and amusement.

"Don't worry. They haven't been out of my sight," assured Blythe. "I figured that if you were so tired you fell asleep in the middle of the Oak & Ash, we'd best let you rest a few hours."

Rew breathed deeply again and shook himself, jiggling his body to wakefulness.

"Come and sit," suggested Blythe. She added, "I stopped by the station."

"I'm sorry I wasn't there to tell you," he murmured, looking away. "I'm sorry I didn't wait."

"Anne told me," said Blythe. Then she chided him, "And you're not sorry you didn't wait. You meant to spare me the sight. I know he didn't tell you, but I'm guessing you knew anyway. You're not as thick as Anne makes you out to be. It was his time. Tate's days were at an end, and I'd made my peace with it. I hate to lose him like this, I really do, but we were going to lose him, Rew. We all have our time. Tate lived a good life, but it was going to end. He lived a good life, Rew, and he'd want us to raise a tankard in his memory, not shed a tear."

Rew didn't answer. He looked at Blythe's red-rimmed eyes, the hair sticking out from behind her ears, the hasty binding she'd tried to tie it back with. Her cheek was scratched, as if from a fingernail, and her lips were white where she'd been pressing them tightly together. She offered him a wan smile and a small shrug. Rew nodded, and there was nothing else they needed to say.

He turned to the two girls. They froze under his gaze, the blonde with a spoonful of soup halfway to her mouth.

"My name is Rew," he said brusquely. "I'm the King's Ranger in the eastern territory. I'm responsible for upholding the king's law in this part of the realm, among other things. At the moment, it seems that all of my trouble is stemming from you two and the lad upstairs." He glanced at the dark-haired girl. "He is your brother?"

"Raif," she said, looking down into her soup. "His name is Raif. I am Cinda. This is Zaine."

"Cinda and Zaine, care to tell me what is going on?" Rew asked calmly, still standing with his fists on his hips, looking between the two girls.

Cinda swallowed uncomfortably and brushed back a dark lock of dark hair. Zaine deferred to her.

"My best ranger was murdered last night," added Rew. "I killed seven men, and I don't know who they were, only that they broke you out of my jail. There is important, dangerous work my rangers and I need to be doing in the wilderness, yet it was in our own station we lost someone. The door to my jail cell was ruined, but I've another. I don't have another ranger like Tate, and I'm at the end of my patience. If you two ever want to experience freedom again, you'd best get to talking. The time for games, the time for secrecy, is over."

"I am Cinda Fedgley," said the dark-haired girl, drawing herself upright, though she still had to look up at him from the table. "My brother is Raif Fedgley. We are the two youngest children of Baron Fedgley of Falvar. We have urgent news for him, and we were rushing to get to him. I am sorry we attempted to steal from this inn, but we'd run out of coin and were desperately low on food. We thought... It was wrong, but it is imperative we get to Falvar. Lives hang in the balance, Ranger. You saw what our enemies are capable of last night. If we cannot reach my father, many more people will die."

Nobles. He'd known it. Not petty thieves. Even worse. Blessed Mother. That was going to complicate matters.

He frowned at the two girls. "Going to Falvar through Eastwatch? Where did you come from?"

"Yarrow," said Cinda. She must have noticed his skeptical look because she added, after cutting her eyes at Zaine, "We thought this would be a quicker route than going through Spinesend… It looks closer on the maps."

Blythe snorted.

Shaking his head, Rew mentioned, "There's no road to Falvar through Eastwatch, lass. We're at the end of the path here."

"I know there's a way!" cried Cinda before sitting back, tossing her spoon into her soup. "I know there's a way over the Spine and down through the barrowlands. I've heard of people coming that way. The Dark Kind migrated south through there two years ago, didn't they! It's closer on the map…"

"Aye, there's a way, I suppose," agreed Rew, taking a seat beside Blythe and studying the girl across the table. "It's not an easy way, though. I mean that. There's no road. I've traveled over the Spine myself a few times, but when we have need to visit Falvar from Eastwatch, we take the road through Yarrow and Spinesend. It's safer, for one, and quicker than rough travel in the wilderness. The son and daughter of the baron, why are you not taking the road yourselves? You ought to be sitting in the back of a comfortable carriage, sipping wine and eating cheese and sweetbreads as the landscape rolls by, footmen ready to set up your camp each evening, a trail of handmaids following behind to attend to your comfort. Nobles don't traverse the wilderness. They don't cross the Spine."

Cinda flushed.

"What sort of trouble are you in?" asked Rew, sitting forward and leaning his elbows on the table.

"You're the King's Ranger?" asked Cinda. "What does that mean?"

Rew frowned at her but decided if he wanted her to talk, to share her secrets, there was no harm in giving an answer, even if it was one he was certain she already knew. "The land around Falvar is ruled by your father, Baron Fedgley, the land around Yarrow by Baron Worgon. They both swear fealty to Duke Eeron in Spinesend, who owes his allegiance to the king. There are the three princes in the regional capitals, but, well, that's complicated, isn't it? Let's keep it simple. Your lands are ruled by your father the baron, the duke, and the king. Here, in Eastwatch, we've no noblemen. There are no other lords or ladies that Eastwatch offers fealty to. This is the king's land. It is only his. There ought to be a governor handling the affairs of government, and there are the rangers—my team and I—handling matters of law and security. Truth be told, though, there's little need for extensive government in the territory, and rarely do I need to enforce the king's laws. Most of what I do, and the rangers who work for me, is monitoring the wilderness to the east of us. That is the prime responsibility of the King's Ranger. Dealing with matters such as your theft are a rare occurrence."

Cinda, tight-lipped, nodded.

"Surely you know all of this," said Rew, hoping it was true.

"I have been taught these things," confirmed Cinda, "but my tutor's focus is rarely on the territories. A noblewoman's education has more to do with sciences and sums, letters and poetry, dress and decorum. I-I wanted to hear it from you about the rangers. You have no allegiances to Baron Worgon, then? None at all?"

Rew scratched his beard and glanced at Blythe, but the junior ranger merely shrugged in response.

"No, lass, I do not," responded Rew. "We stay in touch with the baronies as any good neighbors should do. We share information, occasionally resources, but not directives. I answer only to

Ranger Commandant Vyar Grund in the capital, who answers only to the king."

"Baron Worgon is engaged in a plot against Duke Eeron," claimed Cinda, lowering her voice and leaning toward him. She let her eyes flick from Blythe and back to him. "I don't know all of the details, but I know enough. Worgon's been raising levies for months. He has a thousand men in his command now. He waved me off when I asked him about it, but my brother and I overheard Worgon's lackeys talking. They're planning to assassinate Duke Eeron then take control of Spinesend. After that, they'll take our family's land as well. Worgon means to rule the entire duchy. We fled as quickly as we could, intending to run for Falvar to warn my father."

"Why not go directly to Duke Eeron?" questioned Rew. "It's an easier journey, and if the plot is against the duke…"

"When we escaped the keep, Worgon locked down Yarrow," explained Cinda. "We only managed to slip out with Zaine's help. We figured Worgon would have the road to Spinesend covered in his men. Raif pushed us to travel cross country, but Zaine insisted there was a quicker way to Falvar in the east. We thought… If we can get to my father, he'll know what to do."

"A quicker way," grumbled Rew, rubbing his hand over his hair, feeling the prickly stubble sprung from his scalp after shaving the night before. Blessed Mother, the night before felt like a lifetime ago.

Squabbles amongst the nobles. It was the sort of business he'd come to Eastwatch to avoid. It was the sort of thing he had avoided for the last decade. The nobles were always plotting, always working against each other. It was an endless cycle of marshaling forces, hiring assassins, recruiting spellcasters, and then using them against each other. It never ended. Never would end. The only thing to do was to avoid it.

He sighed. The girl was right.

If Worgon knew the younglings had overheard his minions' plotting, he would have the road to Spinesend covered in spies, but more importantly, he wouldn't be acting alone. If he was preparing to move openly against the duke with armed forces, then he would have allies close by to plunge the knife into his liege's back. With word from Worgon, those hidden blades would be on the lookout for Cinda and her brother as well. Rew doubted the two of them could get anywhere near Duke Eeron's ear before someone snatched them up.

The senior ranger grimaced. It was the Investiture. It was a few years early, but he'd felt the tug, it had to be. The Investiture was the reason the nobles collected their pawns, the event they amassed their forces for. It was why Rew had come to Eastwatch and why he'd spent the last ten years there, hoping to be forgotten on Vaeldon's far fringe.

He kept rubbing his head, studying the two girls, thinking. During the last cycle of Investiture, Duke Eeron had avoided the worst of the conflagration. It was part of the attraction of Eeron's eastern duchy, a buffer between the intrigue of the king's court and the peace and quiet that Rew sought. It seemed that the duchy would be dragged in, though, this time.

"You'll help us get to Falvar?" asked Cinda.

Rew glanced at Blythe again and saw the ranger shake her head slightly. She had no more desire than he to become entangled in the affairs of the nobles.

"What were you doing in Yarrow?" asked Rew, ignoring the girl's question.

She looked as if she meant to press, but answered instead. "My brother and I have fostered there for the last three years."

"Your father was hoping to make a match for you in Yarrow?" wondered Rew.

Cinda shrugged. "I have an older sister in Spinesend. Father doesn't want me to distract her prospects, so where else would he send us?"

"Well, he could keep you home in Falvar, or if not that, send you outside of the duchy?" suggested Rew. "Worgon has no boys, does he? There must be fifty cities in the kingdom with better prospects than Yarrow. In Carff alone there should be dozens of suitable bachelors for a girl of your station."

Cinda flushed.

"You've never been outside of the duchy?" guessed Rew.

She nodded. "Father says the Barony of Fedgley and the Duchy of Eeron are where we will rule, and that is the land which we should come to know. He thought that by fostering us with Worgon, we'd help build a relationship between our families. Of course, now we know that has done us little good."

Rew grunted but did not respond.

"You'll help us?" asked Cinda.

"How many did they send?" asked Blythe.

"Eight," muttered Rew. "One got away."

"There will be more, then," remarked the ranger.

Rew reached out a hand to a mug sitting in front of Blythe. He tilted it but scowled when he saw it was half full of milk. "There will be more."

Cinda, looking between the two rangers, asked again, "You'll help?"

"I don't know, lass," replied Rew, clenching his fist, forcing himself not to smack it down on the table. The mystery of the narjags, the loss of his most experienced ranger… he didn't have time for this.

"We need your help," insisted Cinda. "Our father and Duke Eeron need your help."

Grimacing, Rew allowed, "You'll stay in the Oak & Ash a few days until your brother recovers. He needs rest before you travel, and there's nothing any of us can do about that. If those men last night were Worgon's, there's time still before the runner can make it back to Yarrow and report what happened. There's no immediate danger, I don't think, but I'll station a ranger here at the inn until we've figured out what to do."

Cinda's lips twisted, and he could tell she wanted more, but he had responsibilities to the people in Eastwatch. Even if he wanted to, he couldn't go jaunting off on some adventure to help the young nobles. There was that, but even if there wasn't, he simply didn't want to get involved.

"I've two more rangers on their way back from Yarrow," he said. "When they've returned, we'll know more of what's happening in the city. When they're back, and your brother has recovered, we'll figure out what the options are."

"What about—" began Blythe.

"I'll go and I'll take Jon," said Rew. He held up a hand to stall her protest. "I know he's not the best in the wilderness yet, but he's what we have. While I'm away, I need you here, Blythe. You're the only one I can trust."

Cinda sat back, her head held high. For a moment, Rew wondered if she meant to use her authority as a baron's daughter to try and command him. He was grateful, when instead of speaking, she merely nodded.

Rew told Blythe, "Jon and I will head into the wilderness tomorrow, but before we go, there's something I need to show you."

She raised an eyebrow.

"The narjag party I tracked, they might have had a shaman."

"King's Sake," hissed Blythe.

Cinda gaped at him, her mouth opened wide. "There hasn't been a shaman amongst the Dark Kind in… in fifty years."

"I know," grumbled Rew. "Not even during the last migration did we find a shaman amongst the narjags, but this one had the look."

"Did it-Did it cast a spell?" wondered Cinda.

"It did not, but I didn't give it a lot of time, either," said the ranger, looking at the girl curiously. "It may be nothing. I hope it's nothing, but I must look into it. Tomorrow, I'll go into the wilderness to find where the narjag party had been before I found them and to figure out what they've been doing since our first reported sighting. It shouldn't take me long. When I return, I hope my other rangers will be back from Yarrow. We'll discuss your situation. In the meantime, your brother must rest, and I suggest you two do as well. I'm sure you don't need me to tell you, but no matter what you do, you've long days ahead of you."

"Understood," said Cinda, nodding as if they'd just finalized a trade agreement between cities rather than instructions to quietly rest.

Rew turned to Blythe. "Let's go to the station. I'll show you the artifacts, and we should pay our respects."

Blythe, lips tight, nodded.

"You believe them?" asked Blythe.

Rew shrugged. "They don't seem like they're lying. Not still lying, at least."

"Aye, but they're not telling us all, are they?" she pressed. "A plot by Worgon against Duke Eeron has to be the Investiture, but they haven't said a word about that."

"They weren't alive for the last one," responded Rew. "Duke Eeron has kept his duchy free of most of the royal politics. I don't… Do you think it's possible they don't know? If Baron Fedgley hasn't sent his children from the eastern duchy, it's for a reason. He's protecting them, and maybe he's been keeping them ignorant as well. None of the three princes have visited the eastern duchy in the last decade. Their plotting is taking place far from these lands, and I suppose Worgon would be in no rush to educate potential rivals about that plotting."

"Aye, the princes haven't been to the eastern duchy since you arrived," remarked Blythe.

"It's not because of me," said Rew with a wry grin. "No, I believe in his heart, Duke Eeron wants nothing to do with the Investiture, and the princes are aware of that. It seems Baron Worgon doesn't feel the same as his liege, though."

Blythe crossed her arms over her chest. "How could they not know?"

"Not all nobles are bad people," said Rew.

"What of Worgon, then?" questioned Blythe. "I'd bet my next season's pay that if he's involved in the Investiture it's because he found himself a patron. One of the princes has an eye on the duchy, Rew. Whether Duke Eeron wants it or not, he's going to be pulled into the whirlpool. All of the nobles will be."

Rew could only shrug.

Blythe reached out and grabbed the twisted, torn-open iron bars of the jail cell. "Eight of them and one a spellcaster. Do you think that was a bit much for three children?"

"They're not children," replied Rew. "I carried the boy on my shoulder for three leagues, remember? I can assure you he's a full-grown man. A little extra grown, even."

"That's not what I meant," said Blythe. "Trying to get to Falvar by coming through Eastwatch, the wilderness, the Spine… That's a child's fanciful plan. Without a ranger escort, they'd have no chance of surviving the journey. That girl Cinda said it looked shorter on the map, but I wonder if she's even actually seen one."

Despite himself, Rew laughed. "That bit, at least, I believed. If they overheard a plot against the duke, it stands to reason Worgon would make travel along the roads impossible. Not to mention, I think the other girl, Zaine, is a thief. She may have her own reasons for wanting to avoid the public roads."

"They're all thieves from what I heard," said Blythe with a snort.

"I mean a thief in the guild," said Rew. "She spoke to the thugs who'd taken them like she was high up in the Spinesend guild, like she would have protection. Recall what Cinda said. It was only Zaine who got them out of the city. Who has that skillset? A thief."

"She's a bit young for membership in the guild," said Blythe. "I'm no expert, but I've heard it takes years of apprenticeship before one is allowed in. That's just jabbing over an ale about it, but it makes sense, Rew. The guilds survive because they don't let in inexperienced bunglers. Taking those nobles through Eastwatch on the way to Falvar… That's a foolish move, Rew. A girl that young doesn't get into the guild making foolish moves."

"Maybe she lied trying to save her skin," said Rew, "but if she wasn't lying, what was she doing in Yarrow? How did she stumble into the lives of these nobles?"

Blythe frowned.

Rew kicked a bit of iron that was poking out from the ruined cell door. "I suppose we ought to get down to the blacksmith today and order another one of these. Could be we'll need it."

"Could be," agreed Blythe.

Rew led her back out into the common room where the staff, the necklace, and the other items he'd taken from the narjags were laid out.

"The Dark Kind moving again," said Blythe. "What does it mean?"

"Nothing unless we spy another group of them," said Rew. "These artifacts, can you sense anything?"

Blythe leaned over the staff, peering at it closely. She picked it up and hefted it. She ran her hands up and down its length and sat it back down on the table. She looked at the necklace of narjag ears, but hesitated, and did not touch the withered flesh. "As far as I can tell, there are no enchantments, completely mundane."

Rew nodded, her sense confirming his own. "That's what I thought. Head back to the Oak & Ash, will you? Watch those girls until I come relieve you later today. I'll spend the night there, and in the morning, Jon and I will retrace the trail of those narjags. I hope we can solve that mystery at least."

"And when you get back?" she asked.

"And when I get back, we'll figure out what to do with our errant nobles."

Blythe reached out and wrapped her arms around his shoulders, pulling him close. "Tate was a good man, Rew. He was a bit of a father to me and you as well. You've got some of him in you, you know? That man had a way of making an impression, and he made a bigger one on you than you realize."

"Did he now?" asked Rew, stepping back with a grin on his face.

"I remember the man you were when you arrived here," said Blythe, holding his shoulders in her hands and looking into his eyes. "You're a different man, now. A better man, and that is because of Tate. I'm going to miss him, Rew."

Rew wrapped his arms back around Blythe. They held each other for a long minute before he let go and moved away.

"Why don't you rest?" said Blythe, wiping at her eyes. "Have Anne pour you an ale and take a pipe. I can handle matters here and at the blacksmith."

"I'll have time to rest tonight," replied Rew. He gestured around the room. "I can finish this up. I need to do it. I'm the King's Ranger, and it's my responsibility."

Chapter Six

The first shards of dawn sparkled on the dew-damp grass behind the ranger station. The path the bandits had trampled was dark like a knife wound cutting across that brightness. Headed in the opposite direction was a slender path, one that he had walked with Tate's body in his arms. The ranger was dead, and the thugs that had done it were dead as well. They'd paid the ultimate price for their crime, but it gave Rew no comfort. His friend was gone, and no amount of vengeance would bring him back.

Rew forced himself to look away from the path he'd trod to bury Tate and drew a deep breath of the crisp, new autumn air. He let it go, hoping his sorrow left with the wind. He'd served justice, and there was no use dwelling on it further. Tate wouldn't have wanted him to. Neither of them could have known the three younglings would draw such awful violence, and there was nothing Rew could have done to stop the attack. Unless… unless it had been him instead of Tate. If Rew had been the one on watch, if he had relieved Tate instead of going to the Oak & Ash, talking to Anne, drinking ale… He forced the thought down. It was no use considering such things. He continued to breathe, taking in the cool air and letting it back out.

Minutes later, his newest ranger, Jon, stomped down the back stairwell of the station. The man wore a dark green woolen cloak and was hitching his pack high on his shoulders over it. A long, curved hunting knife hung on his belt, and he was fumbling with a longsword, trying to position it over his shoulder beside his pack where he could draw it.

Rew rubbed his lips. A longsword. When Jon had first been assigned to them, the young man had spent his childhood on a farm and a year training to join the king's infantry. Jon had learned the spear and the short sword in the infantry, though he'd learned neither weapon very well. Now, the young ranger rotated through a variety of weapons. He moved from Rew's and Tate's preferred longswords, to the hatchets that Blythe used, to Vurcell's falchion, and for a brief moment, Jon had attempted to master the swordstaff used by Ang. He traded the blades depending on who he was on expedition with and which one he'd most recently been embarrassed by in sparring.

Rew decided not to comment on how the day before, the young ranger had been hanging up a pair of hatchets like Blythe's, and now he was hoisting a longsword. Today, they had business to attend to. Scolding Jon about not picking a weapon and learning it could wait.

Rew was about to turn toward the forest, but he paused. The wire-wrapped hilt of the longsword that stuck above Jon's shoulder was familiar. The steel pommel, carved into the likeness of a bear, was not standard issue. The young ranger wore Tate's weapon.

Nervously, Jon felt Rew's stare and shifted. He stammered, "Ah, Blythe told me to carry it. She said it was my blade now, and I'd honor Tate by carrying it always. She said… she said she thought the longsword would be good for me. I hope that's all right. Blythe told me it's what Tate would have wanted."

Rew grunted but did not respond.

Blythe was right about what Tate would have wanted, and she was right that the longsword was a good match for Jon.

Rew started off toward the forest, following the narrow track that the rangers had worn through the grass from decades of departing on expedition into the wilderness. Behind him, he heard Jon scrambling to follow, still adjusting his pack, still adjusting to carrying the old ranger's longsword.

Rew had found the trail left by the narjags easily and then allowed Jon to follow it back toward its source. It was easy tracking, and while they were in something of a hurry, there was a limited amount of ground to cover.

Farmer Bartrim had first reported the suspicious activity, and that had been three days ago. The narjags had traveled only a few leagues from Bartrim's farm to where Rew had found their trail the day before. For two days, they'd only moved a few leagues if at all. But when Rew had been following them, they'd seemed in a hurry. What had they been doing before, and where?

Rew walked a dozen paces behind Jon, letting the new ranger follow the trail. They had a mission to be about, and he had to restrain himself, wanting to hurry ahead, but it was the ranger's way to train by doing. If Jon was to be of any use to the king and Eastwatch, he had to learn, and there was no better test than learning on a real expedition. They could take him out for years, following the signs of deer and the feral hogs that populated the shallow forest near Eastwatch, but they'd never know if the young ranger could survive the deep forest or face the Dark Kind until he did.

"Senior Ranger," said Jon, pausing. "Come look at this. I think this might be an… an ayre."

Frowning, Rew hurried to where the young ranger was looking down at the damp soil. A light rain had fallen the night before. It hadn't been hard enough to obscure all of the signs, but it'd softened them. There, in the dirt, was the impression of a paw print. Rew breathed a sigh of relief.

"No, a wolf, not an ayre," he assured the new ranger. He squatted, drew his hunting knife, and pointed with the tip of it. "See here, these marks left by the nails? An ayre's would be twice as long and a little bit thicker. You're right, though. The size of a wolf's and an ayre's paws is nearly identical. The depth of the impression can be the same, too, though if there's a narjag rider on the ayre, you'd expect to see a deeper mark."

Jon frowned. "So it's the nails then, that's the biggest difference?"

"On hard soil, sometimes the only discernible difference," responded Rew. "The back of the footpads are narrower on an ayre, and there's never any mark left by fur. You can't always see that if the ayre is moving quickly or if the earth is dry. The nails are the clearest distinction. With a bit of practice, it's not difficult to tell the two prints apart."

"A wolf…" said Jon, pinching his chin between his fingers. "A wolf tracking narjags?"

Rew nodded, acknowledging that was strange. Natural creatures tended to avoid the Dark Kind. They could sense there was something wrong with them, that their flesh would be rotten, tainted by their ancestry in another world. The scent of a narjag or an ayre was certainly foul enough, but it went beyond that. Those creatures did not belong in the world. They were not native to it, and that was repulsive.

The Dark Kind had been conjured, hundreds of years prior, to build armies. It had been a time of constant war, before the kingdom was united by the original king, Vaisius Morden. The Dark Kind the rangers hunted in the wilderness were the remnants and children of those shattered forces from long ago. The histories claimed that the Dark Kind had grown into massive hordes through feverish breeding, and they'd broken the magical chains their conjurers had used to control them. Vaisius Morden had unified the territories in an attempt to fight back, to save mankind.

And it had worked. Vaisius Morden crushed the hordes of the

Dark Kind and forced them back into the remote places of the world. He'd kept his hold on the people through it all, and on the back of his victories, they'd supported his ascension to king. The lands had remained unified since then, always under the sway of Vaisius Morden's line.

But while the Dark Kind had been defeated, and the conjurers who'd summoned them had been hunted and killed, the Dark Kind hadn't been completely wiped from the world. They'd fled, hid, and continued to breed in the far-off places. From time to time, they emerged again, coming from hiding and threatening the settlements of people.

That was the prime reason why the rangers were stationed in Eastwatch, and that was why they left on expeditions into the trackless wilderness. They were the kingdom's eyes and ears, always vigilant, always looking for signs of valaans, narjags, ayres, and a dozen other lesser Dark Kind that weren't intelligent enough to organize but would still kill a man the moment they saw one. The Dark Kind were all foreign to the world and dangerous. Conjurers and spellcasters occasionally tried to command them, but the truth was, there was nothing to do but kill them.

Someday, the story was, the king would gather forces and march through each far-off corner of his kingdom and eliminate the threat once and for all, but that had been the story for two hundred years and through eight generations of Mordens. The Dark Kind were still out there, and rather than an army, Rew had only five rangers in his command.

He winced. Four rangers. He had four rangers, now that Tate was dead. Four wasn't enough. It had never been enough to cover the hundreds of leagues of forest that he and his rangers regularly patrolled, not to mention the expanses beyond that they knew little of. It wasn't enough, but they did what they could.

Jon, noticing his expression, asked, "What are you thinking?"

Rew huffed and turned his attention back to the print the wolf had left. He looked up and down the path, noting that the creature did seem to be following the trail of the narjags, but it hadn't been when they'd originally picked up the signs. The wolf had followed and then left off pursuit. That was one bit of behavior that wasn't unusual. The wolf had followed far enough to know it wanted nothing to do with the awful monsters.

"I'm thinking there's little we'll learn from one single print," answered Rew. "Let's keep going, see how long the wolf was on their scent, and see if we can figure out what those creatures were doing in the days between Bartrim's sighting and when I found them."

Nodding, Jon started walking again, his eyes scanning the ground and occasionally the foliage around them, moving carefully to avoid stepping onto the impressions that he tracked.

Rew ghosted behind him, watching the tracks and studying the area around as well. It was calm, normal. It meant that whatever the Dark Kind had been doing nearby, they were gone now. A pack of narjags was a disruption, an invisible taint that lower animals could sense. They would have fled if they still felt the narjags nearby, but the song of birds filled the citadel beneath the trees, and small creatures flitted around in front of them, preparing their stores for winter. It was normal, but was it too normal?

Shaking himself, Rew brought his attention back to Jon and his hesitant efforts to follow a trail. Too normal? What was he even thinking?

"Blessed Mother," said Jon.

Pacing around the circle, Rew nodded in agreement.

"A conjurer did this, you think?" wondered the junior ranger, his hand reaching up to touch the wire hilt of Tate's old longsword. "Were they summoned somehow?"

"I don't think so," said Rew. "The Dark Kind were brought through a portal centuries ago from a world that I'm told we can no longer reach. The plane passed too far in the astral nether or something of the sort. The ones we see are the children of those who were conjured. These days, it's demons, imps, and elementals that conjurers are able to call upon."

"What… what is this, then?" questioned Jon.

Rew shook his head. In a circle, twenty paces across, the ground and the foliage were singed, as if from a brilliantly hot, but quick, flame. A thin line bisected it, slicing through a tree as cleanly as a razor-sharp blade, cutting through the earth a finger-width wide trench. It was the mark of a portal that had been opened carelessly, but narjags didn't have the art to cast such high magic, and why would any spellcaster who did have the skill open a portal for Dark Kind? If a spellcaster had opened the portal for themselves, then where were they?

Jon stood, staring blankly at the scene.

"Someone opened a portal," Rew told him. He crouched near the center of the mark and saw whatever fire had blasted the clearing had scoured the soil clear for half-a-finger deep. If a spellcaster had emerged from the portal, they'd blown away any trace of their footsteps. Rew stood, circled the rim of the mark, but saw no impressions left by the boots of a human, just the four-toed marks left by narjags.

"A spellcaster? Why?" wondered Jon.

Rew shrugged. It was a good question.

Both rangers walked out from the site where the portal was opened. There was evidence of a violent spell in the immediate area, but they saw no signs of blood, narjag or human. Whatever the spellcaster had unleashed had not been meant as an offensive or defensive measure, thought Rew. Would they have cast such a spell simply to obscure their footprints? He kept his slow circuit, noting more footprints of the narjags but not seeing anything else.

"Here," said Jon from fifty paces away.

Rew walked to the younger ranger, who was standing at the base of a large rock outcropping. Stone struck from the floor of the forest like a giant's finger, rising a dozen paces into the air, leaning over the ground, and offering a shaded space that was clear of underbrush.

Jon was pointing to the remains of a foul camp.

"Narjags," hissed Rew.

The younger man nodded. "They camped here."

Rew grimaced. There was a fire pit, the torn and shattered remains of several animals, and gourds which smelled of the awful brew the narjags distilled. Their waste was scattered around the area, and the rangers could see plenty of activity where the narjags had stalked around the site.

"They were waiting on something," surmised Jon. "They could have been camped here for days."

Nodding, Rew looked around. "Waiting on the spellcaster, I imagine. Long enough that there are no signs of how they arrived. Narjags holding still for an appointment, a spell was released, and then nothing except the tracks where they left the area."

"I don't understand," said Jon.

"Neither do I," admitted Rew. He kicked one of the broken gourds across the camp where it bounced off the rock outcropping. "We need to speak to an arcanist."

Jon nodded agreement. "There's a good one in Yarrow…"

Rew shook his head. "Falvar. We'll go to see Arcanist Ralcrist in Falvar."

"Blythe told me about the younglings," said Jon, ignoring that he was only a few winters older than the boy, Raif. "You mean to take them over the Spine? That's a hard journey, Senior Ranger."

"I know, Jon," said Rew. "I've done it. I won't go, though. I think Blythe is better suited for this. Blythe and maybe you to accompany her."

Jon fell silent, his gaze darting between the remains of the narjag campsite and to where the portal had opened. Jon scratched his head.

Rew felt a twinge of sympathy for the younger ranger. The only thing nearby was Bartrim's farm, a quarter league west. The narjags had been spotted there in the middle of the night, taking some of the livestock. Feasting, it seemed, and then they'd begun to travel. There'd been enough of them that they could have overwhelmed the farmer and his wife with little difficulty had they wanted to. Bartrim had a small farm, but there were still dozens of animals left alive there, along with the farmer himself. It was enough food to last the narjags several weeks. Why had they not killed everything? It wasn't like the Dark Kind to leave fresh meat still breathing.

And what, for King's Sake, had the filthy beasts been waiting on? Rew shifted his weight, wondering uncomfortably if the reason the narjags had taken so little from Bartrim was because they were attempting stealth. He wasn't sure if the creatures possessed the intelligence to hide and wait, but he was certain he'd never heard of them having the patience to do it for days.

"We don't know where they came from, and we don't know where they were going," muttered Jon, beginning to pace. "It's possible they met someone—or something—here. You said it appeared they were going somewhere or running from something when you were on their trail?"

"Narjags having somewhere to be," groused Rew, hitching his thumbs in his belt. "Can't imagine that's very often the case, but I think it must be. There were no tracks of any pursuit, and I never sensed anything behind me. These creatures were going somewhere, and by the direction of their travel, I'd say it was almost due north."

"Wilderness, the Spine…"

"The barrowlands beyond," added Rew.

"That's a long walk," responded Jon.

"Aye, but there's nothing else around here except Eastwatch, and we haven't seen either narjags or a spellcaster in the village. If there's a caster with talent to travel by portal, why would they appear here, so far from anywhere?" wondered Rew. He forced his arms down and turned to the junior ranger. "Let's swing by Bartrim's place and let him know the threat is over but to remain vigilant. The narjags that were harassing him are dead, but I'm not convinced there won't be more of them. There's something going on here I don't understand, and I don't think we will on our own. We need to get to an arcanist. We need to show them the artifacts I took and describe this site and what we've found. Maybe they'll be able to decipher what's going on."

Jon nodded, and Rew waved for the junior ranger to lead. If the boy could find Bartrim's farm without having to ask for guidance, he was making improvements. Small, incremental improvements. Rew was getting a terrible feeling that soon, those skills were going to be needed.

The next evening, five rangers stood over the grave of a sixth. Around them, knee-high oak stakes rose from dozens of other graves. Some of those spears of wood were recent, signs of a new burial. Other pieces were ancient, decaying as weather and time turned the marker back to the dirt from which it came. Once it did, it was said the memory of the deceased was no longer with its family, that it was in the care of the Blessed Mother.

Tate's grave was unmarked, just freshly turned dirt, partially hidden by plugs of turf that they'd sat down atop it. The rangers had their own rites, and their hope was that the body's return to the earth was speedy, that the memory of the ranger lived on not in the minds of friends and family, but in the sighs of the wind through the living trees of the forest, the laughing of a brook as it bubbled over rocks, and the call of the animals as they roamed where few men dared to go. The rangers gave part of themselves to the forest during their lives, and in death, they gave all. There were no words to say, no incantations to perform, just a final goodbye to a man who had served longer than some of them had been alive.

"I found this amongst Tate's things," said Ranger Ang. He fished a leather-bound flask from beneath his cloak. "It's that brandy from down near the coast the old man bought when he was last in Carff. He said it tasted of dates and sea salt."

Without further word, the ranger uncorked the flask and passed it to his left. Vurcell, Ang's twin, accepted the flask and tilted it up. He sighed and offered a wan smile. "Dates and sea salt."

He passed the flask around the circle, and Blythe, Jon, and Rew all drank their share. Finally, Ang received it back and he tilted it up. He licked his lips and shook the flask, listening to the slosh of the remaining liquid. "Not bad. Not bad at all. Didn't think the old goat had a taste for fine spirits. I can't recall the last time I saw him drink something stronger than a cider."

"He didn't have a taste for it," responded Blythe, a smile on her lips. "He meant it as a gift."

"To whom?" wondered Vurcell.

Blythe winked at him.

"Who?" asked Vurcell again, glancing at Rew.

"He meant it as a gift for Jon," answered the senior ranger. "He was waiting for… I don't know what he was waiting for. Meant it as a gift after an expedition or some other milestone that only Tate would recognize. He wanted to welcome you into our fold, Jon."

"For me?" asked the youngest of the rangers. "I didn't know. He always seemed so… harsh."

"He didn't give it to you," reminded Rew.

They were quiet for a moment. Then Jon asked, "Why not, do you think? Did he not believe I was ready?"

"No, of course not," said Rew. He glanced at Blythe, and she shrugged back at him. "You're just as much a ranger as the rest of us."

"You are," said Blythe, nodding.

"Here," said Ang, handing the flask to Jon. "I'm glad I got to have a final sip with the old man while we're out here, but this was meant for you."

Flushing, Jon reached out and accepted the flask. He looked down at it in his hands, as if unsure what to do with it.

"Drink," instructed Vurcell. "Finish it while we're all here."

Hesitantly, Jon drank, and the rest of them stood quietly, enjoying the company of their fellow rangers, privately remembering Tate.

When Jon finished, Vurcell turned to Rew. "These nobles," started the man. "What's your plan for them?"

"Blythe and Jon will accompany them to Falvar," said Rew.

Blythe frowned, and Jon nodded.

Rew continued, "The sooner we get the nobles out of the territory, the better. Ang, Vurcell, you two will head out and look for more signs of Dark Kind in the wilderness. Go directly east and see if you cross any of their tracks. My guess, if there are more, they'll also be headed north."

Ang, gloved fingers tapping on his swordstaff, muttered, "A portal, Dark Kind answering to the calls of men… that's powerful high magic, Rew. You know what this must be related to, don't you?"

"I know," said Rew.

"Will you answer the pull?" wondered Ang. "Perhaps you should go to Falvar instead of Blythe."

"I will not," claimed Rew. "I'm staying here, in Eastwatch, monitoring the wilderness. It is my duty as senior ranger. This is where I belong."

Ang grunted, and Vurcell appeared skeptical. The two rangers, born a minute from each other and companions since that moment, couldn't have looked more different. Their minds followed the same channels, though. They shared a look.

Vurcell said, "Some might argue that during a time like this, you've another duty."

"Not a duty that I've accepted," responded Rew.

"Accepted or not, the king won't care, Senior Ranger," remarked Ang. "I can see it in your eyes. I know you're feeling the pull, the urge to leave. How long can you fight it?"

"Long enough that things will be well on their way if I succumb," grumbled Rew. "I'm staying here in Eastwatch. You two, take the shift at the Oak & Ash tonight to watch over the children, and then Blythe and Jon can take over tomorrow."

Ang and Vurcell shrugged as one then turned and left, heading in the direction of the inn. Jon sheepishly nodded goodbye and hurried after them. Rew and Blythe were left standing over Tate's unmarked grave.

"I haven't known you as long as those two, and I'm not nearly as sensitive to the swirls of power that course through this world," began Blythe, "but—"

Rew held up a hand to stop her.

She crossed her arms over her chest and said, "I'll lead the expedition to Falvar, but I think you should be the one to do it. I can get us there safely, but once we're there… You can't run forever, Rew. Someday, someday soon, you're going to have to face up to what you are."

"I'm the King's Ranger," he said. "I don't want to be anything less or anything more."

Chapter Seven

"My sister says I owe you thanks," murmured the boy, Raif. Rew inclined his head in acknowledgement, not commenting.

"Will you help us?" asked his sister, Cinda.

"I will," Rew replied. "I'll send two of my rangers to guide you through the wilderness and over the Spine. They'll accompany you to Falvar, but I ask in return you implore your father to allow us access to his arcanist. There's been unusual activity in the wilderness, and we need a more informed opinion than our own."

"Of course," said Cinda. "That is fair."

Rew nodded. "I'll send Blythe, the woman ranger who has been standing watch at the inn, and her apprentice, Jon. She's made the journey over the Spine before, and she knows the way to Falvar."

"That ranger, Jon, he seems little more than a boy," mentioned Cinda.

"He's older than you," observed Rew.

She frowned at him but had no response.

"Rew," said a voice behind him.

He turned to see Anne standing there with a frothy mug of ale in one hand and a stack of plates in the other. Her serving girl,

Jacqueline, stepped around her with a steaming platter of roasted mutton. Carrots, potatoes, onions, and stalks of celery floated in the juices around the mutton, and Rew's stomach rumbled at the rich aroma. Anne sat down the plates and gestured for the senior ranger to follow her to the side of the room.

Eyeing the heaped piles of seasoned meat voraciously, Rew walked after the innkeeper to the other side of the room where she handed him the ale.

"You said you're sending Blythe and Jon to guide those children?" she asked.

He frowned at her. "They're hardly children, Anne."

She shook her head. "That lad is rather large, but he has no experience in this world. At his age, you'd—"

"I know what I'd done," interjected Rew. "I know what I'd done, and that's why I don't think it's fair to call him a child."

"He hasn't lived the life you did," insisted Anne. "I spoke to them while you were gone, and they've been sheltered to an extent that's hard to believe. Falvar, Spinesend, and Yarrow are the only places they've been to, and most of their time in those towns was spent behind the walls of the keeps. They've never been out of the eastern duchy, Rew. They've never been on the road without an escort of their father's men. They are no younger than some we'd consider capable adults in Eastwatch, but they haven't done the living. They don't have the maturity to handle weeks of harsh travel."

"Blythe is my best ranger now that Tate is gone," hissed Rew. "She knows the way to Falvar as well as I do. What would you have me do, Anne?"

"Have her manage Eastwatch and monitor the wilderness," said Anne. "Have her do her job."

He tilted his head and asked, "You want me to accompany the children to Falvar?"

"Children, aye," she said, stabbing him in the chest with a finger.

He shook his head, "I didn't mean—It's just because you were calling them that. I can't leave my post, Anne. I'm assigned by the king to this territory, and this is where I must stay."

"You've left plenty of times before," challenged Anne, "and left for far longer than it will take to get to Falvar and back."

"During times of peace and when I had a good reason," he argued. "I fought a pack of narjags just two days past and a party of men the night after. Eastwatch needs me in uncertain times."

"The answers to that uncertainty lie in Falvar," claimed Anne. "The security of the territory means knowledge, and you won't get it sitting here drinking ale in my inn."

"You gave me…" he spluttered, his tankard held uncomfortably in front of him. He shook his head and decided not to pursue that argument. "I'm sending Blythe. She's as capable as I, and she'll get the answers we need."

"She's a ranger, Rew, but she's not the King's Ranger," said Anne, taking a step toward him and putting a hand on his wrist. "If this is really about the Investiture, you think Baron Fedgley is going to spare his arcanist to discuss a necklace of narjag ears you found in the wilderness? If this is about the Investiture, do you think Blythe will learn what you need her to learn? Even if they don't turn her away at the gates, do you think they'll speak to her like they would you?"

"Fedgley's children will get her an audience with the arcanist," retorted Rew, "and as far as I'm concerned, the less I know about the Investiture, the better."

"Children again, is it?" asked Anne, gripping his wrist tightly. "Whatever Fedgley's designs, if the storm of the Investiture has made it to his barony, he and all of his people are going to be drawn in. No one is going to give a fig about a few narjags in the wilderness. You know that. If you want answers, Rew, you are the only one with the authority to make them listen to your questions. You're the only one with the experience to untangle this knot."

He grunted. "I'll send a note…"

"I'm going with them," said Anne suddenly.

"Wait, Anne, no," he complained. "You're needed here, at the inn."

"I'll be needed there as well, if it's the Investiture."

"You'll join the baron's service?" he asked, stunned.

"The less the baron knows of me, the better," she responded. "I don't mean to be drawn into the noble's twisted games any more than you do, but I cannot sit here on the fringe of the realm when people need me. I can save lives, Rew. I can, so I have to."

"And what of the people who need you here?" he asked. "What of the people in Eastwatch who need a healer?"

"They'll be stitched up by the barber," she said. "When the Investiture begins, it's not in Eastwatch an empath will be needed most. Don't try to tell me otherwise."

"Cinda witnessed your work on Raif, and of course the lad himself knows what you did. The Fedgley children will tell their father what you're capable of," warned Rew. "You won't be able to resist getting pulled into his service."

Anne shrugged. "I've got a few weeks to convince them not to say anything, don't I? I'm going, Rew, and you should as well. We've done good work here, these last ten years, but there are others who can manage things in Eastwatch. There's no one else who can—"

"I'm not getting involved," declared Rew.

"Then don't," replied Anne, "but come with us to Falvar. Come with me, Rew. If it looks like the whirlpool of the Investiture is too strong, that I'll be dragged in, you can only pull me out of it if you're there."

"That's unfair, Anne," he complained.

She smiled at him. "Yes, it is."

He was quiet for a long moment, and she let him chew it over. He guessed she knew what he would say. She'd cornered him like a feral hog led into a camouflaged trap. Now that she'd laid her ultimatum on him, made his decision about her safety, Anne knew she'd given him no choice at all. She was just waiting for the kill.

Finally, he asked, "When will the lad be ready to travel?"

"Tomorrow at dawn," she responded.

Rew sighed and glanced back at the three younglings sitting around the pile of roasted mutton and vegetables. They were talking excitedly, glad to have a plan and someone to guide them. Glad that they'd survived the last few days as well, he supposed. He doubted they had any idea of what lay ahead.

"I'll need to pack," he grumbled.

"Eat first," insisted Anne. "It might be your last good meal for a few weeks."

He frowned at her, put his tankard to his lips, and drank deeply of the crisp ale. When he lowered the tankard, he told her, "Another of these, then."

She winked at him and turned to the bar.

Ambling slowly, like a man on the way to the gibbet, Rew moved back to the table. He sat down, and the children fell silent. "Change of plans, it seems. I'll be the one guiding you to Falvar."

The next morning, Rew stood in the common room of the Oak & Ash Inn, rubbing his hand over his freshly shaven scalp. He was looking at the sparse pile of equipment the younglings had packed, his lips bowed into a sour frown. Finally, he said, "All right, then. I'll sort through my pack and show you what I'm bringing. I should have realized… Ah, you didn't know. We'll get you fixed up with what you need to make a journey through the wilderness and over the Spine."

Standing behind the three younglings, Anne smirked at him.

The night before, he'd finished his ale and his meal, another ale, and had stood to leave. Anne had told him that the younglings would need help packing, that they had little and wouldn't know what to bring on the trek to Falvar. He'd waved a hand dismissively, insisting they'd gotten to Eastwatch somehow, hadn't they?

They had made it to Eastwatch, but after he'd opened up their packs for inspection shortly after dawn, he wasn't sure how. Anne had laid out bundles of food for the younglings, just like she and her staff did every time the rangers left on expedition, but that was the only thing in their packs that was actually correct.

Cursing himself for not paying more attention when he'd rifled through their gear while they were in his jail cell, Rew thumped his pack down on a table in the common room and began pulling out the contents. Food. A pot, a pan. Two changes of clothing and several sets of underclothes. A dozen socks. His razor. Soap. A spare belt knife. A set of needles. Thread for stitching rips in his clothing and thinner thread for stitching rips in his flesh. Packets of herbs that could be used for their healing properties or in cooking. He explained that as often as he could, he selected those that could be used in both. He ignored a whispered comment about eating medicine. He showed them a tarp and a bedroll. Twine. A whetstone to sharpen his blades, oil to polish them. Matches, and a pouch of black powder that could be used as a fire starter. Flint and steel in case that got wet or lost.

"I thought rangers could make fire anywhere," interrupted Raif, scowling at the growing pile of neatly arranged items.

"If I had to, I could start a fire in a rainstorm, but I could do it a lot quicker with this," he said, shaking the pouch of powder.

He sat it down, then dropped a clinking pouch of gold, silver, and copper coins beside it, but did not open that one to show the younglings. They didn't ask, so he assumed they guessed what was inside. Their imprisonment for theft was too recent for anyone to want to discuss how the journey's finances would be handled.

Rew sorted through a number of other items until the big youth interrupted again. "Not a lot for entertainment, huh?"

"We've a spare lute back at the ranger station if you'd like to carry it for two weeks through the wilderness, several days crossing the Spine, and then a few more days in the barrowlands," replied Rew. "Do you know how to play the lute? I don't."

"That seems a rather long way," complained Cinda. "Several

years ago when we went to foster, it took us half that time going from Falvar to Yarrow."

"You were on the roads in a carriage," reminded Rew. "This won't be an easy journey, lass, and I'm worried it will take even longer than I've stated if you cannot keep up. If you want to make it shorter, then my advice is start back toward Yarrow and find yourself a carriage."

The girl's lips pressed tightly together, but she didn't argue. She and her brother needed the guidance of the rangers to avoid Worgon and his men. She knew it. Rew knew it. There was no point begging for that help and then disregarding the advice she was given.

Zaine leaned forward, hovering over the ranger's provisions. "Nothing for spellcasting, either."

"I'm not a spellcaster," replied Rew.

"Rangers are rumored to use low magic," said Cinda, suddenly becoming interested again. "Communing with the forest of course, mysterious abilities to hide their passage. Empathy wouldn't be a surprise, nor would glamours. Some of my tutors speculated whether rangers were capable of transmutation."

Rew laughed. "We're just ordinary people, I'm afraid."

"What's transmutation?" asked Zaine.

"The ability to turn into an animal," answered Cinda. She turned back to Rew. "You don't deny a bit of low magic, then? Can you speak to animals?"

"I can speak to animals, sure, just like you can. I've never heard one respond. And walking quietly through the forest is a learned skill," said Rew. "Avoiding fallen branches, not stepping on soft dirt, hiding oneself amongst the trees and the leaves, these things can be taught to anyone and it only requires a little bit of dexterity and caution."

"Some ranger skills are mundane, of course, but that doesn't answer my question about low magic," remarked Cinda.

"It does not," agreed Rew, beginning to repack his kit.

"I'm most effective if I understand the abilities of the rest of the party," declared the noblewoman.

Rew eyed her, realizing that she was confirming the suspicions he'd had earlier. "You are a spellcaster, then? Why didn't you do something to prevent your kidnapping from the cell?"

She frowned at him, like she didn't want to admit her abilities, but she'd just chastised him for the exact same thing. "I am early in my studies as an invoker. My, ah, offensive capabilities were less than those of the spellcaster who kidnapped us. Then, once my hands were bound, there was nothing I could do regardless."

Rew grunted. A nobleman's daughter neck deep in conspiracy, training in spellcasting, drawn inexorably into the Investiture. Pieces were beginning to fall together. They were forming a picture that Rew wished he didn't see.

"And you?" she asked.

"I know a few cantrips that are useful in the wilderness," he said. "Low magic, as you say."

"Low magic?" wondered Zaine.

"Low magic, like empathy, communion, and illusion, is all based on connections to nature or between people," explained Cinda. "High magic, proper spellcasting, includes conjuring, necromancy, enchantment, and, most commonly, invocation. High magic is drawn from the strength of one's blood. Both types are related, but high magic can be performed in solitude, without the connections required for low magic. High magic is more powerful, of course, and is the province of the nobility. Only those with noble blood are capable of casting it, you see."

"Typically," added Rew, ignoring Cinda's sharp look.

"Did that make sense to anyone?" wondered Zaine. "High magic is for nobles, I get that, but what do you mean a connection is needed for low magic? What kind of connection?"

Cinda pursed her lips. "It's something that's taught to every noble since we are small children. It's ingrained in who we are. Who many of us are, that is." Raif grunted, but his sister ignored him. "I'll try to think of a way to explain it…" muttered Cinda, trailing off and brushing her hair behind her ears.

Rew looked between the two girls. What Cinda said was true. High magic tended to be prevalent in those of noble blood, but there was nothing about a man's or a woman's title that made that the case. It was due to careful breeding by those in power, ensuring their blood was mixed only with that of the other noble families. The nobles attempted to purify their lines and increase the odds that the next generation would possess even more magical power. In the heart of the kingdom, it was common for matches to be made solely to enhance a particular trait in a family's magic. Enchanters bred with other enchanters. Learning and practicing the craft was expensive as well, which meant even those of common blood who had a natural talent for high magic rarely developed it.

Whether it was the pursuit of greater power through marriage which gave nobility their purpose and name, or whether it was as crass as selectively breeding livestock, very much depended on who was doing the explaining.

Rew cleared his throat. "As Cinda explained, high magic does not require a connection. When that spellcaster who kidnapped you threw his fiery missiles at me, he had no connection to the fire or to me, but when Anne used her low magic empathy to heal Raif, it was because she established a connection to him and was able to transfer her power through that channel. It's more complicated than this, but it helps me to think of low magic as a riverbed. It funnels power in a certain direction. High magic is an open plain, and there's no direction at all except that which the spellcaster gives it."

"Nobles shape the power to their desires?" asked Zaine, glancing out of the corner of her eyes at Raif and Cinda. "They've no need of connection to other people?"

"Something like that," agreed Rew, grinning at the thrust of Zaine's question, "but it is complicated. Sometimes, high magic does use a connection. Conjurers, for example, use both elements of high and low magic to open their portals to other planes and connect with the creatures there." Seeing Zaine's look, he grinned.

"I'm sorry, I think any quick explanation will leave more questions than answers."

"If it helps, think of low magic as the art of the commoners," said Cinda. "Empathy and healing. Encouraging plants to grow. Communicating with animals. Glamours. Those types of things. High magic, on the other hand, is the grand art of nobility. It's what you hear about in the stories. Calling lightning, summoning elementals, opening portals, and moving throughout the realm at will."

"High magic sounds like it's mostly useful in battle," mentioned Zaine.

Cinda shifted uncomfortably.

Rew said, "There's a reason the nobles are so keen on it. A duke wants to crush his enemies, not grow turnips in his garden. It's a good point, though, in that the connections formed with low magic tend to build, while high magic is frequently used to destroy. That's not its only purpose, but there are spellcasters who use it for little else."

Cinda opened her mouth to respond, but Zaine interrupted. "The spellcaster who kidnapped us was a nobleman, then? He must have been, if he was able to use high magic. There cannot be many with noble blood in the eastern duchy, can there?"

Rew grinned as Cinda flushed. The noblewoman stammered, "A-A lesser branch of nobility, certainly. If, ah, there are times when one may be of noble blood but without a title. In those cases—"

"A bastard, eh?" questioned Zaine. "Bastards have the magical abilities but not the castles?"

Cinda coughed and rubbed her lips with the back of her hand. She mumbled, "Something like that."

"This is all very informative," groused Raif, "but we are in a bit of a hurry. If this journey will really take three weeks…"

Rew nodded. "You're right. Let's get moving. On the way out, we'll stop by the ranger station to finish your kit. Then, we're off."

"A few more socks, a bit of flint and steel?" asked Cinda.

"What else do we need?"

"Weapons, for one," said Rew, losing his grin. "I will do my best to protect you, but the route we take is not a safe one. Just a few days ago, I tracked down a narjag party out in the wilderness. Unfortunately, when moving through the deep forest, there's far worse we'll need to worry about."

The youths swallowed nervously, but none of them objected. Whatever the risks, it was obvious to everyone it would be better to face them with a weapon in hand.

Grinning, Raif lifted a heavy hand-and-a-half sword. It rose nearly to his shoulder from tip to pommel, and the wide steel blade weighed at least a stone. None of the rangers used such a blade on expedition, but over the years they'd accumulated a variety of armaments for training and emergency circumstances.

Hefting the giant weapon, Raif asked, "What about this?"

"A difficult blade to swing within the forest, and it's quite heavy," said Rew. "That's the first concern I'd have. It's a lot of steel to lug along on a journey like this. Remember, if all goes well, we're going to be doing more hiking than fighting, and there's nowhere on the way you can change blades. A weapon like that is designed for heavily armored opponents."

"It'd do some damage against unarmored ones as well, eh?" questioned Raif. "I imagine sweeping this through a pack of narjags would throw 'em back on their heels, wouldn't it?"

Rew sighed but admitted, "It'd do plenty of damage, of course, but it's heavy. It wouldn't be my first choice on a long journey."

Raif hefted the sword in front of him, pointing it down the aisle of the ranger's armory. He shifted his grip and raised it above his head. He nodded. "I spent most of my training with weapons of this size. This one feels well balanced and of adequate quality. I'll take it."

Rew rubbed his face and did not respond.

"What of this armor?" asked the boy, glancing at a chainmail hauberk hanging near the door.

"No," said Rew, shaking his head. "The armor is definitely too heavy for this trek. If you insist on protection, we have some boiled leather cuirass. Add gauntlets and greaves, and you've got enough to stop a blow from a lesser Dark Kind like a narjag. Chainmail isn't necessary against what we may face in the wilderness. It's either too much or too little, and it will only slow you down."

Pursing his lips, Raif moved on from the chainmail and the shining steel helmets to the sets of tough, leather gear that were stacked beside the steel. There was a great deal more of the leather armor, as it was the only thing the rangers ever took on expedition. Scratching his arm beneath his own leather bracer, Rew tried to make it obvious that the forearm protection was the only armor he wore. In the wilderness, the ability to travel quickly could save your life more often than a metal shirt. Raif didn't seem to make the connection.

Shaking his head and turning from the boy, Rew saw that Zaine had collected two curved, bone-handled daggers that were thinner versions of his own hunting knife. The slender blades were nearly as long as her forearm, and as she felt the weight of them, he saw that it wasn't her first time handling such weapons.

"Using both at once is a skill," he advised her.

She nodded, lips pursed together, posing with the daggers as if she faced some imaginary opponent.

"If you haven't trained with two weapons at once," suggested Rew, "then perhaps a short sword might suit better?"

"I think these will serve me," she said, picking up the belt and sheaths that the daggers had been stored in. "Do you have a bow?"

He nodded toward the back of the room. "I recommend one of the smaller, recurved ones. It's an easy enough draw, with plenty of power."

"Of course, if that's what you suggest," she lilted.

Rew grunted then saw Cinda was strapping a thin, hand-length dagger around her waist. It had a wire-wrapped hilt and a small guard. The dagger was more than a simple belt knife, but it would be terribly ineffective against the Dark Kind or any of the other dangers in the wilderness.

"I, ah…" mumbled Rew.

Cinda wiggled her fingers at him. "If it comes to it, I have other ways of defending myself."

Raif had shrugged into a leather cuirass and was adjusting thick pauldrons on his shoulders. His arms and legs were covered with bracers and greaves. "I find gauntlets restrict my movement," he explained, holding up his bare fist.

Rew closed his eyes and forced himself to breathe slowly.

Zaine squeezed by, a bow in hand, a quiver on her back, and the two daggers hanging from her hips.

Rew followed her out of the room and then out of the station, taking in the fresh air, shaking his head at the choices of the younglings. Making sure they had some weapons was better than nothing, but…

Stiff leather rustling, Raif walked down the stairs to stand beside Rew. The boy tapped the hand-and-a-half sword. "I hardly notice the weight. I don't think it's going to be a problem."

"Wait until we've been hiking all day for ten straight days," muttered Rew under his breath. He looked around the party. "Everyone ready?"

They nodded, and Rew gestured for Jon to lead the way into the forest.

Coming to stand beside him, Anne spoke quietly so that only he could hear. "You're doing the right thing, Rew."

"We'll see," he replied, unconvinced.

"It might be fun," she said. Then, she fell into line behind Raif as Jon led them single file into the wilderness.

Shaking his head, certain that it was not going to be fun, Rew brought up the rear.

Chapter Eight

The party stomped through the wilderness, careless feet disturbing the fallen leaves and twigs on the forest floor, shoulders snapping small branches and knocking leaves from others. There was a trail through the first half-league of forest which the rangers slipped along effortlessly, but one wouldn't have known there was a trail the way the rest of the party smashed through the undergrowth.

When they reached a deeper section of the forest, and the undergrowth thinned and the canopy rose, Rew breathed a sigh of relief. It jarred his nerves, hearing the crash of the younglings forcing their way through the low-lying foliage. At least now, the trees were spread wide, their branches soaring far above, blocking the full light of the sun and choking off the growth of anything trying to come up below. Even the younglings had difficulty finding bushes to casually stumble through in the open forest.

That section of forest was easy travel. It was wide open and flat so close to Eastwatch, but already the party was breathing heavy, and Rew could see that his projection of a three-week journey might have been optimistic. Farther along in the deep forest, there were hills and ridges to climb, thick woods to fight through, creeks and rivers to cross, and dangers they'd have to spend days walking around.

Anne, used to being within the borders of the wilderness to collect herbs and mushrooms for her healing and her soups, walked confidently beside him. She grinned at his disdainful glances at the backs of the others. Her red hair was bound back behind her head, exposing her smooth, pale neck. She wore a blouse, several ties undone, but had a trim vest on so the billowing fabric didn't snag on the branches of the forest. Her pack was hitched high on her back, and her skirts were shorter than usual, coming down to mid-calf. They were practical for hiking through the woods, as were the soft leather boots he spied on her feet.

"Meets your standards?" she asked with a raised eyebrow.

He flushed, looking away.

"Are you really worried about what we'll find out here?" she asked him. "The forest has been peaceful in recent years, has it not? I thought there was nothing in the wilderness that scared a ranger."

He rubbed his chin, feeling the neatly trimmed beard there, and answered, "The wild parts of the world can always be dangerous to those who are not experienced traveling through them. There are animals here that can kill a man with the swipe of a paw or the snap of a jaw, and there are places we'll walk where a fall could be fatal, but those risks are manageable. Even Jon knows enough to avoid the worst of those dangers. I believe I can steer us comfortably through the forest. It's the unknown that I worry about."

"The narjags you tracked?" she asked.

He nodded. "The narjags and whomever they met that came through the portal. There's something afoot, but King's Sake, I couldn't tell you what it is."

"The unknown is always frightening," agreed the empath.

He smirked. "It's more than that, Anne. I'm not some apprentice on my first expedition. I've been walking these woods for the last ten years, and I would have thought I'd seen everything these trees have to hide. Yes, there's some uncertainty that makes me nervous when I find I do not know it all, but that is not what is bothering me. What bothers me is why I don't know. This is not some remote valley that none of us have explored before. It's not a dark cave we're uncertain what creature it hides. If a portal was opened, it's because someone opened it. Someone is out there…"

"And…"

"And what?" he asked her.

Anne gestured to the younglings in front of them. "Nobles appearing unexpectedly in Eastwatch, warning of a conspiracy against the duke. Portals opening in the wilderness, and someone contacting the Dark Kind. You know as well as I what this is related to, Rew. You don't need to ponder why these odd things are occurring. You already know."

He looked ahead, not responding.

"I'm glad you decided to come," said Anne.

"I worry about leaving Blythe alone in Eastwatch," said Rew. "I hope that was not a mistake."

"She's not alone. Ang and Vurcell are there, too," said Anne. "They're all experienced rangers, and the three of them can handle whatever comes up. You trust them, don't you?"

"I do," agreed Rew. "Ang and Vurcell are good men, and Blythe could have earned the position of senior ranger if it wasn't for me. I trust her judgement, all of their judgement, and I trust their skill, but what if she's faced with something beyond her? If it's the Investiture, then no one knows what that madness will bring."

"We're not the only ones who know it's the Investiture," replied Anne. "Blythe is well aware of what may be brewing, but as far as that goes, Eastwatch is as removed from the center of the whirlpool as can be. It's why you came here, isn't it?"

He grunted.

"If you cannot run from it in Eastwatch, then you cannot run from it, Rew," murmured Anne. She walked closer to him. "Are you worried for Eastwatch or for yourself?"

Rew did not respond.

"I spoke to Vurcell," said Anne. "He believes you are feeling the pull. Is that true?"

Rew eyed the empath out of the corner of his eye and did not answer. She snorted, and they walked on silently, watching Jon lead the three younglings through the forest.

After another hour, Cinda dropped back to walk beside them. "There is something you are not telling me," she said, glancing between the two of them.

Neither answered.

"Worgon's plot is against Duke Eeron and my father," she said. "Dangerous times for the duke and the other nobles in the duchy, but this territory is the king's land, and you are the king's man. Everyone knows this. You're not worried about Worgon's plot affecting Eastwatch, I don't think. Not even Worgon is arrogant enough to plot against the king. What is it, Ranger? What do I not know?"

Rew studied the foliage around them, ignoring the girl.

"Surely you've heard of the Investiture?" asked Anne.

Cinda frowned at her. "The crowning of a new king? The elevation of one of the princes?"

Anne nodded.

"Of course I have," said Cinda. "I don't—"

"Do you know how the princes are chosen?" interrupted Rew.

"Merit, I suppose," said Cinda, brushing a strand of hair behind her ear. "It's not like amongst the lesser nobles where birth order is the most important factor, is it? From the histories, it has not always been the oldest prince who was granted the crown. It is the decision of the king, I believe, which prince will ascend to the throne."

"That is true for the most part," confirmed Rew.

"Well, what is the problem, then?" snapped Cinda. "Tell me

what you know. You think this plot of Worgon's is related to the crowning of one of the princes?"

"The Investiture is not a matter of the king simply deciding which of his sons is worthy of the throne," replied Rew.

Cinda walked beside him, frowning. Rew glanced at Anne, raising an eyebrow. The empath shrugged.

"Your father hasn't explained the Investiture to you?" wondered Rew.

"Explained what!" demanded Cinda. "What is there to explain?"

"The princes are expected to compete for the right to the throne," said Rew. "The king does not select them. They prove themselves. You've had history tutors, have you not? What do the scholars say about how they prove themselves? What happens to the princes who do not ascend to the throne? Have you never wondered why each king starts with two brothers, but you never hear of the brothers again the moment one of them is crowned?"

She blinked at him. "I-I don't know. I guess I have never thought about it. You're saying there's no cushy position or quiet retirement for the princes?"

Rew smirked.

"No, lass, not a quiet retirement," said Anne.

"They… They plot against each other?" asked Cinda. "It's a competition, and…"

"All nobles always plot against each other," remarked Rew. "They plot when the prize is a farmer's croft. They plot when nothing more is at stake than pride. When the man who comes out on top sits upon the throne and rules the realm, when the losers are… quietly retired, then even brothers will turn against each other. It's expected, the king demands it. They prepare all of their lives for the Investiture, gathering allies, undermining their brothers' plotting, readying themselves to stab each other in the back. The other nobles are drawn into it like leaves on a whirlpool. They're forced to select a prince to support, and not infrequently, they change sides as the winds of fortune blow.

Armies, knives in the dark, magical attacks... Yes, it is a competition. There is only one prize, and only one person left at the end to accept it."

Cinda shook her head. "I don't understand. You think Worgon has been drawn into this competition amongst the princes... But why? What role is he playing out here on the eastern fringe? The princes never come to the duchy, do they? How would Worgon be serving one of them by plotting against Duke Eeron?"

Rew shrugged. "That's the frightening question."

"If the Investiture works as you say, then why have my tutors not taught me about it? Why has my father not said anything?" demanded Cinda.

"Another frightening question which I have no answer to. There's only one man who can answer that," said Rew. "Fortunately, we are going to see him."

Discomfited, Cinda walked faster, catching up to her brother and leaning close, presumably to discuss what she'd just been told.

"Do you think she really did not know?" asked Anne.

"It's difficult to fathom that a nobleman would keep his children so ignorant," answered Rew, "but I don't think she's lying."

They walked on, and Anne said, "I know you, Rew. I know you better than anyone, and I know you are not worried because some prince is going to assassinate his two brothers. You're not worried that a baron did not tell his daughter how bloody their legacy is or prepare her for the violence that was certain to come into her life. What is bothering you? Is it the risk of war or something else?"

"There may be war," he said. "If knives in the dark and magic don't work, the princes will be forced to rely on their soldiers."

"That's always the case," pressed Anne. "There is more, isn't there?"

"There is more," he confirmed, "but I will not tell you. I cannot."

Anne pursed her lips.

He turned to her, stopping. "Anne, I cannot tell you."

"I don't like secrets, Senior Ranger."

He sighed and shook his head, but he didn't respond. He couldn't.

Anne glared at him for a moment and then hurried ahead, catching up to the younglings and pointing out a short bush that sprouted a dozen yards off of their path. He imagined she was telling them of the medicinal properties of it, but he didn't bother to try and overhear.

The Investiture happened every generation, and if the princes did not act quickly to clear the board of their competition—their brothers—then it would devolve into a blood bath. Tragic, yes, but such were the games of the nobility. Anne was right. The potential for widespread war was always the case with the Investiture, and he'd known that since he was even younger than the younglings. He knew what was coming. Baron Fedgley, Worgon, they would know it as well. Duke Eeron would know it, and he would have prepared. There was more to it, though, that none of them knew. There was a reason Rew had fled to the eastern territory and immersed himself in the wilderness beyond the control of the kingdom and it's nobles. He wanted nothing to do with the princes and their bloody struggle, and he wanted even less to do with their father, the king.

Anne, Blythe, and the other rangers knew some of his past, but they did not know all. Rew couldn't help feeling his time for running, for hiding, was over. The Investiture was drawing him in. Anne and Vurcell had guessed correctly. He could feel the pull of the maelstrom on his soul. It was a tug, an urgency to act. He knew what it was calling him to do, but worst of all, he knew the terrible secret of ascension to the throne. However strong that pull, he promised himself that he would run. He would always run from that awful truth. There was nothing else to do.

He grimaced and then increased his pace to catch the others. The Investitures were always bloody. They always cost a terrible price. This time, he felt it would be worse. He could sense it like a headsman's axe raised above the collective heads of the kingdom. Countless people would die. They would die if he ran, but more might die if he didn't.

The crackling fire cut through the burgeoning chill in the air. The two girls huddled close to it, hands held out, their cloaks wrapped tightly around their shoulders. Rew and Anne sat back from the fire, enjoying the cool autumn air, while Jon attempted to strike up a conversation on the other side of the camp with the young noble, Raif.

Finally, the boy grew tired of the ranger's prodding and scooted over to sit beside Rew and Anne. "My sister told me what you said about the Investiture."

Rew nodded but did not respond.

"You think it will be war, then?" asked Raif. "The Fedgleys have not been involved in a major conflict in generations, but we've trained for such. We have as many men as Worgon, but most of them are tasked with watching the barrows. If we're to pull them from that duty…"

Rew shook his head. "There is little risk from the barrows that your father cannot manage."

Raif raised an eyebrow.

"When is the last time Falvar was attacked by ghosts from that place?" questioned the ranger. "Certainly not in your lifetime and I doubt in your father's."

The young nobleman blinked.

"The shades that haunt those ruins and that forsaken steppe have no interest in the living," assured Rew. "They're tied to their barrows, and it takes little effort to keep them there. It's only when a necromancer releases them that the wraiths become a problem for those who are not attempting to plunder their resting places."

Raif rubbed his fingers over his lips. "You're right. It's been generations since the town itself was threatened. So, you think we could pull those men and march to Spinesend? We could support Duke Eeron there in the brewing conflict with Worgon. That, or perhaps we could assemble a flotilla and head down the river toward Yarrow. There are rapids, but it can be done. He'd never suspect it, I don't think." The boy frowned. "It depends on Duke Eeron, I suppose. He's the liege of both my father and Worgon. If, once Worgon's plot is exposed, the baron doesn't relent…"

Rew shifted, then said, "Baron Worgon won't relent. After Duke Eeron finds out what you overheard, what does Worgon have to lose? He'll face the executioner whether he's taken quickly or whether he's captured on the field of battle. The only chance he has is to fight and to win. But it's not a simple conflict of arms you should be most concerned with. It's what happens in the shadows. If Worgon had a spellcaster to send after you, who else does he have in his employ? He won't roll the dice on facing both Duke Eeron and your father in the field. Even if he's gathered an army, that's a battle he cannot win. He'll have another plan, lad. The hidden blade is the one that should worry you."

Raif grunted and glanced toward the hand-and-a-half sword he'd laid beside his pack. "Whatever he tries, we'll be ready."

"A sword is nice to have when you need it," advised Rew, "but it's best if you never have to use it."

"Worgon will fight," declared Raif. "You said he has no choice. He'll fight, and we'll be ready."

"As ready as you can be," said Rew. The ranger stood and stretched, glancing around the camp. They'd boiled and eaten a pot of rice, beans, and salted ham. They'd washed up and laid out their bedrolls. Rew told the party, "It's the necessaries for me and then my bedroll. Jon, take the first watch, will you? After that, we'll each take a turn, about an hour, as best you can figure. And I'll tell you, in the middle of the night, awake by yourself in the heart of the wilderness, it's going to seem like longer."

The others murmured responses and volunteered for their shifts, leaving Rew with the last one.

"Til morning, then," he told them.

The next few days passed in peaceful, but slow, progress. Cinda and Zaine were clearly not used to the constant physical activity of hiking through the trackless forest. Raif, who had spent hours each day at arms practice, was finding that traveling in armor with a giant sword strapped to his back was an entirely different proposition. Each evening, the younglings would flop down to the ground and complain of sore legs, chaffed body parts, and blisters. Each evening, Anne would make a quick circuit, healing the minor injuries and encouraging them. Even Jon took to accepting the empath's offers of comfort, but when she raised an eyebrow toward Rew, he simply shook his head.

Removing the discomfort of aching muscles was no great burden on Anne, but it was a burden. Rew wouldn't put that on her, not when a good night's sleep would fix the problem quick enough. He told himself it was that, and only that. The connection her empathy opened, the pull he felt on his soul… He wouldn't expose her to that. He couldn't let her feel what he did. It was good for the younglings, though, to get them started on the journey. By the end of it, he hoped they would gain stamina, and perhaps in the open grasslands north of Falvar they could make good time.

But on the fourth morning, as he watched them pick their way across a shallow stream, he despaired. In two weeks, the younglings were not going to turn into expert woodsmen. The nobles had simply spent too much time coddled behind the walls of the keeps in Falvar and Yarrow. When they did engage in physical activity, like Raif's arms training, it was in a controlled environment, constantly monitored and tailored toward their every need. They'd never spent time outside of those sheltered confines, and it was terribly obvious.

Jon and Zaine had gone first and had skipped nimbly across

the rocks in the stream. Cinda had started across hesitantly and then promptly slipped and splashed down onto her bottom, soaking her to the waist. Her brother, trapped behind her, teetering in his armor, suddenly squawked as a rock shifted under his foot, and he crashed into the cold water face first, splashing and flailing between bursts of enraged cursing.

"Do you think he can swim?" asked Anne from where she stood on the creek bank.

Rew shrugged. "He shouldn't need to. That water isn't any deeper than his knee."

Watching the boy for another moment, Rew took a few steps forward, suddenly wondering if he would need to wade in and drag the oaf to the far bank, but finally, Raif got his feet under him and stood, hands held wide for balance.

"Are there no bridges in this place?" growled the boy.

"This is the wilderness," reminded Rew. "There are some who venture into the outskirts two or three days from Eastwatch, but it's rare anyone other than a ranger journeys this deep, so no, we haven't built bridges, and this won't be the only stream we need to cross. There are deeper, wider ones farther north. You'd best learn to walk across those rocks."

Grumbling, Raif made his way to the edge of the water, stumbling once and falling to his knee before finally scrambling up the side of the shallow bank, digging his hands into the soil, and hauling himself up.

Rew walked easily across the stones in the stream then turned to offer Anne a hand. She waved him off and made her own way across, moving slowly but confidently. It was not her first time in the forest, and she'd crossed hundreds of streams looking for supplies for her inn and her healing.

Rubbing his hand over his prickly head and glancing at the soaking wet nobles, Rew suggested, "We'll take a moment to let you all dry off. Walking any distance in wet boots is going to rub your feet raw. Jon, get us a fire started?"

The younger ranger nodded and quickly found a flat piece of

ground where they could rest. He started a fire then helped the younglings string twine between the trees where they could hang their clothes to dry.

Anne began moving about, checking to see if Raif and Cinda had injured themselves when they plopped down into the water. Rew winked at her then told the rest of the party he'd go scout ahead while they rested. Zaine asked if she could come, and he shrugged.

The blonde moved with a lithe grace that would have served her well as a ranger, though it was clear she was a stranger to the forest. Not for the first time, Rew speculated about how she'd ended up with the nobles and whether what she'd said about being in the thieves' guild was true. She was too young, but it was a dangerous thing to claim to a pack of thieves if it wasn't true. Rew had been watching, waiting for her to remove her boots where he could see the soles of her feet. The guilds' marked their members with small tattoos there, a danger if they were caught by the authorities but one they were willing to risk as it ensured complete loyalty. The mark of the guild signified membership in one society but ostracized its bearers from all others. Once marked, there was no going back. So far, Zaine had managed to change outside of Rew's view, and with Anne there, he'd been careful about trying to surreptitiously catch the young girl mid-dress.

As they moved out from the camp, he told Zaine to follow his movements and nodded appreciatively when she fell into his footsteps. She weaved around the low-lying bushes and stepped over fallen branches and leaves as he did. She was slow and hesitant, but the potential was there. He turned to look ahead, letting his lips curl into a smile. One out of three of them who wasn't a hopeless case. It was something.

Quietly, they moved another thousand paces from where the others had set up camp. She asked him, "Anything in particular we're looking for?"

"No," he said, though he wondered if it was true. Was he

merely looking ahead, or was he searching for signs of narjags or other foul creatures? He told her, "Us rangers have a few typical routes we take on expedition when we're patrolling various sections of the wilderness, but there are no truly established paths. Periodically, we venture as far as the Spine, but it's only every few years that we'll actually cross it. The Spine marks the edge of our mandate, and it's quicker to go through Yarrow and Spinesend on the roads if we need to reach Falvar. So, while I've traveled this way several times, this wilderness is too vast to know every stream, ravine, and hillock. We're scouting ahead to make sure the travel is as easy as I can make it."

Zaine grinned. "The nobles aren't used to a long day of hiking. I found the same when I was guiding them to Eastwatch."

"And why were you guiding them to Eastwatch?" asked Rew.

He heard her hesitate, and then she kept walking behind him.

"The roads would have been watched—" she started.

"Nothing to do with the thieves' guild, then?" he questioned, slowing so that they walked beside each other.

She stumbled, suddenly less graceful than she was moments before. "Why do you say that?"

"Had you fallen in the creek like the others, would you have removed your boots to dry them by the fire?" he asked.

"I'm beginning to understand why the empath seems put out with you so often," muttered the girl. She reached out and tugged on the branch of a tree they were passing, trying to pull it off but letting it go so it sprang back behind them.

Rew waited, letting his question settle while they walked side by side through the forest.

"Yes, I would have removed my boots," said Zaine. "What do you know of the thieves' guild? There are no thieves in the territory, as far as I know. Why do you think I would have anything to do with them?"

"I didn't always live in the territory," said Rew. "That, and I overheard what you told those thugs when you were trying to talk your way out of the kidnapping. Did Cinda not catch onto your meaning, or did she already know?"

Zaine, staring straight ahead, replied, "I am not a member of the thieves' guild in Spinesend or elsewhere. I hoped telling those fools I was a member would convince them to release us. It didn't work, as you saw."

"It didn't," he agreed, "but you've a lot of knowledge about the thieves' guild for one who is not a member. You've a curiously thorough knowledge of the law as well. Are you perhaps a judge or a barrister?"

She snorted.

"What's your involvement with the thieves' guild, lass?" he pressed her.

"It's complicated," she admitted.

"An apprentice, then," he surmised.

"I'm not," she said. "I have nothing to do with the guild, but if I did, would you turn me in when we arrive in Falvar?"

"I've no authority there, lass," he reminded. "Besides, if the House of Fedgley wants to punish you for being a thief, then Cinda and her brother already know. I am curious, though, how did you end up with these nobles?"

"A friend of a friend introduced us," claimed Zaine.

Rew laughed.

Sheepishly, the girl shot him another look. "They found me, Senior Ranger. I won't say I've always been on the right side of the law, but I've been as honest with them as I am with anyone. I know you think it suspect I brought them this way, but I'll tell you the truth. I've never seen a map of these surroundings. A friend suggested we go this way, and I figured we'd find passage over the Spine with little difficulty." She shrugged. "Cinda and Raif both thought it a fair idea, and I trusted they'd know the lands better than I. Evidently, they must have thought I knew… Well, none of us were as prepared as we should have been. It started because they paid me to slip them from the city, and I did. Then, we agreed we'd carry on together. You can ask them, and they'll confirm the truth. After helping them escape, Yarrow is no longer safe for me, so I've just as much reason to travel to Falvar as they do."

He studied her, and she turned from him, flushing. She wasn't lying, exactly, but she wasn't telling the entire story, either. Suddenly, he stopped walking.

"I-It is the truth, Senior Ranger," stammered Zaine.

He held a finger to his lips, looked around, and said, "Something is out there. Let's go back to the others."

"Something watching us?" she asked.

"No, not watching us," he said, his stride quickening. "Hurry along. We don't have a lot of time."

No longer practicing stealth, they made it back to the others quickly.

Jon looked up at them in surprise. "Back already?"

Rew glanced over the party. Jon was squatting comfortably near Anne, who sat cross-legged on the forest floor. Raif was standing in his small clothes, shivering in the early autumn air, holding his hands out to the fire. Three bedrolls had been strung in a triangle between the branches of a couple of trees, and presumably, Cinda was huddling inside of them changing her clothing.

For a moment, Rew wanted to comment on the ridiculousness of trying to maintain privacy in the wilderness, but he shook it off and asked, "Do you hear that?"

Raif looked around uncertain, goosebumps pebbling his pale flesh. Anne shrugged. Jon surged to his feet.

"Barking... Yipping?" asked Zaine, frowning. "Are there, ah, dogs in the wilderness?"

"Ayres," hissed Jon.

Rew nodded.

"How far?" questioned the junior ranger, drawing his longsword.

"Two leagues," said Rew.

"They'll come for us?" asked Anne.

"I hope so," said Rew, gesturing at the fire. "They will have sensed us before I heard them. Smelling the fire is probably what's got the ayres so excited. It would be very unusual if they ignored us once they detected our presence."

Raif had moved to his wet clothing and armor and was tugging on his trousers.

"Leave the armor alone," instructed Rew. "You don't have time to put it on. Get your sword. Stand behind Jon and I. Be ready to swing at anything that gets past us." He turned to Zaine. "Do you know how to use that bow?"

"It's been a few years…"

"Do what you can," he said. "Ayres are fast, so you'll have to lead them quite a bit. Unless it's a perfect shot, it won't kill them, so aim for the narjags if they're riding the ayres. Whatever you do, be sure not to hit any of us."

Anne had moved to the bedrolls and was whispering to Cinda. The girl emerged, evidently having already changed into a dry dress.

Cinda flexed her fingers. "I may be able to—"

Rew shook his head. "Jon and I can handle a few ayres and narjags. Stay with Anne, and watch what we do. If you're not skilled at it, spellcasting could do as much harm as good."

Cinda glared at him, evidently put out at being told to stay with the empath, but he meant it. He didn't want to be dodging poorly aimed magical attacks from behind while dealing with the ayres and their riders. A few of them should pose little risk to him and Jon, but they had the added complication of needing to protect the others.

Wordlessly, Rew gestured the group into position, having the women put their backs to the small fire and cluster close together. Raif stood in front of the women, and Rew and Jon stood in front of the lad.

"I don't have time to teach you much, but if an ayre is coming straight at you, and there's a narjag on its back holding a spear, always jump to the opposite side of the spear. Don't let the ayre come directly at you, but don't dodge out of its way too early either. Whatever you do, don't let it get its teeth into you."

They nodded, clutching their weapons, fear growing in their eyes.

Jon leaned close and whispered. "Senior Ranger, I've never faced an ayre before."

Rew slapped him on the back. "Just hold my side. You'll be fine."

"I, ah, I've never seen a narjag, either," muttered the younger man.

Rew gripped Jon's shoulder. "I've sparred with you enough to know you'll be fine."

The senior ranger drew his wooden-hilted longsword and looked into the forest where, at any moment, the ayres would appear. Rew could hear their excited barks and yips and knew their party wasn't going to be ignored.

Listening to the noises of the approaching animals, he told his companions, "Three of them, I think."

Beside him, Jon set his feet and raised his sword to his shoulder. Raif took the other side.

"Back," hissed Rew, but it was too late to adjust.

Through the trees, they could see the bounding shapes of blue-skinned ayres. Narjags clung to their backs, hands gripping the rope harnesses they used to stay on the mounts, their other hands holding short spears. The ayres were fast, running in bounding gaits like wolves but snapping their squared jaws aggressively and whipping their heads from side to side like they'd gone mad from sickness. Their eyes were larger than a wolf's and were watery-yellow. Their skin was hairless, cobalt blue. It bunched thickly at their joints and was as tough as leather armor to cut through. They looked underfed, loose skin draped over bone, but Rew knew that they held their weight and their muscle in their hips and their necks—hips to propel them in leaps to pounce on prey, their necks to rip and tear once they'd sunk their teeth into flesh.

Jon and Raif edged closer to him, nervous.

Rew cursed. "Spread out, you fools."

If they heard him, they didn't respond and only shuffled unconsciously closer still, eyes fixed on the approaching Dark Kind. With the two younger men crowding his sides, Rew's maneuverability was lessened. He would have no chance to dodge to the side, and he couldn't fall back and leave them exposed, either. That left forward.

When the ayres and their riders were a dozen paces away, he charged, running straight into the lead creature's path. It saw him coming and leapt to attack, its rider shrieking a high-pitched battle cry, but Rew had timed his movement so that he met the ayre as it was mid-leap, unable to turn on him.

He breezed past it, his longsword carving a wicked gash across the ayre's throat and down its side. He dragged the point of his longsword through its tough, dark blue skin then brought the blade around in front of him in time to meet a second of the ayres. He thrust forward, stabbing this one directly in the neck, just above its breastbone.

His longsword sank deep, snagging in the body of the charging ayre. Rew let go of the hilt and stepped sideways, letting the momentum of the dying beast carry it by. He raised a forearm and caught the side of the narjag's spear with his leather bracer, shoving it away. With his other hand, he grabbed the throat of the narjag as it streaked past, tearing it from the back of the dead ayre.

The narjag wailed as Rew spun it. He smashed the narjag's compact, muscular body to the ground and pinned it with a knee. Whipping his hunting knife from his belt, Rew punched it into the chest of the narjag and then lurched to his feet, stepping around the dead ayre and tugging his longsword from its motionless body.

The surviving ayre had charged Jon, and the ranger had acquitted himself well, chopping the forelegs of the thing, crippling it. The narjag rider had catapulted over the shoulders of its mount and crashed to the ground, stunned.

The narjag rider from the first ayre that Rew had struck had ridden its ayre to the dirt then jumped off, attacking Raif. The big youth was wheeling his hand-and-a-half sword around and lashing out with a sweeping blow. The narjag raised its own crude blade to parry the attack, but the giant hand-and-a-half sword smashed through the narjag's weapon and took the Dark Kind in the torso, thunking into it hard, cleaving halfway through the narjag's body.

Rew advanced on the lone narjag that survived, the one that had attacked Jon, but Zaine released an arrow, striking it in the shoulder and spinning it. Then, Jon was there, thrusting his longsword into the narjag's chest for the killing blow. Foul, black blood dripping from his weapons, Rew stepped to the ayre that Jon had crippled, and he silenced it with a powerful overhand strike to the neck.

The party was uninjured, and their foes were dead. The younglings began speaking at once, all babbling in amazement at the speed and brutality of the fight.

Rew ignored them, staring at the dead Dark Kind. Three ayres with narjag riders. Why were they there?

Jon walked to stand beside him, and Rew met the younger ranger's gaze. Jon raised an eyebrow in question, shooting his eyes to the dead ayres, but Rew could only shrug.

In years past, ayres and their narjag riders functioned as a scouting and swift attack force for the Dark Kind. They could cover far greater distances than the narjags alone, and the more intelligent narjags kept their mounts on task. The pairs of them were hell to chase down. Fifty years ago, during the last full-scale war with the Dark Kind, Rew knew they'd wreaked havoc behind the lines as the quick-moving groups ravaged small settlements, but that had been the last time Rew was aware the units had operated effectively. In recent years, even during the last migration two years prior, the ayres and narjags seemed to function independently, and only occasionally was a narjag seen atop a mount. Whatever bond they'd held seemed to have been broken.

What had changed? What were three pairs of them doing in an isolated place in the wilderness, and where had they been going? There was nothing to raid, nothing to scout nearby. Rew rubbed at the stubble on his head. Two separate parties of narjags passing through the wilderness seemingly headed in the same direction. Something was going on, but he couldn't fathom what.

He sighed and moved to assist Raif, who still in just his trousers, was trying to free his hand-and-a-half sword from where it'd snagged in the spine of the dead narjag. The boy had raised a bare foot as if he meant to put it on the narjag to help free the blade but cringed at the sheen of ichorous blood that covered the creature.

"Pull," said Rew, stepping on the narjag with his boot. Over his shoulder, Rew called to the others, "Separate the wet clothing and let's wait to dry it until we camp for the night. The stench of narjags isn't pleasant when they're alive, but trust me, it doesn't take long for a dead one to become unbearable."

Chapter Nine

Six days into the journey, they walked along a ridge, looking down into a deep, narrow valley. A band of river cut through dense forest, the water reflecting like crystal in the morning sun. The trees were thick, mostly pine, but the green of the pine was speckled with the colors of autumn as oak and elm broke through the canopy. It was serene and beautiful, but it hid a terrible danger.

"You're certain we're high enough up?" asked Cinda, staring down into the valley.

Rew grinned. "We should be. We've done what we can to stay safe. We're at the top of the ridge. We can't go any higher, and avoiding this valley entirely would add four days to our journey." He pointed down the other side, away from the river valley, where the crest of the ridge they were walking along fell away into an expansive breadth of shorter, scrub-like trees and outcroppings that burst randomly through the foliage. "It's difficult to see from here, but the land down there is broken, shattered. The soil is thin, so there are no tall trees blocking the undergrowth. It's covered in brambles, and we'd have to chop our way through. There'd be as much climbing as there would be walking through that stretch. It's all short, jagged outcroppings and boulders, but here on the ridge, the travel is as easy as it is anywhere in the wilderness. We've just got to be careful not to venture down the wrong side of the slope."

"Easy, unless one of these… what did you call it, a simian?" she asked. "Unless one of these simians comes up here after us."

"There's a reason this is wilderness, lass," he said. "Look around you. This land is beautiful and verdant. If it was safe to live here, Eastwatch wouldn't be the fringe of the kingdom. But it's not safe. East of Eastwatch, it'd be difficult if not impossible to form a settlement in this forest without encroaching on something a lot bigger and nastier than we are. The narjags are just the start of it. Dark Kind are dangerous in large groups, but as long as they don't gather, they're little problem. It's the natural creatures that pose the greatest risk day to day. Simians, bears, wolves, primal sloths that have shoulders as high as the roof of the ranger station, silver-breasted harpies when we near the Spine, giant marrow spiders, rock trolls, and even forest drakes. Believe me, the last thing you want to do is go anywhere near the hunting grounds of a forest drake. If people tried to build a village out here, it wouldn't be long until something came along that viewed them as food."

Cinda shuddered.

"Your home has its dangers as well," he advised. "Everywhere does. Outside of Falvar in the barrowlands, you've wraiths to worry about. They don't frighten you because your people have charted which barrows are active, and it's easy to avoid those. If you were to stumble into the wrong crypt, though… There's little danger when you have knowledge of your surroundings, whether you're in the wilderness or Falvar. It's when you're on unfamiliar terrain that the risk is serious, and that's true anywhere that you are. Even the civilized places like the capital have courtiers, and truth be told, I'd rather deal with a simian than one of those."

Cinda laughed, and Rew grinned, happy to have taken her mind off the dangers of the world. The girl was bright, and he imagined she was normally inquisitive and thoughtful, but the stress of fleeing Yarrow, the kidnapping in Eastwatch, and the attack by the narjags and ayres two days prior had sent her into a terrible depression. She'd shuffled along, one foot in front of the other, and it'd pained him to watch. It pained him even more to know that worse was ahead. Not even the girl's brother had been able to cheer her.

They walked on, and after a moment, she asked him, "You've been to the capital, or were you jesting?"

"I've been to Mordenhold," he admitted.

"Can you tell me of it?" she asked. Flushing, she added, "I've never been outside of Duke Eeron's duchy. Spinesend is the greatest city I've seen, and from what my tutors have told me, it's a speck compared to Carff or Mordenhold."

"Not a speck, I wouldn't say," said Rew, grinning at her, "but yes, it's much smaller than those two cities. Carff is a beautiful place, as you might expect for the capital of the eastern province, though it's rather crowded for my taste. It's filled with arches and domes, formed of the red sandstone that surrounds the city, but instead of blending into the terrain, it seems to burst from it. The sandstone is painted in a myriad of bright colors. Tiles decorate most of the doorways and windowsills. Colorfully stained glass is set in the windows of those who can afford it, and who cannot hang sheer curtains. Shimmering domes of copper and tin adorn the buildings, and the people wear light linen robes dyed in vibrant hues. Poets spend volumes describing Carff, but to me, it looks as though a drunken artist stumbled and spilled his entire palette over the city."

"It's a hub of commerce, isn't it?" asked Cinda.

"It is," confirmed Rew. "It's the largest sea port in the kingdom, and one of the few places that interacts with the lands beyond the realm. Carff's streets are filled with strange languages and scents. It's both wonderful and overwhelming." He waved a hand around them. "You may have guessed, I prefer solitude."

She grinned at him. "And Mordenhold?"

Rew's smile wavered. "It's less crowded than Carff and less

colorful. Mordenhold sits deep in the mountains, only accessible by a few roads that are guarded by stout walls and watchtowers. Where Carff is a city that grew up because of its access to the sea trade and the wider world, Mordenhold grew because it's inaccessible. The original king, Vaisius Morden, prized defense above all. His capital reflects that attitude."

Cinda nodded, her eyes sparkling.

"It sits athwart a major east-to-west highway, and merchants have a much quicker time passing through than going all the way around the mountains, so there is commerce," continued Rew, "but the purpose of the city is rule and war. Mordenhold is a grim place of dark stone and soaring battlements. The streets are filled the clank of steel instead of the babble of strange tongues. The military and the courtiers all wear the black livery of the Mordens, and even the burghers favor darker shades. Where Carff smells of the sea and exotic spices, Mordenhold smells of snow and oil on metal. The smithies are fired constantly, crafting weapons and armor for the king's soldiers."

"There's an academy there, is there not, for spellcasters?"

Rew grunted. "Yes. It's… Yes."

Cinda frowned at him.

He kept walking and finally decided that he may as well explain. "There's an academy but not one I recommend you ever visit. It's not a place of study and thought as you might imagine. High magic passes through the blood, as you know, and there's no blood purer than that of the king's line, so while the masters spend some time developing their students, they spend just as much trying to strengthen the bloodlines. It's a cold, callous environment, filled with people who think only of themselves and their own standing."

"They try to strengthen the bloodlines?" questioned Cinda.

"Many of the matches between the highest-ranking nobles are concocted within the halls of the academy. Unions are directed by scholars and genealogists in the king's employ," explained Rew. Before she could speak, he kept on, "And there are the bastards, children of high-ranking nobles with the talent that comes with their blood but without the income and opportunities. The bastards are collected in the academy and trained there for service to the king. They're bred as well, with little choice in their mates, and no one to look out for them. The progeny from such relations have even less freedom. The only life they know is in the academy, and the indoctrination they receive there. Powerful practitioners of high magic are too dangerous to be allowed freedom, so they're held captive, by psychological and magical means. It is not pleasant, being forged into a tool for the realm."

Cinda brushed a strand of hair behind her ear. "I… I've never heard it described in this way."

"I did not find Mordenhold a joyful place," said Rew. "If you have the opportunity to visit one of the kingdom's great cities, then I recommend Carff, or Jabaan in the west."

She nodded and opened her mouth as if she would have a question, but he held up a hand to stop her. Rew paused then slung his pack off, setting it on the ground and flipping open the top.

"What?" asked Cinda, glancing around nervously.

"See down there by the river, where it curves around the bend? Look at the inside of the elbow, on the rocky beach."

She frowned. "That's a bit far away."

"I know." He stood, offering Cinda a small, leather-bound, brass spyglass from his pack. "Look through this."

She took it and turned, adjusting the spyglass and trying to find the curve he'd mentioned on the river.

"Blessed Mother!" she cried, drawing the attention of the others. As they scrambled back to see what the matter was, Cinda asked, "Is that a simian?"

Rew confirmed that it was.

"It's big," she said.

"A full-size adult may have three, four stones of weight on your brother," said Rew. "They're strong, too. I guess swinging from tree to tree and holding on with those long arms of theirs builds muscle. You can't let one of those get a hold on you, or it's over. They have no claws, but they can tear a man's arm off with ease. Their teeth are dangerous, too. Most are like ours, but they've two big fangs the size of my pointer finger. If they chomp down on you with that, well, you can imagine."

Nodding, Cinda held out the spyglass to her brother and pointed where she'd been looking. "It has an animal its eating. A deer, maybe, but I can't be certain."

Rew told her, "They'll take a deer if they can, though simians are not quick hunters. They tend to wait high in the trees and drop when something walks below them. Deer are nervous and always ready to bolt. A quick-footed one can be away before the simian is on them. Wild hogs are common prey, but those either learn to avoid the territory of the simians, or they're gone soon enough. Hares, birds, squirrels, and other small creatures are what the simians feed on most often."

"People?" asked Cinda.

Rew grinned. "If they have the chance. The rangers know the territories of all of the simians within a week or so of Eastwatch, and we avoid them. Every now and then, though, they wander out or we accidentally wander in. Fortunately, simians tend to keep to the deep forest, so there's little risk in the vicinity of Eastwatch."

"When you described it," murmured Raif, "I thought it'd be cute like a monkey. I've seen those in the markets in Spinesend. They're sold as pets, there. This is… It is not cute."

"I wouldn't be surprised if simians and monkeys are related," said Rew with a laugh, "but simians are ten times the size of the largest monkeys and twenty times as mean. I'd guess their branch of the family tree came from some ancient, angry, and drunk uncle."

Raif, shaking his head, passed the spyglass to Zaine and gripped the hilt of his hand-and-a-half sword. "If one came up here and attacked us, what would we do?"

"Get behind me," advised Rew. "That or run. Simians are solitary creatures, only coming together to breed. The young stay with the females after birth for about a year. Then, she kicks her offspring out of her territory, and they're on their own until they're mature enough to earn their own breeding partner. As long as it's not mating season, you can safely assume there will only be one of them. I've faced them before and know what to do, so just let me handle it."

Raif rolled his shoulders. "Hide behind you. That's your answer to every danger we come across."

Rew raised his hands, palms up. "That's because it's what you should do every time we come across something dangerous. I've been out here ten years, lad, and I've faced just about everything this wilderness has to offer. Trust in my experience, and I'll get you to Falvar."

"You keep calling me a lad, but I'm a full-grown man, you know," remarked Raif gruffly. "I had my eighteenth winter this last new year. I could inherit and rule."

"Fair enough," said Rew.

After the younglings had spent enough time awing over the simian far below in the valley, they began to hike again, moving along the crest of the ridge, the land falling away below them on both sides. It afforded them an excellent view of the surrounding forest. In the distance they could see the gray face of the Spine rising up toward the sky. That day, its top was obscured in thick, white clouds, but Rew hoped it would blow off before they descended from the ridge so he could get a good look at the peaks. It was early autumn and still comfortable in the forest, but at height, it wouldn't be unusual to see a bit of snow. Rew wanted to see what they would face when they ascended to the passes.

"How are we going to get across that?" asked Raif.

"There's a way that I'd prefer to take if it's open," explained Rew as they walked along. "It's narrow and is blocked easily when there is snow and ice. Another month, and I wouldn't bother even trying for it, but if it's open, it's the quickest route. You know the old border forts out in the barrows? There's one of them on the other side of the pass. I don't know the name of it, but for as long as I've been in the east, it's been a base for a mining operation. If we can get to it, the trek down will be much easier. There's an established road between the old fort and Falvar."

"I'm familiar with the place," said Raif. "I visited the fort once, as a child, but I don't recall anything about a pass through the mountains above it."

"It's rarely used," said Rew. "One, because it's rare anyone travels through the wilderness at all, and two, it's a bit risky to brave the pass."

"Risky?"

Rew nodded. "Not particularly more dangerous than hiking through the forest, but there are different dangers. Rock trolls instead of simians, that sort of thing."

Raif swallowed uncomfortably.

"Outside of the boundaries of the realm, the world is ruled by beast, not by man," added Rew.

"So it seems," said Raif. He hurried to catch up to his sister, presumably to tell her about the rock trolls.

Jon fell in with Rew, letting the younglings take the lead as it was simple enough to follow the line of the ridge. He slowed, and Rew mimicked him until the others were out of earshot.

"I've been thinking. Those ayres the other day were headed north," mentioned the younger ranger, "just like the narjags you tracked down."

Rew nodded.

"We're headed north."

"The same occurred to me," said Rew. He kicked at a pinecone, sending it tumbling down the side of the ridge. "Both parties of the Dark Kind were headed north, away from Eastwatch and the farms and homes scattered around the region. Neither party of the Dark Kind seemed to be roving about, looking for food. Instead, they were going somewhere."

"What do we do?" wondered Jon.

"We keep moving. We keep an eye out for tracks," said Rew. "I've seen what I believe are some more signs, but they're old. If it wasn't for the younglings, I'd be following the narjags, going north, just as we are. Is it another migration? I hope not, but what else could it be?"

Jon nodded.

"The answers to all of our questions about the Dark Kind and these younglings seem to lie in the same direction, and that worries me, Jon."

The younger ranger cringed, and Rew offered a grim smile. Somehow, the arrival of the youths, the Investiture, and the movement of the narjags, were related.

For days, they moved through the wilderness, avoiding the haunts of known creatures, and trying to avoid the unknown ones. They had to scare off a curious bear with shouts and clapping, and Zaine had woken them all shrieking one night as a swarm of bats burst from a cave set into a hillock they'd camped beside. They'd all laughed about it until a giant marrow spider came bounding out of the cave after the bats. The spider, its legs splayed as wide as a man was tall, had flung a glob of disgusting thread from its spinneret and caught Anne's leg. The huge arachnid had attempted to reel the empath in, but Rew arrived in time to stab his longsword through its soft body. No one had slept the remainder of the night, and it'd been a foul-tempered party that had started hiking shortly after dawn.

The next evening, they'd spied a red-bearded primal sloth strolling across an open field in front of them. Each of its legs was taller than even Raif, and its feet were as wide as a shield. They'd crouched, holding their breath, as the giant animal passed without noticing them. They'd walked nervously until they saw the normal forest resume without the crushed trees and deep impressions the sloth left in its wake. That night as the sun was setting, the younglings had thought they'd seen a drake far in the distance, though Rew guessed it was more likely another bat and much closer. Drakes were rare, even a week's walk from the nearest settlement. The creatures avoided people.

"If they avoid people, how do you explain the stories?" questioned Raif. "I grew up on tales of knights fighting giant drakes, and I'm told my father's grandfather slayed one of the monsters. His enchanted greatsword hangs behind my father's throne as a reminder of the strength of the Fedgleys."

"Could be," allowed Rew. "I don't know your great grandfather's tale, but I know that most drakes, most of the time, avoid people. When they're disturbed or angered, they don't. There is little in the natural world more frightening than a drake angry enough to seek out people."

Raif grunted, peering into the night where he thought he'd seen the flying lizard.

"Have you ever seen a drake up close?" asked Cinda.

"I haven't seen a drake in the wilderness," said Rew, "though, in the deep forest, we have found signs. Years before I became a ranger, there was an encounter with one, and all I can say is that I'm glad I was not there. We've had plenty of other odd appearances. It's part of the role of a ranger, of course, to keep those stray wanderers within the forest and away from the rest of the king's lands. Almost ten years ago, shortly after I arrived in Eastwatch, we had one of those red-bearded sloths walk right down the street. It went from one end of the village to the other. Then, it crushed the brewer's shop. That alone was a tragedy, but the brewer and his family attacked the sloth, and it killed three of them. The senior ranger at the time just watched and let it go when it headed back into the wilderness. Said if we confronted it, more people were going to die, so the best thing was to stay out of its way. Good advice for a lot of situations, I've found."

"Oh my," said Cinda, glancing behind them, clearly thinking of the giant animal that they'd seen. "In the village…"

"Exactly," said Rew.

"That's the job of the rangers, then?" asked Zaine. "You patrol these lands, making sure what's out here stays out here? Thought you'd said some bit about hunting the Dark Kind."

"We monitor the beasts in the wilderness," explained Rew. "Keeping order within the territory is part of our role. Much like we enforce the king's laws, we'll deal with anything that threatens the safety of the villagers in Eastwatch. For the most part, though, we try to leave the natural creatures alone as long as they stay within the deep forest. The Dark Kind are different. Those, we hunt. You're familiar with the migration that happened two years ago when the Dark Kind crossed the Spine?"

"They were fleeing the barrowlands," said Raif. "We were driving them out. My father and his men rode against them before they made it into the crags of the Spine. Killed hundreds of them, but I suppose some got away."

Rew nodded. "Hundreds of the Dark Kind crossed. It was our role as rangers to track them and to finish them."

"Only you and the other rangers we met?" questioned Cinda. "You fought hundreds of narjags? You killed them all?"

Rew shrugged. "We killed all that we could, though certainly some got away. With so many, it was impossible to hunt them all once they scattered."

"Impressive," muttered Raif, shaking his head in disbelief.

Rew winked at him. "They began to fragment nearly the moment they made it out of the foothills of the Spine, so we didn't fight them all at once. Narjags are disagreeable and fractious creatures, and without a valaan commanding them, they don't stay together long. We didn't attempt to face the entire group. We waited until they split apart and then hunted those smaller groupings."

"Ah," said Raif, giving a satisfied nod.

"What would the Dark Kind do in the wilderness?" wondered Cinda. "Would it be better to leave them unmolested as long as they did not try to enter the lands of men? Let the sloths and the simians deal with them…"

"The Dark Kind are anathema to the natural beasts," said Rew. "Those creatures would avoid them, allowing the Dark Kind a chance to procreate. They'd build their ranks then have the strength to fight the natural beasts in these woods. They'd fight those creatures and us. Narjags reproduce like rabbits, and they'll kill and eat nearly anything. It wouldn't be long before there would be enough of them to form an army. As I mentioned, it's not easy to organize a large group of narjags, but if a valaan or some other creature did… Your father and his men can face a few hundred Dark Kind in the field. Maybe even a thousand if the baron was warned and had time to prepare, but ten thousand? That's enough to overrun Falvar. Fifty years back, there were hundreds of thousands of Dark Kind. It was more than any individual baron or duke could stand against. We lost that many people before the king arrived with his army and the Dark Kind were stamped out, forced to break up and flee."

"Hundreds of thousands of them," whispered Cinda, shaking her head.

"I understand they think of nothing other than killing us and the creatures of this world," said Raif. "Who could control such an army of them?"

Tight-lipped, Rew raised an eyebrow.

"What?" asked Raif.

"No one knows who organized them," explained Rew.

Raif stared back at him, startled.

"There were valaan captains," continued the ranger. "You're familiar with them, yes? They're the most intelligent, or perhaps I should say cunning, of the Dark Kind. Deadly fighters as well. Tall, thin, and strong. Unlike the other Dark Kind, they are also able to coordinate and work together with those of their own species. The narjags are terribly afraid of them, and a single valaan can control hundreds of the lesser Dark Kind. But while the valaan loathe us as much as their cousins, they are sly enough to avoid direct confrontations with men that they cannot win. They know that even hundreds of thousands of Dark Kind are not enough to unseat mankind as the rulers of this world, so why did they lead the armies? Who directed the valaan?"

The younglings stared back at him, as if waiting for an answer, but he didn't have one.

As the days passed, and they drew closer and closer to the foothills of the Spine, Rew became more and more nervous. He and Jon were sharing looks, furtively pointing to tracks that narjags and ayres had left passing before them. The Dark Kind were traveling in small groups, but the rangers were seeing evidence that dozens, maybe hundreds, of the foul monsters were headed due north, just as they were.

There was a river that ran along the base of the Spine, and when they reached it, Rew was frightened of what they'd discover. One evening, just a day from the river, Anne cornered him and Jon while the younglings were busy preparing the camp.

"What is it?" she asked, her eyes darting suspiciously between the two rangers. "The longer we've been out here, the more nervous you've gotten. What are you seeing that we do not?"

"Tracks," Rew said, eyeing the younglings, not wanting to worry them. "Several parties of narjags headed the same direction we are."

"A reverse of the migration?" asked Anne.

Rew shrugged. Two years prior, he and the other rangers had hunted and killed all of the Dark Kind they could find, but they hadn't gotten them all. The creatures still lurked in the wilderness, though to no purpose anyone understood. No one knew why they'd left the barrowlands, and no one knew if they ever intended to go back. It was certainly possible that's what they were doing now.

But he wondered. Was two years long enough for the Dark Kind to have repopulated to the point they could face whatever they had fled from? Rew didn't think so. Surely it took longer than that for the creatures to achieve maturity, to be able to produce their own offspring, and to do so again in large numbers. Of course, maybe he was seeing the tracks from all that was left. Maybe all of the surviving Dark Kind were headed north, instead of a small representation. Rew wasn't sure which was worse, but neither scenario was good.

He grimaced, thinking that it was quite possible they were going to walk right into the back of a massive gathering of narjags. At that point, it wouldn't really matter why they were there. If there were dozens, he worried he wouldn't be able to protect the others. A hundred, and he wouldn't be able to protect himself.

By the time they reached the river that ran along the base of the Spine, formed from the crystal clear rain water and springs that dribbled down the side of the mountain, Rew decided he could not keep the secret within the Eastwatch contingent. The signs were clear. They were traveling the same path as the narjags, and there were a lot of them. They had to decide if they should turn around or proceed. And either way, it was important the younglings were alerted that the danger of the wilderness was no longer the usual threats. He hadn't wanted to worry them, but they had to know.

On the bank of the river, Rew squatted down and pointed at the earth. "Look here, between the stones."

The youths clustered around, staring down at the dark soil and the pale gray rocks that were scattered thickly near the water. Tumbled down from the heights above, the stone formed the bed of the fast-moving stream, slowly dissolving under the constant flow of water or being swept ashore in rocks ranging from pebbles to giant boulders. Where the party had emerged from the forest to the clear space around the river, the rocks were small, the size of apples or grapes, and in between the stone, impressions were obvious.

"Narjags," guessed Raif.

Rew nodded. "They're traveling the same direction we are. At least several dozen, I believe, though not all together in one group."

"What do you suggest we do?" asked Cinda.

"There are two choices," responded Rew. "We can turn around and go back to Eastwatch, and we can reconsider our options there. Or we can proceed, but with the knowledge we may stumble into a small army of Dark Kind."

The girl winced.

"We can't afford weeks of delay going back to Eastwatch," declared Raif. "We have to reach our father."

"He's right," said Cinda. "During the weeks it will take us to return and find another path to Falvar, Baron Worgon will have made his move."

"You don't think we should return, either," said Zaine, studying the ranger.

Rew crossed his arms on his knees, still squatting by the tracks. "If I was alone or just with my rangers, I'd continue. It's our role to find out what is going on in the wilderness, to see where these creatures are headed. I'd stop them if I could or gather reconnaissance if there were too many for me to face alone."

"It seems clear, then," said Cinda.

"Dozens of narjags," reminded Rew. "If we're forced into a fight with them, we might not win."

The group was silent for a long moment, everyone considering that.

"For us," murmured Cinda, "I don't think there's a choice."

Rew stood and looked around the group. "Allow Jon and I to lead. If we see narjags or ayres, follow our instructions quickly and exactly. Have your weapons ready at all times. If we're faced with more of them than we can handle, our only choice is to retreat to defensible terrain. If we can limit how many come at us at once, we may still have a chance. In the open, surrounded, I cannot protect you all. If we face a small group, a dozen or less, I'll take the point. I'll break their grouping, and you fall out on my sides. If they have ayres, focus on those first. They're faster, and those jaws and necks will rip a chunk out of you that Anne cannot put back. Raif and Jon, it's on you to cripple any of the ayres that I miss. Zaine and Cinda, do what you can from a distance, but keep your attacks well clear of the rest of us. Keep your eyes open, and yell if anything is coming at our backs. If you've a choice of not attacking or risking a strike close to us, don't attack. Zaine, use your bow and don't engage with those daggers unless it's against something wounded, or you truly have no choice. Until you've trained extensively with the daggers, the lack of reach could be fatal in a fight against a large group."

Anne asked, "Rew, could you conduct some training with the children? Even a little…"

He shook his head. "We don't have time."

"We're not children," complained Raif, "and I've been training for years. You saw what I was capable of last time, Ranger. Don't discount what—"

Rew held up a hand. "It's different when you're not facing a single opponent. That blade of yours could devastate a narjag, of course, but they're small and fast. If there are several of them, you'll swing at one, and the rest will slip behind your guard."

Raif grunted, and Rew could see the boy had no intention of staying back behind the two rangers. Rew wasn't sure what to say to convince him. Like all young men, Raif believed he was invincible, and the words of a man who was mostly a stranger weren't going to convince him otherwise.

"If there are enough of them, Rew, we'll need all the help we can get," mentioned Jon.

Rew sighed and turned to Raif. "I know you want to fight, but if we see them, will you at least hear my advice? We'll be most effective if we work together, and I ask that you listen to my tactical instructions if I have time to give them."

"Of course. We'll be most effective working together," said Raif, staring at the ranger, throwing his own words back at him.

Rew rubbed his head then turned to Cinda. "You wanted to engage the last time we faced a party of narjags. What spellcasting are you capable of?"

The noblewoman glanced around at the others and admitted, "Not much. I've some natural talent, but high magic takes study, and I've done little. If I may borrow that firestarter you showed us, the black powder, I believe I could send it on a cloud and ignite it. It will be more than just dust in their eyes. It could blind them. I don't think it will kill anything, but if they cannot see…"

"That's good. That's good," said Rew, taking off his pack and searching for the pouch of firestarter. He got it and tossed it to the young spellcaster. "I want you to walk with Anne from now on. She'll find out what you know of casting and teach you what she can. It won't be enough to make a big difference in such a short time, but even a little is worth trying."

Cinda frowned at the empath. "What do you know of spellcasting?"

"I know some," replied Anne with a smile.

"You're not…"

"Of noble blood?" guessed the empath. "No, I am not. I have no high magic, but I've seen spellcasters at work before. I know some of their methods."

"You've seen spellcasters in Eastwatch?" questioned Cinda, disbelieving.

"I wasn't always in Eastwatch, and I wasn't always an innkeeper," replied Anne.

"What, ah… you aren't from Eastwatch?" stammered Jon.

Anne laughed. "It's a story for another day."

Scratching at the back of his neck, the young ranger looked around. "Are we ready, then?"

"I'll lead," said Rew.

Chapter Ten

※

With the river to the left of them and the forest to the right, they began moving again, heading northeast toward the source of the river where they would turn and start into the foothills of the Spine.

Looking across the clear band of water to the thin fringe of forest there, above it to the foothills, and then craning her neck to stare high up at the peaks of the Spine, Cinda asked, "We're really going to climb that?"

"We'll have to climb about halfway up," said Rew. "There's a pass. On the other side is the mining encampment, and from there, the travel should be a good deal easier."

"Well, that's something, at least."

He grinned at her.

"How did you become the King's Ranger?" she asked.

He frowned.

Cinda waited for an answer.

"I joined the king's service in Mordenhold and traveled a great deal to the cities and military encampments scattered around our kingdom. I was looking for a quieter assignment that had less interaction with people," explained Rew, after walking several hundred paces beside the silent noblewoman. "It doesn't get much quieter, or farther away from people, than patrolling the wilderness. After the first time I visited the eastern province, I knew this was where I belonged. I requested a transfer of assignment, and it was granted."

She asked, "And what were you doing in the king's service previously that required all of this travel?"

Tight-lipped, Rew shrugged. "A little bit of this, a little bit of that. A scout, most of the time. Good training for a ranger."

Mercifully, she glanced back behind them toward Jon. "And him?"

Breathing a quick sigh of relief, Rew answered, "He was training in Mordenhold for a position in the king's infantry. When we requested an additional ranger, he was assigned by our commandant, Vyar Grund. Grund keeps an eye on the recruits, picking out those suitable for ranger assignments and sending them to the frontiers when they're needed."

"How many rangers are there?" wondered Cinda.

"On the eastern front, myself and five under my command," answered Rew. "Across the kingdom including in the capital, I'd guess fifty of us. We're scattered broadly, though. Grund comes through once or twice a year, but other than that, it's only every few years that we'll see a ranger from outside of our territory."

"I can imagine," said Cinda. "Travel from one end of the kingdom to the other would take months if one could not portal. Is Vyar Grund a spellcaster? Travel by portal seems the only practical way to manage such an expansive area."

"Commandant Grund can open a portal," said Rew, "and you're right. Without portaling, managing the rangers would be entirely impractical. Even with the portals, it is only one-way communication. It takes ages for our messages to reach the capital, and we can only hope Grund is around to receive them. Ideally, we'd have a network of rangers who could travel back and forth, but good spellcasters are hard to come by. As it is,

Grund spends a good deal of his time portaling around to the far reaches of the realm, ferrying instructions, people, and supplies."

Rew stopped walking, a frown growing on his face.

"What?" asked Cinda.

"A portal," he muttered. "The first party of narjags I found were waiting in the wilderness for someone to come through a portal. We found no signs of the spellcaster, so they must have left after relaying instructions. That's why the Dark Kind are traveling north, because the spellcaster told them to."

Cinda brushed a lock of hair behind her ear. "Dark Kind working for a spellcaster… Has that happened before?"

"It was two hundred years ago when they were first conjured, and the Dark Kind were used by spellcasters then," said Rew. "Fifty years ago… As I said, no one knows who was commanding those foul armies during the last war." He smacked a fist into his hand. "We were wondering why a spellcaster of talent would be coming into the wilderness and not stopping by Eastwatch. It's because they weren't looking for a place or a person but for the Dark Kind. The spellcaster was organizing the narjags."

"Why would someone do that?" questioned Cinda.

"The only way to find out is to find out where they are going," declared Rew.

As they moved along the river, Rew and Jon saw more signs of narjag activity. It became apparent they were not going to be able to continue unnoticed. They and the Dark Kind were traveling the exact same path, bound by the river on one side and the wilderness on the other. It did not surprise Rew when at midday, he began to get a creeping sense that there was danger ahead.

The river bubbled by, clear and unconcerned, and the wind stirred the branches of the trees, crackling the dry leaves and sending flurries of them down to carpet the forest floor and the bank of the river, but the sounds of animal life had stilled. The birds and other small fauna that normally filled the day with their songs and rustling had gone silent. It wasn't the presence of man that had driven them into hiding. It was the uneasy sense of wrongness that they would sense near the Dark Kind.

Rew warned the party to be alert and had everyone check their weapons. He considered moving into the forest, guessing that whatever was ahead was near the bank of the river, but that might only be putting off the confrontation. If there were narjags ahead, they were going to run into them sooner or later. Best do it during the day when they were prepared.

After another league of travel, he called for a rest. When the party paused, he told them, "I'll go scout ahead. Stay here and keep an eye out."

Moving alone, Rew began to jog along the riverbank, his feet falling softly, his attention focused ahead. He made it a quarter league before he slowed and moved into the forest, creeping along, but still faster than he could travel with the others. It was difficult, now that the autumn leaves had begun to fall in earnest, but he'd spent decades of his life practicing moving quietly, and he was able to ghost between the trees until he found what he was looking for.

There, on the bank of the river, a dozen narjags were clustered around a kill. Rew circled them, staying well back, peering between the pine boughs and bushes that provided him cover. He raised a hand, feeling the wind. It blew down from the north, off the mountains and following the course of the river, but wind was a temperamental force. Within the forest, he was confident of his ability to stay hidden, but the narjags had exceptional noses, and they would smell him before they could see him.

He raised a hand to his lips, pressing the five points of his fingers there. He whispered a simple cantrip and then waited a moment, feeling the lethargy that seeped through his bones at the casting and then the tingle over his skin as his spell began to work. His scent was contained for a time. He began to move again, placing each step with care. The narjags wouldn't be able to smell him now, but if he was clumsy-footed, they could still see and hear.

Rew peered between the leaves and the boughs, studying the scene in front of him. Twelve narjags, no shaman, no ayres. There was a bloody kill in the middle of them, and he wondered briefly if they'd been chasing something or someone, but as he circled the site, he saw it was a bear they'd felled, a small one that had no chance against a dozen narjags. They were gorging themselves on the animal's flesh, and he knew they wouldn't pause long once they were finished.

Rew had seen what he needed to and skulked back the other direction, staying within the cover of the trees for a thousand paces before he came back out into the clear on the riverbank and released his cantrip. He sighed in relief as the pressure faded from his skin and the weariness leaked from his bones. Jogging south, he made it back to the party in a few minutes and described what he'd seen.

His plan was quite simple. He didn't trust their party to be able to move through the forest with stealth, so a quick ambush wasn't going to work. Instead, Rew had Jon and Raif take the lead, and they walked with the others along the river, heading straight for the narjags. The two swordsmen would try to slow the attack of the creatures, while Cinda let loose a handful of the firestarter powder into their eyes. Zaine would strike as many as she could with her arrows, and then Rew would come at them from behind as the party held the attention of the narjags.

He was counting on the women to slow the Dark Kind with their ranged attacks and the men to hold them for a brief moment. Unseen, Rew could cause devastation as he came at their opponents from behind. If the party could hold out for just a moment, it would work.

From the cover of the forest where he'd gone ahead to hide, Rew watched as the party first appeared walking along the riverbank. He gripped the wooden hilt of his longsword and shifted nervously. If something went wrong, they were visible and alone out there.

In front of him, the narjags had not yet noticed the party's approach. Rew waited, forcing himself to breathe slow and steady, holding his longsword in his hand, ready to chase after the creatures as soon as they attacked.

It was a good plan. It should work, but plans had a way of falling apart the moment blades were drawn. The younglings were untested, and even Jon had only faced his first narjag days ago. They'd all handled themselves well during that fight, but they were facing more of the enemy now, and Rew wasn't standing with them. He hated letting them approach on their own, but it would give him the opportunity to strike quickly and ruthlessly. Striking by surprise, without the others to foul his movements, he could fell most of the narjag party in the space of half a dozen heartbeats. It would work. He hoped it would work.

The narjags, shoving and snapping at each other as they finished gorging on the last of the bear carcass, took longer than he expected to notice the approaching people. When they did, they suddenly sprang to their feet and turned south, grasping crude weapons, snarling in their bestial tongue to each other.

Rew waited.

Jon shouted as if surprised to see the narjags there, and he and Raif drew their swords, the ranger holding his longsword comfortably, Raif gripping his hand-and-a-half sword like it was a child's comfort blanket. Behind them, Zaine nocked an arrow and let fly.

The narjags were startled, and one of them screeched as the feathered shaft of the arrow flashed past it, gouging a bloody trench on its arm. Rew grimaced. The wound was inconsequential and wouldn't even slow the creature.

The narjags took the attack as impetus to charge, and they did so in a disorganized, howling pack. Rew waited three breaths. Then, he darted out of the forest, letting the narjags outpace him before speeding up, running after them.

Zaine fired another arrow, and this one flew true, catching a running narjag in the chest. The creature tumbled, rolling across the rocky ground, kicking and squealing, clutching the shaft of wood that had bloomed in its torso.

Cinda threw her hand up, tossing a cloud of the firestarter and whispering a quick incantation. The powder drifted by her to fall gently on the ground, and even from the other side of the narjag pack, Rew could see her frustration as she stared down at it. Whatever casting she'd attempted had failed, and there was no time to attempt it again. When the narjags reached the party, the Dark Kind wouldn't be blinded as they'd planned.

Rew sped up, racing after the narjags at a full sprint, giving up his attempts to reach them unnoticed. Nearly the whole pack was going to reach the party unmolested.

Raif glanced over his shoulder at his sister, white-faced. Jon crouched, like he was the lone spearman facing a full company of charging knights, and Anne drew her belt knife, though she stayed back and didn't look eager to use it.

Zaine, with the narjags a dozen paces from the men, got off another arrow. It was a panicked shot, but with eleven targets right in front of her, she managed to strike one, and that narjag went down, though Rew couldn't tell if it was a killing shot or not. The hastily aimed arrow had slowed one of them, at least.

Jon shouted something, and both he and Raif charged, evidently trying to shock the narjags into pulling up on their attack.

Raif swung a mighty blow with his hand-and-a-half sword, sweeping it across the narjags, making a clean strike against one across the throat, nearly chopping through the head of a second, and battering a third, knocking it astray. But the blow pulled him off balance, and his sword was terribly out of position. Two narjags were on him, one punching at his torso with a rusty-tipped spear, the other jumping at him, yellowed teeth snapping at the boy's face. Already teetering from his sword swing, Raif stumbled to his knees on the rocky riverbank from the force of the attack.

Jon had easily dispatched one of the narjags, parried a strike from another, but then saw Raif was in trouble, so he tried to turn, lunging toward the youth. The ranger thrust with his longsword, taking the narjag clinging to Raif's shoulder in the side. Jon had left himself open, though, and three narjags smashed into him, surprised he was undefended, swinging at him wildly with their small blades.

Jon cried in pain, and Raif roared, tossing the dead narjag aside but then taking another strike from the spear of the first in the torso before he could bring his sword back around to kill it. The narjag fell away, and two more darted in, attacking inside the guard of Raif's longer weapon.

The boy dropped the hand-and-a-half sword and grabbed for the narjags. He was strong, but the little creatures were surprisingly wiry. One of them slashed at him with a short blade. The other sunk teeth into Raif's arm.

Then Rew was amongst them.

He wielded his longsword in a tight pattern, sweeping it across the backs of the narjags but not allowing himself to be thrown off-balance by the force of the blows like Raif had. In heartbeats, he'd carved through four of the foul creatures, and then he swung the blade low, hacking into the narjags on Jon like he was scything the grass behind the ranger station, sweeping them away in a tangle of flesh, blood, and shattered bone.

The young ranger was lying on his back, bleeding, but Rew could see the panic in his open eyes. Jon was alive, for now.

Rew spun, thrusting his blade into the back of the creature stabbing at Raif, and then Zaine was beside him, carving up the one biting the fighter like she was filleting a fish, one of her long daggers plunging into its side, the other raking across its abdomen, spilling its guts in a disgusting pile at its feet.

Raif tried to rise, but he stumbled and collapsed onto his side.

Rew turned and saw the last injured narjag approaching, its blade raised. Casually, the ranger stepped forward and chopped its head off. The twelve narjags were dead.

"I'm sorry. I'm sorry. I'm sorry," babbled Cinda, falling to her brother's side.

Rew moved to help her, seeing Anne was already with Jon, the empath's confident fingers poking at the bloody gashes in the young ranger's side.

Gently, Rew moved Cinda's hands so she was holding her brother's head and so he could see the boy's injuries. Raif's leather cuirass had taken a solid strike, but the armor had held, and there were several nasty-looking impressions from teeth on his bracer. Rew's hand came away bloody when he put it underneath the cuirass. He winced. One of the narjags' spears had found a gap in the protection.

Rew began to unbuckle the breastplate. With Cinda's help, he tried to move it aside, but the heavy youth was laying half on it.

Zaine stood above them, glancing between the two injured men then at the forest as if she was afraid more narjags would come pouring out of it. Rew thanked her for keeping watch and told her to keep doing so. In times of trauma, it helped for everyone to have something to do.

Zaine nodded tersely and retrieved her bow from where she'd dropped it.

"Hold him while I undo these buckles," Rew instructed Cinda, turning her brother so he could reach the other side of the armor. "We need to get this cuirass off of him and then cut away his shirt to see the extent of the damage."

"How is he?" questioned Anne from where she was working on Jon.

"A puncture from a spear, I think," said Rew, talking over a continuous litany of curses from Raif as the boy writhed in pain. Rew leaned on the big youth and held him down long enough to free the buckle on the cuirass. "It's pretty deep. Close to going all the way through him, but I don't think it hit any organs."

"Let's switch," suggested the healer. "Jon's got a dozen lacerations, but they're all shallow cuts. Make a poultice to patch him up and to slow any infection. I'll tend to Raif and come back to Jon when I've recovered."

Rew pressed the fighter's hands against the wound in his side and told him to keep pressure. Then, he stood and collected his pack from where the party had dropped it just before the fight began. He opened it, looking in at dozens of pockets stuffed with a variety of herbs.

Teeth gritted, Jon watched as the senior ranger began to pull out packets and jars.

"Chew this, but instead of swallowing the juice spit it out," said Rew, handing Jon a pinch of dried flower buds. "It will help a little with the pain, a lot with any infection."

Anne had already sliced the ranger's shirt and peeled it wide open, so Rew had no problem identifying nearly a dozen slashes on Jon's ribs and stomach where the narjags had hacked at him with their dull blades. Blood streaked Jon's side, but Anne had been right. They were all superficial cuts, though rather painful looking.

"Blythe's going to kill me when she sees this," jested Rew, trying to take the young ranger's mind away from his injuries. "You keep it up at this rate, and you'll have half as many scars as the rest of us in no time, though there'll come a day when you decide it's best to not let the Dark Kind chop you up. Everyone's gotta learn the hard way, it seems."

Rew bound a hasty bandage around Jon's side to staunch the bleeding then went to rinse his bloody hands off in the river. He returned with some water in a bowl and began dropping herbs into it. He ground them with a pestle, making a slick paste. It would be better if he could boil the poultice, but it would provide some benefit as is. He just had to keep the younger ranger alive until Anne could tend to him. Rew kept joking with Jon, keeping the other man's attention on his words and not on what he was doing.

Behind them, Raif's breathing was still coming fast, but Anne's voice was low and calm. Rew took that as a good sign, that the empath thought she'd have little problem closing the wound. When she was stressed, her words took on a brusque, demanding tone. As long as she spoke softly, Rew wasn't overly concerned.

Looking down into the bowl, he decided the poultice was good enough. Rew pulled back the loose bandage and began to slather the mixture on Jon's side.

The younger ranger gasped. "It's cold!"

Rew grinned. "It's the water from the river and the oils from some of the herbs. Don't worry. It will help numb the pain. There are other herbs in this mix to fight potential infection, to stop the bleeding, and to speed healing, though hopefully Anne can get back to you before those have a chance to work. Just stay still and try to breathe evenly."

Rew pulled his bedroll off his pack and slid it under Jon's head. Gratefully, the younger ranger laid back and relaxed. Glancing at Anne, Rew saw she'd sat back on her haunches and was rubbing at her temples. She looked tired but unworried.

Cinda, tears in her eyes, was still babbling apologies to her brother over her failed attempt at casting.

"How is he?" the senior ranger asked the healer.

"He'll be fine," Anne said with a groan. "I know we'll need to move from here, but I recommend we stop for the rest of the day as soon as we can. I need a few hours before I can address Jon. By morning, everyone should be capable of travel, though we cannot push it. Rew, you might need to scout ahead."

Rew met her gaze, and he could see in her eyes that she meant it. The party would be well enough to hike a few hours the next day, but they wouldn't be near anything like fighting shape.

Rew stood, torn between staying with the party and moving off into the forest to find them a safe place to recover. If the narjags were all doing as the tracks indicated, heading directly for the river and then following its bank, then their current location was an awful place to make camp. They were right in the path of whatever Dark Kind may come shuffling along next, but with Jon and Raif both injured, they couldn't waste hours exploring their surroundings. Zaine was the only one proven effective in combat who was still standing. Rew couldn't leave the party unguarded for long.

He glanced at Zaine. "Nice shooting, by the way."

She offered him a wan smile.

"I mean it," he said. "Firing into the face of a charging enemy is never as easy as hitting a stationary target."

"I failed us," hissed Cinda from where she was still sitting on the ground, cradling her brother's head in her lap. "He could have been killed."

"You didn't stab him," remarked Rew.

"I didn't manage to blow the powder into the faces of those narjags, either," lamented Cinda. "I tried to light it when it fell to the ground, hoping to distract them, and I couldn't even do that. All I could do was watch."

"You've had no chance to practice," consoled Rew.

"I had enough time," said Cinda, looking up to meet his eyes. "Anne helped me with some of the technical aspect. This is a spell I know, Ranger. I've done similar before, but when it mattered, I couldn't cast even the smallest of sparks."

Rew glanced at Anne, but she was not looking at him. Instead, the empath sat forward and put a hand on Cinda's thigh. "High magic is not easy, lass. It takes years of study. Be calmed. You will learn it but not in a week and not while spending most of the day hiking. You need rest. You need focus. You need time, and we have none."

"She's right," said Rew. "You will learn but not today. Today, you can help us carry the packs so we can get Jon and your brother to a place they can rest." He looked between the injured men. "Can you move now, just a few hundred paces?"

They gave assurances, and with Rew's help, they struggled to their feet, clutching their sides and cursing fervently.

Grinning, Rew gripped each of them on the shoulder. "It could have been worse."

"It would have been, if you weren't there," said Jon.

"That's why I'm here," said Rew, feeling Anne's eyes on him. He looked away and pretended not to notice her smug look.

Chapter Eleven

For two days, they traveled half the day, walking slowly so their injured could recover. Anne doled out healing, taking their pain but not so much that she affected her own ability to travel. At the end of the second day, they made it near the source of the river. It was a slender finger of water compared to the arm that flowed farther south, but they'd passed hundreds of feeders where water poured down from the pale gray mountain on the other side.

Beside the river, there was a pair of shoulder-high piles of rock. The stones were worn, weathered by wind and rain, but they'd been placed and fitted together carefully to signal a shallow place in the river. It would take more than a storm to topple the two markers. Between the stones were the bodies of five narjags.

"We're not the only ones out here killing narjags," remarked Jon, "or do you think it was some sort of tribal disagreement?"

Rew walked up to observe the bodies, wrinkling his nose at their awful odor. "These five have been sitting out for some time. I'd guess four days, and they weren't killed by other narjags."

Everyone, reluctant to get too close to the stench of the bodies, was intrigued enough to pinch their noses and try. The five narjags had huge, brutal slashes on them that cut them open as cleanly as if on a butcher's table.

"Sonic lashes," murmured Rew, walking a slow circle around the bodies. "A spellcaster did this. Afterward, it appears someone looted the bodies. I'm guessing these were killed, then another party of Dark Kind took their belongings."

"They don't bury each other?" quipped Zaine.

Rew offered her a tight smile.

"A spellcaster, out here?" asked Jon. He gestured around them. There was nothing but wilderness, and no other people within several days' walk of them. He scratched his head. "I suppose it could have been the same one who opened that portal we found near Eastwatch, but why would they portal there and then to here? I can't imagine there are two spellcasters out in the wilderness, but I also can't imagine anyone with the skill to open a portal would do so and then hike so far. And if they didn't hike through the wilderness like we did, it seems rather odd they'd choose these two locations to portal to."

Rew nodded. "Spellcasters in the wilderness, spellcasters choosing to hike, spellcasters appearing somewhere like this crossing? I agree. None of it seems likely, but all the same…"

The younger ranger didn't reply. All the same, they'd found evidence of a portal opening, and now, they were standing above the bodies of five narjags killed by a spell. Whether or not the options seemed likely, there was evidence that something of the sort had occurred.

"But why?" wondered Cinda. "Spellcasters use portals to save time moving between the places they'd want to be. Eastwatch maybe, but here? What reason could they have to be here?"

Rew merely grunted in response.

Continuing, Cinda added, "Perhaps they didn't know exactly where they were going. Without an established target destination, travel by portal can be erratic, I've read. Maybe they didn't realize how far off they were, and maybe they are appearing in random locations to try and figure it out."

Rew shook his head. "I disagree. If it's the same spellcaster, they've been traveling by foot or by portal with an awful lot of precision for someone who's lost." He pointed to the stacked rocks marking the crossing. "They came to the exact point I was guiding you to after two weeks in the open woods. The odds of that are unfathomable. At the other site, they appeared within one hundred paces of a waiting pack of narjags. No, if it's the same caster, they arrived in these locations because they meant to."

"Could they be tracking us?" wondered Jon.

"This happened about four days ago," remarked Rew. "If they were tracking us, why would they appear here four days before us and at the other site before we'd even gone looking for the narjags?"

Cinda frowned, crossing her arms over her chest. "You said you've seen tracks by the narjags, right? What about tracks that could have been from a spellcaster?"

Rew shook his head. "I've seen nothing. That means they could have traveled by portal, or they could have cast a glamour to obscure the signs of the passage. A spellcaster who could cast a glamour to fool me in these woods… I think it unlikely, but perhaps it could be done."

"I'll take your word for it," responded Cinda.

"Could this spellcaster be traveling to your father's domain the same as we are?" asked Rew. "Maybe it's someone in your father's employ, and for some reason, they're unable to portal directly to Falvar."

Cinda shook her head. "My father has no spellcasters of his own. It's part of the reason he sent me to Yarrow to foster. I was to be trained there. I… I don't think he has any spellcasters of his own."

"There's much we do not know," mused Rew. He glanced down at the bodies of the narjags again. "Come on. Let's drag these to the edge of the forest where they can rot out of the path, and then let's cross. You'll want to get rinsed off after touching those, I suspect."

He winked at the younglings, but none of them laughed at his jest.

The trail up the side of the mountain wasn't much of a trail, but it was up the side of a mountain. The first league felt similar to traversing the wilderness but at a sheer incline. After that, the ground became rugged, not just scattered bits of rock but boulders jutting out of the earth and patches of raw stone that they had to scamper across, leaning against the slope so they didn't slide hundreds of paces back down.

That first league into the foothills was littered with the corpses of narjags and ayres. Three dozen of them, Rew counted, before the trail of bodies ended. At the end of the grisly line, it appeared a concussive blast had been unleashed, pulping the bodies of ten narjags, knocking over several trees, and blasting huge chunks of stone a score of paces away.

"Maybe the spellcaster was tired of being followed," speculated Jon.

Rew didn't respond. Whoever had killed three dozen narjags while on the run, leaving not a trace of their own passing, was a frightfully talented spellcaster. Blessed Mother, what were they doing out there?

"Sonic lash spells, for the most part," advised Cinda, looking the way they'd come then back toward the site of the explosion. She admitted, "I don't know what that was."

Shaking his head, Rew kept going, and for the rest of the day, they did not see any more corpses of narjags. He wasn't sure if they'd moved off the path that the spellcaster and his pursuers had taken or if all of the narjags had finally been killed.

"She," said Cinda from the other side of the fire when he'd commented on it that evening. "The spellcaster could be a she."

He blinked at her and shrugged. "Of course."

Raif, tossing his empty bowl on the ground, groaned, "I don't know about the rest of you, but I'm ready to eat something other than beans and rice."

"I think the narjags have been running off all of the wildlife the last few days," said Rew. "Maybe tomorrow we'll have better luck with fresh game. You're right. It'd be good to mix in something new. There are mountain goats on these slopes. If we see one close, we may be able to chase it down. Of course, any that survive up here are quick and careful. They've got to avoid the rock trolls, after all."

Raif cringed, and Rew grinned at him.

"I'm just glad it's not me cooking any longer," remarked Zaine.

"As are the rest of us," mumbled Anne.

They all laughed, and the mood lifted.

Anne usually cooked their evening meal, but after the healing of Raif and Jon, she'd been exhausted. To everyone's dismay, Zaine had taken over the responsibility, and they'd spent two days scraping burnt bits off the bottom of their pots and tossing inedible hunks of overcooked slop into the fire.

"If you take a rabbit tomorrow with that bow, we'll consider it even," said Rew.

She hefted the weapon, accepting the challenge.

Jon leaned forward and put another branch on their fire. "Getting chilly in the evening, isn't it?"

Rew rubbed at his beard, thinking it was getting a bit wild and that it was past time for a trim. He said, "The next few days we're going to need to collect some spare firewood. A bundle of wood is no fun to carry uphill, but the pass will take us two days to navigate, and there are no trees in there. The wind blows through like the breath of a banshee, and we'll want what heat we can make for ourselves."

"Anything you can do?" Zaine asked Cinda, wiggling her fingers.

Cinda pursed her lips. "There are a number of castings which could provide heat, but I worry too little heat isn't going to do us much good, and too much…"

Zaine grunted. "Firewood it is, then."

"I've an idea," said Anne, and she searched about until she found several fallen leaves. She cleared a space near their fire and set the leaves down in a row. "A dome of mild heat is not a terribly complicated spell, but you're right, it's the control which is difficult. Maybe we can do some practice this evening. These leaves, if exposed to too much heat, will ignite. We can begin by adjusting your range. See if you can enclose one of them at a time, and then we'll start adjusting the temperature. We probably won't get it right away, but winter is approaching, and you never know when such a skill might be useful."

"Hopefully by the time winter gets here," declared Raif, "we'll be sitting in front of our father's fire, drinking giant goblets of mulled wine and doing nothing more exciting than scratching the hunting dogs behind the ears."

Anne offered him a mirthless smile, and Rew wondered what the empath suspected. She didn't know any more than he did about the mystery of the spellcaster and the narjags, but she knew people. Was she inferring something about Baron Fedgley's plans from what the children had said or what she'd sensed through her empathy? He'd learned her senses were as sharp as anyone's. If she felt something was coming, even if she couldn't articulate what it was, he was inclined to believe her.

With grim thoughts and unanswered questions, Rew told the group half-jokingly to keep an eye out for rock trolls then laid out his bedroll and retired for the night. An hour after midnight, he was woken by Zaine crouching down next to him. She nodded when she saw his eyes open then moved off to her bedroll. Rew yawned. He felt like he hadn't slept a wink.

Soundlessly, he slipped out of his bedroll and stretched. His body was used to sleeping on the hard ground, but two weeks of near constant travel and now the incline up the mountain were taking a toll on even him. Anne was still offering her healing to him and the others, and Rew knew he could not accept it.

Shaking his head and donning his cloak in the cool air, he rifled through his pack for his pipe and his leaf. He thumbed the fragrant leaf down into the bowl and found a small stick on the ground. He put another thick hunk of wood onto the flickering embers of their fire then lit the small stick. He held the tiny brand to the bowl of his pipe and inhaled, drawing the fire in and watching it dance across the dry leaf. He puffed several more times to get it burning hot and then flicked the stick into the fire. He began to pace, circling the camp at the very edge of the firelight, looking away from it, out into the rocks and trees around them.

They'd lost much of the cover they'd had at lower elevations, and sometime tomorrow, they would pass the tree line. There would be no cover from the vegetation after that point. The rocks would provide a little shelter to camp beside, but there would be few places that could hide all of them if they saw narjags or the spellcaster.

Again, Rew wondered if he should travel ahead and scout the safety of their path, but again, he worried the others couldn't survive against a larger group of narjags without him. Against just twelve of the Dark Kind, the two men had taken serious wounds. Cinda had been ineffective, and Zaine had caused some damage but not enough to make it a fight the swordsmen could win. No, the party needed him close.

His feet falling silent, Rew moved with a grace that came from twenty-five years of practice. He did it without thinking even in the dark of night. He circled out farther, enjoying the cool air as he left the warmth from the fire entirely behind, the pipe smoke trailing behind him as he walked.

When his pipe was finished, he tapped it out and stuck it into his belt. He kept walking, taking slow strides, his mind unfurling directionless. He had some thought that such unfocused consideration might tease loose a piece of the puzzle, but instead, it nearly brought the end of him.

With a jerk, he stopped walking, one foot hovering just above the soil. Carefully, he lowered his foot, looking up into the trees ahead of him.

There, perched on a branch, was a vivratu. Its neck, curling like the body of a snake, waved sinuously as it stared at the camp. Its body, the size of a dog, was hunched down, clawed feet gripping the wood of the tree. Its wings were pulled tight on its back, but as Rew watched, the creature flexed them, the thin membranes looking solid in the dark of the night.

Vivratu weren't unknown in the wilderness, but it'd been five years since he'd last seen one. They were Dark Kind, conjured from the same realm as the narjags but with none of the intelligence or ability to follow commands. Vivratu were thoughtless but cunning hunters. They would wait until prey came within range then glide down from a tree on spread wings. They would dart with their long necks to strike, sinking fangs into a victim, and then, they would flap away where they would claim another perch and wait patiently for their victim to die.

Their venom wouldn't kill instantly, but there was no known antidote. The creatures were not of this world, after all. Instead, the choices came down to amputating a limb, if that was where the fangs sank in, or granting a swift end to avoid the agonizing, half hour-long descent into body-wracking spasms. Eventually, the spasms would grow powerful enough to crack bones, ending when the victim's spine broke or their head thumped one time too hard on the ground from the convulsions.

It was better if the victim died, then, because even paralyzed, they would be aware of what came next. Vivratu had small mouths, so they could not swallow a person whole and didn't have the strength to tear off a hunk of flesh. Instead, they bit down and allowed acid to seep from their mouths, dissolving skin and muscle until it was soft enough for them to strip it away, gobbling the mushy, acid-soaked bits down their gullets. And like that, they would slowly consume a person while the person was trapped in frozen agony, watching themselves being dissolved and eaten, bite by bite.

Rew shuddered. Of course, he'd never seen it. If someone was bitten by one of the creatures, any true companion would immediately end the suffering. If the victim was alone, their best bet was to do what they could to end it themselves.

All of this flashed through his mind as he stared aghast at the vivratu in the tree. He knew little about the capabilities of the thing's senses, but it hadn't heard him yet. He thought it possible they had little ability to smell, or maybe his pipe had covered his odor. The disgusting creature could see, though. It was watching the sleeping companions around the campfire, its sinuous neck bobbing, like a child selecting which delicacy to take from the baker's counter. The vivratu spread its wings to their fullest extent, and on slender legs, it raised its fat body, its snake-like neck coiling tight. It hissed and gave a little hop then launched itself from the branch.

Rew surged after it, leaping over a fallen log and dodging beneath a low branch. The vivratu glided through the forest, its awkward body somehow looking comfortable in the air as it coasted around the thin trunk of a tree. Then, it was in the clearing, and half a second later, Rew burst out after it.

He bellowed, "Watch out!"

The party, exhausted from days on the road, dead asleep, did not react quickly.

Rew yanked his longsword off his back and, in the same motion, threw it. The blade, not meant for throwing, spun in the air. He kept charging after the vivratu, drawing his hunting knife and shouting a cry of celebration when the longsword thunked into the vivratu.

The creature, focused on its prey, didn't see the blade until the length of steel pierced it, skewering its fat body. The vivratu flapped its wings, twisting its neck to see what had happened to it. It crashed to the ground, clawed feet kicking in the dirt, wings flapping helplessly

"Stay back!" yelled Rew as Jon staggered to his feet, longsword in hand.

The vivratu, spitted by the blade, was not dead yet. Its long, sinuous neck twisted violently, black eyes reflecting the light of their fire as it searched for its attacker. It opened its mouth, baring its fangs and showing off the acid sacs on the sides of its cheeks.

Rew circled it, coming from behind. He reached out with one hand and gripped the vivratu's snakelike neck. It jerked against his grip, and he nearly lost his hold, but he kept it long enough to bring his hunting knife around and slash through the neck, severing the vivratu's head.

His heart hammering, Rew tossed the severed head into their fire and then immediately went for water and a rag to clean his blade. Left untouched, the acid from the vivratu's neck could ruin the steel of the knife.

"Sorry about that," said Rew to the startled party. "By the time I saw it, it was already poised to strike."

"What-what is that?" stammered Zaine, wide eyes fixed on the corpse of the creature.

Rew glanced down at it. "Vivratu. A Dark Kind from the same plane as the narjags and ayres. They were brought here but never used by their conjurers. They're no more intelligent than our native animals, but they're extremely dangerous. I imagine that those conjurers of old realized the vivratu could not be controlled and then simply ignored them. Through the years, they've persisted in the wild places of the world."

"Dangerous..." said the thief, shivering, peering at the fire-blackened, shriveled head as it popped and sizzled in the embers of their campfire.

"Are they common?" asked Anne, shivering in disgust at the dead, bleeding body. "I don't think I've ever heard of them."

"Not common," said Rew. Then, he ushered everyone back into their bedrolls, encouraging them to try and get back to sleep.

He and Jon dragged the vivratu off into the forest and kept watch while the others covered themselves back up. Fitfully, they tossed and turned. Sleep was a long time coming for each of them.

Whispering, Jon said, "Senior Ranger, if anyone else had been on watch…"

Rew nodded. He couldn't bring himself to say it, but he'd been thinking the same. If anyone else had been on watch, they would have lost one of the party. It was a grim thought.

"Get some rest," said Jon. "I don't think I'll be able to sleep for some time."

"I'm wide awake as well," replied Rew.

Jon turned to him. "Rew, if a vivratu was in this area, it's safe to assume there is nothing else out there that will come at us tonight. You and the other rangers told me how protective they are of their turf. Bears, rock trolls, even a simian would avoid that thing. Now is the time for you to rest." The younger ranger looked to where they'd deposited the body. "You're going to need it because we're going to need you."

Grunting, Rew walked to his bedroll and crawled in. He set his longsword beside him and pulled off his boots, but otherwise remained clothed. Jon was right. In the vivratu's territory, they wouldn't be bothered by anything else. But the next day and the day after… someone would have died if he hadn't been on watch. He had to stay alert if he was to protect the younglings.

Chapter Twelve

❦

They hiked farther up the side of the mountain, and as they rose in elevation, the temperature dropped. The party wrapped their cloaks tight and kept moving during the day to stay warm. At night, they attempted to shelter behind rocks or the backs of ridges, but once they passed the tree line, there was no escaping the bitter wind. It blew over them constantly, chapping faces, tugging at their clothing, and pouring a constant deluge of cold air over them.

"Now that I think about it," muttered Rew, "the last time I crossed this pass it was summer."

Her jaw shut tight to keep her teeth from chattering, Anne glared at him.

"It won't be so bad once we get to the other side and start down," he offered. "That's, ah, just three more days. Of course, it will be a bit worse in the actual pass."

They pressed on, placing steps carefully on the scree-strewn slope of the mountain, angling their way up in a zigzag pattern, hiking a dozen paces apart so any rocks they dislodged as they walked didn't go tumbling back into one of their companions. Below them, stones bounced and slid, and Rew worried they would come across more of the narjags. The side of the mountain would be an awful place to fight the creatures, and amongst the pale gray rocks, there was no place they could quickly hide. But fortunately, they saw none of the Dark Kind, and they hiked higher with only the desolate landscape to challenge them.

By the end of the first day past the tree line, the world had transformed into pale gray. Looking ahead, all they could see was the chalky stone of the Spine and the steel-colored clouds that wreathed its crown. It was only during sunrise and sunset they could differentiate between the two. The stone of the Spine evoked the bones of some fallen giant crashed down upon the ground, crumbling and eroding over the ages. Regularly, Rew looked behind them, absorbing the comfortable green of the forest far below. He felt those quick glances at the verdant woods were the only thing keeping him sane.

"I suggest we no longer have a fire at night," advised Rew. "It will be cold tonight, and it's only going to get colder, but outside of the cover of the trees, it will be visible from half a league away. And the wind is strong enough tonight that it could carry the scent of burning wood and meat for leagues. It will be uncomfortable, but it's too risky."

The others grunted. They'd gone silent, their thoughts kept to themselves, their energy conserved for the difficult uphill trek.

Rew added, "It's one more steep push tomorrow morning, and then we'll be into the pass. It's relatively flat hiking there, but it's not easy. We'll be in the narrow for two days, and I'll be honest, it's not an enjoyable place to walk."

"The narrow?" asked Cinda.

Rew nodded, not bothering to explain, and the noblewoman evidently couldn't summon the energy to inquire further.

After they ate a cold meal and cleaned as best they could with limited water, the group moved around, kicking rocks and trying to find a flat place on the stone to lay their bedrolls.

"I don't think I slept a wink last night," complained Raif, picking up a fist-sized rock from where he'd been trying to lay down, glaring at it, and tossing it down the slope. "Not sure I will tonight, either."

"You can catch up when you're on your feet tomorrow," jested Zaine, though no one laughed. It was too close to the truth.

"Not much more of this," assured Rew. "You wanted to avoid the roads, and we have. I can't imagine anyone chasing you is going to be able to follow us all this way. Without a ranger to guide them, they probably couldn't even make it to the Spine, much less figure out where to climb over it."

Cinda smirked. "I'm willing to admit, Senior Ranger, I finally understand why you were so shocked we weren't taking the roads. Perhaps we should have spent a little more time studying the maps and figured a way around Worgon's forces on the way to Spinesend. It wouldn't have been easy, but…" She gestured to the towering peaks that rose out of sight above them.

Rew nodded in acknowledgement but did not respond.

"When we reach your father," said Jon, settling down beside the fire and helping Anne stow away the iron pots and wooden dishes they'd used for dinner, "what do you think will happen? A message to Duke Eeron, of course, but do you think he'll assemble the army and call to the capital for more help?"

Cinda and Raif glanced at each other. They hadn't shared the details of what they'd overheard in Yarrow, and no one had bothered to press them. It didn't surprise Rew that there was a conspiracy afoot, and he didn't need the details. Whatever it was, he wanted to avoid getting entangled in it, and the best way to do that was to stay ignorant.

Jon, unaware of the nature of the Investiture like most of the common folk, was filled with curiosity. He must have noticed the nobles dodging his questions, but he couldn't help prodding them.

"To be honest," said Cinda after a long pause, "I don't know. Of course my father will want to alert Duke Eeron, but… I think it will depend on the duke what happens next."

Jon nodded. He looked to Rew. "And we'll return to Eastwatch?"

"That's where we belong," said Rew. "It's our responsibility to keep an eye on the wilderness and to maintain order in the village." Turning to the younglings, he said, "It's not that I'm uncaring, you understand, but you've a responsibility to your family, your lands, and your people. Mine is to the territory."

"We understand," assured Raif, clenching and unclenching his fist as if he was preparing to face Baron Worgon that very moment. "We appreciate your help, Senior Ranger, and I hope you'll learn what you need to about these narjags. I can't say I understand what is happening with them, but it's one more complication in a complicated time. I'd like for you to get to the bottom of it."

"I hope your father's arcanist can help," said Rew. "Is it still Arcanist Ralcrist that serves in Falvar?"

"It is," confirmed Cinda.

"Arcanists," said Zaine. "They're not spellcasters, are they?"

Rew shook his head. "Not at all. Usually, they've no magical talent whatsoever, but they have a burning curiosity about it. Arcanists are scholars who've dedicated their study to the magical and unnatural, the arcane. Most of them have some specialization, but out on the frontier, they ought to be familiar with the information I seek. Who could have opened that portal near Bartrim's farm? Who could have cast those attacks against the narjags, and is there any explanation for the narjag's behavior? Whatever those foul creatures are up to, I believe it's tied tightly to this spellcaster we keep seeing evidence of, but how are they related? I have no idea. I can't understand the actions of the narjags or the spellcaster. I hope the arcanist does."

"Arcanist Ralcrist served my father well and my grandfather before him. He's a wise man," assured Cinda. "He's been in Falvar as long as I've been alive. Maybe as long as my father has been alive. Ralcrist could have been in Falvar during the last war against the Dark Kind, now that I think of it. He has the experience you seek."

"If he doesn't have the answers, then no one does," agreed Raif.

Rew smiled a tight-lipped grin. The nobles meant that to be reassuring, but it wasn't. Would the arcanist be able to shed light on what was occurring? Maybe. Maybe not. Rew couldn't decide which was better, to leave the answers unknown and return to Eastwatch or to find out who this spellcaster was traipsing through the wilderness and why the narjags were on his heels. Either way, Rew was becoming concerned it would be nearly impossible to untangle himself from the mess, whatever it was. The Investiture was coming, and staying away was always going to be difficult. In Falvar, in the heart of a conspiracy… He sighed and turned to his bedroll, stretching it across a flat bit of rock, grimacing at the sharp pebbles he felt underneath of it. It was going to be a long night.

The next morning, they woke early. As expected, no one had slept well the night before on the windy, rocky side of the mountain. They stretched out sore muscles, rubbed at bruises they'd acquired from lying atop the hard ground, and made a quick breakfast before pressing on. The slope steepened as they rose in elevation, and in places, they were climbing on hands and feet, leaning into the rock face, fingers numb from contact with the cold stone. They tried to ignore the long fall below them.

After two hours of strenuous hiking and climbing, they came across another scene of a fight. It was at the end of a gully, just two hundred paces below the start of the pass. Rew was leading them up when he began to get whiffs of an awful smell.

"Weapons ready," he called back.

But it was unnecessary. Ahead of them, they found a dozen broken and ruined bodies of narjags and blue-skinned ayres. The end of the gully looked to be the site of small avalanche, shattered rock blocking the way forward and covering several of the Dark Kind.

"They're still chasing him," muttered Jon, shaking his head at the scene. "What is driving them?"

Rew rubbed his beard, long and tangled after so much time in the wilderness and shook his head. "More than fresh meat, I'm certain of that. Narjags are lazy. They'd only come up here if they were motivated, if they were on the hunt."

"They're not hunting very effectively," said Raif with a grin, gesturing at the dead bodies. "Whoever they're after, we haven't seen a sign of them. No blood, nothing."

Rew nodded. "Had they gathered together before they attacked, maybe they'd have a chance, but it's clear this spell-caster is capable of handling a small group with little difficulty."

"Rew," said Jon. He pointed to a bit of wood sticking out from the tumbled rock at the end of the gully. "Look familiar?"

Rew squatted down next to the shaft of wood and tried to tug it free, but it was trapped under dozens of heavy stones. He didn't need to see it, though, to guess what it was. "A staff like the one we found near Eastwatch."

"That's what I thought," said Jon. "A shaman?"

"Not a very good one," muttered Rew, glancing around and seeing no signs of narjag spellcasting, unless the shaman had accidentally brought the pile of rock down onto itself. "What if instead of shamans, these staffs and attire are signs of a pack leader?"

"Could be," agreed Jon. "We've never seen that sort of, ah, fashion amongst narjags before, have we?"

"Back during the war, the Dark Kind raised standards much like a human army would," said Rew. "It was assumed that was the valaan's doing, and they did it for the same reasons we do, to try and maintain order during an engagement. It could be the narjags have their own totems to signify tribe or leadership. To be honest, no one has spent much time studying them."

"Why would you?" muttered Raif, staring down at the legs of a narjag which poked out from under the rock pile.

Rew, beginning to pace back and forth across the gully, frowned. "Back in the wilderness, we saw the tracks of what could be hundreds of Dark Kind. We've seen several dozen that have been killed. Where are the rest of them?"

None of the companions had an answer.

Rew looked back out the gully, past the mountain to the forest days below them. He scratched his beard. "There are no signs of the spellcaster, but there are tracks for more narjags than we've discovered. It's clear that a lot of them are on the move, but from the campsites, they are not moving together. It's almost as if individual groups are getting periodically slaughtered."

"They are a fractious race, are they not?" asked Raif. "Maybe when the different groups stumble across each other, they fight. Well, I suppose they didn't pull these rocks down to kill each other, and I can't imagine they are the ones using those sonic lashes either."

"If they had those capabilities, they would have used them on us," agreed Rew. He stood at the end of the gully, staring at the bare stone around them, looking for tracks, but knowing he would find none. "I've spent years in the wilderness, and Jon and I are both trained to notice anything outside of the usual. If that spellcaster traveled through the forest, even with spells assisting his stealth, I think I would have seen some sign. They had to sleep, right? If the spellcaster traveled the wilderness, they must have camped, eaten, made waste…"

"You're thinking the spellcaster is periodically checking in on the narjags by portal?" wondered Anne.

"It could be," said Rew.

"But why?" she asked.

He held up his hands helplessly and didn't respond.

"I'm glad the narjags are dead, and if there is some spellcaster killing them, they have my blessing, but what are we supposed to be doing here?" asked Cinda. "There's no path."

Rew nodded and pointed at the fallen rock which blocked the end of the gully. "The path used to be right through there."

Cinda crossed her arms over her chest.

Rew kicked a fallen rock with his boot. It would take them half an hour to move back out of the gully. Then, he'd have to leave the party or drag them along while he scouted for another route. Assuming they could even find one, that might take hours or days. They were worn out, and up past the tree line, there weren't a lot of options for fresh water. With so many narjags in the area, he didn't want to risk running low in case they ran into trouble and didn't have time to search for more. For comfort and basic needs, they needed to move quickly.

"We climb," he said.

Raif shifted nervously, eyeing the steep sides of the gully and the fifty paces they would have to ascend to get to the top of it.

"You shouldn't have brought all of that armor," mentioned Rew. He moved to the wall. "I'll go and check things out up top. Then, I'll come back for the rest of you. While I'm gone, strap your gear on tight and make sure you've got a full range of motion. In a few minutes, up we go."

Behind him, the party began to do what they could to prepare, putting weapons on their backs, pushing aside their cloaks, taking off their gloves, and cinching their packs tight so they didn't jostle around as they climbed.

Rew put his fingers on the wall, feeling the chill of the stone immediately seep into his skin. He hauled himself up, finding toeholds with his soft boots and scaling the side of the gully like a spider. He traversed it toward the corner where the rocks had fallen, seeing they'd been shattered free by an incredible force. The climbing would have been easier there, except pieces of rock were loose. Inexperienced climbers might not see the risk, and if they lost their grip when the rock fell away under their hands, they would go tumbling down.

He skirted back out toward where the rock was stable and plotted the easiest route up. It wasn't difficult for him, and he imagined Jon and Zaine would have little trouble, but the nobles were not used to such activity, and Anne hadn't climbed anything steeper than a stairwell since she'd come to Eastwatch.

At the top, he saw the way was clear yet again, and he could see the opening into the pass. The mountain had split there due to some geological event ages earlier. It must have been torn apart, but it looked as if a giant had cleaved the peaks with an axe. It left a narrow passage through, the bottom filled with rubble and scree from above. It was just a dozen paces wide, and in some spots, it narrowed even further. An easy hike, as long as you weren't bothered by tight, confined spaces with a long way to go in either direction to escape.

Rew shuddered, thinking of the last time he'd passed through. The center of the narrows was a particularly tight squeeze. Shoulders brushing against both sides of the pass, he'd wanted to run the two hundred paces through it. He would rather face an army of narjags than spend more time than necessary in such a constricted area, but they had to do it. The only other places they could pass over the Spine would add over a week to their journey to Falvar.

Rew looked down at the party below and grinned. They looked as nervous about the climb as he felt about walking through the narrows. Misery loves company.

He drew a deep breath, glad to be free of the stench of the gully where the dead narjags lay, and frowned. He sniffed again and detected old smoke. He moved away from the gully, and fifty paces east of the pass, he found the remains of a giant fire. Scattered around it was the refuse of a feast. Skin, bones, hair… He swallowed uncomfortably, realizing he was standing in the middle of a campsite for a huge party of narjags. They must have spent the night there before entering the pass. Circling slowly, he walked out from the fire, spotting waste the foul creatures had left and the marks on the stone where they'd disturbed them. He saw several bodies, but they looked like they could have been killed by their companions. Common enough, amongst a group of narjags. There was no soil so high up on the mountain and no growth that could give away more details, but he was confident a very large party had rested there. A hundred of them, at least.

Walking back to the fire, Rew toed through it with his boot. There were the stubs of logs that must have been extinguished by the wind before they could be entirely consumed in the fire. There were bits of animal that had been thrown in as well. Few scraps or other signs outside of the fire, but narjags traveled light. He scratched his beard. Narjags traveled light and never with the foresight to bring firewood with them for when they passed the tree line. And where had they gotten the animals? Any animal wily enough to survive in the heights of the Spine wouldn't be easy to catch for such a large group of narjags.

He couldn't figure what it meant, that a large party had camped at the top of the gully while a dozen more had been trapped and killed below. After seeing the rock up close, he was certain spellcasting had caused the small avalanche, and he didn't think the narjags were capable of such. Were the creatures working with the spellcaster or chasing him?

Rew picked up a charred piece of wood and sniffed it. Two days old, he guessed. The narjags that had camped beside the fire could already be through the pass now. They would have no clue his party was coming behind them, so he felt it safe enough to continue, but where were the Dark Kind going? What were they up to?

Heavy thoughts pressing on his mind, he scaled down to the others, taking more time than the climb up. He told them what he'd found and assured the younglings there was no cause of immediate concern. Then, he began describing how they should ascend, where the finger- and toeholds were, and giving the party what pointers he could.

Jon was the first to climb up, demonstrating the route for the others, and then Zaine went behind him. Both of them, limber and strong, made decent time with little problem. The thief confidently followed in the ranger's shadow, and Rew briefly wondered just how much experience she had. She had the body of a climber, and her movements had the confidence of someone who'd done their share of scaling under stressful circumstances. Too young to be a full member of the thieves' guild, but...

His thoughts were cut short as Cinda began the climb. The noblewoman wasn't used to such hard labor, but she was light and determined. Slow compared to the other two, she crept up the rock face, taking her time and testing each finger- and toehold before she trusted it with her weight.

Rew nodded for Anne to go next, and she frowned but then looked at Raif. The big fighter was watching his sister, trepidation evident on his face. His arms and legs were the strongest of any in the party except for Rew, but he weighed twice as much as Anne and the girls. If he fell, he would take out anyone who was ascending behind him.

As Anne began after Cinda, Rew asked Raif, "Care if I haul your armor and sword up?"

The boy shook his head, unwilling to bend his pride. "I've got it."

Rew sighed then stated, "I'm going to carry your armor and sword up."

Raif drew himself upright.

Rew met the boy's gaze without blinking. "It's a difficult climb, lad. We're going to need you if we encounter another band of narjags up there. Your sister and father are going to need you when we reach Falvar. Don't risk yourself on something so foolish as carrying armor up a sheer rock wall. A leader knows when to delegate, and traversing this wilderness is what I do. Let me do it."

With a grunt, Raif unslung his pack and untied his armor. He insisted, "I'm taking the sword myself."

Rew shrugged and picked up the heavy leather armor. It was better than nothing. "After you, then."

The pass, with its sheer rock walls, narrow passage, and bitter cold wind blasting into their faces like water off the edge of a waterfall, was every bit as unpleasant as Rew recalled. They huddled together, leaning into the wind as they forced their way forward. Tears leaked from their eyes, and they had to shout to keep their words from being blown away by the gusts. It made the walking exhausting, constantly leaning into a wall of wind that tried to force them back, but it was manageable, and compared to hiking up the side of the bare mountain, it wasn't much more strenuous.

But at night, there was no respite. Instead of laying down on fist-sized rocks, they had to contend with the screaming wind blowing over them in a constant howling rush. In the morning after they'd spent the night in the narrows, they were all awake before dawn and agreed to start moving, eating a cold breakfast as they hiked. Their skin was chapped. Their ears rang from the unceasing wail of the wind, and none of them had gotten more than a few hours of fitful rest.

Rew led the way, his body getting battered by the wind, but he broke it for the rest of the party, and they followed behind, tightly clustered in his wake. The others offered to take turns in the lead, but he shook his head and pressed on. He could deal with exhaustion. He could deal with wind, and he could survive the cold, but the awful feeling of being trapped between the towering rock walls made his skin crawl. He would rather face the wind and have the passage open in front of him than be buried within the party, people in front and behind. He knew his discomfort wouldn't pass until they cleared the narrows and he could stand in the open, so grimly, he trudged on.

Shivering, he glanced up, seeing sparse clouds streaking across the blue sky. They were visible in a thin band a thousand paces above, where the tops of the Spine's peaks reached. He paused, thinking how the narrow pass looked just like a giant version of the gully and how the end of that gully had been sealed by a landslide. There would be no climbing a thousand paces up the smooth rock walls to escape the pass. His heart racing, Rew started walking again, his breath coming in tight, nervous bursts.

It was near nightfall when they finally reached the end of the narrows and he saw shards of the sunset leaking into the gap of the pass. The white stone at the end of the passage was splashed with shades of red, pink, and gold like a banner welcoming them out of the horrid stone tunnel. The wind roared as hard as it had since they'd entered the pass, and he knew the sun would set soon, casting a deep chill over the land, but Rew's spirit felt like it was free, racing toward that opening.

"Come on. We're almost there," he called back to the others, and not a one of them complained as he increased the pace to nearly a jog.

That evening, they flopped down to rest, still in the upper reaches of the mountain, still laying on hard rock, still battling the numbing cold at the high elevation, but they'd found a hollow to lay down in and avoid the scouring wind.

"Ah, that's nice," murmured Jon, speaking in a voice lower than a shout for the first time in two days, touching his bright-red cheeks, worn raw by the force of the wind. "Happy to be done with that bit of the journey, and it should be smoother travel from here on out, no?"

"Well, there's the barrows..." mentioned Rew.

Jon blinked at him.

"You know what a barrow is, right?" asked the senior ranger.

"I-I thought they called it that because it's rolling hills?" stammered the younger ranger. "Surely not all of those are—They aren't, are they?"

"The legend is that three hundred years ago, even before the arrival of the Dark Kind and Vaisius Morden uniting the kingdom, there was a titanic battle in the barrowlands," said Rew. "The people who lived here, and who eventually joined the kingdom as we know it, battled some enemy that has been forgotten through time. We must have won, since it's people like us who rule these lands, but the stories say the losses were catastrophic. They say the dead lay like a carpet for one hundred leagues. An exaggeration, I'm sure, because where would you even find so many people to kill, but there probably were an awful lot of bodies. Too many to return home for proper burial, so they buried them out there, in the steppes, in barrows. It's only the wraiths that live out there now."

Jon swallowed.

"He's jesting with you," assured Anne, rolling her eyes at the senior ranger. "Those low hills just look like barrows. Walking through the barrowlands is quite pleasant, actually. Lush grass as far as one can see and easy, open travel. In the spring, wildflowers bloom everywhere. It's like a giant painted an emerald green canvas with the most vibrant colors you can fathom."

"Some of the hills are real barrows," insisted Rew.

Chuckling, Anne admitted, "Yes, some are barrows. And yes, there are wraiths which haunt them, but those can be found anywhere in the ancient, hidden places of the world. The barrows along the road we'll follow were cleaned out ages ago. Unless we venture deep into the grasslands, there is nothing at all to worry about."

Rew winked at her.

"Wraiths?" whispered Jon, shifting to look over the rim of the hollow they'd camped in, down at the vast expanse of darkness that lay beneath them at the foot of the mountain. "There truly are wraiths out there?"

"Anne is right. There are no wraiths along the path we'll be walking," assured Raif. "There's a, well, not a proper road, but there is a track between the mining encampment and Falvar. It's well-traveled, and there's no danger on the route. It's safer even than the road between Falvar and Spinesend. In my lifetime, there's never been a wraith spotted close to the road or the town, and there are no bandits out in the barrowlands. Who would bother to steal from a bunch of miners?"

"But… real wraiths?" worried the young ranger, looking at Rew out of the corner of his eye. "You're not jesting with me? You're serious?"

"Our family has spent generations cleaning the wraiths from the barrows," declared Raif. "Within a day's ride of Falvar and along the road, there is no danger."

Rew, rubbing the back of his hand on his lips, tried not to laugh at Jon's worried expression.

The younger ranger, eying him suspiciously, evidently decided he was more comfortable with a different topic. He asked, "What are they mining for?"

"Iron ore," answered Raif. "It's why the road is so safe. No one's going to try to steal a shipment of ore. The barrowlands are well patrolled by my father's men, but the truth is that there is little need for it. In Falvar, not even the children are scared of wraiths or bandits from the barrowlands. It's as easy travel as one can find in Duke Eeron's duchy."

Jon scowled at Rew.

Rew winked back at the younger ranger. "It's been a long journey, you can't blame me for having a little fun."

Settling himself down on the opposite side of the hollow so his back was no longer to the barrowlands, Jon did not seem to agree.

"I went to the old fortress once as a child," said Raif. "Before we fostered in Yarrow, my father would take me on tours of our lands. It's been years, though, and we did not pass beyond the tower up into these mountains. How long, do you think, until we reach the tower?"

"A day and a half then four more down to Falvar from there," said Rew. Grinning at Jon, he admitted, "And it should be easier travel from here on out."

A day and a half later, they were following a rocky, twisting cart path. It wove between the open mouths of half a dozen mine shafts, sunk into the sides of the mountain at odd intervals and random seeming locations. The mouths of those tunnels yawned, dark and vacant. They were a bit creepy and would have been the perfect lairs for rock trolls, but Rew knew the miners regularly traversed the area and entered the tunnels. As the nobles claimed, the area was quite safe. They did not see anyone as they walked, but the trail showed recent use. Rew had no problems picking out places in the rock dust where cart wheels had bounced up with supplies and then back down filled with hunks of rock and ore.

He didn't know how long it had been since this side of the Spine had seen rain, but sometime since then, people had been on the trail. Surprisingly, it was only the signs of man that he was able to find. There were no tracks of the Dark Kind, no signs of their waste or campsites. He'd seen evidence in the pass, but from there, the signs vanished. They could have taken a different path down the mountain, but it would have delayed them by days and would have added difficulty to their journey. Narjags were lazy, and Rew couldn't picture them circling around the mining encampment to be stealthy. Of course, none of their other actions made sense, either.

"It's a tough life out here on the edge of the world," said Raif, peering into one of the open mine shafts. "Nothing to do, just a handful of miners to keep you company. I don't think I could stand it."

"Oh, I don't know," said Rew. "Doesn't sound so bad to me."

Anne laughed.

"What?" asked Rew.

"You'd cut off your own arm before you went down into one of those mines," said Anne. "I don't care how much you want to be away from people. That's not the kind of lonely life most would enjoy."

Rew chuckled and nodded in acknowledgement. "That's true."

Raif kept on, discussing the lonely lives of the miners, not seeing through the jest that the rangers and Anne had chosen a similar life. Of course, few of the miners would have chosen the profession for the isolation. They would have done it because they had no other option. There were few jobs that entailed more risk than mining. Fumes, disturbed deep beneath the ground, could kill a man without warning. Cave-ins were common, and there were always accidents when men were swinging heavy equipment at even heavier rocks in the dark. No, it was not a profession that many would grow up wanting to pursue.

As Raif continued, Rew mused that arguably, one would be better off as an untrained grunt on the front lines of the king's army, storming some arrow-bristling, boiling oil-spilling, rebellious castle. At least the king's army only marched when there was war. A miner had to go down into those dark, dank caves every day.

He was still thinking about it, peering into the mouth of another tunnel they were passing, when strange sounds began to rise on the winds that blew up the face of the Spine. Rew frowned, trying to identify what he was hearing. They walked on another hundred paces when he called a halt.

"What is that?" wondered Jon. "Dogs? Do miners use dogs?"

"Ayres," hissed Rew. "I don't know which way they traveled from the mouth of the pass, but I'm guessing this is the group we've seen so many signs of." He looked around the party. "That means there will be a lot of them."

Raif drew his hand-and-a-half sword, looking around nervously, his elbows in tight, perhaps recalling what had happened last time he tussled with the Dark Kind.

"Weapons ready," said Rew. "We've got a bit to go before we see them, I think."

"How do you know?" questioned Raif.

"I'd bet good silver that they're assaulting the tower," explained Rew. "It's where the miners would have fled if they were attacked, and it's stout enough they could hold out against the Dark Kind for a bit. They're not tacticians, but maybe the Dark Kind avoided this road to sneak up on the fort. Maybe that's been their goal all along."

They walked another half hour before Rew slowed them and started taking time to peek around every turn on the narrow mining path. Moving quietly, they finally found an outcropping where they could peer down at the fortress below.

It was one of the old border forts, left over from the great war that spanned the barrowlands three hundred years earlier. Built to last, it'd been repurposed as a home for the miners and a storage space for their equipment. Its legacy as a fortress was the only thing saving the people inside now.

Surrounding them, Rew guessed there were at least sixty narjags and a dozen ayres, though the mounts were moving rapidly, yipping and barking, trying to leap up to the battlement of the tower, making it difficult to count them. Some of the narjags were flinging rocks up toward the tower's battlement or brandishing their crude weapons, but most were using carts they must have found abandoned outside. They were gathering piles of rock which they dumped on the side of the tower and forming the beginnings of a ramp to the top. At the edge of the action stood a giant narjag, adorned in necklaces and brightly colored scarves. It clutched a staff in its hands and gestured with it, directing its charges in the harsh, guttural language of the Dark Kind.

"A shaman?" wondered Jon.

Rew twisted his lips but did not respond. The narjag was dressed in the manner of shamans, but if the creature had spells to cast, it was not making use of them. Instead, it appeared many of the narjags were attempting to harry the defenders while their counterparts built the ramp. Rew saw that once the ramp was built, the narjags and the ayres could pour over the wall of the battlement with no difficulty. With so many of the Dark Kind, the fight would be over quickly.

There were a dozen miners crouched behind the walls. Two or three held swords or spears, and the rest held tools that they'd repurposed as weapons—a scythe that may have used to clear grass around the fort and an awful lot of heavy-looking hammers. In the doorway to the keep stood a man dressed in black, high-necked robes. They were embroidered extensively in silver, and he wore a black, velvet cloak around his shoulders. In contrast to the disheveled miners, the man's dark hair was swept straight back with spots of vivid white gracing his temples. He had a slender mustache and goatee as well, and even in the midst of battle and from a distance, it was obvious he had recently groomed himself. He couldn't have been a sharper contrast to the dirty, gruff-looking men around him.

"King's Sake," snarled Rew.

"What?" asked Jon, following the senior ranger's gaze, seeing the well-dressed man staring back at them. "Is that… Who is that?"

"That's our spellcaster," said Rew, glaring at the man. "Why isn't he doing anything? He killed dozens of those narjags on the other side of the Spine. Behind those walls, he could pick these off with no problem."

"He's staring at you, Rew," mentioned Anne.

Growling, Rew looked back to the narjags below them.

"Why is he staring at you?" wondered the empath.

"He's waiting for me to get him out of this mess," barked the ranger. He motioned for them all to duck back behind the outcropping of stone they were hiding behind. "We won't be doing that for him or anyone else if those narjags spot us."

They crouched down on the road, just around the bend. Rew smacked his fist against the rock outcropping that hid them, issuing a foul string of curses.

"That man is waiting on us?" whispered Raif. "What of the miners? Do you think they knew we were coming?"

"I don't think they are waiting on us. I think they had no choice but to hunker down behind those walls," said Rew. "You can see that they're scared witless and aren't even trying to put up a defense. If they flee, they'll be run down. The walls of that fort are the only thing keeping them alive. Those miners might be capable brawlers, but against a large group of Dark Kind, they don't stand a chance. And for some reason, Alsayer isn't casting."

"Alsayer?" asked Cinda, her voice tight.

"Alsayer," confirmed Rew. He clenched his jaw. "He's the one we've been following, and though I'd rather jab porcupine quills into my arm, I need to talk to him. He'll have the answers we're looking for."

"I'm not sure now is a good time…" said Raif.

Rew shook his head. "Not now. After we free the tower from the Dark Kind."

"F-Free the…" stammered Jon. "Ah, do you have a plan?"

"I'm thinking of one," snapped Rew. He closed his eyes. "Give me a moment."

Chapter Thirteen

Sixty narjags and a dozen ayres. Twelve miners armed with hammers and picks and a spellcaster who wasn't casting. A healer, three untrained youths, an apprentice, and a ranger.

Rew realized immediately that it wouldn't take long for the Dark Kind to build their ramp high enough to swarm over the battlements, and if Alsayer declined to join the fight, the miners would be quickly overwhelmed. Rew's party wouldn't fare much better against so many. They had nearly crumbled against a force the quarter the size of this one.

Rew glanced at Anne and saw her worried face. Raif clutched his hand-and-a-half sword, but the blade was trembling in his grip. Cinda was pawing through her pack, though the ranger knew there was nothing in there which could help their situation. Worry lay on Jon's face like a mask, and the young ranger had not yet drawn his longsword. Zaine seemed inexplicably calm, holding her bow lightly, an arrow set on the string.

"Behind those walls, they can hold out, can't they?" asked the thief. "Should we make haste for Falvar, alert Baron Fedgley, and get these people some relief? I think if we go several hundred paces back up the slope, there's a—"

Cinda shook her head and interjected, "We're four days from

THE KING'S RANGER

Falvar. That's over a week before assistance could arrive"

"Those miners must have weeks of supplies inside," argued Zaine. "Within the walls of that tower they could hold indefinitely. It's not like the narjags will bring in siege equipment."

"The narjags are building a ramp," said Rew. "By dusk, they'll be over the walls. The miners are tough characters, and they won't go down easy, but they're outnumbered seven to one. They aren't trained for a fight like this."

"The spellcaster?" wondered Cinda.

Rew scowled. "There's a reason he's not using his spells. I can't fathom what that reason is, and even if he told us, I wouldn't trust his explanation, but we all saw what he's capable of on the journey here. If he wanted to, he could make short work of the Dark Kind. My guess, there's some reason he won't use his spells, or he's waiting and will only act to save his own skin."

"You know him?" asked Anne.

Grimacing, Rew nodded. "From a long time ago."

That evidently satisfied the empath, and she didn't ask for further explanation.

"Cinda, can you provide a distraction, and then we can charge into their backs?" asked Raif. "Just like the last time, but this time we'll all have surprise on our side."

No one spoke. The last time, Cinda's distraction hadn't worked, and even with surprise on their side, the boy might take down several narjags, but he wasn't going to take down sixty of them. The Dark Kind would overwhelm him in moments, and there was no way the rangers could protect everyone against such a large pack. The younglings were more of a liability than a help against such a large force of narjags.

Rew sighed and looked to Jon and Anne. "Keep the younglings here until it's clear. When you have a route, make for the tower. If the miners hesitate, the spellcaster's name is Alsayer. Tell him you're with me. He'll let you in."

"What will you do?" questioned Jon, looking confused.

At the same time, Anne said, "You don't have to do this."

169

Rew shook his head. "You have another plan?"

She held his gaze but didn't respond. There was nothing to say, nothing else they could do.

"I don't understand," said Cinda. "What do you plan to do?"

"Stay here. Run for the tower when it's clear," repeated Rew. He shrugged his shoulders, stretched his legs, and then nodded to Jon and Anne.

"Wait. W-What—" stammered Jon. His eyes widened as Rew drew his longsword and rose into a low crouch, shuffling to the edge of the outcropping they were hiding behind. "You can't! It's too—"

Rew ignored the other ranger and scampered down the trail, finding a scattering of large rocks on the slope below, slipping behind them, and making his way stealthily down the mountain. He moved silently, hiding from the narjags and their mounts, but with the higher elevation, he knew he would be visible from the fort. He didn't look to the people there, but he could feel Alsayer's eyes on him. He knew the spellcaster would understand his plan.

Rew seethed as he got closer, cursing Alsayer for holding back his magic. Why was the man not unleashing his skill upon the Dark Kind? From behind the wall, he could pick them off cleanly with no risk to himself or anyone else. It'd been years, but Rew was certain the man's reserves were deep enough he could take care of a handful of Dark Kind. Besides, assuming he was the spellcaster that had portaled into the wilderness, they'd seen evidence of what he was capable of on the other side of the Spine.

The ranger reached the bottom of the slope and crouched behind the last rock of any size. Rew drew deep breaths, steadying himself and ignoring the voice in his head that told him this plan was stupid, that he wouldn't survive. He shook himself, adjusted his grip on his longsword, and peeked around the corner of the boulder. He might not survive, but he could survive long enough to give his companions time. Behind the walls, their strength added to the miners, they had a good chance. Well, a better chance, at least.

Rew waited patiently as several of the narjags flung fist-sized stones at the miners, mostly missing, occasionally forcing the men to duck behind a crenellation. Other narjags gathered rocks and piled them at the base of the tower, building their ramp higher and higher. The ayres yipped at the miners, springing fruitlessly against the walls, falling down, and then sprinting in agitated circles. Rew waited until a trio of those ayres came racing nearby. Then, he sprang from hiding.

He swept his longsword in a wide arc, clipping two of the creatures across the backs of their legs, sending them tumbling into a tangled, yipping heap. The third ayre was racing behind the other two and leapt at him.

His longsword out of position, Rew threw up his forearm, his leather bracer catching the ayre on the bottom of the chin, clacking its jaw shut and stunning it. It crashed against him, and he stumbled back, but he remained standing. He swung around his longsword, stabbed it into the surprised ayre's chest, yanked the blade out, and ran.

Nine ayres. Sixty narjags. Behind him was the rock-strewn slope that hid his companions. Ahead of him was the stout tower that the miners were defending. Everywhere else was the enemy.

Rew darted to his left, arms and legs pumping in a full-out sprint toward the trees that bound the space around the old tower. In fifty paces, he would be in the cover, in his element. The ayres would be slowed, darting amongst the trees. The narjags unable to come at him in full force. Between him and the trees was the narjag shaman and two creatures that appeared to be its bodyguards.

Guttural shouts of alarm were rising from the narjags and howls from the ayres. The shaman raised its staff and opened its mouth, its harsh voice bellowing. A spell or commands to its followers, Rew didn't know. He didn't plan to give the thing time to finish, whatever it was trying to say. On the run, he feinted at one of the narjag guards. The creature hissed and raised its spear in a defensive crouch.

Rew dodged to the side, avoiding that narjag and slamming his shoulder into the second guard. It was surprised and flew backward from the impact, its smaller body bouncing like a rock off a wall as Rew smashed into it.

The shaman's cry stalled, and Rew thrust at it with his longsword, not pausing to ensure a clean blow, just making sure to wound the thing, to make it and its followers really mad. The tip of his steel dug into the shaman's chest, piercing half-a-hand deep. Then, Rew was by, tearing the sword free, still running to the forest.

He didn't think he'd killed the shaman, but whatever he'd done prevented it from launching any spells after him. Not pausing to look over his shoulder, he made it to the trees and ducked into the forest, the barks of the ayres telling him he'd have moments at best before they were on his heels.

Branches of thin pine whipped against him as he barreled through the forest, dodging the narrow trees, leaping over rocks and fallen tree trunks, striving to gain some distance between himself and his pursuers. He passed an older tree and darted to the far side of its wide trunk, pausing a beat.

Seconds later, two ayres crashed past him, paws scrambling on the rocky soil, teeth bared at him. They growled from deep in their throats, but they'd been at a full run and stumbled, trying to make the turn back to him.

Rew jumped after them, slashing two efficient strikes, taking one ayre in the throat, the other in the skull. The second beast fell back, whimpering, and Rew hoped he'd struck it a fatal blow. He didn't have time to wait or to finish it, and he was on the run again before the first creature fell to the earth, kicking and squealing.

Behind him, he heard the thrash of dozens of bodies storming through the forest. He clambered up the slope, getting elevation and a defensive advantage. He glanced over his shoulder as he hauled himself up onto a head-high boulder.

The ayres were coming close, and the narjags were in bunches behind. The ayres would have little difficulty outpacing him, even in the forest, but he would be able to keep ahead of the narjags. Their squat legs were muscular, and they could propel themselves into impressive jumps and short sprints, but they had little stamina and weren't as dexterous as he was moving over terrain.

He had to cut down the ayres. After that, he could take his time moving ahead of the narjags, carving them off one by one as they got close. He would be exhausted once it was over, but as long as he didn't let the entire group pin him down, he might survive.

If he could cut the ayres down.

One of the beasts came hurtling at him from above, evidently curving high on the hill to cut off his escape.

Rew ducked as it sprang at him, thrusting up with his longsword, catching it in the gut, and disemboweling the ayre as it soared overhead. Its momentum carried it over the edge of the boulder and it crashed down into the brush beyond.

He started up the hill as another ayre leapt at him from the bottom of the boulder, teeth snapping shut near his boot. Swinging a wild slash at it, he missed as it twisted away, but the strike slowed it, and Rew was running again, heading uphill and looking for a position he could hold for a moment to fend off the ayres.

Already, his breath was coming in quick bursts, and he knew there was only so long he could charge straight up the side of the mountain before it would wear him out. If he got tired and sluggish, he didn't like his odds against so many Dark Kind.

He looked back again and saw three ayres pelting up the slope at him, the narjags a hundred paces behind. The other ayres seemed to have disappeared. Were they back at the tower? He grimaced then spun, running straight at the three blue-skinned creatures on his heels.

They were shocked at the sudden reversal and skidded on splayed paws to stop. One veered off its course, fouling the path of the second creature behind it. The third one launched itself at

Rew. Its jaw was open wide, its paws raised to smash into him, to tear at him with its giant claws, and pin him on his back where it could work him with its powerful bite.

Rew darted to the side and headed toward the ayre that had turned. It tried to run from him, but he caught its rear leg, severing its foot. The ayre collapsed, howling and gnashing its teeth.

The one that had stopped attempted to come at him while his back was turned, but he spun to meet it, his free hand snatching his hunting knife from his belt, burying the blade in the ayre's neck, twisting it, and yanking it free. The creature's body fell into him, knocking him back, and he let himself collapse, rolling over his shoulder and back onto his feet.

The last ayre was standing, growling, and trying to block his line of escape so the howling pack of narjags could catch up. Rew ran right at it. The ayre snarled, crouching to attack, but Rew lunged forward, thrusting his longsword down its throat. The ayre, surprised at the direct blow, stared at him stupidly as the steel rammed down its gullet.

He was running again, the first of the narjags ten paces behind him. Jumping from boulder to boulder, scrambling up the slope, he tucked away his hunting knife and used his free hand to steady himself against the rocks and dirt as he recklessly climbed.

Two hundred paces upslope, he found a dry creek bed. He turned and watched as the narjag swarm approached. If they were smart, they would wait and hold him in the narrow defile while others found a different path up the ridge and circled around him, pinning him in the confined space between two parties of several dozen. With that many on both sides of him and no room to maneuver, he would be in trouble, but narjags were aggressive and not known for their well-considered battle strategy.

They came at him in a tight group, forcing themselves three abreast into the narrow chute of rock he'd backed into. Holding their crude spears and rusty short swords, they stabbed and swung at him, fouling each other's strikes and making it easy for him to lunge forward and use the length of his blade to strike and then retreat back to safety.

The narjags elbowed and swiped at each other as they came, others tugging at the ones in front and throwing their companions off balance in their rush to come at him. Rew made them pay for it. His longsword, flicking like the tail of a scorpion, struck over and over. He held his hunting knife in his off hand, using it to turn the thrusts from the narjag's weapons.

With just a few at a time able to face him, their attacks were uncoordinated, wild, and easy to defend. He kept an ear open, extending his senses behind, worried the three remaining ayres would appear at his back. Against those beasts and with narjags in front, it would get ugly, but as he backed up the creek bed, nothing came from behind, and one by one, he cut the narjags down.

Their bodies littered the defile like carpet, following him higher and higher. His arms burned from the exertion of absorbing their attacks and dealing his own, but in minutes, he'd felled dozens of the Dark Kind. Suddenly, behind the first rank, the others began to fall back, and then, they turned and ran.

He stabbed one in the face, slinging its body aside. The last narjag charged him, and he casually brushed aside its spear and whipped his hunting knife forward, burying it in the Dark Kind's chest.

The narjag fell, desperate hands scrabbling at the rocks, quickly bleeding out. Several others twitched and wailed, but he saw it was only a matter of time before they expired. Their wounds were grievous, and if their companions returned, they wouldn't offer assistance. They would come to consume the flesh of their fallen brethren. There was little love amongst a pack of narjags.

Breathing heavily and letting his arms relax but not yet sheathing his weapons, Rew studied the forest. Thirty of the narjags lay piled in the creek bed like leaves fallen from the trees above. Beyond them, he could see the corpses of the ayres he'd felled and a few scattered narjags who darted down the slope, fleeing.

With satisfaction, Rew noted that they were fleeing away from the tower, away from his party and the miners. He waited, listening, sensing for another attack, but after several minutes he decided that as a group, they had indeed all fled.

Cleaning his longsword as best he was able, he sheathed it then moved back down the creek bed, stepping cautiously and pausing whenever he discovered a Dark Kind that still lived. He knelt, and he killed them. It gave him no pleasure, wading through the gore, but the creatures were evil. Should any of them survive their wounds, it was only a matter of time before they attacked someone. They were not of this world. They did not belong, and there was nothing to do but eliminate them.

Rew made his way back through the scrub pine forest, moving slowly and looking for signs of the Dark Kind, but he found none other than those he'd killed. When he reemerged near the fort, he saw his companions clustered on the old battlement, staring in a mixture of relief and horror. He glanced down at his clothing and winced. He was covered in dark, fetid blood and gore from the Dark Kind.

Miners opened the sturdy tower door for him, watching in awe as he walked by them. No one spoke as he climbed the open stone stairs up to the battlement.

"Is any of that yours?" asked Anne when he reached the top.

He shook his head, looking over the group. "Not much of it. Everyone make it in safely?"

They nodded.

"Three of them remained near the, ah, the leader, but we took care of them. Most ran after you or fled," stammered Jon. "You… Did you kill them all?"

Rew shook his head. "Half of them. The rest disappeared down the slope of the mountain."

"Oh," said Jon, eyes wide. He looked confused and scared, like his best friend had suddenly mentioned that he had wings and spent the occasional afternoon flying.

"Where's Alsayer?" asked Rew.

"Inside," answered Anne.

Rew found the door to the interior and walked in. The first floor was one giant open room where the miners did their cooking and eating and had their entertainments. Alsayer was seated in a worn chair near the fire, his feet propped up in front of him, a mug of ale in his hands. He watched Rew as the ranger walked directly toward him.

The spellcaster stood, glancing at the ranger's bloodstained clothing. "Perhaps a change and a bath before we speak?"

Rew strode forward and gripped the front of the man's robe in his fist, shoving the spellcaster back and shaking him. "Why were you hiding behind the walls? Why didn't you kill those things?"

"Whoa, there," said Alsayer, raising his mug of ale. "This is no good, but it's all that they've got. Let's not spill it."

Snarling, Rew shoved the man back, pushing him half a dozen paces until Alsayer's back smacked against the stone wall of the tower. Rew stared into the spellcaster's eyes, waiting for an answer.

Alsayer raised his tankard as if to take a sip, and Rew hauled him forward and then slammed him back against the wall. Anger flashed in the spellcaster's eyes, and ale spilled down the front of his silver-embroidered black robes.

"Rew…" murmured Cinda.

Around Alsayer's free hand, blue lightning crackled, but the man left it by his side, fingers curled into a claw, the energy staying tightly clustered around his hand. The spellcaster stared back at Rew with murder in his eyes.

"Rew, he's—" started Cinda.

"He won't do it," growled Rew.

"Don't test me, Ranger," snapped Alsayer.

Rew hauled the man forward with one fist and smashed him back against the wall again.

The spellcaster's head bounced off the stone, and Rew could see the shock and pain in his eyes.

"Rew!" cried Cinda.

The ranger drew his hunting knife, still crusted in blood from the narjags, and held it in front of Alsayer's eyes.

Cinda moved a few steps behind them and warned, "Rew, he's built power. He could unleash it in a blink."

"He won't do it," repeated Rew. "He knows what I'll do to him if he does."

"It's been a long time, Ranger," hissed Alsayer. "Since we've last seen each other, I've—"

Rew hauled the man forward and slammed him back against the wall again. He demanded, "What are you doing here, Alsayer?"

A smirk twisting his lips, but pain in his eyes, the spellcaster raised his hand beside his head, his palm and fingers crackling with coruscating flashes of pale, blue lightning.

"Talk now or I'm going to gut you like a fish," said Rew. "Try any of your parlor tricks on me and I'm going to take my time doing it."

Alsayer paused, his hand still raised, the lightning still crackling. Then, suddenly, it blinked out. He told Rew, "Despite your ill treatment of me, I am not your enemy. We should talk in private, cousin."

"Private?" questioned Rew, wondering if it was a trick, or if the spellcaster truly had something he would tell only Rew.

"I'm on a mission, cousin," explained Alsayer, "and my words are for the ears of Baron Fedgley alone. For the King's Ranger, though, perhaps I can make an exception."

"Fedgley?" asked Rew. He nodded back toward Cinda. "That's his daughter. The big lad is his son."

Alsayer, suddenly curious, leaned around Rew to stare at the young nobles. "Now, what are you two doing way out here in the middle of nowhere? I expected you would be in Falvar by now."

Rew twisted his fist, gathering another turn of the spellcaster's robe, and snarled, "I asked you the same thing, Alsayer, and I'm done waiting for a response."

Sighing, the spellcaster said, "Very well. Let me go, and I will tell you."

Backing up, Rew released the man's robes but kept his hunting knife in hand. If it came to it, he thought he could defeat the spellcaster, but Alsayer had not lied when he'd said it had been a long time. The spellcaster had always been dangerous, and over the years, he would have gotten more so.

"There's a plot afoot, and Baron Fedgley is at risk," confessed the spellcaster, brushing his black, silk robes where Rew had wrinkled them, frowning at the wet spot of ale that had been spilled. He looked around the room, noting the collection of strangers, and said, "It's been twenty-five years, you know. Even out here, on the fringe of the realm, you must still keep track of the years." Alsayer eyed Cinda and Raif again. "Of course, what am I saying? You know, Rew. You know what's coming. You can feel it. Traveling with the Fedgley children, though, I did not expect that. I thought you'd come to the eastern province to stay out of our family entanglements."

"I did," muttered Rew.

Alsayer looked to the miners. "Give us a moment, will you?"

The gruff-looking men, faced with a spellcaster and a ranger who'd slaughtered three-dozen Dark Kind, moved outside without complaint. Rew's party stayed, and Alsayer frowned at them.

"They're trustworthy," assured Rew.

"I'm sure they are," said Alsayer, walking around the ranger and heading toward the ale barrel.

Rew, looking at the man's back, reminded himself that while his companions may be trustworthy, Alsayer most certainly was not. Cousins, yes, but both bastards. More outcasts from their family than a part of it, which suited Rew perfectly well. Alsayer had chosen a different life, one that Rew had spent the last twenty years trying to avoid.

His ale refilled, Alsayer turned. "There's a plot against Duke Eeron and Baron Fedgley. I was sent to warn the baron. The roads between Falvar and Spinesend are dotted with spies, and there's a ward cast across this land that dampens the efficacy of high magic. I didn't know how far it extended, so I couldn't risk portaling in too close without risk to myself. So, I've been bouncing around the wilderness on my way here, where I've found I can go no farther."

Rew grunted, shaking his head. "A barrier against high magic that covers such a distance?"

Alsayer nodded. He flashed an arrogant smile but then admitted, "Yes, a barrier that covers such a distance that I cannot pierce. Believe me, cousin, I was as surprised as you are."

"I haven't felt any ward against magic," murmured Cinda.

Alsayer eyed her, pursed his lips, and then suggested, "Try casting something right now."

The young noblewoman looked back at him uncertainly. Rew wasn't actually sure if she could cast a spell. So far, she hadn't in his presence, and it seemed she wouldn't now.

Rew turned to Alsayer and suggested, "There's no spellcaster in the eastern province with the skill to lay such a ward."

"That's my assessment as well," lilted Alsayer, "but all the same, the ward is there."

"How many casters are there in the kingdom who could do such a thing?" questioned Rew.

Alsayer shrugged. "Not many. None of them would be happy to see you."

Rew began to pace back and forth across the room. Alsayer's and the others' eyes followed him as he walked. He could hear Cinda and Raif whispering to each other, speculating on what Alsayer's message could be.

"An artifact?" Rew asked Alsayer. "Could an artifact power a barrier like that?"

Alsayer nodded. "Sure, though I've never heard of such an artifact."

Rew glared at the man. "We saw where you arrived outside of Eastwatch. There were narjags waiting for you, and all along your path, they've been with you."

Alsayer nodded, his lips twisting. "Following me, cousin, following me. Every time I stepped through a portal, it was not long, and they were on my heels. This is rather embarrassing, but I believe someone has affixed a beacon to me. It's a magical… a call, you could say. It's attracting the Dark Kind to me like a flower attracts a bee. If you followed my path, then surely you saw the bodies."

Rew frowned, then sheathed his hunting knife without responding.

"Unfortunately while the beacon explains the Dark Kind swarming after me, it doesn't explain why they're there in the first place," said Alsayer. "You keep the forest clear, don't you, cousin? Why are so many of these foul creatures nearby? My patron has suspected some danger from these quarters, and that's why I'm here, to warn the baron and to provide what assistance I can, a helping hand and a sharp pair of eyes."

"I don't understand," said Jon.

Anne, from the far side of the room, guessed, "One of the princes is rousing the Dark Kind for the Investiture. Where are they gathering? The barrowlands?"

"Who are you?" asked Alsayer, looking at Anne as if he was seeing her for the first time.

"Don't answer that," said Rew. He then asked Alsayer, "You came to tell Baron Fedgley the Dark Kind are massing, but someone has attempted to lock down the area, to prevent you or other casters from portaling in and interfering. Someone tied a beacon to you to make your job more difficult. Do I have the right of your story?"

Alsayer nodded. "You have the right of it."

"Who is conspiring against the baron?" asked Rew.

The spellcaster nodded at Raif and Cinda. "I believe they can tell you that, cousin."

"Worgon," growled Rew, stalking around the spellcaster, finding a tankard beside the beer barrel and dipping it in. He tilted it up and took a deep swallow. Shuddering, he said, "This is awful."

"It is," agreed Alsayer, "but given the circumstances, I thought it best to have a few."

Rew strode across the room and flopped into one of the miner's sturdier-looking chairs.

"What is going on?" demanded Cinda. "Dark Kind massing, a plot against my father and Duke Eeron… Do you think these narjags are meant to keep my father from getting involved to assist the duke? Who is behind all of this? Surely Worgon himself does not have the strength to raise an army of Dark Kind. The Worgons are a family of enchanters."

Alsayer smirked. "Fedgley's kept you as innocent as rumored, hasn't he? It was suspected, of course, when you never left Eeron's duchy, but no one was certain. I cannot believe it. You really know nothing of this, lass?"

Cinda glared at the spellcaster.

"She doesn't know," confirmed Rew.

"Then, I suppose it's time you tell her," remarked Alsayer. He looked to Raif. "And the lad, of course. He'll inherit these lands one day, if they're still in Fedgley hands."

Setting his tankard down on a table beside his chair, Rew scrubbed at his face, feeling two weeks of road dirt and the blood of the narjags coating him like a second skin. He looked up and told Alsayer, "You tell them."

Grinning, the spellcaster turned to Raif and Cinda. "Every twenty to thirty years, the kingdom of Vaeldon requires a new king. Each cycle, the current king's children are assessed, and the strongest is chosen to take the throne."

"Assessed?" asked Cinda, looking at Rew and Anne. "Is this what you told us in the wilderness? Assessment seems a rather mild explanation, doesn't it?"

"They compete against each other," Alsayer laughed. "To the

winner goes the spoils, as they say. To the loser... well, that's the last of the loser."

"So we've heard," growled Raif, looking at the spellcaster suspiciously. "The princes try to kill each other."

Alsayer winked at Rew. "So you have told them a little. Yes, the princes try to kill each other. Whichever of the three is left standing inherits the throne. It's all rather terrible, but I do not believe that is what our ranger wants me to tell you about."

"What?" asked Cinda.

"It's more than just the princes," answered Alsayer. "It's more than just their magic and their assassins. They raise armies. They enlist allies."

Raif and Cinda frowned back at him.

"For Worgon to plot against Duke Eeron, he must have one of the princes as his patron," explained Alsayer. "Otherwise, it'd be beyond foolish for him to defy his liege. Worgon and those like him around the realm are responding to the first stirrings of the Investiture. They feel it's time to begin, so they're enacting plans they've spent years or even decades putting into place."

"Does the king know of this?" demanded Cinda. "Treachery and betrayal—"

"The king demands it," clarified Alsayer, interrupting her. "King Morden the Eighth's hand is not a benevolent one looking to shelter the innocents. Just like his father before him, just like all of the Mordens since Vaisius Morden the First, the king is the one pushing the princes toward each other. He'll let them struggle and then place the crown on the one who is left standing."

"Worgon's allied with a prince," said Raif, disbelief dripping from his voice like water from a melting icicle.

"Worgon and..." said Rew, glaring at Alsayer.

"What?" asked Cinda, her eyes darting between the two men.

Rew raised an eyebrow at the spellcaster.

"Why are you looking at me?" asked Alsayer, his eyes fluttering, the picture of innocence.

"Which one are you working for?" demanded Rew. "Which prince is Baron Fedgley working for?"

Cinda gasped, but the spellcaster smirked at Rew. "Come on, now. You know that is something I cannot tell you, no matter what sort of threats you make with that big knife of yours."

Rew grunted. He hadn't expected the man to admit his allegiance, and he wouldn't have trusted the answer had Alsayer given one, but it was worth asking.

"Are you saying…?" stammered Cinda. "What are you saying about our father's involvement in all of this?"

"Nothing, nothing at all," claimed Alsayer, "but I do have a favor to ask of you."

Rew groaned.

The spellcaster chuckled, seeing the ranger's reaction. He turned to Cinda and Raif. "I must travel with haste to warn my ally, your father. Unfortunately, I am prevented from casting beneath this ward. I've little ability to defend myself without my magic, and your father needs to hear what I have to say. You, ah, you saw what my cousin did to me. He's fortunate we're under the ward because I could do nothing to stop his rough behavior. I couldn't have flung that lightning I was holding much farther than my nose. With the narjags on my heels, well, I'm at a rather large disadvantage with no sword, no armor, no one to protect me. I cannot make it through the barrowlands alone. May I travel in your party, under your protection, for the good of Falvar and your people?"

Both of the younglings turned to Rew. He laid his head back on the chair, staring at the ceiling far above. He refused to comment.

"Good," said Alsayer, his voice bubbling with enthusiasm. "What say we spend the night here and then leave at dawn? And cheer up, cousin. It's been too long. This will give us an opportunity to catch up."

Rew, still staring at the ceiling, groaned again.

Chapter Fourteen

In the corner of the room, Alsayer hunched next to Cinda, scratching on a piece of scrap paper the miners had given him. From what Rew had overheard, the spellcaster was teaching Cinda the theory behind the sonic lash spell he'd used against the narjags. A practical bit of magic, Rew supposed, though he thought it ridiculous to attempt to teach a girl with her skill an attack. She would be better served with something she could easily practice or a defensive measure.

Rew grunted and looked away. There was no sense inserting himself between the noblewoman and the spellcaster. Alsayer would teach what he wanted. Cinda would listen if she was interested, and Rew would avoid getting involved.

A miner, a brooding, silent type that Rew could appreciate, raised a bushy eyebrow and gestured to Rew's empty ale mug. The ranger nodded, and the miner picked up the tankard and went to dunk it into the open beer barrel. Foul stuff, but it was the only drink being served.

Beside him, Raif frowned at his own tankard, still half full.

"Not much of a drinker?" Rew asked the boy.

Grimacing, Raif whispered back, "Not of this."

Rew winked and nodded his thanks as the miner returned

with a full mug. The man stood there a moment, hesitating, then walked off to a far corner of the room. The miners, dark with dirt and dust from beneath the earth, acted like they were walking on burning coals around the party. They weren't used to nobles in their midst, and a spellcaster was even worse. They'd been generous, though, and Rew hoped that when they left, Raif and Cinda would give the men proper thanks. He sipped the warm beer and wondered if he needed to tell the younglings that. Surely, they'd have been taught etiquette? They hadn't been taught about the Investiture and other life and death matters, but their tutors must have taught them something.

Rew sighed and leaned back, cradling the mug on his lap. Around them, orange light danced across the pale stone walls of the tower. Half a dozen miners were playing some game that involved dozens of chips of stone and a lot of bellows and curses followed by embarrassed looks at the women in the party. Another of the miners, evidently trying to impress Anne, played a merry little tune on a battered fiddle. He wasn't doing such a bad job, for a man with fingers used to crushing and hauling rock every day.

Jon was sitting near the fire, attempting to teach Zaine how to mend a torn pair of trousers, but it was evident the thief was paying him no mind. Instead, she was listening to the fiddle player, tapping her foot to the man's simple jig. She had been partaking freely of the open ale barrel.

Rew studied her glassy eyes and broad grin, wondering if he should stop her from drinking so much, but she was a woman near grown, and it wasn't like there was much trouble she could find herself in stuck in a mining encampment on the outskirts of the kingdom. He turned back to Raif and saw the boy was staring up at the ceiling, his eyes following the heavy, age-darkened wooden beams that towered three stories above them.

"It's nearly as high as in my father's throne room," remarked the boy, evidently feeling Rew's gaze on him. "There are four more stories in the tower above this room, and there's huge space beneath our feet. It's all storage down there, not practical living quarters, but it's space. On the four floors above us, they house a dozen miners, but they could fit five times that many comfortably. When this was a fortress, that storage below could have held enough food to feed this tower for, I don't know, six months maybe. These walls, they're nearly as thick as Falvar's. If those Dark Kind hadn't begun building a ramp up the side, they never would have gotten to the miners. This place is built to stand."

Rew nodded.

"Why?" asked the boy.

Rew grinned at him. "As the future ruler of this land, I figured you would already know that."

Raif frowned. "I've been taught combat since I was old enough to lift a sword. I've been taught my letters and how to write them beautifully. I've been taught figures, and I could give a clerk in a counting house a run for it. I know a bit of engineering. I know a little of agriculture. I know how our taxation scheme affects the commoners living on our land, but I don't know our history. Not of my family, not of the barony."

"Curious," replied Rew.

"It is," admitted Raif. "My father has made sure that Cinda and I know how to run the barony, but he's made equal efforts to disguise how our family came to rule it. I thought it was to cover some shame in our family's past and never gave it much thought beyond that. I imagined some ancestor of ours performed a treachery to earn these lands. Now... now I am unsure. What you and the spellcaster have said about the Investiture has gotten me thinking. Do you know the history of my family?"

Rew shook his head. "I don't know much. Not enough to answer your questions, anyway. From what I recall, your family has ruled these lands for... Well, I don't think I've ever heard of any other ruler."

Raif nodded. "The story is that an ancient Fedgley won these lands through incredible valor in battle. No one has been able to tell me who he was, who he fought, or when that happened. I am certain my father knows more, but he can be a difficult man. As I said, he's told us little about our past."

Rew sipped his ale, coughing at the sour taste. He drew a deep breath then sipped some more. "While I know little of your family's history, I do know the history of this land. Perhaps they are intertwined."

Raif raised an eyebrow.

Gesturing with his tankard to encompass the room, Rew explained, "You were right, this tower is far larger and far more secure than these miners ever would have needed. It dates back some three hundred years to before the kingdom of Vaeldon."

Raif, forgetting himself, drank from his own ale mug.

"Three hundred years ago, this land was controlled by a different people," said Rew. "They were much like us but not entirely. Your family has stumbled across their shades, you know, in the barrows?"

Raif nodded, letting Rew speak.

The ranger continued, "The people were different enough that we must have considered them mortal enemies. From what I understand, it was a time of constant war, and I suspect it was our people who were the aggressors. You've been to the top of the fort, or the others like it? There's a signal fire there, and when lit, it can be seen from the next fort out in the barrows, and that way, they could share information by blocking and revealing those fires. They used these forts to learn when the other race was nearby, and then, they'd send out forces after them."

"We built these forts to stage our own attacks, then, rather than to defend ourselves?"

Rew nodded. "The histories are unclear, but that's the way I always believed it was."

"And Falvar itself?"

Rew shrugged. "It's an old town, but is it three hundred years old, far older? I cannot say."

"There's a greatsword that hangs above my father's throne," said Raif. "It's said to be the same blade that my ancestor used when they earned us the barony and later to slay a drake. It's a symbol of our past strength, but my father treats it like a trophy. It's a powerful, enchanted weapon, but like the rest of our story, the history and properties of the weapon are lost to time."

"Enchanted, really?" asked Rew, surprised. "You don't know the nature of the enchantment?"

Raif shook his head. "My father has placed his faith in the strength of our family's magic rather than our strength of arms. In my lifetime, I've never seen him or anyone else take down that blade. It's still sharp, though. You can see the gleam along the edge of the steel. When I was younger, I would ask my father if I could hold it, but he always told me it was too dangerous for a child. Now that I'm no longer a child, I know better than to ask. He relies on magic, our noble blood, and he believes trust in arms is a weakness."

"But you've no magic," mentioned Rew.

Raif looked away.

"I'm sorry," murmured Rew. "I didn't mean it like that."

"It's all right," said the boy. "It's true. My father commands high magic, and he believes it's how our family will rise above our current station. Maybe he's right, but we earned our land with muscle and steel. It's who we once were. It's who we could be again. Someday, I hope to take down that sword, to prove to my father that the strength of the Fedgleys need not be reliant only on our spellcasting."

Rew lifted his tankard of ale and clinked it against the boy's. "To a strong arm and sharp steel."

Raif returned the toast, and they both drank the sour ale.

"Your cousin is a rather accomplished sorcerer," said Cinda, taking the seat her brother had vacated minutes before.

Rew nodded.

"You two know each other well?" questioned the noblewoman.

Rew shook his head. "Before today, I hadn't seen him in years. It's been over a decade, I suppose."

"You must have known each other well," said Cinda, frowning. "He knows a lot about you."

"It's Alsayer's job to know as much as he can about everyone he can," responded Rew. "He's a... a trader of information, you could say. If he comes across something interesting, he'll remember it until he finds a use for it."

"And why does he find you so interesting, Senior Ranger?" wondered Cinda.

"I have no interest in revisiting my past, lass, and I doubt the spellcaster does either," said Rew. "It's been a long time since Alsayer and I knew each other, and even then, we were not close. I've moved on, and I no longer want any part of that life. I've moved on and forgotten."

Cinda pursed her lips as if she didn't believe him, but she didn't ask further questions about his past. Instead, she said, "I don't think anyone thanked you for what you did earlier today. Rushing into that pack of narjags, drawing them off... I thought you were going to be killed."

He laughed. "I nearly was."

"Thank you," she said. "Without you, we wouldn't have made it into this tower. More than once now, you've saved us, and we haven't shown our appreciation. I mean to change that. You have my thanks, Senior Ranger, and when we reach Falvar, you'll have the baron's favor. Whatever you ask, we'll grant you."

Rew shook his head. "I have everything I want, lass."

"No one has everything that they want," claimed Cinda.

"I did before you arrived," said Rew with a wink.

Cinda rolled her eyes at him. "Think about it, Senior Ranger. When we arrive in Falvar, my father will be grateful for our return and grateful to be warned of Worgon's betrayal. Assistance like that deserves a reward."

"I need to see the arcanist, and that is all," said Rew. "Get me an audience with Arcanist Ralcrist, and I'll consider us even. As soon as I've finished with him, I plan to leave. Eastwatch is my place, and it is the only boon I ask of anyone."

Cinda tilted her head, studying him, then stood and left without word.

Zaine leaned against the battlement, her head hanging loosely between two crenellations. She didn't notice as he stepped beside her, and he stood there silently for a long moment. Around them, the wind pounded the slopes of the Spine, but they were on the lee side of the tower, and the centuries-old building broke the onslaught. They stood in the calm while the wind howled around them. The young thief stared out over the dark barrowlands that lay far below, or maybe she stared at the stone in front of her. It was hard to tell.

Rew smiled, thinking of the last time he'd felt as Zaine must feel now. Eastwatch had been toasting the betrothal of the blacksmith's apprentice and a farmer's daughter. Two families that had been in the village for generations were coming together and celebrating the fact that their children would likely stay there instead of seeking far horizons. The fathers of the two children had rolled out the ale and cider barrels, and Rew had helped himself to rivers of the free drink. It helped that he hadn't had to ask Anne for each refill. The innkeeper cast a judgmental eye when he'd had more tankards than she thought sensible. The innkeeper didn't mind him having a few ales, but after a point, she made her opinions on drinking too much known. It was a constant battle between the two of them, the ranger trying to slip in another drink, the innkeeper crossing her arms, tilting her head, and scowling at him, trying to limit his intake through the sheer force of her glare. He smiled, recalling how much of a fool he'd made of himself that night, and how Anne, perhaps herself too many cups into it, hadn't said a word.

"Is this tower spinning?" wondered Zaine, finally realizing someone was standing beside her.

"I'm sure it feels like it," said Rew, "but I can assure you, it's anchored tightly to the mountain. Is the fresh air helping?"

"I think so," muttered Zaine, letting her head fall down onto her crossed arms.

"I brought some water," Rew told her, holding up a tankard he'd filled in the rain barrel. "Plenty of this and a bit of rest should sort you."

"You're not going to chastise me for drinking too much?" asked Zaine, her head still buried in her arms.

"If you're like me, then no amount of lectures will convince you," replied Rew with a laugh, leaning against the stone of the tower beside her. "The misery you'll be in on the hike tomorrow morning will do more to keep you sober than anything I could say. Until the next time, at least."

"The next time," groaned Zaine. "King's Sake, you say it isn't the tower that is spinning, so I must be."

Rew put his hand on the girl's shoulder and instructed, "Drink the water, and then I'll help you up to bed. You'll feel better in the morning—sorry, that's not true. You won't feel better tomorrow. You'll feel worse, but the morning after that, you'll feel much better."

Standing and looking like she regretted moving quickly, Zaine hesitantly accepted the mug of water. She drank, and Rew waited patiently. Finally, she finished most of the cup, spilling the rest of it down her chin.

"To bed, then," said Rew.

"When you came out here," responded Zaine, her voice thick with drink, "I thought you meant to take advantage of my circumstance and question me about my past."

"Not tonight," said Rew.

"Good," slurred Zaine. "My secrets are mine."

"They won't be if you keep telling people you have secrets," mentioned Rew.

Frowning to herself, Zaine let Rew drape one of her arms over his shoulder, and slowly, the two of them went back into the tower and up the winding stairwell, looking for one of the empty rooms that the miners were not using. When they found one, Rew laid Zaine in the bed, removed her boots, and paused. The girl cracked a massive yawn and then stilled, her chest rising and falling steadily.

Setting her boots down at the end of the bed, Rew stared at Zaine's socked feet. Finally, he bent forward and removed her socks. In the dark room, he peered at the soles of her feet, looking to see if there was a mark there from the thieves' guild. When he saw her skin was unmarred, he gathered some blankets and laid them over her. He turned to go, thought better of it, and scooted the chamber pot close to the bed where it would be obvious if she got sick in the middle of the night. He walked to the door and stood in the hall for a moment, looking back at the young thief. She seemed settled, so he closed the door, leaving it slightly ajar. She was done for the night, but he wouldn't mind another ale.

Anne looked disapprovingly at the full tankard in his hands when Rew settled down in the chair opposite of her. She was sitting in front of the dying fire, letting the glowing red embers warm her toes. "Another, really?"

"The children are finally in bed," remarked the ranger. "This is the first one I've been able to enjoy."

She shook her head at him.

"You want one?" he asked her.

"No," she responded, "and don't think I will heal your hangover in the morning."

He grinned at her. "Zaine's going to be suffering a brutal one, but perhaps it's best to leave her to it. Nothing teaches you your limit like waking up the next morning with something to do."

Anne grunted. She said, "That was rather reckless of you, earlier. The others may sing your praises, tell you how brave you were, but I saw it for what it was."

Rew sipped his ale and did not respond.

"There must have been a better way," insisted the empath. "Charging off like that… You could have been killed, Rew."

"If you had a better idea," replied the ranger, "I would have loved to have heard it then."

"I don't know what we could have done, but we could have done something," declared Anne.

Rew looked into the embers of the fire and scooted his boots closer, feeling the heat seep through the leather. He wasn't sure how to respond to her comment.

"This cousin of yours," said Anne. "Is he like the rest of your family?"

Rew nodded.

"Then he'll betray us," said the empath.

"If it suits his purposes, then yes, he'll betray us," agreed Rew. "I'll be honest, though. I can't fathom how that may be. If he'd wanted to harm the children, he could have done so easily when I was off in the forest with the narjags on my heels. And if not then, he's devious enough he could have figured a way this evening while we're all stuck in the tower together."

Anne ran her hands through her hair, untying it in the back and shaking her red locks loose. She massaged her head, kicking her feet gently in front of the fire, wiggling her bare toes in front of the smoldering embers.

"Alsayer is up to something," said Rew. "It's not a coincidence that he was here when we arrived. I am certain he was waiting for us, but I don't know why."

"The children, you think?" asked Anne. "He wants them to play some role in the Investiture?"

"Probably," agreed the ranger. He drank his ale, cringing at the sour taste and wondering if a final mug was really wise. He glanced at Anne and decided he wasn't ready to admit in front of her that it wasn't, so he took another drink. "Alsayer has been preparing his entire life for the Investiture. He eats and breathes intrigue, and he does it to amuse himself. Oh, he'll try to improve his standing with whichever prince comes out on top, just as all of the other nobles will, but that's not why he gets involved in these sorts of things. He does what he does because of the thrill, and that's what makes him truly unpredictable and dangerous."

Anne let her hands drop to her lap. "So, what should we do?"

"We're going to drop these children off in Falvar, talk to the arcanist, and then leave," said Rew. "We'll make sure they're safe with their father, so don't worry about that, but I want nothing to do with the Investiture. If Alsayer is here… We should leave as soon as we're able."

Anne pursed her lips but did not reply.

Sighing, Rew set down his half-full mug. "I know you don't believe it, but I am serious. As soon as the children are in the caring arms of their parents, we'll leave. Falvar is the best place for them, Anne, and there's nothing else we can do to help once they're there."

"If you say so," said Anne. She eyed his mug on the table nearby and asked, "To bed, then?"

"To bed," agreed Rew.

Chapter Fifteen

The walk down from the miner's tower as dawn broke over the mountains behind them was a far easier leg of the journey than the walk up had been. There was a wide road pounded flat by decades' worth of wagons hauling ore from the mines. In front of them, the barrowlands spread out like a rumpled green rug, sparkling with dew in the morning sun.

From their perch, they could see the thin thread of road that cut along the outskirts of the barrowlands, hugging the mountain range as tightly as it could without traveling into the actual foothills. They couldn't see Falvar, but it was there, somewhere in the distance, hidden by the morning haze.

At the front of the party, Alsayer walked with Raif, complimenting the boy on his weapons and his courage and inquiring about every detail of their journey through the wilderness and the encounters they'd had there.

The spellcaster was ingratiating himself with Baron Fedgley's family, Rew knew, trying to earn himself some measure of trust before his arrival in Falvar. Whether it was because he had plans for the children or because he wanted to ensure his message was heard by their father, Rew wasn't sure. Alsayer, whatever his purported role in the Investiture, whatever his professed allegiances, was steeped in chicanery. His loyalties changed as often as he changed his underclothes.

Rew had thought to intervene, to tell Raif to stay away from the spellcaster, but he decided there was little point. Alsayer was good at what he did, and if he meant to befriend the Fedgleys, he would. It was better to let Alsayer have his way than force the man to spend the four-day journey undermining Rew.

"Your cousin?" asked Cinda, walking beside ranger, nodding ahead to the spellcaster. "If he's capable of high magic, then he must have some noble blood. If he has noble blood and the two of you are related…"

Rew grunted and did not respond.

"Do you have a title other than the King's Ranger?" she asked him bluntly.

"I do not," said Rew.

"Who is he?" she asked, staring at the back of the spellcaster.

"He's a creature of the court," replied Rew. "All of the courts, I suppose. I haven't seen him for years. When I last did, he'd declared no particular affiliation, but was a regular in each of the princes' entourages. I doubt any of the king's sons believed he was loyal to them, and I can't imagine they trust him, but he's useful when he wants to be, so they make use of him. He might be running an errand for one of them as he says and really is coming to alert your father of a threat to the barony. There certainly are Dark Kind swarming around, and you and your brother overheard the plot by Worgon. It's not inconceivable Alsayer may help your father with these matters. I warn you, though, do not trust the spellcaster. It's just as likely he's up to something other than what he says. You could fill an arcanist's tome with the list of betrayals he's been responsible for."

"He betrayed you?" wondered Cinda.

Rew shook his head. "He's never needed to. I've no interest in the pursuits of Alsayer and those like him. I've always done my best to stay apart, to avoid the politics of Vaeldon."

"But now you cannot," said Anne from behind them.

He looked back at her. "Nothing has changed."

She snorted and gestured at Cinda then at Raif and Alsayer ahead of them. "For a man uninvolved, you appear rather involved, Senior Ranger. Admit it or not, but everything has changed."

"We'll get everyone safely to Falvar. I'll speak with Arcanist Ralcrist, and then Jon and I shall return to Eastwatch," he declared. "You should come back with us, Anne. This… You should come back."

"If you return to Eastwatch, perhaps I'll come with you," she said. "If you return."

He sighed and looked ahead.

That evening, they clustered around a campfire, and Rew stared out into the darkness. Several ayres and half the narjags involved in the assault on the tower had fled, but they'd be drawn to the beacon affixed to Alsayer like iron to a lodestone. They, and whatever other Dark Kind lurked in the area.

The party had made camp beside the road on the edge of the barrowlands. In front of them, the grasslands stretched for weeks. Behind them, the bare stone of the mountains, broken by scattered stands of the tough trees that survived on the northern slope, rose up toward the peak. There was little cover if something approached them, and they should have been safer now that they were in the barony, but Rew couldn't relax. The ranger glanced at the younglings, seeing the smiles and noting that not a one of them looked out into the darkness around the camp.

"Your ranger, you trust him?" asked Alsayer, joining Rew where he stalked the perimeter of their campsite.

Rew nodded.

"Then you, I, and he should split the watch," advised Alsayer. "I gather the empath has seen more than some backwater wilderness town, despite the fact she's playing dumb with me, but these others are just children. Given what we know is out there, I'm not sure I could sleep if they are the ones watching over me."

"What worries you?" asked Rew.

"The Dark Kind," said Alsayer, his hands clasped behind his back as they walked. "The Dark Kind and the unknown."

Rew glanced at him out of the corner of his eye. "Do you expect we'll meet something out here?"

"Anything other than narjags and a few ayres? No, I don't expect anything," said Alsayer. He held up a hand to stop Rew's response. "I'm counting on you, cousin, to ensure my safety. I spoke the truth. My magic is dampened here. Any casting I attempted would fizzle out as little more than a pop. It is only your steel that we can rely upon. If I knew of some specific threat other than the narjags, I'd tell you. But you know as well as I the games the powerful will play during the Investiture. If one of the princes is gathering the Dark Kind, what other cards do they hold? I confess, cousin, I am nervous without my spells."

Pulling a long blade of grass from beside their path and swishing it in his hands, Rew nodded.

"The Investiture is always a time of bloodshed and death," said Alsayer. "Blades in the back, poison, it's what should be expected. It's been several cycles, though, since outright war broke out within Vaeldon. I worry that this cycle… I worry that it will be bad, cousin. Can you not feel it? The three princes are all strong. They're well protected. No mean cutthroat is going to slip through this cycle and remove a player from the board."

Rew grunted but did not respond.

"I've spent years in each of the princes' courts," continued Alsayer. "None of them have any obvious weaknesses. If I was unable to find the chinks in their armor, then I do not think anyone else will be able to, either. Their magical skills are equally matched, and I don't think they'd risk an outright confrontation against each other. Even if one of them thought they'd best their brother, they'd be weakened for the third one to strike. If none of the three are felled from assassination, it's going to devolve into a drunken tavern brawl that draws in every spellcaster and army in the realm. I have a bad feeling it will come to that, cousin, a very bad feeling."

"If the princes called to the Dark Kind, do you think any of them could control what answered?" questioned Rew. "Would they? It's been, well, a very long time since a conjurer attempted to control more than a handful of narjags. I'd think whichever brother risked it would be in danger of the other two uniting against him. Certainly, the winner does not want to ascend the throne and immediately have to deal with a war against the Dark Kind."

"What you say is logical, but the princes do not think like that. They think only of winning. This cycle is going to be a bloody one," insisted Alsayer. "They've hidden their capabilities from each other, even from me. I can feel it in my bones, cousin. This kingdom will be flooded with fire and death. The realm will need good men to step in and pick up the pieces when it is over."

"Pick up the pieces? I never would have guessed that would bother you," said Rew with a snort.

His cousin's lips tightened, but he admitted, "That's fair, I suppose, but what is the point of my plotting if there is no one left to rule when all of this is finished? I aim to attach myself to the winner, you know that about me, and I'd guess the princes do as well, but what if these fools destroy the kingdom in their pursuit to rule it? What shall I do with whatever favor I have earned?"

Rew walked on in silence.

"Truly, you mean to return to Eastwatch?" questioned Alsayer.

"If I can," muttered Rew. "If I can."

Two days later, they hiked along the dirt road, following two lines worn into the turf by countless wagons that had passed that way. The impressions were stamped into the soil, packing it hard so that nothing could grow in the wheel ruts, but everywhere else, the grasses were wild and a rich, emerald green. Low hills surrounded the party, obscuring their vision past a couple of hundred paces, but it was enough they should have some warning if they were attacked. Troubling, though, was that they had not been attacked.

Rew had begun to wonder if perhaps Alsayer was wrong, that there had been no beacon affixed to him or that its effect was also dampened by whatever affected the spellcaster's own magic. Rew shivered and tried to ignore the sneaking suspicion that the spellcaster had been lying about the beacon, but then they came across the site of a battle.

They heard it first, the neighing of horses and the shouts of men. The party had glanced at each other, surprised there would be enough people out in the barrowlands to make such a racket, but when they moved along the curling road and cleared one of the low hills, they saw why.

Men, clad in the azure livery of the Fedgley's, dull chainmail shirts beneath their tunics and helms on their heads, were moving about a trampled field covered in dead Dark Kind. There were dozens of the men and near a hundred dead narjags and ayres. At the edge of the battlefield, a tent had been set up, and Anne immediately started toward it, ignoring the surprised calls of the armored men when they saw the party appear.

"Let her go," said Rew. Then, he gestured for Raif and Cinda to lead the way to the warriors. When the nobles moved off, in a lower voice, Rew asked Alsayer, "Could the Dark Kind have been preparing an ambush for you? I didn't know they were capable of such tactics without a valaan to lead them."

The spellcaster smirked and pointed to a giant narjag surrounded by his peers. "That's the shaman from back at the tower. Led by one of those, yes, they can conduct some simple tactical operations. You should have killed the thing when you had the chance."

"A true shaman?" wondered Rew. "There hasn't been a Dark

Kind capable of casting a spell in... Could its magic have been blanketed like yours?"

Alsayer shrugged. "It's dead. We'll never know."

"We're lucky we didn't run into this," remarked Jon, coming up to walk beside them, watching Raif and Cinda conferring with their father's men.

"A hundred Dark Kind," said Rew, raising a hand to rub his head. "Out in the open like this, nowhere we could hide, just these low hills to set up a defensive position. We're very lucky these soldiers happened to come by."

"Should we, ah, should we return to Eastwatch, sir?" asked Jon, watching the baron's soldiers gather around the younglings. "It seems they're safe, and we have the answer we needed about why the Dark Kind were moving about the wilderness." He gestured at Alsayer, who winked back at him.

Rew looked at the road behind them, the twin dirt tracks cutting through the barrowlands. His gaze lifted to the sharp peaks of the mountains, and he sighed. Anne was in the tent with the wounded. He knew she would be reluctant to let them travel to Falvar without her care.

"No, we'll continue on," said Rew. "It's just another day to Falvar, and with Tate down, I need to send a letter to Commandant Grund. We need another ranger to replace him. Sending the post from Falvar will save us several weeks. We can restock our rations and see if there's a carriage headed over the roads we can hitch a ride on. It's a long walk back through the wilderness back to Eastwatch."

Jon nodded, and Rew glanced at Zaine, who seemed to be hiding behind the men.

She scowled and asked, "What?"

Giving a wan smile, Rew started forward, joining Cinda and the others as the young noblewoman explained to her father's captain what she knew.

The walls of Falvar rose like a leviathan out from a grass sea. Pale rock, quarried in the foothills of the Spine, was stacked thirty paces high. The battlement was wide, extending in a sheer cliff for a quarter league. Atop it, flags fluttered and soldiers patrolled, but not like they once did. The fortress had been constructed in a different era, when the threats to the peace of the kingdom were external rather than internal. Now, the grasslands were empty except for the herds of the shaggy cattle that roamed beneath the open skies and the occasional shade that was disturbed when man or beast breached its prison. Despite what they'd seen in the last few days, Rew knew that it'd been generations since there had been a real threat to Falvar. Even the last migration of the Dark Kind had been easily repelled before the creatures crossed over the Spine and fled into the wilderness.

But a fortress built is a fortress that must be maintained, lest the defenses of the kingdom fall fallow and those external threats return. Baron Fedgley was tasked by the king with protecting the distant edge of the realm, so he did, though there was little to protect it from.

Rew considered that as they drew closer. The war party they'd stumbled across was made up of thirty well-equipped soldiers. They'd had reports, they'd said, of Dark Kind near the road. Rew had no reason to disbelieve, but thirty mounted men was a strong contingent, and as he began to pick out the troops upon the walls, he counted dozens more. Beyond the fortress, near the bridge and the river it crossed, he saw the low-slung hovels of the working folk and a scattering of azure-tabarded men moving amongst the buildings.

He counted close to one hundred men in Baron Fedgley's livery, all purported to guard an endless, quiet graveyard. Rew had himself and five in his command to cover the entire expanse of the wilderness, which was packed full of dangerous beasts. He guessed if there were a hundred men in uniform and on duty now, there had to be hundreds more off duty somewhere within the town of Falvar, and he could only speculate how many out in the barrows. A sick feeling began to grow in Rew's stomach as they walked closer, and it got worse when Alsayer showed no surprise at the strength of Baron Fedgley's forces.

"We should have turned around and gone back home," hissed Rew under his breath.

Beside him, Jon looked confused, but Anne stared ahead, her lips tight. She'd helped to heal several men who'd been injured in the engagement with the Dark Kind, and she had promised to accompany them back to the barracks where their own physicians could take over. She felt an obligation to them, forged by the connection an empath establishes with a patient, but even she could tell there were far more soldiers present than ever would be necessary in such a remote outpost.

Cinda and Raif walked far ahead of them, in between Alsayer and the captain of the soldiers.

Rew turned and found Zaine close at his heels. "Lass, is this many men normal? It's been years since I was in Falvar, and I don't recall such a strong garrison."

Zaine shrugged. "It's been some time since I was here as well."

Rew's eyes narrowed. Seeing his look, she swallowed uncomfortably but was spared having to respond when the captain of the baron's soldiers came trotting back on his horse.

"Senior Ranger," he called, turning his mount so he paced them in the grass beside the road. "When we reach the city, Baron Fedgley would like a word with you."

"He would, would he?" asked Rew with an eyebrow raised skeptically. "He told you that?"

The captain flushed. "I am certain he would like to see you. You saved his children, after all. They've told me everything. That sort of heroism deserves a reward, I should say."

Rew watched the man as he squirmed atop his mount. A military man used to direct words and direct action. The subterfuge was killing him.

"I suppose I ought to see him, then," allowed Rew.

"When we first arrive, along with Spellcaster Alsayer," said the captain.

"Not before his own children, surely?"

The man swallowed. Glancing at the backs of the younglings, he said, "We shall see, but I think it best if we proceed immediately to the keep and don't leave the baron waiting."

"Very well," said Rew.

The captain trotted back up to the nobles and the spellcaster. Alsayer turned and winked. Rew glared at the man.

"I understand I owe you my thanks," boomed Baron Fedgley. "My thanks, and perhaps a reward?"

He sat upon a raised dais in an ornate wooden throne. Beside him, his wife's throne was empty, but Rew had seen the woman on the way in. She'd nodded but not spoken as she glided out to find Raif and Cinda.

Rew offered the baron a shallow bow. "No reward is necessary, Baron Fedgley. I was merely doing my job."

"The King's Ranger," said the baron, fidgeting with a fat, emerald ring that graced his finger. "A bit of an archaic position, is it not? I've never understood why the king does not install a nobleman and a proper garrison in the territory."

Rew held the baron's gaze but did not respond.

Fedgley turned to Alsayer. "And you, I'm told you have a message for me? Shall we discuss it privately?"

"I believe the senior ranger can be trusted to hear it, m'lord," said Alsayer. "Who knows? Maybe he will have some useful comment to add."

Rew clenched his teeth.

"What does Prince Valchon have to say, then?" questioned Fedgley.

Rew clutched his hands in front of his waist to stop himself from throttling the spellcaster. Prince Valchon, so that's who

Alsayer was claiming to work for. Alsayer and, it seemed, Baron Fedgley. Despite the children's ignorance of the Investiture, Rew had no doubt now that their father was up to his neck in it.

"The prince is wondering how the recruitment of the wraiths is coming," said Alsayer. "As I am sure you've realized, the Investiture has begun earlier than expected. Not all of the prince's preparations are complete, but we've no choice except to proceed."

Rew forced himself to breathe evenly, forced himself to stand still. Recruitment of the wraiths! Blessed Mother, what was Alsayer playing at?

"Of course…" murmured the baron. "My men have been harried constantly by the Dark Kind while working in the barrows. We've lost three necromancers just in the last two weeks."

"Three?" questioned Alsayer.

Baron Fedgley waved a hand dismissively. "They weren't very good ones. Still, it's slowed us down."

Alsayer nodded. "I myself had some encounters with the Dark Kind on the way in. It looked as though your men are clearing the roads, though?"

"As best we can," grumbled the baron.

"Do you have more necromancers?" wondered Alsayer.

"I have two left, though neither one is much more talented than the three who died," complained Baron Fedgley, standing and beginning to pace on the dais. "Can the prince send me more? As you know, we've a lot of ground to cover out in the barrowlands. It can take days for the necromancers to move between the far crypts, and when they breach them, we find more than half are empty. Even when they're not, there's no guarantee of success. It's a tricky business, capturing those old souls. These two necromancers I have out there, well, I suspect even if the Dark Kind don't catch them, they won't last long against shades of this vintage."

Alsayer, tugging on his neatly-trimmed goatee, declared, "I'm afraid resources have become suddenly constrained with the start of the Investiture. You must finish your task with what tools you have available, Fedgley."

"If the prince wants his wraiths, he must give me the spellcasters to collect them!" thundered the baron, suddenly losing his temper and stabbing a finger at Alsayer. "What he asks is not easy. It's impossible to speed our efforts without help."

"If you mean to advance from this backwater barony, you'll figure out a way to do it," replied Alsayer calmly. "The prince allies himself with those who can handle their responsibilities and rewards those who do so successfully. If you cannot manage your part without the prince's help, then what good are you to him?"

"You threaten me?" snapped the baron.

Alsayer shook his head. "I am only sharing that the prince has requested an update on your progress and that he expects it to be significant. If it's not... he's authorized me to take what actions I deem necessary. If you cannot finish the task, Fedgley, then I will."

Rew shifted, his heart hammering, his mind screaming to fight or to flee. Alsayer looked over and grinned at him. The ranger bit his tongue, struggling to remain quiet, to not reach out and smash his fist into that smug face. Blessed Mother, the baron was raising an army of wraiths for Prince Valchon! If those miserable creatures were let loose, they would wreak havoc on the world. The things were nearly impossible to control. It was reckless, completely—

"There's another necromancer who could command the wraiths," stated Alsayer, raising an eyebrow at the baron. "Perhaps it's time you got off that throne and made yourself useful, Baron."

"I'm needed in the city, not lost days away from here in the grasslands," growled Fedgley.

"Prince Valchon expects results," said Alsayer coldly. "If it's another necromancer you need... What should I tell the prince, Fedgley? You need him to send you someone because you're too comfortable here in your own hall? You're too, what, frightened to venture out on your own?"

Fedgley looked away, his face red as a beet. "You know not of what you speak, Spellcaster. My family has been dealing with these wraiths for generations. There is no one who—"

"Worgon suspects what you're up to," interrupted Alsayer. "Has he attempted to interfere?"

Fedgley shook his head. "Not yet, unless it is he who sent this plague of Dark Kind against us."

"Your children are spreading word to everyone who will listen that Worgon is plotting against you," mentioned Alsayer. "There will be no avoiding the coming conflict. I'm here to ensure you collect the wraiths as promised, but it's important to tend to your mundane defenses as well. I saw the men in the city. When it comes to it, will they fight for you? And, Fedgley, make no mistake, it will come to it before all is done."

"I believe we're getting into territory that should be discussed privately," grumbled the baron, still fidgeting with the emerald ring on his finger. "I know the king's agents are to remain uninvolved in the Investiture, but…"

"Senior Ranger Rew is my cousin," stated Alsayer.

"Your cousin?" asked Fedgley, suddenly looking at Rew with interest.

"He can be trusted," assured Alsayer.

Rew, not wanting to be trusted with the information the men were sharing, not wanting to hear any of it at all, returned the baron's look without speaking. Alsayer was not a man who carelessly spilled his plans to any open ear. There was a reason he wanted Rew to listen to his plotting, and that terrified the ranger.

"I planted rumors of an insurrection in Yarrow against Spinesend," said Baron Fedgley, crossing his wrists behind his back and continuing to pace the dais. "Duke Eeron will believe that Worgon is plotting against him, and he'll deal with the man for us. I suspect any day now, the duke will begin marching his troops. Whichever of the two comes out on top, they'll be severely weakened, and then the Duchy of Eeron will be in my sole control within months. I'd planned to consolidate the lands under my banner as we continued our work in the barrows, but as you say, the Investiture has begun. We must all adjust our plans."

"Your children know nothing?" questioned Alsayer, glancing at Rew from the corner of his eye. "If they do know, I must commend them on their acting. They had me convinced they were innocent."

Baron Fedgley snorted. "They're not good actors, as far as I know. I thought it best if they believed the lies I intended them to spread. I sent them to Baron Worgon in Yarrow years ago, knowing no one would suspect I would move against the man while my children were in his possession. Who would believe I would risk fostering my heir and his sister while plotting against the baron? And if I'd told them... You traveled with the two for several days, and you must have seen they're just as much children as they are adults. They wouldn't understand the import of what we do."

Alsayer nodded. "Of course. What children would?"

Fedgley grunted. "After the Investiture, after Prince Valchon takes the throne, I will explain all. They will understand, but until then, I believe it best if they are ignorant of the way the world really works."

"Wise, m'lord," said Alsayer, his voice slick like soap.

"I must go see them," said the baron, rolling his eyes and chuckling. "If not, Cinda will be battering down those doors trying to get in here to warn me about Worgon."

"She seemed rather strong-willed," agreed Alsayer with a smile. "She'll grow into a fine woman."

Baron Fedgley, ignoring the compliment, asked the spellcaster, "Is there anything else?"

"I will remain here for several days, Fedgley," said Alsayer. "I will monitor your progress and suggest improvements where I see they can be made."

"I'll accept your help, but do not think to threaten me," growled the baron.

"It is best if we work together," responded Alsayer, "but the prince sent me here for a reason, and I for one, will not fail him. We will procure the wraiths he needs, Baron, and we will do it quickly."

Baron Fedgley grunted then waved the spellcaster and the ranger to depart. "Tell the guards to send for my children on the way out, will you?"

"Of course," said Alsayer, a predatory smile curling across his face.

They walked out of the baron's hall, Rew two steps behind the spellcaster, his hands still held tight so he didn't instinctively reach out and strangle the treacherous bastard right there in the baron's foyer.

The spellcaster murmured, "The baron had the right idea. A private word?"

Rew followed the other man as he asked the guards to send for Raif and Cinda and then led Rew to a secluded alcove near the side of the keep's expansive foyer.

"Wraiths?" hissed Rew the moment they were away from anyone who could overhear them. "The baron is gathering an army of wraiths? That's dangerous, Alsayer, incredibly dangerous. And if you meant for me to learn of it, why didn't you just tell me yourself?"

Alsayer shrugged. "I believed it would be best if you heard it from the lips of the baron. If I'd told you, you would have suspected it was some intrigue of mine. It's not, cousin, as you heard from the baron himself."

"I still suspect it is some intrigue of yours," snapped Rew.

Grinning, Alsayer admitted, "Fair enough."

"If Prince Valchon is gathering the wraiths, then which of the princes is working with the Dark Kind—Heindaw or Calb?"

"I don't know," said Alsayer, glancing over Rew's shoulder as a soldier clanked by in heavy chainmail. "One of them or their minions attached a rather clever beacon to me, and until I can figure out how to slip it, the Dark Kind will be relentlessly drawn to me. Not much of a problem when I'm in the capital, but out here on the frontiers, it's going to be rather inconvenient. If I knew which prince had attached it to me, I'd have a better chance to counteract their magic. Unfortunately, I have no idea."

"An arcanist cannot detect the beacon?" wondered Rew.

"None of the untrained fools who reside out in the hinterlands," complained Alsayer. He tugged at his goatee and admitted, "There's no one back in Mordenhold I can trust."

"While you're here, you'll draw the Dark Kind to the town," warned Rew.

"Falvar is well defended," replied Alsayer with a wave of his hand. He studied Rew. "What do you think of the baron not telling his children of his plans? This entire time, they've been risking their lives, rushing to warn him of a false conspiracy that he himself dreamt up. Does that ill treatment bother you?"

Frowning, Rew admitted, "Of course it does. Everything about the Investiture bothers me."

"Rather rough on them, don't you think?" pressed Alsayer. "Can't trust their own father, don't even know what's about to happen to them, eh? Nobles with no clue the Investiture is breathing down their necks. Makes you feel for them."

"What do you want?" growled Rew.

"Nothing. I'm just saying it's an awful situation those children are in," claimed Alsayer. "They're good kids, don't you think?"

"They're not children," muttered Rew.

Alsayer laughed.

Changing the subject, Rew asked, "Do you really mean to assist in gathering the wraiths? You know what kind of destruction they could cause. The baron's family may be a talented line of necromancers, but a wraith is a two-edged knife, Alsayer. It's foolish to attempt to use the things, no matter how desperate Prince Valchon is."

"I will assist, and I do know what kind of destruction they will cause," agreed Alsayer. "I told you, cousin, this cycle is going to be different. It's going to be bloody, and before it ends, it's going to draw us all in. My advice to you, cousin? Pick a side."

"Pick a side as you've done?" questioned Rew. "Are you even working for Prince Valchon, or is that another deception?"

Grinning, Alsayer replied, "You know me, cousin. I always leave my options open."

"Your options open and your hands bloody," accused Rew.

Alsayer raised his hands, turning them as if to inspect them for blood, and replied, "Everyone is going to be drawn in, cousin. Everyone. Before it's over, your hands will be just as dirty as mine. Don't you think it best if you're the one who decides whose blood they're covered in?"

"I will have nothing to do with the Investiture and the king's games," snapped Rew.

"And you don't mind the children dying because of that?" questioned Alsayer.

Rew glared at him. "What do you mean?"

Alsayer merely looked back, his smile gone, his eyes dead serious.

"What do you mean?" repeated Rew.

"High magic passes through the bloodline, cousin," reminded Alsayer. "If the baron is capable of commanding a wraith, don't you think... Ah, but you've no desire to get involved, do you? That information means nothing to you. The children are here with their father who loves them deeply. Why should Rew worry about their fate? Why should the senior ranger of the eastern territory worry about whether Prince Valchon needs another necromancer on leash in case Baron Fedgley fails? And it's not your concern if one of the other princes sees an opportunity to recruit a powerful necromancer of their own. If the wraiths are put on the board, a necromancer strong enough to manage them will be a valuable target for any of the princes, but I'm sure the children will be just fine."

Alsayer offered a mock bow, slipped around Rew, and walked away.

Scowling at his cousin's back, Rew turned and strode deeper into the keep, looking for Arcanist Ralcrist's chambers.

Chapter Sixteen

Rew rapped on the door and listened to the muffled reply. He thought it may have been unwelcoming, but he wasn't sure, so he tried the door. It was unlocked, and he swung it open.

"King's Sake!" screeched a voice. "I said I was busy."

"My apologies," offered Rew, stepping inside and closing the door behind him.

A man dressed in sleek silk robes the color of new grass was standing opposite a polished mahogany table. On it was a complex contraption of twisted, gleaming silver wires. Suspended above that framework was a large, scintillating, cerulean crystal.

The man, his stomach-length, white beard trembling in outrage, was clutching a large pair of tweezers in his gnarled fingers. Spitting curses at Rew, he tugged on the silver framework beneath the floating crystal, moving a strand of wire slightly toward him. He then adjusted the tweezers, pinched another piece of the wire, and pushed it deeper into the structure of the framework.

"Ralcrist?" Rew asked him.

"We're being tested," growled the man, not acknowledging the question. "People prodding at my ward, searching for gaps, and all the while, the baron is asking for gaps, giving me this foolish map, telling me to uncover this barrow, cover the other back up. I have work to do, real research! These interruptions are maddening."

Rew stepped close to the table, crouching down to see what the man was working on. "Yes, I'm sure they are."

The arcanist leaned to the side to glare at Rew around his device. One eye was made huge by a large, gold-rimmed, oval piece of glass that he stared through. The other was startlingly blue with a prescience that belied the man's advanced age. The arcanist blinked and caught the glass monocle in his hand as it fell from his eye. "Who are you?"

"I'm the King's Ranger," replied Rew. "I have a few questions for you."

The arcanist grunted then turned on his heel, stalking deeper into his rooms, calling over his shoulder, "I have no time for questions."

Rew followed.

"I said, I've no time for you, Ranger," shouted the arcanist. He moved through sitting rooms, through a library, and into a workshop. "Why are you following me? I've no time, no time at all. Does the baron know you are here? I told him I could suffer no more distractions if he means for me to keep this ward working properly. Leave me be!"

"That crystal, it is what is dampening the use of high magic in the region?" inquired Rew.

"You're a spellcaster!" accused the arcanist.

Rew shook his head. "Who is testing the ward?"

Mumbling to himself, Arcanist Ralcrist began collecting empty beakers, vials of powders, an old leg bone of what may have been either a rather large chicken or a particularly small child, and an acid-stained notebook. He licked his finger and began thumbing through the crisp pages of the notebook.

Rew craned his neck and saw the small pages were cramped with writing. He asked again, "Who is testing your ward against high magic?"

"Spellcasters!" snapped Arcanist Ralcrist. "Who else?"

Rew leaned against one of the man's worktables and then quickly stood as glass beakers rattled at the disturbance and one filled with a noxious looking green-brown liquid nearly tipped over. "You should have the leg of that table looked at, Arcanist. What spellcasters are trying to breach your ward? Where are they coming from?"

Glaring at him, the arcanist spluttered.

"I just came from meeting with the baron, and he didn't say a word about not bothering you," said Rew, electing not to mention that it was because the baron didn't know he was going to see the arcanist, "so bothering you is what I intend to do until you've answered all of my questions."

"What do you want?" growled the arcanist. "What are you doing here?"

"As I said, I'm the King's Ranger, and I've come to ask you about recent phenomena that are outside of my experience. It's my duty to protect the territory, you know, and I need your advice."

"You're a long way from the eastern territory, Ranger," responded Ralcrist.

"Yes, and I'm ready to get back as soon as I can," said Rew. He walked over and closed the book that the arcanist had been thumbing through. "I can't stand being within these walls, but I have questions that must be answered before I go."

"How long will this take?" muttered Ralcrist.

"Quite long, if you keep dodging my questions," threatened Rew. "If you answer, though, less than a quarter hour."

Grumbling to himself, Arcanist Ralcrist waved Rew after him and led him back into the library. He pointed to a decanter of wine. "Care for a glass?"

"Do you have ale?"

"No," replied the arcanist.

"Then wine will do," allowed Rew.

"Good. Pour me a glass as well," instructed Ralcrist.

The arcanist stalked to one of his stuffed couches and plopped down, folding his arms over his chest and scowling at Rew as the ranger poured the two of them wine. Rew handed the man a glass and shook a table laden with manuscripts and ancient-looking tomes. Incongruously, it felt sturdier than the rickety bit of furniture holding up the potions in the workshop, so Rew leaned against it.

"Senior Ranger Rew," spat the arcanist. "I know who you are."

Rew nodded, sipping the wine and finding it surprisingly good.

"What do you want of me?" asked Arcanist Ralcrist.

"The crystal out in your foyer," said Rew. "Why?"

The arcanist snorted and looked away.

"I've no interest in the baron's plots," said the ranger, "but it may have something to do with what we've been finding in the territory."

"No interest in the baron's plots? If that was true, you wouldn't be here," stated the arcanist.

Rew frowned then shook his head. "No, I came here to ask you about odd happenings out in the territory. There was a portal that opened, and it appeared narjags were waiting for whoever came through. We followed the tracks of narjags for two weeks, and they were always headed in the same direction, as if following someone. I was told it was a beacon, affixed to a spellcaster."

The arcanist shifted on his couch, trying to look annoyed, but he couldn't hide his interest in the problem. It was the sort of thing men joined the profession for, to untangle esoteric clues, to get to the bottom of a mystery.

He told Rew, "Narjags have no way of sniffing out high magic, Ranger. As they are anathema to our world, high magic is invisible to those of their world. It's why high magic is so effective when combatting the Dark Kind. They can see, hear, and feel the flame of a fireball thrown into their face, but the casting of it doesn't raise their hackles like it would us."

Rew frowned. "There's no way they could follow a magical beacon?"

"It's not likely," claimed the arcanist. "A beacon like that would surely be formed of high magic, and with no affinity for it, I cannot imagine the narjags detecting it, though there are many strange things in this world. Do you have a particular spellcaster in mind who is supposed to have opened this portal and attracted the narjags?"

"I do," confirmed Rew.

"And where is this person?" asked Ralcrist.

"Here," said Rew. "In Falvar, in the keep."

The arcanist swallowed and steepled his fingers in front of his face. "I see."

"These probes against your ward, can you see where they are coming from?" wondered Rew.

"From elsewhere," said the arcanist with a wave of his hand. "They're coming from elsewhere. Spellcasters are trying to open portals into our city. They could be in the vicinity of Mordenhold, Carff, even Jabaan. Nowhere in the barony, and that I am sure of."

Rew stood off the table and began to pace. "Many of them?"

"Dozens every day," said Ralcrist.

"Is that normal?" asked Rew. "From what I recall last I was in Falvar, there were no practitioners of high magic outside of the baron's family. Is there a reason so many are now trying to portal here?"

"The Investiture, of course," said the arcanist. He held up a hand. "No, do not ask me what sorts of plots and maneuverings they're attempting. I do not know, but it's the only reason there'd be such a spike in activity. They mean to either join the baron or to thwart him."

Rew stalked back and forth.

"What is your involvement, Senior Ranger?"

Rew turned to Ralcrist. "None."

"I said I know who you are," reminded the arcanist.

Shaking his head, Rew began walking again. "I have no

interest in the Investiture, and I mean to do everything I can to avoid it. It's the reason I came east, the reason I assumed responsibility for the territory. That is my place, Ralcrist, and I will stay there as soon as I can finish in Falvar."

"I'm afraid the baron has gotten himself deeper than he realizes," said the arcanist. He picked up his wine and leaned back on the couch, tugging on his beard with his other hand, looking tired. "I was the arcanist in Falvar twenty-five years ago, you know. Baron Fedgley's father kept the family out of it, and Falvar escaped unharmed. Some may have been worried the king would retaliate, as we did not support him, but the truth was he couldn't have cared less what happened out here. We're on the outskirts of the realm, and we've little to offer the plotters and the backstabbers in Mordenhold. Little other than the baron's own skill, that is. Oh, that Fedgley had followed in the footsteps of his father."

"Your ward that prevents the spellcasters from opening portals here?" asked Rew. "How does it work?"

The arcanist smirked. "It's complicated, Senior Ranger."

"The broad brushstrokes," said Rew.

"High magic is drawn from the spellcaster," said the arcanist. "Not their blood, exactly, but it's a good enough way to think of these things. I found a way to interrupt that flow of power. Years ago, I fashioned physical restraints using my theories, thinking it was a practical way to safely capture lawbreakers who can cast high magic. Simple manacles, clamped on the wrist, and the spell caster's abilities are blanketed. Unfortunately, it seems those who can cast high magic are rarely given forgiveness, and my devices were never used as part of enforcing the law. Instead, I found they were exclusively used by those with political designs. They locked their opponents in the manacles and held them until some condition or payment was met. I found it abhorrent, so I stopped making the things."

Rew sipped his wine, slowing his pacing and letting the man talk.

"I expanded on my research, though, and created the crystal

you saw in my foyer. It is the only one of its kind," said the arcanist, sitting up and raising his head. "Like the manacles, it interferes with the ability to cast high magic, and I've found I can extend it for dozens of leagues. This way, practitioners cannot use their magic as a weapon against each other. When Fedgley demanded my assistance, it was the only way I would agree to do it. No spellcasters can come against him while my device is in use, but he cannot use his necromancy within the bounds of my ward. Currently, I've blanketed the entire region from the Spine, across the barrows, and two dozen leagues on the other side of the river. No high magic can be cast within two days' journey of Falvar."

"I'm surprised he was amenable to that," remarked Rew. "One thing I know about spellcasters is that they become addicted to the power their magic provides. I cannot imagine any of them voluntarily giving that power up."

Ralcrist's lips twisted, and he let go of his beard. "Fedgley threw quite the fit, but he needed me. Without my wards, he can't achieve what he's trying. He and those working with him would be under constant attack, and the man has little experience with combat, despite the family history. No, the only way he can maintain the focus he needs to, ah, to do what he's attempting, is without the distraction of hostile spellcasters arriving in Falvar or stalking the barrows, hunting his minions. He's promised his patron results, and you know the danger of that as well as anyone, don't you, Ranger?"

"His patron, Prince Valchon?" asked Rew.

Arcanist Ralcrist's eyes flashed, and he nodded. "Prince Valchon has heard of my research. I understand he even possesses a pair of the manacles I crafted years ago. Fedgley told me Valchon wanted more of them, but I refused. A risk to refuse a prince, but evidently Valchon believes my expanded ward will be quite handy."

"What do you know of their plans?" prodded Rew.

"Senior Ranger," declared the arcanist, "my role in this is to dampen high magic. As far as I'm concerned, when it comes to the plotting around the Investiture, that is the single most helpful thing I can do for the baron and for the common people who will be harmed by this bloody process. You know what havoc high magic can wreak. If I can prevent that from happening to Falvar, even if it allows the baron and the prince to conduct their mischievousness, then I have done a good thing. I don't like what it is they do, but I have done what I can. Falvar is safer if high magic cannot be cast here."

"And what if your ward was laid over another city, and then the baron released the wraiths he's collecting?" wondered Rew. "Without high magic, the only way to defeat the shades is with prayer, and we all know how the Mordens view true fealty to the Blessed Mother. Against your device and the baron's wraiths, a city may be entirely helpless."

Ralcrist looked away, his face pale.

"You have thought of it, then," said Rew.

"Falvar is my responsibility," murmured the arcanist. "My charge is to support the baron and to protect the people who live here."

Rew snorted. "Protect your own, eh, and forget the thousands of others that may die because of your actions?"

"Look to yourself, Ranger," snapped Ralcrist. "High magic is a scourge on this realm, and as long as it's the chief tool the nobility use to keep their seats and squabble amongst themselves, it will remain so. I'm trying to put an end to it, Ranger. What are you doing to help?"

"An end to high magic. A curious position for an arcanist to take," muttered Rew.

Ralcrist drank deeply of his wine and then said, "I know the evil that men hold in their hearts, and I've learned what power magic gives them to make it reality. I study the forces, as any scholar does, but it does not mean I like what those forces can do. High magic is dangerous, Senior Ranger. It's dangerous, and much of my study has been figuring out how to stop it. What would you have me do instead? Run from what I know?"

Rew didn't respond. Instead, he walked around the man's library, glancing at the titles of the books on the shelves, battling with whether he should ask the man what he was wondering or whether he should leave. Leave Ralcrist's chambers, leave Falvar.

Finally, Rew turned back to the arcanist. "If a beacon was attached to a man, and that beacon was drawing the Dark Kind, would that beacon work within the area of your ward?"

"'You haven't been listening, Senior Ranger," chided the arcanist. "The Dark Kind cannot sense the presence of high magic. With or without my ward, a beacon like you speak would not draw them. Whatever that spellcaster told you, it was a lie."

Rew winced. "What about an enchantment? A device or symbol that—"

Arcanist Ralcrist shook his head. "The Dark Kind are anathema, Senior Ranger. They are not of this world, and their senses are not the same as ours. They cannot detect high magic. Whatever call magic sends would be meaningless to them. It is like us waving a flag to a blind man or wafting a fresh baked roll beneath the nose of one who cannot smell. Feeding a berry to a man with no tongue. Clapping our hands beside—"

"I understand," grumbled Rew. "I understand, but how then, can one manipulate the Dark Kind?"

"Simple instruction, of course," declared the arcanist. "The same way that the Dark Kind have always been controlled. Make them more afraid of you than of what you're telling them to do. Narjags are vicious creatures, but they are sentient. They understand fear and have the instinct for self-preservation. It's how the valaan control them. It's how the spellcasters of old controlled them. Even amongst the packs, the biggest and strongest of the group may fight or kill their rivals to cement their command. They rule through fear, Ranger, and fear alone. Kill enough of them, and the rest will fall in line."

Rew cringed, thinking of the clusters of dead narjags they'd stumbled across in the wilderness and on the slopes of the Spine.

"The Dark Kind were summoned through high magic, of

course," continued Ralcrist, not seeing Rew's expression, "but even then, when they first poured through the portals, the conjurers controlled them through fear. They'd find the most aggressive of the new arrivals and make examples of them. They displayed their power, and the narjags trembled before it. Valaans are trickier, of course, but it's the same—"

Rew closed his eyes, pausing in the center of the arcanist's room.

"Why are you asking these questions, Senior Ranger?" demanded Ralcrist, suddenly noticing Rew's reaction. "Does this have to do with the gathering of Dark Kind that was discovered by our patrol?" He shook his head. "The spellcaster you mentioned, is it the same one who arrived with the baron's children?"

Rew did not respond, but he did not need to. Ralcrist could see confirmation in his face.

"You thought the man had a beacon affixed to him, that he was drawing the Dark Kind to him," guessed Ralcrist. "The man is in the employ of Prince Valchon, is he not? The Dark Kind we've seen in the barrowlands have been thwarting Baron Fedgley's plan. If this spellcaster is allied with Valchon, then he cannot be behind the attacks from the narjags. No one would be foolish enough to betray Prince Valchon in such a manner. Betraying a prince? That would be suicide. There must be another spellcaster in the vicinity, one who is supporting Prince Heindaw or Prince Calb."

Rew ran his hand over his hair, thinking he needed a shave—and to leave Falvar as soon as he could.

Arcanist Ralcrist pointed toward his foyer. "You see, Ranger, why I've invested my life's study in fashioning this ward? We are safe here from the machinations of these spellcasters because of me. This man who arrived with you and the baron's children, whoever else is out there plotting against him and the baron, they are helpless in Falvar because of my ward."

"Do you know the old border fort adjacent to the Spine?" asked Rew. "The one converted to an ore-mining operation?"

Ralcrist nodded.

"Does your ward reach that far?"

Ralcrist frowned, appeared to do some calculations, and then answered, "No, I don't believe it would. My ward extends twenty-five, thirty leagues from here. That tower is a four-day journey, is it not? You came that way, didn't you?"

"I did," said Rew. "It was four days walking, outside of your range."

"Do not fear, Ranger. Whatever these spellcasters are up to, they are impotent in Falvar. I've made sure of it," cackled the arcanist.

"Impotent only while your crystal is operating," warned Rew.

Ralcrist winked at him. "No spellcaster can stop it. The reverberation to their magic if they came within my rooms would be too much for them to bear. It'd be like their blood was boiling. It'd drive them to their knees, and if they struggled close enough to touch it, the crystal would shred them to pieces. Have no fear, Ranger. Not even Baron Fedgley can enter these rooms."

Rew grunted.

"What worries you, Ranger?" wondered Ralcrist.

"I don't know," replied Rew. "I don't know, and I don't—I don't want to know what these scoundrels are plotting. It's time for me to leave, Ralcrist. I need to tell my companions to prepare, and we'll start our journey home as soon as we can."

"Best of luck to you, Ranger," offered the arcanist. "I'm told the pull of the Investiture is impossible to resist, but best of luck to you."

Rew headed for the door without responding, but then he paused. Over his shoulder, he suggested, "Ralcrist, perhaps some guards outside of your chamber? A spellcaster may not be able to enter, but you're not immune from a mundane attack. Don't let a man with a knife be the end of your life's work."

"No hammer or sword can destroy that crystal, Ranger, only a staff designed by my own hand, which is the key to making it operate," said Ralcrist, "but I'll consider your advice. We'll all be pulled into this, and a wise man takes precautions."

Rew grunted and opened the door.

"For what it's worth," called Ralcrist, "I think you're doing the right thing. The Investiture is a terrible ritual, and I'm glad to see you want nothing to do with it. Their blood gives the nobles the powers to practice high magic, but it does not give them wisdom. They waste the gift their blood grants them by using it to try and spill the blood of others. Magic and noble blood, Ranger, they're helplessly intertwined. Us commoners would be best off without either of them." The arcanist cackled then hastily added, "Don't tell the baron I said that. He needs me, and despite how much I loathe it, I need him."

Rew walked out of the man's rooms, closing the door on the arcanist and his floating crystal. He needed to find Anne and Jon. They needed to leave Falvar.

Chapter Seventeen

"It was Baron Fedgley, not Worgon," said Anne, shaking her head, leaning close so that no one else in the tavern could hear what she said, "and his children never suspected?"

"Evidently not," said Rew. "Perhaps they never will. Not until all of this is over, at least. The baron hasn't told them he's behind the conspiracy, and I certainly don't plan to get involved."

Anne frowned, looking unsure.

"What are you going to do, Anne, march up to the palace and tell them their father is behind it? That he is the one who planted the false story about Worgon's betrayal and sent them on this quest?" questioned Rew. "Even if they believe you, and the baron doesn't find out and toss you in a cell, what would that accomplish? With the Investiture starting, the duchy is going to be embroiled in conflict no matter what we do. The children are safest in the baron's keep, under his protection."

"There has to be another way, Rew," responded Anne.

"Not while the king is on the throne in Mordenhold," said Rew. He reached over and put a hand on hers. "The Investiture has been going on for two hundred years, and each cycle brings tragedy and devastation, but it's the way of things. We don't have to like it, but there's nothing we can do to stop it."

She shook her head in disagreement, but she had no answer. He was right. The Investiture had been the way of things for two hundred years, and until someone overthrew the king, it's the way it would be.

Neither of them spoke, letting the noise of the busy common room fill the silence between them.

Jon returned from the bar, sitting down at their table and placing an ale in front of himself and Rew and a mug of wine in front of Anne. "They told me it'd be half an hour on the food. Seems the inn is quite crowded with the soldiers in town. We were lucky to get rooms, I gather."

"We came down from the keep," said Rew. "That didn't hurt."

Anne, looking over the place with a professional's eye, remarked, "They'd do well to hire more staff and do a bit of cleaning. Doesn't look like they've properly swept the floors in a week. The rooms upstairs, well, I'm glad it's only a night we're staying. I'm choosing not to think about what's taking place behind that kitchen door."

Grinning, Rew winked at Jon over the rim of his ale mug. "It's the cleanest inn we could find, Anne. If you don't like this place, you should see some of the sinks we've had to stay in when we visit Spinesend."

Anne cringed, feigning terror, and the two men laughed.

"It's decided, then?" asked Jon. "Just one night in Falvar, then we return home?"

Rew sat down his tankard and stretched. "Aye, it's decided. Eat supper, get some rest, stop by the post tomorrow with a letter for Commandant Grund, pick up supplies for the journey, and then back to Eastwatch."

Out of the corner of his eye, he watched Anne. He knew she'd originally thought to stay and help the commoners, as they were drawn into the Investiture, but the Dark Kind and the gathering of the wraiths had given her second thoughts. Baron Fedgley planned to march with his army against Duke Eeron and Baron Worgon. His men might need healing after, but they were the aggressors. If Anne announced herself and stayed, it would not be the common people she would be forced to heal. It wouldn't be the victims she would be helping.

The truth was, the best thing the commoners could do was to flee, but Rew admitted, there may not be anywhere to go. If what Alsayer claimed was true about each of the princes' strength, then the entire kingdom was going to be drawn into the conflict. Eastwatch, though, Eastwatch could still benefit from the help of a good ranger and an empath. Rew would keep the territory out of it, as much as he could, and keep the people free from the whirlpool that was forming around Mordenhold. He and Anne couldn't help everyone, but they could help some, and that was worth doing.

He hoped so, at least.

They sat and drank for a moment, savoring the chance to enjoy a decent cup in comfortable seating for the first time in weeks, even if the cleanliness of the floor wasn't up to Anne's standards.

"That man, the spellcaster, he called you his cousin," said Jon. "What did he mean?"

Rew twitched, nearly spilling his ale. "History. He was talking about history."

"You are related, though, aren't you?" pressed Jon. "You didn't act surprised."

"We're related," admitted Rew, "and that's all I want to say about it."

The younger ranger eyed him curiously, but Rew did not comment.

Changing the subject, Jon mentioned, "I'm surprised the baron did not invite us to stay in the keep tonight. We did just bring his youngest two children through the wilderness safely. That, and helping to spread word of the plot by Baron Worgon against Duke Eeron. A little thanks should be in order…"

Jon glanced between Rew and Anne, but both looked away, pretending to study the room.

"You're like my parents, never wanting to admit there's a

problem when it couldn't be any plainer that there was one," grumbled Jon. "Senior Ranger, I know I'm the least experienced man on your staff, but I am a ranger. If there's a threat to the territory, you should share it with me. I can help."

"Investiture isn't just a threat to the territory, Jon," replied Rew. "It's a threat to everything."

"That'll be one gold, three silver, sir," said the postman.

Rew winced. "Take it from the king's account, authority of the senior ranger for the eastern territory."

The postman, a thin-faced grouch whose skin looked as if it hadn't seen the sun in years, eyed the ranger up and down. "I'll need your name and signature."

"Of course," said Rew.

The man turned his logbook and pushed it across the simple wooden counter. Rew scrawled the necessary information on the book, noting that the majority of the entries were in the same hand. The postman's own, presumably. Rew wondered if the man was testing whether he could read the columns and make his marks in the appropriate places. Suspicion was growing everywhere, and it was only going to get worse.

"How many days to Mordenhold, do you think?" asked Rew, handing back the man's quill.

The postman scratched his head, the ink from the quill scrawling across his temple. "There's a number of stops along the way where the parcel will be transferred. Delays are always possible, but the roads should be in good shape going into winter. A month if all goes reasonably well and a month back once the recipient has sent their reply. Shall I be expecting a return letter?"

Rew shook his head. "No, the answer will arrive in Eastwatch."

The postman nodded, made a few final marks in his logbook,

and stuck Rew's envelope containing the letter to Commandant Grund below the counter. The ranger nodded his thanks and left.

He glanced up and down the stone streets of Falvar, feeling like he was trapped in a prison. The city's walls rose in a box. They were visible between the roofs of the shops and down each open street. Those tall walls were like a pen, caging him inside. The streets themselves were fashioned like the buildings, from the pale rock of the Spine. It gave Falvar a washed-out feel in sharp contrast to the verdant grasslands that surrounded it.

Rew yearned for the freedom of those grasslands and the forests he could reach beyond them, but he had a bit more to attend to in Falvar, so he steeled himself, content knowing that in the afternoon, he, Anne, and Jon would be leaving, and he would yet again feel the comfort of the open road, the wind across his face, and dirt beneath his feet.

All around him, burghers jostled, moving about on their errands. Housewives picked up packages from the grocers. Workmen made deliveries to the shops. Vendors called out their wares from kiosks, and the more successful merchants who owned their own storefronts stood outside, prepared to welcome in prospective customers. Down the center of the street, groups of armored men walked slowly, their gazes roving over the citizens, the shops, and the walls of Falvar.

"Where is he getting them?" muttered Rew under his breath as a group of five liveried soldiers strolled past.

One of the soldiers turned to study Rew, his gaze resting briefly on the ranger's longsword then moving up to his eyes.

Rew met the look, seeing the man's thick black beard and swarthy complexion, and guessing the soldier hailed from the Southern Province. What was such a man doing at the far fringes of the kingdom's eastern border? The soldier, glaring at Rew, appeared miffed his look didn't intimidate the ranger, but he kept moving.

No authority over the citizenry, guessed Rew as he watched the soldiers walk away, another group appearing at the far end of the street shortly after the first vanished. But if they had no authority over the people, what were they doing on patrol?

Grunting, trying to forget his questions, Rew started toward the market where Jon and Anne were supposed to be collecting supplies for the journey back to Eastwatch. He moved down Falvar's main avenue, glancing up at the dark sky. High above hung steel gray clouds that did not look promising for an evening on the road, but Rew was eager to leave, to get out of the town, to avoid the draw of the Investiture. Still looking up, purposefully ignoring the crowd around him, he nearly stumbled into another squad of azure-clad soldiers. He stopped several paces in front of them, but the men kept marching without pause.

"Clear the way," barked the squad leader.

Rew eyed the man then stepped aside.

The squad leader stopped and jabbed a finger at him. "I suggest next time you move faster unless you fancy a night in the baron's jail."

"For what crime? Walking down the street?" asked Rew.

The soldier drew himself up and clamped a hand around the hilt of the broadsword hanging at his side. "Trying to make trouble, are we?"

"No, not at all," said Rew, studying the big man. "Just walking down the street, as I said. Are you trying to make trouble?"

The soldier blinked at him, confused.

"Where are you from, soldier?" Rew asked the man. "What brought you to Falvar?"

"That's none of your business," growled the uniformed man.

"A mercenary, then," responded Rew.

The man stepped forward. "You are trying to make trouble, aren't you? Come with us, and maybe that night in the cell will sort you out."

"I don't think so," said Rew.

The soldier puffed his chest out like a bird standing over his nest, his hand still on his broadsword, his shoulders working like he was winding himself up. Rew waited, wanting to see what the man would do. He was not worried. A mercenary called to the edge of the realm was unlikely to have been given authority to arrest anyone and certainly had no authority over an agent of the king, even if they were in Baron Fedgley's domain rather than the territory. The soldier paused, on the verge of action, surprised Rew did not seem intimidated. Behind him, his companions shifted nervously, evidently unsure how to respond to a challenge.

"You were hired to be out in the barrows," guessed Rew. "Why are so many of you in town? Is Fedgley expecting an attack?"

The soldier spluttered, his face going red. He opened his mouth, but a hand fell on his shoulder. The soldier turned in surprise.

"You don't want to cross this one," remarked Alsayer.

Rew snorted at the sight of the spellcaster.

"He's being disrespectful to the baron's men," growled the soldier. "Disrespect toward us leads to disrespect of the baron himself. I've seen it happen before, Spellcaster, and the baron'd be wise to make sure it doesn't happen here. I wasn't planning to hurt this man. I just wanted to let him cool off in a cell, teach him a lesson."

Grinning, Alsayer remarked, "I don't believe he'd willingly walk into a jail cell with you, my friend."

"It's not his choice," barked the soldier.

Alsayer winked at the bigger man and suggested, "I think it is, Soldier. This man is the King's Ranger. He's not subject to the baron's law, and even if he was, you'd need two or three times as many men to take him in. Go on, now, and meet the rest of your fellows at the barracks. You should be getting ready to depart. I'm heading that way as well to speak with Commander Broyce, and I expect you to be there before I am."

The soldier seemed to deflate under Alsayer's gaze. He shot a final glare at Rew then turned and gestured for his men. Grudgingly, they marched up the street.

"I thought you were leaving, cousin," said Alsayer.

"I am," assured Rew. "I just posted a letter to the ranger commandant in Mordenhold and I'm going to meet the rest of my party now. We've some supplies to buy, then we'll be leaving later today."

The spellcaster glanced up at the menacing clouds above them. "Not a pretty day for travel, is it?"

"I've hiked through worse," said Rew, trying to edge away from the spellcaster. "Don't let me keep you from meeting with the commander."

"The baron and his commander are getting their men organized, sending them out to the barrows as I requested," said Alsayer, waving a hand dismissively. "The baron understands the circumstances, and I'm just going to ensure the commander does as well. A few veiled threats go a long way with such men. Really, Rew, you're leaving today in this weather? I guess that means no goodbye for the children you brought here. I saw them this morning, and they said they hadn't seen you."

"I did what I promised. I got them here safely," responded Rew. "They're not children, Alsayer, and nothing more is needed from me."

"Ah, I thought maybe you'd grown fond of them," remarked the spellcaster in his silky, patronizing voice. "You certainly risked your life for them back at the miner's tower."

"I did what was needed," snapped Rew. "Do you have something to say or not? I told you, I'm headed to meet my companions."

"So angry, Rew," murmured Alsayer. "What is bothering you, cousin?"

"You are," growled the ranger. "A beacon drawing the Dark Kind to you, isn't that what you told me? What'd you do, Alsayer, jump around the forest finding those creatures? How'd you talk them into traveling back over the Spine? What was it you said, a few veiled threats? I suppose with the Dark Kind you've got to remove the veil and kill a few of them."

The spellcaster held up his hands innocently. "I know not of what you speak."

"Don't play me for the fool, Alsayer," warned Rew. "I know it was you portaling all over the wilderness collecting the Dark Kind, even if I don't know why."

"You were never an easy one to fool," admitted the other man.

"What are you doing with the Dark Kind, preparing to betray the baron?" questioned Rew. "Does Valchon know, or are you stabbing him in the back as well?"

"I thought you didn't want to get involved," said the spellcaster, leaning close. "Are you sure you want the answers to those questions?"

"I'm not getting involved," snarled Rew, stepping back.

"I'm only here to help the baron with his task," claimed the spellcaster, his eyes wide and hands clasped in a mockery of innocence on his chest.

Frustrated, Rew turned and began stalking down the street, walking away from his cousin and wishing he and the other man had both kept their mouths shut. The more he knew…

"Rew," called Alsayer.

The ranger paused, cursing himself for listening, but unable to stifle his curiosity.

"I told you before. The strength of a spellcaster is in their blood," said Alsayer, stepping close to Rew's back and pitching his voice low so that only the ranger could hear. "High magic requires a carefully bred bloodline. When the unions are properly managed, the child is always more powerful than the parent. Prince Valchon selected Baron Fedgley to command the wraiths he is assembling because Fedgley is the strongest necromancer in the realm outside of the royal line. Did you know the baron's wife is an invoker? But her father was an accomplished necromancer, as was his father before him. It's in both her and the baron's blood. It's in the children's blood. The prince knows about them, Rew. He knows about the girl and what her potential is. What she is capable of if she left off her fruitless training in invoking and studied necromancy. If something were to happen to Baron Fedgley, I suspect Prince Valchon will immediately start looking for the daughter."

Rew sensed the spellcaster move away, felt him stride up the street into the stream of traffic, headed toward the barracks. The child is more powerful than the parent. Prince Valchon knew. Alsayer was preparing to betray them all.

Rew barked a curse then headed for the marketplace, hoping to find Anne and Jon there ready to go, ready to leave Falvar. He had to get out and get away, or it would be too late to avoid being dragged into the building maelstrom of the Investiture.

Rew made it to the market and was looking over the tented-stalls and open tables, searching for Anne's red hair or the steel bear head on the pommel of Jon's longsword. He was surprised when they appeared at his side. "What… You haven't started your shopping, have you?"

Anne offered a guilty smile. "I wanted to check in on the injured before we left, and I brought Jon along with me. We'll get started and move quickly, Senior Ranger."

Rew reached up and rubbed his face with his hands.

Jon pointed at the thick gray clouds above which obscured the sun. "To be honest, Rew, it might not be such a bad idea to spend the night indoors again." He sniffed the air. "It's hard to tell in the walls of the city, but it smells like rain."

"The longer we stay here…" muttered Rew.

"Rew, if you mean to drag me out into this weather, I'm going to gather supplies first," insisted Anne.

"Anne, we cannot delay," he said.

"It'd be quicker travel if we took the roads," muttered the empath.

Rew shook his head. "If we're to avoid the Investiture, we have to avoid Spinesend."

"Get yourself an ale while we shop," advised Anne, pointing to a small stand with a cluster of tall tables and stools outside of it. "It may be your last one for a couple of weeks, so savor it. And just think, if we'd been ready, you would have missed getting the ale. See the upside, Rew."

"We have to leave," he declared.

"We will, Senior Ranger, soon." Anne turned, and Jon followed her as they headed toward the market stalls.

Scowling, Rew made his way to the kiosk and ordered a tankard of ale from the man working behind the counter. He watched as Anne and Jon made their way deeper into the market, the empath turning toward the dried herbs that lined one row and the ranger headed toward several vendors selling general goods. No doubt, he would turn later to the weapons. The market stocked stuff that hopefully the young man knew better than to purchase, but Rew had decided on the journey to Falvar that he needed to give Jon room to make his own decisions. The ranger was young, true, but with Tate dead, the core group of rangers was only getting younger. It was important that Jon get ready to step into a ranger's full responsibility as quickly as possible. Bleakly, Rew admitted they were going to need all of the skilled hands they could get.

Rew watched as Anne bent forward to sniff a bundle of dried herbs. From the distance, he couldn't see what they were, but he could see her asking the seller about them and eventually handing over a small pile of copper coins for the purchase. Something she thought might be useful in healing and couldn't be harvested on the edge of the wilderness, Rew supposed. None of the spices in Falvar's market were any more exotic than those in Eastwatch. Anne moved down the aisle, passing out of sight, and Rew turned to see Jon haggling with a cobbler over a pair of soft leather boots.

Rew sipped his ale and looked up at the sky.

Jon hadn't been wrong. If the senior ranger knew anything of the weather, he knew it would rain that evening. A downpour, most likely. He weighed his desire to get out of Falvar against the accusing looks he was certain to receive from Anne if they were forced to huddle together under a rain-whipped tarp all night with no fire and no fresh provisions. If he forced them to stop their shopping early, and they couldn't keep a fire going to boil their beans and rice, that left only handfuls of jerky…

Rew ordered another ale, deciding it was worth letting the empath resupply, but then they would leave, just as soon as she and Jon finished.

Periodically, he'd see the two of them walking amongst the aisles, filling their packs, gathering the provisions they would need for nearly three weeks on the road. Neither of them appeared to be in a rush, and Jon frequently shot surreptitious looks at the clouds overhead as if counting the moments until they broke loose with a deluge of raindrops.

Rew noticed the crush of soldiers had thinned, and after half an hour, he heard the distinct sound of men marching. Leaving, he supposed, heading toward the barrows to collect the wraiths, just as Alsayer had said.

Over the din of the market, Rew listened to the soldiers moving from the barracks toward the north gate, their heavy steps and rustling chainmail like the noise of some ancient drake sliding through the town. Rew tried to guess how many there were. Certainly well over one hundred of the men, but it was impossible to know for sure. He decided it was at least two hundred, maybe as many as three hundred, as the final sounds of the stomping boots faded. It had to be a third of the men garrisoned in Falvar.

Jon appeared and dropped off a package of dry goods. Peeking inside, Rew saw salted meats, wheels of cheese, and a few loaves of fresh bread. The younger ranger then went back into the market, picking up a few additional items.

Rew opened his pack to stuff in the victuals and saw a rough sack in his pack. He grimaced. It contained the necklace of narjag ears he'd recovered near Eastwatch, and the head of the narjag shamans staff. He'd meant to ask Arcanist Ralcrist about the items. Sighing, Rew shoved the food into his pack and flipped it closed, pulling a leather strap through a brass buckle to tighten it.

He was on his third ale and was beginning to appreciate the time to drink it when he saw a familiar face slipping through the crowded aisles of the market.

Zaine, still armed with the two daggers and the bow she'd gotten in the ranger station in Eastwatch, was moving gracefully through the crowd, sliding around shoppers and passing like a ghost.

Briefly, Rew thought to chase after her to collect the weapons. They'd been meant as a loan to get the party safely through the wilderness and over the Spine, but in the rush of arriving at Falvar and going to see the baron, he hadn't had the chance to ask for them back, and she'd vanished into the town without offering to return them.

Rew glanced down into his ale then sat back. Allowing the girl to keep the weapons was a small price to pay for avoiding another entanglement in Falvar. The king's treasury could suffer the blow, and the Eastwatch armory had plenty of other weapons until he purchased replacements.

It was like a nagging itch between his shoulder blades, the urge to get up and leave. He could feel it, that they had to get on the road, or they wouldn't. He'd finish the ale, he decided, and then he would round up Anne and Jon. They'd had enough time to shop, and he was sure they could survive without whatever other goods they were missing. It was past time to be gone.

Zaine, a hundred paces away, near the entrance to the market, paused, and Rew saw her chop her hand behind her back. A dozen paces behind her, a man stopped and waited a moment then moved to a stall and began examining a pile of brightly colored head scarves.

Shopping for his wife, wondered Rew. The ranger picked up his ale and took a sip, his gaze still on the man over the rim of his tankard. Scattered around the market, several other men who'd been striding purposefully along had suddenly moved toward nearby tables.

Rew frowned. Half a dozen men had moved at the same time to various stalls. They were all dressed in plain cotton tunics and trousers, light cloaks on their shoulders, their hair and clothing indistinct but in the style of the locals. They'd been moving along with the current of the market traffic, but now they were not, cutting across other shoppers so that they could stand in front of the closest tables. Outside the entrance to the market, a pair of men strolled by, dressed in Baron Fedgley's livery, walking on patrol.

When they passed, Rew saw Zaine gesture again, and she exited the market, a line of plainly dressed men following, walking a dozen paces apart from each other, but all at the same pace that Zaine set. None of the men carried any goods that they'd purchased on their stroll through the market.

Rew, without putting thought into it, marked the faces of the men he thought were following the girl. They were following her, taking her direction, and avoiding Baron Fedgley's soldiers. What was the girl getting herself into?

"Is that Zaine?" asked Jon.

At the same time, Anne said, "Well, I think we should stay the night, but if you insist— That is Zaine, isn't it?"

The girl vanished up the street.

Anne continued, "I was hoping to say farewell. Do you think we can catch up to her?"

"Let's try," said Rew, knowing he would regret it.

Chapter Eighteen

❧

He led the way out of the market and to the pale stone street beyond. To his left was the river gate, the main entrance and exit from the walled portion of Falvar. To his right, Baron Fedgley's keep, and beyond that, the north gate which led to the barrowlands. Groaning, Rew started toward the keep, his pace slow, his eyes scanning the people and the buildings around them. He opened his senses, like he would in the forest, and tried to sort through the overwhelming deluge of stimuli that battered him.

"We'd best hurry if we want to catch her," said Jon.

Rew did not respond. Fifty paces in front of them was one of the men who'd been following Zaine. The man moved at a casual stroll, glancing around much like Rew was and frequently peering ahead as if he was looking for something. Rew followed his gaze and saw their quarry was eyeing another of the plainly dressed men. They were strung out, keeping their distance from each other like baby ducks following a mother. Rew slowed down and kept walking.

"Are... Are we following someone?" wondered Anne.

"We're seeing where Zaine is going," replied Rew.

Behind him, he could feel the empath and the younger ranger give each other a look, but he didn't explain. Zaine was leading a troop of men toward the baron's keep. Zaine who'd claimed to be a thief in good standing but did not have the markings of the guild. Zaine who'd told him she hadn't been to Falvar recently but had slipped away to meet with someone as soon as their backs had turned. There was more to her story. Rew had known it, but he hadn't wanted to get involved. He still didn't want to get involved, but he couldn't help himself. Curiosity had caught him, and it wasn't letting go.

The man they were following paused, and Rew risked bringing them closer. He looked ahead, trying to pick out more of the plainly dressed men. It was difficult to tell from behind, but he thought he spied four of them now, and then they all started moving again at an identical pace, still headed toward the keep.

Overhead, thunder rumbled, and Anne hissed, "If you mean to drag us out onto the road tonight…"

He held up a hand, and she quieted. Beside her, Jon remained silent as well, clearly sensing something was afoot and just as clearly not having any idea of what it was.

Moments later, drops of rain began to plonk down on their heads and shoulders, and behind him, Jon and Anne grumbled, rearranging their cloaks and cinching their packs tightly shut. The thick wool of their garments would keep the water off them for a while, but the raindrops were falling fat and hard. Rew ignored the patter of the rain on his bare scalp, keeping his eyes on the scurrying men in front of them as they made directly for the keep.

"Jon," he asked, "when did you first think it was going to rain?"

The young ranger shrugged. "Ah, on the way out of the infirmary, I suppose. The clouds had gotten thick by then, I think."

Rew nodded, glancing up at the dark gray mass that hung overhead. The light of the sun had been cut off completely, and along the street, the lamps had not yet been lit.

"What's going on?" asked Jon, his eyes darting nervously around the street in front of them. "Where are we going?"

"Zaine is leading a group of men to somewhere near the

keep," answered Rew. "They're hiding from Baron Fedgley's soldiers, and they must have started moving shortly after the bulk of those soldiers departed and cleared the gates of the town. The men behind her are professionals, used to moving stealthily. Thieves' guild, I can only assume."

"But—But she's not in the thieves' guild, is she?"

Rew shrugged. Then, he nodded to the left and had them take a narrow alley that was dotted with open doors to small clothiers' shops. The tailors and seamstresses were bustling about, lighting lamps outside of their doors or closing up, balefully eyeing the stone-paved street that recently would have been filled with potential customers.

With the scattered rain, it seemed everyone was headed for home. Another peal of thunder rang from above, and Rew saw a shopkeeper throw up his hands, snuff out the match he'd been about to light his lamp with, and storm inside his shop, closing the door behind him.

On the main street they'd turned away from, Rew had seen one of the men he recognized pausing, staring back the way he'd come. The others had streamed by him while he watched their tail. Professionals, no doubt. With the strange group covering their rear, Rew didn't want to risk staying too close to them, but he suspected he knew which way they were headed.

From that point on the street, he could see all the way to the main gates of the keep, and Zaine was not there. She'd either gone inside somewhere nearby, or she'd turned. Several blocks away, there was a second entrance to the keep, one reserved for guests of the baron, where they could come and go without having to wade through the throng of commoners at the main gate. It was the gate that Rew had used the day before after leaving the arcanist. If Zaine and her men were not at that secondary gate, Rew doubted he would find her again, but he had a feeling she would be there.

They moved quickly through the empty, rain-splattered streets. After several blocks, Rew slowed their pace, and they peeked down a tree-lined boulevard that led from the wealthier enclaves of Falvar to the small, private gate that bored through the keep's stout walls.

It was a massive oak door, bound with steel, and it rose twice the height of a tall man. Zaine was standing in front of it, banging on the door with her fist. A window set at head height slid open, and Rew could see a face peering between the steel bars that protected the peep hole. The ranger could not hear what was being discussed, but clearly, Zaine was presenting herself for admittance.

Rew couldn't see the side street she must have emerged from or where the men who followed her were hiding, but they would be nearby. Zaine had spent several weeks traveling with Baron Fedgley's children. She'd assisted them in their escape from Yarrow, and she'd been by their sides in Eastwatch's jail. She'd traversed the wilderness with the pair. The Fedgleys owed her compensation for her role in their escape, or maybe they'd just agreed to an audience with someone they'd grown close to. It didn't matter. It was plain enough that someone, likely the thieves' guild, was using Zaine's connection to get them inside of the keep.

The door swung open, and Zaine stood in the entrance, glancing around. Behind her back, she held up two fingers.

"She's signaling the others," hissed Rew.

There was a streak of motion, and two darts flashed past Zaine into the open doorway. Rew saw one of them land in the neck of an armored guard. The man held up his hand, a startled look on his face. Two of the plainly dressed men came running out of hiding and rushed into the doorway. One of them caught the guard and carefully lowered him to the stones inside of the keep. He gestured with his hand, and four more men came out of hiding and entered the keep.

Zaine stood in the entrance, trembling, staring down at the bodies of the guards. When the last man drew next to her, he slipped a hand beneath his cloak and lifted a truncheon. Without pause, he swiped it down, bashing Zaine on the back of the head with the short club. Anne gasped, and Jon looked on, stunned.

Zaine collapsed into the man's arms, and he dragged her inside of the baron's keep, tossing her down where Rew imagined they'd left the bodies of the guards. The doors swung shut, and Rew realized the entire breach had taken less than a dozen breaths. Professionals, no doubt.

"I don't understand," muttered Jon.

"Thieves' guild," said Rew, rubbing at his smooth scalp and brushing away the rain that was beaded there. "They must have found her when we arrived in Falvar and convinced her to show her face at the door to get the guards to open it. If these men are known, there's no way they could make it into the front gate, and even if they did, they'd be surrounded by dozens of guards guiding them into the public areas. An attack in broad daylight, though, and they've already killed two guards… They're not going in to pilfer a handful of silver candlesticks."

"What do we do?" asked Jon.

"We go warn the guards at the main gate that they're under attack," said Rew. "Come on."

They ran back through the streets of Falvar, headed toward the main gate, but when they got there, they found the gates were shut.

"W-Why would…" stammered Jon.

Rew shook his head. Minutes before, they'd seen the gates, and they'd been wide open.

A bell began to clang, and on top of the battlements, they saw soldiers hurrying, pointing out somewhere over the walls of the city. Rew spun and looked down the broad avenue toward the northern gates that led to the barrowlands. At the end of a long boulevard, through the shroud of heavy raindrops, he saw those gates had swung shut as well. The rain obscured anything beyond the walls, but it was clear. The soldiers scrambling about in their azure livery were preparing for an attack.

"I don't understand," said Jon, spinning in the street, looking from the keep to the city walls and then back again.

"Neither do I," admitted Rew.

Denizens of Falvar were opening windows, peeking out, or stepping out into the rain to look up and down the street with the same confused looks on their faces as Rew and his friends.

A man, wearing the azure tunic of Falvar, raced toward the keep from the northern gate. He came to a skidding stop before the looming walls, wiped a hand over his face to brush his wet hair back, and yelled up to the guards on the wall, "Dark Kind, hundreds of narjags. Could be more we haven't seen yet. We're closing the gates and preparing to defend. Alert Commander Broyce and—Ah, he's gone. Alert Baron Fedgley!"

The guards atop the walls of the keep conferred then shouted down, "You're right. Commander Broyce just left an hour ago on an expedition out into the barrows."

The messenger shifted, looking behind toward the city gate. "I know. I know. We've got minutes until the Dark Kind are at the walls. Captain Marsk is requesting all soldiers to the northern gate where he can position them to defend Falvar."

Between the crenellations of the keep, Rew could see the soldiers shifting irritably.

"Come on, man!" shouted the messenger. "Open the gates and get out here!"

"Protocol is to shut the gates and keep them shut during an alarm," said the soldier on the wall. "Only Commander Broyce and Baron Fedgley have the authority to open these gates and reassign our positions."

"Well, go get the baron!" demanded the messenger. "We're under attack. We're outnumbered. We need more men."

"We've sent someone to find the baron," called the soldier from the top of the wall. "I—It's protocol, you understand? You know as well as I do what happened to Eames just three days past for violating the baron's orders."

Seething with frustration, the messenger glanced back toward the city gates then tried imploring the soldiers on the wall one more time, "If we can't hold the walls…"

"It's protocol," insisted the man up top. "If the baron decides we shouldn't have violated protocol to open the gates, it's my head, mate."

Rew could see the crestfallen look on the messenger's face. The ranger guessed that in the service of the baron, it was well understood the punishment for violating orders.

"Give us time," said the soldier on the wall, his hand held over his brow to block the rain, looking out past the city walls were he must be able to see the approaching Dark Kind. "Tell Captain Marsk to hold, to buy us time. As soon as the bell started ringing, we sent a man for the baron. The messenger could return any moment now, and we'll start cranking these gates open and send a company to assist."

The messenger cursed and raced away, headed back toward the city gate. Watching him, the townspeople looked disgusted and scared. Nervously, they shuffled back inside, shuttering windows and barring their doors. The clanging of the alarm bell rang out over the city, and handfuls of soldiers streamed out from where they must have been resting in the city barracks to man the walls. The gates of the baron's keep remained stubbornly shut.

"Should we yell up to them? Tell them someone snuck inside?" asked Jon.

Rew shook his head. "Zaine and her thief brethren snuck in the minute before the Dark Kind were spotted. That was an hour after half the town's defenses disappeared into the barrowlands and out of earshot for the alarm bells. It cannot be a coincidence these events happened in that order. Whatever they are doing inside of the keep…"

"You'll stop it?" asked Anne.

Rew glanced to the closed northern gate. They might be able to slip out the southern gate, if it was still open. That was the way they should return home anyway, taking the roads rather than the difficult crossing over the Spine, but he doubted those gates would be open. They would have been closed as soon as the alarm rang just like the others. Until the Dark Kind were dealt with, no one would be leaving. And even then... Blessed Mother, what were the thieves doing inside the keep? If they were planning an assassination or some other terrible attack...

Smacking a fist into an open palm, Rew growled, "There's nowhere else to go. We can't leave, so we may as well help."

"How do we get in?" asked Jon.

They were surrounded by locked gates, locked doors, and a handful of citizens running through the streets, rushing toward their homes. The keep was four stories of tightly mortared stone with a wide avenue circling it to prevent anyone from scrambling over from the nearby buildings. When guarded with a full complement of soldiers, it would be nearly impregnable to any attacking force that didn't come with the necessary siege equipment, but at the moment, the soldiers on the walls were clustering along the battlement, pointing and gesturing to what must be the growing presence of the Dark Kind north of the city.

"We could wait until they open the gate," suggested Anne.

Rew shook his head. "This was well planned. The thieves are probably to Baron Fedgley by now, if that's where they were headed. The soldiers won't be opening the gate unless some officer disobeys orders. Let's go around back, away from prying eyes, and find a way inside."

Fifteen minutes later, Rew rolled over the top of the battlement. He removed a rope from his pack, grateful Jon had bought the length in the market following the last climbing adventure. He looped it around a crenellation, cinching it tight and dropping the tail toward Jon and Anne.

With the rope, they climbed quickly, and in moments, they were throwing their legs over the edge of the battlement. The section they were on was clear. All of the soldiers on the north side were looking out to where the Dark Kind must be assaulting the walls of the city now. The din of battle rose, but so far, it wasn't the panicked screams that would sound if the Dark Kind had found a way inside. The soldiers had gotten the gates closed in time, and with only crude tools, narjags would have a hell of a time battering their way through.

Dark Kind, for all of the danger they posed, were fairly ineffective at siege warfare. They had little skill with crafting. They weren't particularly smart, and they were frightfully impatient. Once a gate was shut, during the wars of years passed, they would bring crude ladders if they were prepared and giant trunks of trees if they were not. They would attempt to bash down the gates, but unarmored and poorly lead, their casualties could be catastrophic.

It gave mankind an advantage when they were able to crouch behind their walls, but the danger was what the Dark Kind would do outside of those walls. They were vicious and offered no quarter. Anyone caught outside the walls would end up in a narjag's belly, screaming as they were torn apart and then eaten. And if the narjags did breach the walls, they would go into a frenzy, and even trained warriors would tremble in the face of a frothing pack of them.

Luckily, it seemed the Dark Kind had struck from the north, the same gate that Rew and their party arrived through. If the Dark Kind realized that there was an unprotected settlement to the south... Rew could only hope the soldiers would act and race to defend their exposed citizens instead of leaving them unprotected in their hovels by the river. He could only hope the untested mercenaries had the leadership to fend off ladders or a battering ram. But for now, he could not worry about any of that. They had a keep to assault.

He led the trio down the stairs into the interior of the keep, telling his companions, "Act like we belong here. Word is out that the alarm is for Dark Kind, so no one should be particularly suspicious of us, but the less we have to do with the soldiers, the better."

"We shouldn't simply alert them?" wondered Jon.

"We could have done that from outside the gate," mentioned Rew. "No, I think there's too much going on here that we don't understand. The thieves slipping in? That's one thing. The bulk of the town's forces being diverted away, the thieves slipping in, and an attack by an army of Dark Kind? This is something else, and we won't know who we can trust until we figure out what is happening."

Jon grunted, and Rew led them into the inner hallways of the keep. There were two people who might be able to do something about the attack on the city and the thieves that slipped inside the keep—Baron Fedgley and Arcanist Ralcrist. Rew hoped the soldiers were already with the baron, convincing the man to open the gates and to protect the city walls, so he headed toward the chambers where he'd met Ralcrist. The arcanist had known they were under threat, and Rew guessed the wily old geezer had prepared. Seeing no one but panicked staff, they raced through the corridors.

The tapestries, carpets, and sconces that dressed the halls of Baron Fedgley's keep were in stark contrast to the madness happening outside of the place. Stately, refined, all of it carefully put in order until they reached the arcanist's rooms. The door hung open, its oak surface scarred with twisting lines of char. One of the plainly dressed thieves lay in the entryway.

"He's dead," said Anne, studying the man from a dozen paces away.

Rew didn't respond. Instead, he hissed for his companions to be quiet and cautiously approached the open door. He jumped when he heard a sizzling crackle inside followed by a shriek of agony. There was another shouted command that was unintelligible outside of the room, and then the sounds of a struggle. Rew rushed inside.

In the center of the room, the giant cerulean crystal was still there, pulsating with subtle light, suspended in the air above the table and the wire framework. On the other side of the crystal, two bodies lay on the floor, black, acrid smoke drifting up from them. Near them, the arcanist was wrestling with the remaining three thieves, trying to wrench a gold-capped staff from their grip.

As Rew raced into the room, he saw one of the thieves draw back a blade then stab forward, slamming the weapon into Arcanist Ralcrist's stomach. The thief ripped it out violently, disemboweling the old man. Ralcrist cried out in pain, gasping for help. His voice barely a whisper, he cried, "Don't let them—The staff, Ranger! The staff!"

The thief turned to look at Rew and his party. He barked, "Attack them!"

Two of the thieves split up and began circling the table, blades held confidently in their hands.

"Take the left, Jon," instructed Rew, trying to quickly evaluate which of the killers was deadlier. There was no time to decide, and he could only hope the young ranger could defend himself.

Longsword already in hand, Rew approached his own foe, one eye on the man in front of him, the other on the thief who'd stabbed Ralcrist. That thief had collected the arcanist's staff, though he made no move to advance on either of the rangers with it.

The thief facing Rew looked nervously at the senior ranger's longsword then flipped his dagger in his hand and whipped it back to throw.

Rew didn't give him time. He lunged forward and stabbed with his longsword, taking the thief square in the chest. The man squealed a gurgled cry and fell back. Rew turned to the leader of the thieves, but instead of attacking with the arcanist's staff, the thief thrust it into the crystal on the table.

Lightning crackled and danced along the length of the staff. The man let go and jumped back, but the intricately carved shaft of gold-capped wood remained stuck in the crystal, sticking up from it, snapping with incandescent bands of light. Thick, white smoke billowed out of the crystal and filled the room. Rew raised a hand toward it, but hesitated, unsure what would happen if he grasped the staff. Then, the crystal shattered.

Rew cringed, holding up a hand to shield himself from flying shards of the broken gem.

Jon cried out and stumbled back against the wall of the room, clutching his chest. The man he'd been facing was lying face down on the floor.

Laughing, the surviving thief turned and lunged for Ralcrist's open balcony. Rew ran after the man, but nimbly, the thief jumped onto the balustrade, leapt out to catch a branch of a fruit tree outside in the courtyard, and shimmied down it as nimbly as a monkey.

Rew sheathed his longsword and was about to follow, but he heard Anne exclaiming at Jon's injuries. Cursing, Rew ran back and knelt beside the empath. "How is he?"

Anne had her belt knife out and was sawing through the young ranger's tunic. Blood pumped from a deep cut in his chest, staining her hands and his clothing. Jon's face was pale, and his breath was coming in short, pitiful bursts. Placing her hands over the furiously bleeding wound, Anne closed her eyes.

Around them, the room was dead quiet. Rew frowned. He heard soft feet running in the hallway outside. It wasn't the heavy trod of boots or the panicked rush of servants startled by an attack. It was deliberate. Rew stood and moved to stand by the doorway. In moments, a woman burst into the room, a shouted warning dying on her lips as she surveyed the room. Rew caught her arm and spun her, slapping away her wrist as she reached for one of the daggers on her hip.

"You," said Zaine.

"Me," agreed Rew. "You've got some explaining to do, lass."

"I, ah… Ralcrist is dead?" asked the thief, peering around Rew's shoulder.

Rew nodded.

"I overheard there'd be an attack. I came to warn—"

"You let these men into the keep, Zaine," accused Rew. "Don't deny it."

"I-I... No, I—" she stammered.

"I watched you talk the guards into opening the gate," said Rew. "I watched you signal to these men, and I watched them murder those guards."

Zaine's eyes flashed. "Then you saw what happened to me?"

He nodded.

"These men, they're thieves' guild. They forced me to do it," she claimed.

"Rew," said Anne from where she was kneeling beside Jon. "He'll live, but it's not safe to move him. I think the blade nicked his heart. I need to make sure the wound is sealed."

Rew nodded. "It should be safe in these rooms. They've done what they came to do. Stay here until I can return." He asked Zaine, "What did they plan to do after killing the arcanist?"

The thief swallowed and looked away. "No one said anything about killing him."

"What did they say, then?" asked Rew, his voice low. He took a step toward Zaine. She tried to back away, but he caught her arm.

"They told me they'd destroy the crystal and then we'd leave. They said they would just knock out the guards, and after... All I knew was that they meant to take the arcanist's staff. I didn't know anything about anyone getting killed!" she insisted. "My head's aching like the worst hangover I've ever had. I woke up near the gate, beside those bodies. I saw them... I saw what happened, and I knew the thieves had lied to me. I knew they would hurt the arcanist and anyone else who got in their way. I came running here as quickly as I could. I meant to... I meant to warn him."

"What'd they offer you?" asked Rew, but before she answered, he guessed, "A place in the guild?"

Lips pressed together, she nodded.

"They came to destroy this crystal, and that's all?" asked Rew, glancing at the shattered pieces of ice blue stone on the table.

"They only told me about the staff," said Zaine.

"Blessed Mother," cursed Rew.

"What?" asked Anne from where she'd laid Jon down on the floor.

"The crystal dampened high magic in the vicinity of Falvar," said Rew, gripping his longsword and scowling. "The strongest practitioner of high magic in this city is the same man who sent half of Baron Fedgley's soldiers out into the barrowlands today. That treacherous bastard Alsayer is behind this. Of course he is. I knew he would be. I—King's Sake. I should have done something to stop this."

"But… why?" questioned Anne. "Why would Alsayer do this?"

Rew snarled, "I don't know, but I'm going to find out."

"I didn't know anything about… about the killings and the spellcaster," pleaded Zaine. "I swear it. I did not know."

"I'll come—" said Anne, starting to stand.

"Stay with Jon," Rew instructed her. "Alsayer will know the thieves were successful in destroying the crystal, so he'll have no reason to come to this room. You'll be safe here."

"I'll stay as—" began Zaine.

"You're coming with me," snapped Rew. "You're not leaving my sight, lass, until we've sorted out a few things."

Zaine winced but didn't object.

"Here," said Anne, standing and touching the back of the girl's head with her bloody hands. "Find me after this is over, and I'll give you a thorough check, but for now, I can ease your pain."

Tight-lipped, Zaine nodded.

Rew wiped the blood from his longsword and instructed, "When we find Alsayer, stay behind me, and be ready to leap. He's an arrogant ass, but it's deserved. If he starts flinging his magic, find cover and stay out of sight. Let me deal with him."

"As you say," murmured the thief.

Rew led them out of the arcanist's tower, listening for the eruption of spellcasting he was sure was about to come.

Chapter Nineteen

They rushed through the corridors, and it wasn't long before Rew heard what he'd dreaded—the concussive thump of high magic.

"Is that Alsayer?" wondered Zaine as a deep womph echoed down the stone hallway.

"We can assume so," said Rew. "Sonic lashes, I'd guess."

"That's what he used against the narjags?"

"The same," confirmed the ranger, slowing as they passed a cross-hallway. He looked up and down both corridors but saw no one. He began jogging again, headed toward the throne room. "Sonic lashes are no more than incredibly dense bands of sound. They're dense enough that they can cause serious damage, as we saw on the bodies of those narjags. They're quite simple and are easy to control, so they're a favorite amongst spellcasters when they're in a battle with the luxury of targeting their attacks. If we see him, hide behind something substantial. Wood can shatter beneath a sonic lash. Stone should hold."

"Why's he doing this?" asked Zaine. "If the thieves killed Arcanist Ralcrist, couldn't they have killed the baron too? Or, better yet, could Alsayer himself not have killed the man? He might not have had access to his magic, but if he requested an audience alone with the baron, I imagine he'd get it. Alsayer looks healthy enough. Even without his magic, a dagger to the heart, a drop of poison in the wine… Surely he could figure something out?"

"He could," agreed Rew, "and that's what concerns me."

They made it to the hallways before the throne room, and Rew worried that yet again, they were too late. There were a dozen guards crumpled against the walls and sprawled on the center of the plush carpet. They were mutilated with giant wounds, like a huge battle axe had been taken to them—the results of Alsayer's sonic lashes. Rew and Zaine had witnessed the efficacy of the man's castings on the narjags, and it was just as brutal when unleashed against a human foe. The wooden door of the throne room had been punched open, and as they drew near, they could see Alsayer's back. The spellcaster was standing in the center of the room, and in front of him, two score guards were arrayed in defensive postures.

"Can he get through all of them?" whispered Zaine.

Rew nodded as they padded silently into the room.

Alsayer, evidently hearing Zaine's whisper or detecting them with some spell-enabled sense, glanced over his shoulder. "Ah, cousin, I hoped you would still be here."

Rew raised his voice and called, "Do not do this, Alsayer."

The spellcaster smirked. "You saw the guards outside, cousin. It's too late to turn back now, don't you think?"

Rew, silently admitting the man had a point, raised his longsword and stalked closer.

"I need a moment, cousin," said the spellcaster. He tore a pendant from his neck and hurled it at the floor behind his feet. A glass orb, the size of grape, shattered on the floor, and a billow of thick, green mist boiled up from it.

Alsayer turned back to the soldiers in front of him and swept a hand out, flinging a sonorous, rib-rattling thump. A narrow band of sonic energy took two soldiers in the chest, slashing through their chainmail and into their skin. The men's startled cries were quickly silenced as they were blasted back into their companions. Alsayer waved his arm again and unleashed another band of sonic power. The squad of soldiers retreated as a second group of them were torn open by the invisible assault. Their faces were locked in rictuses of panic, and the men were visibly trembling.

"Attack him!" bellowed Rew, trying to dodge around the growing column of foul smoke that emanated from Alsayer's broken pendant. "You have to attack him, you fools!"

In a fight with a spellcaster, it never paid to let them fling their magic with impunity. The only way to defeat a spellcaster was to charge right at them. You couldn't give them time or let them work the range of their attacks to their advantage, and above all, you couldn't show them your back. The soldiers, terrified of facing a spellcaster with an expert control of high magic, were doing exactly the opposite of what they should.

Rew started forward, but the green cloud roiled, and he was blocked as two giant conjurings stepped forth from the mist. Creatures conjured and then bound into the artifact were released on its destruction. There were two of them, and they stood sentry behind the spellcaster, forced to serve as his guardians. They walked on short legs and thick arms, their knuckles balancing them as they tottered closer to Rew and Zaine. On top of their heavily muscled shoulders were a second pair of arms, and round, hairless heads sat on squat necks. Despite the extra set of arms, they looked vaguely humanoid, except their mouths were filled with giant teeth that protruded from fat lips. They were an awful variety of imp, the largest Rew had ever seen, and he shuddered at the thought Alsayer might be capable of conjuring such. The monstrosities drooled and snarled, shuffling closer, their arms moving with the dexterity of an ape, their hind legs hopping along, landing in-between the arms and then pushing off to move them forward.

"W-What the..." stammered Zaine.

"Stay behind me," advised Rew, looking at the giant imps in disgust. Conjured from another plane, perhaps amalgamated from several creatures of that horrific world? He wasn't sure, but the huge imps' bodies bulged with taut muscle, and Rew thought it a safe assumption the things would be terrifically strong.

He moved forward, feinting a charge, and watched as the creatures' second set of hands reacted, following his movement, while the pair they used to walk kept propelling them closer.

One of the creatures reared up on its short legs and cried a high-pitched challenge, flexing both sets of arms and then dropping and charging him in a lurching trot. With no chance to form a strategy, Rew leapt at the monster, chopping at it with his longsword. The creature didn't pause, but it screamed in rage when his steel bit into its leading arm, drawing a line of crimson blood across its forearm. The imp scrambled sideways, as if confused, and Rew attempted to pursue it, but its companion reached for him, a massive paw grasping at his head.

Rew dodged away, cursing under his breath. Behind the two conjurings, he could see Baron Fedgley's soldiers being torn apart by Alsayer's magic. Rew had no love for the baron, and he suspected the man deserved everything that was going to happen to him, but whatever the spellcaster's goals, Rew was certain they would end in torment and loss for innocent people. Whatever Alsayer was attempting, Rew decided he would stop it.

Rew dodged to the side, and the two massive imps followed him, swiping at him with their giant hands. They were slow and evidently slow-witted, but they were huge. Even in the open throne room, there was little space he could slip by them to get to the spellcaster. And if he did, he would be facing high magic with those two things at his back. Rew growled and attacked again, taking the one on his left this time, spinning his longsword and then dragging it across the monster's knuckles, tugging against the bone and leaving a deep, bloody laceration.

He darted away, and the thing began a limping hop, its bleeding knuckle leaving crimson smears on the floor as it moved. It cried out, angry at the pain, but such a small cut would do nothing to disable the giant.

Ducking beneath a raised arm, Rew ran at the summoning on his right, slashing a wild blow to one of its upper arms, twirling his longsword, and stabbing deep into a lower appendage on the opposite side.

Retreating again, he spared a look back and saw he was already halfway to the entrance of the throne room. He was running out of area to dance around and avoid the imps. He feinted at them again, attempting to push them back on their heels, but they just kept coming. The one on the right was bleeding profusely, but for a creature that size, Rew guessed it would take a day to bleed out from the wounds he'd given.

He spied Alsayer between the mammoth imps' bodies and shouted, "Stop now, or I'll have no choice."

The spellcaster paused for a moment, glancing back over his shoulder. He grinned at Rew when he saw it was only a distraction.

"Enjoying my friends, cousin?" called the spellcaster. He gestured and flung another sonic lash to decapitate a charging soldier.

Cursing that his ploy failed, that Alsayer hadn't reacted by instinctively flinging magic at the perceived threat, Rew ran at the monsters again. His back was about to be at the wall, and if he didn't get through quickly, it would be too late. Whatever Alsayer was intending would be done.

The creatures turned as Rew ran into their midst, and he feverishly hacked his sword into arms, legs, and torsos as they came in range, carving brutal wounds but not having the reach to inflict a fatal blow.

He dodged as arms swung at him, crouching low then jumping a forearm that swept at his legs. While he was in the air, he caught the back of a fist from the second imp that smashed against his side. Rew was flung across the room. Tucking his shoulder, he thudded to the carpeted floor of the throne room. He rolled and sprang back to his feet, groaning at the twinge in his arm and shoulder where the imp's fist had struck him.

The conjurings came after him, seeking to pin him against the wall.

Rew launched himself at one, desperation forcing reckless action. Aiming low with his longsword, he pulled back as if he meant to unleash a strike powerful enough to sever the creature's arm. Perhaps hesitant now that he'd sliced several bloody gashes in it, the giant imp drew back the arm and reached forward with the top pair.

Rew jumped, stepping on the lower pair of limbs and hurtling over the upper pair. He swung a thunderous overhand blow at the imp, striking it on the top of the head. The edge of the blade met the thick skull of the monster, and Rew heard the crack of bone. He saw the look of stunned pain in the imp's eyes. The conjuring slumped, and Rew slammed into it, his thighs hitting its shoulder, the rest of his body flipping over. He rolled down the monster's back and thumped onto the floor.

Behind him, the beast collapsed, and then, the second one scooped him up.

Arms with incredible strength wrapped around him and lifted him into the air, trapping his own arm with his longsword against his side. His bones creaked beneath the crushing pressure, and he felt a drop of hot saliva on his neck. He imagined the imp's maw opening, preparing to clamp down on his head.

Frantically, Rew scrambled for his hunting knife, the creature's arms shifting, its hand gripping his shoulder. Another arm wrapped around his waist and sword arm. In a panic, Rew realized the imp was preparing to rip him in two.

He felt the bone hilt of his hunting knife, barely above the monster's arm, and yanked it free. Blindly, he stabbed behind his head, over and over, his blade meeting resistance, punching into flesh and bone. The imp howled in anger, until Rew felt the blade sink deep. He shoved on it, guessing he'd found an eye socket.

The imp wailed a bestial cry of agony and let go of him.

Rew fell, stumbling as his feet hit the floor. He spun, thrusting up with his longsword and burying the steel in the imp's chest. He twisted the blade and yanked it free.

"Rew!" shouted Zaine.

He flung himself to the side.

A black cloud filled with glittering sparks flashed above him and smashed into the wall, dozens of gleaming silver flakes embedding into the stone and sticking there like tiny saw blades. Had he not ducked, those flakes would have shredded him like arrows punching through a paper target.

Rew rolled across the floor and jumped up in time to see Alsayer raise an open palm to Baron Fedgley's wife. All around the imposing woman were dead soldiers. The baroness stood on the dais before her throne, her arms crossed in front of her, a pale shield of blue-white magic raised in defense. Her eyes blazed behind the translucent barrier, and she shouted, "You've gone too far, Spellcaster!"

Alsayer, a smile plastered on his face, launched a melon-sized globule of liquid fire at the baroness.

She stood calmly, ready to absorb his attack with her shield, but the fire hissed on contact with the barrier and burned through her magic in the space of a breath. Drips of molten fire fell onto one of the baroness' hands, and she screamed, looking in terrified shock as her wrist melted away to nothing but bone, and then, that fell away too. The end of the baroness' arm was nothing but ash.

Transfixed in pain and surprise, the baroness stood still, not defending the next globule of fire that took her directly in the face, incinerating her skull in an instant. Headless, the baroness wavered and then collapsed, her body tumbling down the short stairs of the dais.

"Mother!" cried Raif, bursting into the room from a side door in time to see the grisly death. Wild-eyed, the boy looked around the room before settling on Alsayer. He bellowed, "You!"

Raif charged, and Alsayer cackled.

Rew sprinted across the room, knowing he couldn't reach the

spellcaster fast enough, so he hurled himself at Raif, smashing his shoulder into the side of the charging fighter, taking him off his feet and knocking them both clear as a jagged spear of ice blew past them, shattering against the wall into a thousand shards that exploded in a cloud of sharp ice, cutting Rew's face and hands as they pelted against him. Rew rolled clear, only to see Cinda striding past him, her hands raised, coiling electrical energy crackling between her fingers.

"Stay back," snarled Baron Fedgley from before his throne, gesturing wildly at his daughter. "I just need another moment!"

Casually, Alsayer flung another of his dark clouds at Cinda, sparkling flakes inside of it shimmering like the stars at night.

Rew spun on his back, kicking the girl's feet out from under her.

She flopped onto her side, her lightning blinking out. Another of Alsayer's dark clouds speckled with the razor-sharp flakes flew overhead, tinkling into the wall behind them.

Baron Fedgley raised his arms, and the room darkened. "You've erred, Spellcaster. You should have struck me down first. I did not want to do this, not in my own hall, but you've left me no choice. Your time in this great game is over."

"King's Sake," cursed Rew, rising to his feet. Next to him, the younglings stirred, and he demanded, "Stay down!"

Either aware of what their father was capable of, or sensing the panic in the senior ranger's voice, they stayed down. Rew stood, frozen in indecision. He didn't know if he should attack the spellcaster who'd just murdered scores of soldiers and then had tried to kill him, or the necromancer who just called upon the power of a barrow wraith in the middle of a populated town.

"How many can you control?" wondered Alsayer, speaking to Baron Fedgley.

"Enough," snarled the baron, his face ruddy with exertion, his arms splayed, his hands curled like claws.

A chill wind swept through the room, and the terrifying wail of the undead sent a shiver down Rew's spine. He stepped toward

Fedgley then glanced down at the man's children who were huddled together on the floor, eyes wide at the sounds of the approaching wraiths.

Rew turned to Alsayer. The spellcaster was standing calmly, not attacking. Fedgley certainly had invoked defenses around himself, but with the ease Alsayer had burned through the baroness', Rew couldn't understand why Alsayer didn't even attempt to strike the baron. Was the man waiting for the wraiths to appear? That was madness. Why was he not—

"He's not going to kill you, Fedgley," warned Rew, raising his voice to be heard over the approaching cries of the wraiths. "He's going to capture you."

"He's going to try," boomed the baron, the man's mad grin baring his teeth, sweat already pouring from his bright red face. The baron's hands were raised, his fingers twitching as he pulled upon some invisible binding to the wraiths. He exuded confidence, certain that Alsayer could not deal with the spirits he was drawing into the room.

Rew shivered, unsure. Alsayer knew the baron had the capability to call upon wraiths, and he was waiting for them to arrive. He hadn't attacked the necromancer earlier because he'd known exactly what the man could do and that calling wraiths took time. Alsayer had planned this entire attack so that Baron Fedgley would muster his undead minions.

A stifling sense of fear assailed Rew, and he turned. Five terrifying shades drifted into the room. They floated, insubstantial but frighteningly real, like a passing shadow or a reflection of light off a mirror in a dark room. An agonizing wail echoed around the stone walls, though Rew knew it was only in his imagination. The wraiths were dead silent, and it was only their psychic energy that pierced his conscious and made him quake. The wraiths congregated on Alsayer, but the spellcaster waited calmly.

"These are from before the Great War?" the spellcaster asked, amused. "It's true, then. An excellent vintage indeed."

Rew watched in surprise as the spellcaster removed a small,

silver box from within his robes and opened it. The wraiths, like smoke pulled into a chimney, were sucked into the box. Alsayer snapped it shut as the fifth shade disappeared, and the room seemed suddenly brighter. "We'd hoped you could summon more than five, but so old, they will be quite powerful. It's a pity there are not more, but this began before any of us planned, didn't it? We'll work with what we have."

Rew started forward, raising his longsword, but Alsayer swung his hand, and a visceral thump resonated, echoing through the throne room. Rew wouldn't have been surprised if they'd heard it throughout the keep and even in the town.

A wall of pure sonic energy flew from the spellcaster, and Rew dropped to his knees, stunned Alsayer could call upon such a potent spell after the devastation he'd already wrought. The man's stamina was greater than the ranger ever would have guessed. Rew crouched, his arms rising to cover his ears in the instant it took the spell to smash into him.

He was shoved back along the floor, his body ringing like a bell struck by a mallet. His guts twisted, threatening to blast forth every meal he'd eaten in days. His eyes watered, and his ears pounded, on the verge of bursting. Then, the wall passed behind him, and he jumped to his feet.

Alsayer was at the dais, gripping the front of Baron Fedgley's intricately embroidered doublet. The spellcaster glanced at Rew and cut his eyes to where the baron's children were coughing and gagging after being swept across the room by the sonic wall.

"Remember, cousin, the power of high magic lies in the strength of the blood," said Alsayer. He twisted his free hand. Next to him and the baron, a circular vortex appeared, violently churning purple slashed with silver and gold. "At least two of the princes are interested in the baron and his talents. It won't be long before they turn their eyes to his progeny. Watch the children for me, will you?"

Alsayer flung the startled baron through the open portal, winked at Rew, and then stepped through himself. The opening in the fabric of reality winked shut, and Rew fell to his knees, staring in shock at where Alsayer had just vanished.

The throne room was silent, but the keep was filled with alarmed shouts and the sounds of running feet. Outside the windows and the walls, he could hear the roar of battle. The bells atop the keep's highest tower rang frantically, signaling no pre-arranged message, but one that was nonetheless understood. Panic.

Rew looked to Raif and Cinda and saw they were still alive, though looking as if they wished they were not. Raif was on his hands and knees, coughing viscous yellow bile. Cinda was curled on her side, clutching at her stomach, her eyes squeezed tightly shut. Without steeling themselves against it, Alsayer's spell could have crushed their internal organs, destroying critical parts of their anatomy on the inside, but they were breathing. Their lungs were working. Rew thought that was a good sign. He suspected Alsayer pulled his punch and released his hold upon the magic the moment it passed Rew. The devious bastard hadn't lied about that. He wanted the children alive because he was planning to come back for them.

"Zaine," barked Rew. The girl ducked her head around the doorway where she'd been hiding just outside of the throne room. Rew pointed at Raif and Cinda. "Run to the arcanist's tower and tell Anne that they were struck by a sonic wall."

Zaine, her jaw hanging near her chest as she saw the aftermath of the fight in the room, didn't seem to have heard.

"Get them to Anne!" shouted Rew, "and when I'm done, you'd better still be here."

"What—What will you do?" asked the thief.

"Falvar is under attack from an army of the Dark Kind," growled Rew, glancing at the empty dais and the forty bodies of mutilated soldiers lying around the throne room. "Since no one else is left, I believe I'd better go assume command and organize a defense of the city."

Chapter Twenty

Rew strode out of the throne room, out of the building at the center of the keep, and into the courtyard in front of the still-closed gate. Fifty men were milling about in the open space and atop the walls. He demanded, "Who's in charge here?"

The men blinked at him, horrified, and he looked down. He was covered in the blood of the two imps he'd battled, and maybe a little bit from the thief in the Ralcrist's tower. Combined, it was a lot of blood.

He growled, "Well?"

"I am," said a man, taking a hesitant step forward. "I am Sergeant Gage—What, ah, what's going on inside of the keep? We heard noises, but no one has come out… Could've been, well, some of the lads thought it was thunder. We couldn't abandon our post to go find out. Dark Kind are outside. We sent two messengers—"

Rew interrupted the man. "We'll speak of it later. For now, you should know that Commander Broyce left the city and has not returned. Baron Fedgley is indisposed. I am Rew, the King's Ranger, and by the authority of the king, I am taking control of Falvar's garrison. Can anyone tell me the disposition of the narjag forces outside of these walls?"

"The baron is indisposed?" asked the unnamed sergeant. He sounded incredulous.

"You haven't received orders from him, and the two messengers you sent haven't returned, all in the middle of an attack by an army of Dark Kind," snapped Rew. He looked around the men. "If the baron was capable of coming out here and taking charge, don't you think he would have by now? I am sorry to say those messengers are not going to return. Surely one of you was on duty at the gates or in the throne room when the baron received me yesterday. One of you must know that I am who I claim."

The man in charge shifted uncomfortably.

"Anyone have family out there?" cried Rew. "If we don't act, thousands of people are going to die for no reason."

"He is the King's Ranger," said a voice from the side. "I saw him meeting with the baron yesterday."

"Do you really have authority to take command of the garrison?" wondered the sergeant.

"Probably," said Rew, "but we don't have time to go sort it out with the legal scholars now, do we?" Growing frustrated, he shoved through the crowd of soldiers and climbed the stairs to the wall above the gate. Immediately, his heart leapt into this throat. "King's Sake, you fools! I don't give a damn about your protocol. What are you still doing behind these walls?"

The city gates of Falvar had been breached, and in front of them, Dark Kind were furiously storming through. A narrow line of soldiers held the street before the gate, but even from afar, it was evident they couldn't hold long. There were as many soldiers lying on the ground as standing, and beyond the gates, even in the pouring rain, Rew could see the dark mass of more narjags attempting to force their way into the breach.

"Most of 'em is mercenaries," hissed a man by Rew's side.

Rew scowled and turned to find the sergeant had ascended the stairs with him. The man was looking out, hopeless, scared.

The sergeant continued. "The baron has put severe punishments in place for breaking the rules, and the mercenaries don't have family or friends in Falvar. They're more afraid of the gibbet than the Dark Kind."

"I'm going to order this gate opened," called Rew, raising his voice over the tumult of the rain and the battle so that every man in the courtyard could hear him. "When I do, I want archers moving two blocks off to the left then making directly for the walls. Get up on the battlements, shoot the narjags outside. You can't miss. Thin them out. Get them looking up instead of ahead. Every man that doesn't have a bow is behind me. We're going to assist the men holding the gate, and if we can find an engineer, we need to clear space for them to get those doors repaired. If there is any man that does not do as I instruct, I'm going to come find and personally hang them the moment this fight is over."

Around him, men swallowed and glanced at their fellows.

"Ranger," said a man down in the courtyard, "you might have authority over the baron's men, but most of us is—"

"I'm the King's Ranger, Soldier, not the baron's. You may not be from Falvar, but you are a subject to the king, are you not?" interrupted Rew. He raised his longsword so that the men could see the dark blood staining its length. "Besides, as far as I'm concerned, you signed the baron's contract, you're wearing the baron's colors, so you're the baron's men. As the baron's men, you've a responsibility to this city and these people. If you think to shirk that responsibility, tell me, and we'll settle this now, so I don't have to waste time tracking you down later."

Rew pointed the tip of his longsword down at the man, looking at him blank-faced. He'd hoped he could appeal to the men's honor, to the idea that they needed to rush out and play the hero, but if that didn't work, he would do it the other way. There was no time for anything else.

The man below raised his hands, backed up, and protested, claiming it wasn't what he meant. His companions shifted away from him, not looking at the man or at Rew.

Rew could see some of them looked resigned to their fates— the mercenaries. Others looked scolded and ashamed—the locals.

They knew what was happening outside the gates, even if they'd been too scared to open them on their own. Whether they were scared of the penalty for breaking protocol or scared of the mercenaries stabbing them in the back if they tried, Rew didn't care. If need be, he would give them something to really be afraid of.

Shaking his head in disgust, Rew pushed his way down the stairs, calling for men to get the gates open and for the archers to grab a second bundle of arrows from the storage lockers alongside the courtyard. If they were going to get on the walls and start firing into the narjags, they may as well make sure they had plenty of shafts.

Rew walked to the center of the gate and waited. The cranks turned, and the chains pulled tight. Inch by inch, the huge wooden slabs swung open, and the steel portcullis rose.

Rew guessed the soldiers had managed to get the barriers closed a lot quicker than they were getting them open. Cowards, he wanted to call them, but the truth was that most of them were just following orders. It was easier to do that, to lead where someone else pointed, particularly when that way seemed to be the safer route. It was why they were opening the gates now, because Rew had taken responsibility. Without someone to direct them, too many people were willing to sit there and watch others die. As long as they had their own walls to hide behind, a place to run to. An escape. As long as—

He grunted and forced the line of thought away. It would do him no good, thinking like that, it was too close to... He shook it off. There was nothing but trouble down that road.

The gates had swung open, and as soon as the portcullis rose to shoulder height, Rew moved forward, ducking beneath it, and stood on the other side. Ahead of him was the long, broad avenue which led directly to the northern gate. He could see the narjags swarming, threatening to overwhelm the thin band of defenders.

"Hope you men know how to run," shouted Rew.

Then, he broke into a trot, the curtain of rain falling around him, his boots splashing through shallow puddles. He gave a grim smile at the clink of chainmail and the heavy stomp of booted feet. The soldiers fell in behind him, and he slowed his pace slightly, setting a pace the armored men could match.

They rushed down the avenue, the soldiers around him breathing heavily and struggling before they were halfway to the gate. As they ran, they saw their fellows ahead of them falling. They saw the swirling mass of Dark Kind that threatened to overwhelm the town. Maybe some of them had families in the buildings and structures around them. Maybe some of them came to the simple conclusion that their fate was tied inexorably to that of Falvar. Maybe they finally understood what it was they faced, the Dark Kind, anathema to all natural life. Maybe some of them were scared of what the ranger would do if they didn't join him, but as they ran, Rew began to feel the determination growing in the men. This might not be their place, and they might not have been hired for this fight, but the Dark Kind were their enemy, and it was impossible to see them so close and not know it. Their guts would be telling them to fight or run. Luckily, these men were ready to fight.

Men died, and narjags howled. A handful of the awful creatures broke loose, racing down the avenue, weaving drunkenly as if they couldn't decide which homes to break into first, which place to begin their slaughter.

And then Rew and the soldiers from the keep arrived. Speeding up, jogging out ahead of the others to give himself room with his longsword, Rew met the first narjag, swinging his blade and hacking through the thing's neck. Then, he continued the motion and skewered another, twisting the dying creature's body as he ran past and jerking his blade free. He darted through the scattered narjags that had gotten loose, trusting the men behind him to take care of them, and he headed directly for the back of the line of Falvar's defenders.

Rew picked a gap that had broken open in the line and plunged in, drawing his hunting knife as he slammed into the first of the narjags. He punched a fist into the chest of one of the short creatures and tried to shove it back to give himself and the other men room. Rew felt like he was pushing a wagon. He realized there were too many Dark Kind pressing against the backs of their first rank, so the ranger changed tactics and slashed his hunting knife across the throat of the startled narjag. He began to thrust over its shoulder with his longsword. The elegant steel weapon moved like a needle sliding in and out of a length of cotton, stitching its way across the narjags, felling half a dozen of them in moments.

The narjags, attacking in an unorganized, ferocious pack, had sent the soldiers reeling, and where the men still stood, they did so crouched behind heavy wooden shields. The soldiers were attempting to hold their ground, but their efforts to fight back were stilted by the power of their fear. Sensing the weakness, the narjags came at them with little thought, clawing and biting at each other as often as the men in vicious attempts to force their way farther into the town.

The Dark Kind must have already sensed victory and were not prepared for the violence brought by the ranger. Rew tossed aside the body of the narjag he'd been stabbing over the shoulder of and stepped forward, using the length of his longsword to thrust into the second rank, holding his hunting knife close to deflect any strikes from narjag spears.

Around him, he felt the lines flex as the men from the keep joined the fray. Rested and motivated, perhaps embarrassed it took so long, they joined their exhausted brethren and gave them hope.

Rew pressed forward, stabbing and swinging his longsword in narrow strikes, holding his knife close. In such tight quarters, much of his skill was wasted, but on the other hand, every time he attacked, he couldn't help but find Dark Kind flesh to slide his blade into.

Beside him, the soldiers of Falvar began to advance as well, bolstered by fresh arms and swords. In minutes, they'd pushed the smaller narjags back to the gates. As the line of men narrowed and the flow of Dark Kind was bottled up in the broken-open gate, Rew took a moment to step back behind the line and look up at the walls. There, dozens of archers lined the battlements, frantically firing arrows down between the crenellations. From such a distance, with so many targets, even a child would hit something. Rew knew the archers would be wreaking devastation amongst the Dark Kind.

The sergeant who'd been in charge at the keep stumbled up beside Rew. He'd gained a cut on his scalp since Rew had last seen him, but otherwise looked hale. "Sir," he breathed, wiping rain and blood from his face, "the archers just called down to me. There's still one hundred of the bastards outside, but half of them are wounded, and they're breaking up. They're falling back, sir. Should we give pursuit and chase them out over the barrowlands?"

Rew looked around. With the narjags outside fleeing, they would have little trouble cleaning up the handful still within the walls of the town. The archers were healthy, and most of the men from the keep appeared to be in good shape, but the men who'd been guarding the gates from the beginning had suffered terribly. Dozens of them were lying dead or wounded on the cobblestone street. The sergeant didn't know it yet, but another two score of the baron's soldiers had been torn apart by Alsayer in the throne room. Rew had to assume that the men standing with him were the only soldiers left to defend Falvar.

"No sign of Commander Broyce's company?" he asked the sergeant.

"None, sir," replied the man.

Rew shook his head. "We don't have the men to take the fight out into the barrowlands, Sergeant. We've got to tend to Falvar before we go looking for more trouble. The first thing we need to do is get someone to secure this gate, and we need men on these walls, Sergeant. We cannot allow night to fall without every corner of this town… Blessed Mother, has anyone reported on the settlement by the river? Were they hit?"

"I-I don't know, sir." stammered the man. "Sir, I'm just a sergeant. Should, ah…"

"Is there anyone here who outranks you, Sergeant?" asked Rew.

The man looked around helplessly.

Rew noticed that several other men had clustered nearby, listening to his instructions. He called to them, "Which sergeant was born in Falvar and has been in the baron's service the longest?"

They all looked around confused, and the man Rew had been speaking to raised his hand. Despite being draped in chainmail, the crimson blood on his scalp, and the filthy black blood of the narjags on the edge of his broadsword, he had the look of a tradesman rather than a warrior. His eyes looked sharp, though, and he kept his head high. "I suppose that'd be me."

"Sergeant," stated Rew, "by my authority as the King's Ranger, you are now a captain. What's your name, Captain?"

"Gage, sir, Serg— Captain Gage."

"Good, Captain Gage," said Rew. "I want you to assign one sergeant to establish a triage area for the wounded and ensure anyone with skill at healing is brought there. I want another man responsible for carting the wounded to the area, working with the healers to separate the wounded into groups, and collecting whatever supplies they require. Put a third man in charge of the watch and this gate. That man is tasked with gathering whatever soldiers are needed and to conscript from the townspeople if necessary. We must make sure every span of this wall is covered and nothing gets within five hundred paces of Falvar without us seeing it. And finally, a fourth man needs to get out to the settlement by the bridge and bring those people in. Let them take whatever they can, lock down their homes and shops as best they can, but every man, woman, and child should be behind these gates before the sun sets. We don't want to incite panic amongst the people by dragging them in by force, but those narjags could come back under the cover of night."

The new captain swallowed and slowly nodded.

"Assign your men now, Captain," said Rew. "If you don't have enough sergeants, make some more."

Captain Gage turned, surveyed his fellows, and began designating roles. Then, he began immediately berating them for not moving quickly enough and called after them as they started to hurry off, collecting their own assistants and issuing the next layer of orders. "Hurry up, now, boys. You heard the man. You've got an hour, then, ah, I want a report in an hour, and you'd better tell me you've made progress! Go, go!"

The soldiers scurried about, still disorganized and afraid, but men like them required direction, and they were finally getting it. Rew hoped that in a little time, they would fall into their roles and handle them adequately enough.

Captain Gage turned to Rew. "And me, sir, what would you have me do?"

"I want you to oversee these efforts, Captain," said Rew. "Make sure it's all done properly. I'm afraid that will mean a long night for you, but first, you're coming with me to the keep. I may need your help figuring out what the hell just happened."

Chapter Twenty-One

Rew stopped by the arcanist's tower first but found Anne and Jon had left. Other than their disappearance, little had changed. There were no new signs of violence, which Rew took to mean that Zaine had found the healer, and they'd determined Jon would be easier to move than the other two.

Captain Gage, following quietly in his wake, gaped like a dying fish at the wreckage in the room. "What—What happened here, sir?"

"Wait until we get to the throne room," replied Rew.

The newly promoted captain clearly wanted to ask more, but he refrained, and when they got to the throne room, he panted like he was waking from a terrible nightmare. Rew worried for a moment the soldier might be having a heart failure, but after a while, the other man got himself under control.

In the throne room, they found sheets had been hung to give some privacy at the edge of the room, and servants were scurrying in with piles of pillows, pitchers of water, and towels. Jon was slumped in a chair against the opposite wall, where petitioners could sit while awaiting their turn with the baron. The young ranger looked sweaty and in pain. His gaze was locked on the corpses of Baron Fedgley's soldiers, but when he heard

Rew enter, he tried to stand. Rew waved him down and walked over.

"I'll live," claimed the junior ranger through gritted teeth.

"Glad to hear it," said Rew.

"The attack outside of the city?" asked Jon.

"It was a bit ugly, but we've chased off the Dark Kind," responded Rew. "They're working on securing the walls now. Anne?"

"In with the nobles," said Jon, gesturing at the shroud across the room. "The staff is checking on me. I'm all right out here if you want to go in. Just need a bit of rest, I think."

Rew nodded and turned toward the sheets.

"Where's the baron and—" Captain Gage cut off as Rew pointed to the immolated body of the baroness. Even without her head, it was clear from her attire who it was. The captain staggered to the side and was violently ill.

"Can we get a sheet over the baroness' body?" Rew asked a passing servant. To Captain Gage, he said, "Catch up when you can."

Rew walked to the curtained area and ducked inside. Raif and Cinda were both there, propped up on pillows, their clothing drenched, their hair matted from sweat. Their faces were bright red, and their breathing was heavy, but their eyes were open and turned to him as he entered the enclosed space.

Anne was tending to a small censer which spilled a nearly transparent smoke. She was feeding herbs into it and then waving the smoke toward the two ailing nobles. Noticing him enter, Anne remarked, "They said Alsayer hit them with some sort of invisible wall. Said it felt like being hit with the real thing. They had severe internal bruising, but luckily, none of their organs were damaged irreparably. I don't think it would have been fatal, but it would have taken months to recover if I wasn't here."

"Sounds about right," confirmed Rew. "Alsayer used a twist on the sonic lash, I believe. I've never seen anything quite like it. He's more dangerous than I anticipated."

The ranger left it there and didn't comment on the destruction laying outside of the curtained alcove. Anne would have seen the scores of dead bodies on her way in. Rew had known Alsayer was a killer, and he'd known the man was treacherous, but he hadn't taken the time to see what was happening. He should have known that Alsayer was lying, was using them to get access to his target. He should have... He should have what? He'd known Alsayer was a back-stabbing bastard, but even if he'd suspected a betrayal was looming, he never would have guessed what the spellcaster had planned.

"They said this sonic wall struck you as well," remarked the empath, jolting him from his thoughts.

"It did," he admitted.

She paused and turned, looking at him over her shoulder.

"I'm fine," he assured her. "A few scrapes and some bruises that are feeling tight, but nothing worse than I'd get in a normal day's work."

Anne frowned at him, disbelieving, but he returned her stare. Snorting, she turned back to her herbs and her censer.

"How?" asked Cinda.

Anne shushed her, but the girl kept talking.

"That wall struck you full on before it hit us. I could see it warping around you," Cinda said. "He meant it for you, not us, and you took the brunt of it. We were merely caught the wave that broke over you. It still nearly killed us."

"He meant to slow me down," acknowledged Rew.

"How did you fight it?" asked Cinda.

Rew frowned, not responding, and when she opened her mouth to ask further, he held up a hand and explained, "There are a few tricks one can do to defend against high magic. Some are simple physical acts like dodging out of the way. Others are similar, like bearing the weight of an attack where you're most able to absorb it. Taking the blow on your shoulder instead of the face, for example. Then, there are more complicated responses that can diminish the effect of a spell. Cantrips one can whisper, wardings one can maintain, ways to anchor oneself to your surroundings and leverage external strength."

"Low magic," gasped Cinda. "You're saying you used low magic to combat high magic."

"Aye, I used low magic," agreed Rew. He gestured to Anne. "Nobles assume high magic is superior, and many times, that's the case. But not always. Low magic can be just as effective when used in the right circumstances. When someone knows what they're doing…" He shrugged, hoping he'd given enough to satisfy the girl.

Cinda made as if to speak again, but Anne shushed her. "Girl, you're right, you nearly died. I know you have questions, but they can wait. High magic, low magic, you're not doing anything with either one of them before you recover."

"Our father?" asked Raif, rasping out the question.

Rew winced. "Taken by Alsayer."

Raif closed his eyes.

Cinda whispered, "I saw what happened to mother."

"There's nothing anyone can do for her," said Rew. "I had someone put a sheet over her body. The servants will treat her with respect, and when things settle, you can make arrangements for proper—"

Behind him, the curtains parted, and Captain Gage entered. He gasped at the sight of the younglings and immediately offered a bow.

"Senior Ranger," asked the captain, "if the baroness was the body out there, then where is the baron?"

"He was betrayed and captured by the spellcaster that came bearing warnings yesterday," explained Rew. "Captain, Raif here is Baron Fedgley's heir. For now, he's in command."

The captain bowed again, a nervous hand rising inadvertently to tug at the collar of his chainmail. Raif and Cinda stared back at the soldier, lying slumped on their backs on the floor of the throne room, propped against a pile of pillows. It was a pathetic sight, all around.

Raif raised his hand and said, "Ah, Raif Fedgley. Pleased to meet you. I, ah…"

"I'll retain command for the moment, I suppose," said Rew, rubbing his hand over his freshly shorn head and looking down at the boy. "Raif, Cinda, this is Captain Gage, newly promoted to the role. He's the most senior man I can find in your service, and he seems a good sort. I took temporary command of the garrison to fight off the Dark Kind, but as soon as you're back on your feet and able to shoulder your responsibilities, I'll happily return command to you, or I can grant the authority to Captain Gage, if you'd prefer."

Raif stared back like a rabbit surprised by a fox.

"Dark Kind… what do you mean? What has happened?" asked Cinda. "I mean, aside from… from what happened here?"

"You haven't heard?" muttered Rew. He turned to pace but stopped. With five of them in the curtained area, there was nowhere to go. "Where were you before… Ah, I've more questions than we have time. Of course you haven't heard. The city was attacked. Hundreds of narjags mustered outside shortly after Commander Broyce left with the bulk of the garrison. A pack of thieves snuck in and struck down Arcanist Ralcrist. Then, they used his staff to destroy the artifact he was maintaining that dampened high magic in this vicinity. When the crystal was destroyed, Alsayer attacked your parents, killing your mother, capturing your father, and escaping through a portal. Following the attack, I ran out and saw that there was no one left in authority. I took command, and we defended the city against the narjags. The Dark Kind were driven off, but there are still close to one hundred of them loose in the barrowlands. We've made preparations to secure the city and provide what care we can to the injured. We're bringing in everyone from the outlying areas, and I believe that's everything."

"Arcanist Ralcrist is dead?" asked Cinda, a catch in her voice.

Rew nodded. He watched the young noblewoman, thinking she seemed more upset about the arcanist than her own parents.

He supposed that before she'd been fostered to Worgon in Yarrow, Ralcrist must have been her tutor in high magic. Her tutor and perhaps a parental figure as well. After speaking with Baron Fedgley and learning the man had fostered his children to his enemy as a distraction, Rew found it hard to imagine baron and baroness had ever shown much love.

"We have to go after Alsayer," hissed Raif. "We have to recover Father."

"Maybe," said Rew. "First, you've the town to look after. You've hundreds of soldiers to bury. You've got to get in touch with Commander Broyce and get him back to help fortify Falvar. Then, there are still the Dark Kind roaming the barrowlands. They must be hunted but only after the people are safe."

"I will not leave Father with that... that man," growled Raif, tears leaking from his eyes.

"Quiet," said Anne, wafting more of the smoke in his direction. "You're larger and it will take you longer to heal than your sister. My healing will be most effective in the first few hours, and the more you speak and move about, the longer your recovery. So stay still."

"With Mother and Father gone..." stammered Cinda, "I don't know where to start."

"Start by healing," advised Rew. He turned to Captain Gage. "The baron is in enemy hands. His children were subject to a magical attack but will recover. The baroness is dead. There are still Dark Kind out in the barrowlands, and we don't know where Commander Broyce is or, frankly, if he still lives. You understand the situation, Captain?"

His lips twisting in consternation, Captain Gage nodded.

"Get back into the city, then," instructed Rew. "Get it into order, but share little of what you saw here. For now, the rumors won't be any worse than the truth. I want the men focused on the Dark Kind and rebuilding the gate, not on what's happening in the keep or with the baron."

"Father," croaked Raif. "You are talking about our father."

"I know, lad," said Rew, turning back to him. "I know. We've got to sort Falvar first. We'll sort Falvar, and then… then we'll talk about the baron."

The captain ducked out, and Anne looked up at Rew, a question in her eyes.

He sighed and looked away. He was quiet for a moment before turning back to her, "I want you to care for the younglings, Anne. When he left, he told me… Alsayer isn't done with them. That man and his plans! These children… They're at the heart of it, Anne."

"I will do as much as I can," promised the empath.

"They need to be healthy," insisted Rew. "Quickly, Anne."

Cinda and Raif looked between the ranger and the empath, confused. Neither Rew nor Anne bothered to explain.

"Healthy even at the expense of others?" she asked quietly. "During the attack outside, how many were—"

Rew took a step forward and put a hand on Anne's shoulder. His mind screamed at him to turn away, to leave instructions for Captain Gage, to flee. He could feel it, a relentless pull. He could feel the swirl of need building around him. He closed his eyes. "At the expense of others. Alsayer felt it, and I can feel it too. I don't know how, but they've a further role to play in this drama. Falvar is just the beginning."

Anne drew a deep breath, let it go, and stuck more herbs into her censer. "I understand."

Nodding, Rew stepped back. The pull was like a fishing line, hooked into him, tugging, inescapable.

He frowned. "Where is Zaine? I didn't see her outside. She was supposed to wait with you."

"I don't know," said Anne. "She came to find me and helped me bring Jon here. I looked at the back of her head again, and she didn't seem badly hurt…"

Rew sighed. "If Captain Gage needs me, I'll be back shortly. I've got to go collect a—No, I've got to go collect two thieves."

Rew walked back to Arcanist Ralcrist's tower, Jon following in his wake. The younger ranger was moving slow, and his hand kept rising unconsciously toward his chest where the thief had stabbed him, but he was moving more comfortably than he could have several hours before. It seemed the movement was helping to stretch his muscles, loosening them from the strain of Anne's healing. After the short walk, his breathing was even, and Jon gave Rew an encouraging nod before they stepped into the room.

"Stay behind me and just watch, no matter what we find," warned the senior ranger.

Jon murmured agreement, and Rew ducked inside.

He'd tried to talk Jon out of coming, knowing the man needed time to rest, but the younger ranger insisted, perhaps feeling guilty that Zaine had slipped away while he was there. It was true that she had, but that didn't mean the man was in any kind of condition to do something about it. Jon felt responsible for her, which he should, but the situation was what it was. Jon's presence was more likely to be a burden than a help. It hadn't mattered what Rew said, though. The younger ranger had insisted on coming. Rew had tried to drag Jon to Anne, to discuss it with the healer, knowing she would refuse to let her patient go, but Jon must have known that as well. He'd started hobbling off toward the arcanist's tower the moment Rew had mentioned Anne. Now, Rew was responsible for the young man.

Shaking himself, Rew forced his attention back to the present and to the wrecked room in Arcanist Ralcrist's tower.

The dead thieves were still there, along with the body of Ralcrist himself. The crystal was still shattered. Nothing had changed since Rew had last been in the room except Jon was walking about instead of lying on death's door.

Rew walked out onto the arcanist's balcony and looked down at the lawn where the thief had made his escape. From the second floor, it was obvious where he'd dropped from the tree onto the soft turf. There were marks in the soil even a layman could spot. Rew followed the footsteps he could see to where they disappeared into the keep. It wouldn't take a ranger to follow the trail across the grass, but not even Rew could see footprints on bare stone unless there were some traces of mud or crushed grass left on the thief's boot. It was worth looking for, though Rew did not have great hope they could follow any signs for very far.

Rew glanced at Jon, assessing the younger ranger. Jon was in no shape to shimmy down the tree outside, so Rew took them back out into the hall where they found a stairwell down to the lower level.

"You think Zaine went this way?" questioned Jon as they reached the floor below and started walking, looking for any marks the escaped murderer had left. "Why'd she leave? What do you think she's doing?"

Rew shrugged. "I think there are two possibilities. One, she may have gone looking for the thieves who betrayed her. They knocked her over the head on the way in, remember? Perhaps she wants revenge, or maybe they owe her some reward. Two, she's afraid of the consequences of helping the thieves into the keep, so she fled and is trying to find a place in the town to hide until she can escape Falvar."

"Fled from us?" questioned the younger ranger.

"She was involved in a conspiracy against the baron," reminded Rew. "The baroness died along with hundreds of soldiers. Zaine might try to explain to the soldiers that she was coerced, but what are the chances they will believe her? The penalty for conspiring against nobility is death, even when it's not successful. She's guilty, Jon. I cannot say I blame her if that's the reason she fled."

The younger ranger swallowed, evidently his feelings for the girl clouding the facts of her actions. After a moment, he asked, "If she's in hiding, how will we find her?"

Glancing back at Jon, Rew shrugged again. "Find someone she knows. Find out who would be willing to hide her. We use the tools of the investigators, but I'd rather we find her before they do."

The younger ranger nodded.

"You feel responsible for her," said Rew, pausing to crouch down and peer at a rug that ran down the center of the stone hallway.

"She slipped away on my watch," remarked Jon.

"Anne's watch," reminded Rew.

"You won't blame Anne," retorted Jon.

Rew stood, his eyes picking out a series of tiny smudges of dirt. Moving slowly so as not to miss any of them, walking bent half over, Rew followed the trail.

"I was in position in the throne room," continued Jon, "I should have known better when I saw her walking out. I should have stopped her."

"You were injured," said Rew. "You almost died."

"You would have stopped her," replied Jon.

Rew didn't respond.

"I'll get her back," declared Jon. "Whatever we have to do, I'll get her back."

Rew snorted. "And then what?"

"She'll…"

"Do you mean to protect her or punish her?" asked Rew. "We're not in the territory, Ranger. What happens to Zaine will be up to the Fedgleys, not us."

"I—We can question her, get to the bottom of this, find out what she knows," said Jon. "Before anyone decides anything, we should know the truth. She could have been forced into their conspiracy. It may not be her fault."

"It's worth keeping in mind," said Rew, "that the answers you get from the lass may not be the ones you want to hear."

Rew followed the faint scuffs of mud to a door. He looked up and down the hall and then opened the door. It led to another hall, another door, and then exited into an open space that circled between the buildings of the keep and the wall that encircled the place. Fifty paces from them, a handful of guards were milling about near the small private gate Zaine and the thieves had entered.

"Well, we can assume the man is no longer inside of the keep, I think," said Rew.

Jon grunted, and they walked toward the soldiers.

The men looked up.

Rew asked them, "What did you find?" When they looked unsure if they should answer, Rew added, "We're tracking the perpetrators of an attack against the baron and his family. It appears they came this way."

The soldiers, evidently deciding there was no reason not to share what they knew, pointed to the bodies of two armored men and then to the open gate. "Looks like someone attacked these men as they were escaping, sir."

"They came in this way," corrected Rew. "They killed these men when they entered, not when they left. There were witnesses who saw it happen, but you're right. I believe this is also the way the assassins exited. The gate had been shut after they slipped inside."

"Oh..." said one of the soldiers.

"Your group familiar with Sergeant Gage?" asked Rew. "He's been promoted to captain, and at the moment, I believe he's the most senior official in Falvar. Send a runner to find him and tell him what happened here. And men? Close this gate once we're outside."

Rew and Jon stepped around the confused guards and left through the open gate.

"Zaine could have exited there just as easily as the thief," said Jon.

Rew didn't respond. He was looking around the area, seeing it would be impossible to track the faint traces of dirt through the public streets of Falvar.

He suggested, "Let's go to the market."

Chapter Twenty-Two

They walked through deserted stalls. The vendors had gathered what they could and closed quickly. Rew guessed all of them were currently huddled in their homes, doors barred, families clustered around them. Word that the Dark Kind had breached the gates would have sent the citizens of Falvar scrambling. Most of them would have hidden behind whatever rudimentary barriers they could quickly erect. A few of them would have rushed out to help the soldiers. None of them would be shopping.

"What are we looking for?" asked Jon.

Rew shrugged and did not reply. He didn't know.

In the forest, he was comfortable. After a decade as the eastern territory's senior ranger, he knew the wilderness like the back of his hand. In any wild place, he felt more at home than in a town. Not that he was unfamiliar with towns and the peculiar rules that they operated by, but the signs and the tells were a mystery to him. Rew didn't know the first thing about how to identify a thieves' lair or how to get in contact with members of the thieves' guild. He'd never needed to know such a thing, and even if he had, he suspected that sort of information wouldn't be widely shared. They had to do something, though, and going to the place he'd first seen Zaine and the thieves stalking through the town seemed a logical place to start.

He'd watched as Zaine had appeared, the thieves in tow, and they'd come from the far side of the market. There wasn't a main road there going to and from the city's gates, so whatever lair the thieves had, Rew guessed it was somewhere within the city walls. It wasn't on the far side of the keep, and it wasn't easily accessible to the most heavily tracked thoroughfares that ran through Falvar. If it had been, the thieves would have come from the other direction or used busier streets. They needed the flow of the other citizens to mask their movement.

That narrowed the search considerably, but it left them with five by ten square blocks of Falvar that Rew suspected could hide the thieves' lair. Fifty individual blocks, hundreds of buildings. He grimaced, thinking about searching each of them, but maybe they would see something or find some person who might know more.

At the edge of the market, Rew stared down an empty street that he thought was where Zaine and the others had come from. It was lined with small shops that would have been doing brisk business while the market was open. Now, they were shuttered, their owners barricaded inside of the stores or in the apartments over them. Those places were too small, Rew thought, to hide a meeting place for the thieves. They would want something larger, somewhere it wouldn't be unusual for people to walk in and out of. It would have to be open all hours as much of their comings and goings would be at night.

A shop with a back entrance? He frowned. Maybe. Would the neighbors complain, or would they be content to have suspicious characters operating next door? Rew guessed the thieves wouldn't rob their neighbors. No, they would be good to those who lived in the immediate vicinity, hoping to tamp down suspicions and to give no reason anyone would go scuttling off to the baron's soldiers. The thieves couldn't rely on goodwill alone, though. They would need secrecy.

Rew and Jon strolled down the street, eyeing the small shops and the housing where the proprietors lived above. An inn, maybe? It would offer an excuse to have strangers coming in and out at odd hours. It would also give the thieves reason not to spend time building relationships with those they shared a street with. Inns had ale, and he supposed a thief might enjoy a celebratory drink following a heist as much as he did after an expedition.

This quarter of the town didn't seem to have any inns, though, and as they walked, he realized it was because those places were clustered near the city gates or the keep. Travelers would have no reason to venture into some quiet, residential quarter of Falvar to find a bed for the night. There were taverns instead where people could get a mug of ale or wine and a simple dinner.

A tavern, then? It offered many of the advantages of an inn, and he saw some of them on the corners of the streets they passed, but he kept walking, unsure what else he was looking for, but not convinced the thieves' guild would be upstairs of some tavern. He wasn't sure what signs he searched for, or if he'd recognize them when he saw them, but in the forest, he'd learned to trust his instincts. Out in the wilderness, it was the absence of a thing that sometimes was just as important as the thing itself. Animals moved naturally, looking for food, mates, and rest, until their base senses alerted them of a threat. People, civilized and removed from the forest, lost that incredible ability to know when something was wrong. Their higher skills robbed from the lower ones, Rew supposed, but he had learned to watch the animals, to watch them react to the signs he himself could not detect.

The movement around the taverns, as quiet as they were, did not seem suspicious. Most of the ones he saw were open, and hesitantly, people were ducking their heads in. Maybe to get a drink to steady their nerves or maybe to glean information about what had happened. The Dark Kind had attacked and were repelled. What had occurred at the keep? Taverns in a town like Falvar would be central places for gossip, the way people got their news, and Rew saw they appeared to be operating as usual.

Like animals at the watering hole, the people were approaching, and they did not seem afraid of what they would find there.

He kept walking, Jon pacing at his side, both of them quiet.

Then, Rew stopped. Down a dead-end cross street, there was a large building that looked much like an inn except all of its windows were shuttered. It was three stories tall, and as Rew watched, a man stepped outside, glanced around, and tugged at his belt to make sure it was secure and still held up his trousers. The man walked off. In the cul-de-sac, Rew spied a decrepit-looking tavern, an herbalist, and a coin changer.

"Let's stop in there," he suggested.

"What is that place?" wondered Jon.

Rew snorted. "When you were in training for the king's army, did you not spend some wild nights on the town?"

"You think... you think it's a brothel?"

"Yes," said Rew, "I think it's a brothel, and maybe it's more."

Jon adjusted his belt, making sure his longsword was in reach. Rew, thinking of how the man had done much the same on the way out of the building, rubbed at his lips with the back of his hand, trying to hide his smile.

"Stay behind me," warned Rew, forcing his voice to be stern. "You're not well, and if you put yourself at risk, you'll put me at risk too. No matter what we find, stay behind me. That's safer for both of us."

Jon nodded. "Understood."

"And if you draw steel, which you shouldn't, don't go immediately for your longsword," advised Rew. "Inside a building, without room to swing, a dagger or a knife will serve you better."

They strode into the cul-de-sac, reached the front of the building, and pushed the door open to walk inside. The entrance was boxed by wooden posts hung with diaphanous silk curtains. The curtains lent a hazy aspect to everything beyond, but it was clear enough that it was a house of ill repute. There was a bar against the far wall, and low couches strewn about the floor around it. One side of the room looked to have tables for gambling and another a stage for performances. In the middle of the day after an attack on the town, the stage was empty, and no one was gambling.

A girl stood behind a podium and smiled at them as they walked inside. "Good day, sirs. Welcome to the Two Eggs. What can I do for you today?"

"The Two Eggs?" asked Rew.

"Your first time here?" asked the girl. She nodded to a sign hanging above her head. Two eggs, cooked sunny side up, were carved out of wood and adorned with the name of the establishment. In the context of the place, they looked rather a lot like breasts.

Rew nodded. "First time."

The girl had the look of one who would work in such a place. Young and pretty, though her pale skin was dusted in powder and rouge. She wore modest clothing, but it clung to her tightly. Her attire was meant as a promise of what lay beyond the silk curtains, he supposed.

"Visitors to Falvar, then?" she asked them, her welcoming smile painted on her face as carefully as the kohl around her eyes.

"We are," agreed Rew. "Normally, we don't pause long, but you heard there was a bit of trouble outside of the city today? We figured no one is coming or going until it's all sorted. If we're here, we may as well enjoy the stay, eh?"

"I heard there was a bit of trouble," said the girl, looking at their clothing.

Rew winced. They should have taken time to clean up, but it was too late now. "Aye, more than a bit, I'm afraid. Dark Kind breached the gates, and we got caught up in it. I don't mind a bit of a tussle, but well, we're looking for something to take our minds off it, you understand?"

"Yes, I can imagine," said the girl with her false smile. "You've found the right place. What's your pleasure, then?"

"A drink to start with," said Rew. "After that, ah, I gotta wet my throat afore I think of what else."

The girl looked them up and down, clearly unhappy with their openly displayed weapons and filthy appearance, but evidently, it wasn't enough to turn them away. She turned to open the curtains for them.

"The bar is in the back, and once you're settled, some girls will be along to see if there's anything else we can do to make your time in the Two Eggs more comfortable," said the girl. She paused and added, "We have baths finer than anything you'll find outside Baron Fedgley's keep. You can soak there by yourself for a bit, or some men enjoy having the girls accompany them. I'm afraid we've no laundry."

"The bar first," said Rew, and he stepped through the curtain.

He led Jon toward the bar, having to step quick so the younger man didn't walk on his heels. Rew shot the younger ranger a glare, but saw Jon wasn't paying attention to him. Jon's attention was on the rest of the room. The place was sparsely populated, which made sense in the middle of the day after an attack on the town, but there were people there, a dozen girls in skimpy attire and several men lounging comfortably throughout the space.

The barman offered them a smile and a cheerful greeting, and Rew ordered himself an ale. He turned, leaning back against the counter as he waited on the drink. He pretended to study the girls. They might be eyes for the thieves' guild, but a very quick look let him know they were not carrying any weapons of serious size. The men, though, could have been.

Dressed in clothing that would be typical for a burgher in Falvar, those men wouldn't have looked out of place except they were sitting in a brothel and weren't speaking to any of the women working there. Why come to such a place if you weren't going to do business?

At the far side of the room was a staircase covered by a curtain. As Rew watched, one of the working girls stopped by one of the men and spoke a few words into his ear. Then, they both disappeared through the curtain up the stairs. A working girl and client going to complete a transaction, or were they going to inform someone that two armed men had arrived at the bar? The ale came, and Rew sipped his while Jon lifted a glass of spirits. The senior ranger raised an eyebrow.

"I need something strong," muttered Jon.

"Keep your wits about you," advised Rew, still leaning against the bar so he could survey the room.

It was several moments before the woman who had taken the man upstairs returned, and now she had another man with her who walked down from the stairs and found a couch to lounge on. The woman bent near the man, as if to kiss his cheek or to hear some instructions, then went back to circling the room, eventually finding her way to Rew and Jon.

"How are you doing today, gentlemen?" she asked, putting a hand lightly on Rew's wrist, a floral scent wafting around her. "My name is Rachel."

"The truth, it's been a wild day," responded Rew. "We got tangled up in the mess by the gates. I'm not ashamed to admit I needed something to steady my nerves. You heard about the attack by the Dark Kind? Several hundred narjags, it was."

The woman bit her lip and nodded. "Terrifying. You fought them?"

"We did," acknowledged Rew.

The woman shuffled closer, moving her hand from his wrist up his arm. "I'm glad you were here in Falvar, then. It looks like you were injured. Is it painful? A man like you, I bet you didn't even notice. Why don't we go to the baths? I can help clean you up and get you to relax a little. You feel so tense."

"Maybe later," said Rew. He tilted his ale mug so they could both look in and see it was half full. "I don't want to waste a drop of this. Not sure I've ever wanted an ale more in my life."

He winked at her and laughed. She smiled back at him, her lips curling, but her eyes looked like short bits of broken glass.

"Mind if I keep you company while you drink?" asked the woman, Rachel. "It's quiet today, and I don't want to let a man like you slip into the clutches of the others."

"Sure," said Rew, taking a sip of his ale.

"How'd you get drawn into the fighting?" wondered the woman. "You don't have the look of merchant's guards, and you're not soldiers." She let her hand drop from his face down to the hilt of his longsword. "A man doesn't carry a blade like this unless he plans to use it. You don't think you'll need it in here, do you?"

Not answering her question, Rew raised his mug and quaffed the rest of his ale. "Maybe it's time we find somewhere private. I'm aching for something to take my mind off the day, and you're just about the prettiest thing I've seen since we got to Falvar."

The woman smiled, turning away coyly, but there was no flush in her cheeks, and the glint in her eyes did not change. "To the baths?"

"Do you have a room upstairs?" asked Rew.

"For six silver an hour I do," she said, turning back to him and leaning close. "Four if you bathe first, but either way, I'm worth every coin, I promise you."

Rew turned to Jon, meaning to ask the younger ranger to stay downstairs at the bar, but the other man spoke up. "Is that six silver for both of us?"

"Both of you?" wondered the woman, looking back and forth between the two men.

Seeing no way to back out without raising suspicion, Rew simply shrugged.

"Fourteen for the both of you," said the woman.

Rew frowned. "Come now, Rachel. That's more than twice the rate for one. How about twelve, and we'll buy you a drink?"

The woman eyed Jon up and down with a professional's appraisal. She pursed her lips, put a finger to them, and then turned back to Rew with a wink. "Your friend doesn't look like he'll take long. Sure, twelve silver and a drink."

Rew paid the barman for the most expensive glass of wine he'd ever bought and followed Rachel to the stairwell, Jon tight on their heels. From the corner of his eyes, Rew could see that a few of the other girls and several of the men in the room were watching them, but two men accompanying one girl upstairs wouldn't be unique in such a place, even if it was unusual. The woman who was leading them gave no indication anything was wrong, so none of the watchers moved to stop them as they walked up the stairs and the curtain fell behind them. They reached the second floor of the place, and the woman turned down the hallway.

"Hold on," said Rew, pointing to a door he was certain hid another flight of stairs. "What's up there?"

"More rooms, more girls," said Rachel, "but my room is on this floor."

"Mind if we go and look?" asked Rew. "I'm curious if we can see the town gates from up there."

"It's just a bunch of rooms," said the woman, stepping back toward him. "All of the girls on the third floor are asleep. They work late nights, and if we wake them, they'll throttle me. Come on, you two. The hour started when we left the bar. If you want your coin's worth, we'd better get started."

"Just a peek upstairs," said Rew. "I promise I won't wake any of your, ah, colleagues."

The woman shook her head and looped an arm around his waist. "The only thing you need to see is beneath this dress."

"Are you worried about the thieves?" asked Rew, wrapping his arms around her.

The woman gasped and tried to wriggle out of his clutches, and when he didn't let go, she screamed.

"Upstairs!" barked Rew, shoving her away and spinning toward the door.

He and Jon flung open the door and charged up the stairs to find a second door, this one a heavy, iron-bound barrier at the top. Rew shook the handle and found the door was locked.

"W-We could..." stammered Jon, as if saying the first part of the sentence would lead him to a solution. It didn't. Lamely, he offered, "They're probably all fleeing now. Maybe if we go outside, we can—"

Rew shook his head, hearing the sounds of stomping feet coming from below. "Getting out isn't going to be easy. They've been watching us since we walked in here, ready to close the noose if necessary. With just the two of us… I'm hoping they're curious who we are and will take the risk to question us."

They didn't have long to wait, as several men appeared below them on the stairs, compact iron crossbows in hand, deadly quarrels pointed directly at the two rangers.

"You boys have a key to this door?" asked Rew.

The thieves raised their crossbows, their fingers shifting near the triggers. None of them proffered a key to the door.

"Zaine sent me," claimed Rew. "Said she'd found out something in the keep after the job was finished earlier today. She said the guild needed to know immediately."

Behind the door, a bolt slid, then another, and another, and finally, the door swung wide open. A man was standing in the entrance. He commented, "That's a lie."

"It is," agreed Rew, looking the man up and down.

He wasn't one of the thieves they'd seen earlier, but he was dressed in similar attire. He was an older man, but his back was straight, and he held himself with the confident assurance he could still move quickly when he needed to. His appearance was unremarkable, which Rew assumed was the point. The man asked Rew, "What do you know about the job that took place earlier today?"

"Same thing that everyone does," responded Rew. "Zaine helped your men inside. They killed two guards at the private gate. They killed Arcanist Ralcrist and shattered the crystal on his table with his own staff. That allowed high magic to be cast again in Falvar, which facilitated a spellcaster attacking the baron's family, killing the baroness and scores of guards, and abducting the baron. Oh, and the spellcaster trapped a handful of wraiths as well before escaping by portal. Five of your men were killed in the operation."

"That's the same thing everyone knows?" questioned the white-haired thief. "Not even I know all of those details." He paused. "I suspect not even the leader of the job knows all of those details."

"It sounds like we have something to talk about then, don't we?" drawled Rew.

The man's jaw bunched, as if he was chewing the thought over. Finally, he stepped back and gestured. "Come inside."

They walked onto the third floor of the Two Eggs and found it was a giant room that extended the entire length of the building. There were a score of people there. They were mostly men, all dressed like burghers of Falvar, with a few women who could have been housewives of shopkeepers in the city. There was a rack of arms, a wall of closets Rew guessed were filled with supplies and disguises, a large table with several chairs arranged around it that could be used for guild meetings, and a woman in the center of the room bound to a chair.

"They're going to kill you!" Zaine shouted to the rangers when she saw them enter. "Run!"

Beside her, the thief that Rew had seen in the arcanist's tower turned and smiled at them.

The white-bearded man pointed for Rew and Jon to walk farther into the room, and they followed the instructions without complaint. The crossbowmen came up as well and spread out, keeping their weapons trained on the rangers.

"Axxon," called the thief beside Zaine, "in a lucky turn of fortune, these are the only two men who can identify me. It seems as if our problems are all congregating here, begging to be solved."

"Your problems," murmured the older thief, Axxon. The guild leader, Rew guessed, from the easy way the man carried himself and the way the rest of the people in the room turned to follow his movement. "Though, it seems I have a problem as well. Everyone who is looking for you is coming directly to the right location. Why do you think that is, Balzac?"

"They found us, but they won't get a chance to tell anyone about it," claimed the thief beside Zaine.

Axxon turned to Rew. "How did you find us? Who told you the location of our guildhall?"

Rew smirked. "Finding you was simple luck. I'd seen your men traipsing through the market earlier today on the way to the keep. We started there and walked back, looking for a likely location."

Axxon's lips pressed tightly together.

"I have a few questions for you," added Rew.

"And I a few for you," replied Axxon. He put his hands behind his belt, tucking his thumbs into it, his stance tense. "First, who are you?"

"I'm the King's Ranger of the eastern territory," answered Rew.

"The King's Ranger?" guffawed Balzac from beside Zaine. "A bit far away from your territory, are you not? The King's Ranger has no authority in Falvar. Shouldn't you be hiking in the wilderness or something?"

"I've taken temporary control of Falvar's garrison in the absence of Commander Broyce and Baron Fedgley," replied Rew calmly. Ignoring the startled reaction of the thieves, he walked in front of Zaine and told her, "I asked you to stay in the keep."

"Perhaps I should have," murmured Zaine, unable to meet his gaze. "Maybe that would have kept us both alive."

Balzac chuckled, glancing around at his companions.

Rew looked to him and said, "Balzac, yes? I witnessed you murder two soldiers of the king as well as Arcanist Ralcrist. I'm afraid the penalty for those crimes is death, whether under the king's law or the baron's."

Balzac grinned, pointing at Rew. "Is anyone else hearing this?"

"Did you come alone?" wondered Axxon from behind them.

"Just the two of us," confirmed Rew.

"A rather bold plan, is it not, coming alone and threatening my thieves within our own guildhall?" questioned Axxon.

Rew met the man's gaze. "I didn't think I needed anyone else. Give me the girl and this man Balzac, and I'll leave you in peace. I'm only taking command in Falvar until things settle and security can be reestablished by the proper authorities. I have no interest in your petty thefts, but I'm afraid I must respond to someone killing the baron's arcanist as part of a plot to abduct the baron himself. At the moment, I only have proof that Balzac was involved. He'll hang for the crime, but until the baron's soldiers are able to investigate the matter thoroughly, the rest of you will have time. I suggest you use it to flee."

Axxon gestured to the trio of crossbowmen that were arrayed beside him, still pointing their quarrels at Rew. "I think you've miscalculated, Ranger."

"The job did not go as planned, did it?" asked Rew, crossing his arms over his chest. "The spellcaster tricked you, as he did everyone. I'm guessing you had no idea the baron would be kidnapped, no clue the amount of attention this job would bring."

Axxon tilted his head and acknowledged, "It did not go as we were told it would."

Rew watched the man, seeing how he maintained control, breathing evenly, his gaze steady. The thief's spine was straight as a rod, but his arms trembled slightly from the tension of clasping his hands behind his back. Rew was certain, beneath the thief's still exterior, he was roiling inside. It was a familiar feeling. The leader of Falvar's thieves' guild would be uncertain, thrown off by a situation he'd never found himself in before. To survive the day, the ranger needed to keep the man off guard. He needed time to let the thieves' tension eat at them like acid, clouding their minds, helping them make a mistake.

Rew told Axxon, "You said you had questions for me. Go ahead and ask them."

"Who was the spellcaster?" asked the leader of the thieves' guild.

"You did business with a man you did not know?" wondered Rew, shaking his head and looking at the other thieves in the room. "You risked everyone's neck and you don't even know who your client was? That does not sound like the thieves' guilds I'm familiar with."

Axxon grunted, and Rew saw his eyes flick toward Balzac.

Rew turned to Balzac, making sure all of the other thieves saw it. "Ah, I see."

"Who was he?" questioned Balzac. "I was about to get that information from the girl, but—"

"She doesn't know," interjected Rew. He began walking, pacing in a wide circle around Balzac and Zaine. He didn't come close enough to anyone for it to be perceived as a threat, but he wanted the thieves comfortable with his movement. As he walked, the thieves shifted, responding to him. Their hands stayed close to their weapons, but no one interfered. They wanted to know what he knew. "Zaine first met the spellcaster in the old mining tower north of here, the one that sits next to the Spine. He had traveled there on foot because he couldn't portal into Falvar. That crystal you destroyed in Arcanist Ralcrist's chamber, it dampened high magic in the vicinity. It was protecting Baron Fedgley from men like this spellcaster."

"What did you say the spellcaster's name was?" asked Axxon.

Rew, still pacing, smirked at him. "The lass has only known the spellcaster for a few days. She only traveled with him down from the mining tower. I've known him for years. Almost my entire life, in fact."

None of the thieves spoke.

"Let her go," instructed Rew. "She cannot tell you what you want to know. She cannot tell you what you need to know if you plan to live through the night."

"Are you threatening us?" snapped Axxon. "At my word, there will be three crossbow bolts sticking through your body, Ranger."

"Maybe," said Rew, "but I was not threatening you. I was

merely pointing out that the man you are concerned about, the spellcaster, is exactly the man you should be worried about. He single-handedly killed forty of the baron's soldiers earlier today in the keep. He blasted through the baroness' defenses with ease and trapped the five wraiths the baron called. He portaled out of the throne room to escape, you know? If he can leave Falvar so easily, did it occur to you that he could return the same way? You are men beyond the law. What would you do if you were elbow deep in a conspiracy and some of your associates still lived, and were talking to a man like me? Do you think the spellcaster will be content to let you keep his gold and spill his secrets, or do you think he'll be back soon to tie up loose ends?"

The thieves as a whole shifted uneasily at that.

"Forty soldiers, the baroness who commanded substantial magic of her own, and the baron himself. Wraiths!" said Rew, still walking the slow circle. "The things I am telling you are easily verifiable if you do not already know them. Surely word has escaped the keep by now. Forty heavily armored soldiers are dead. The baron and his wife, both accomplished spellcasters. I see you have twenty men in this room. Do any of them happen to be exceptionally talented spellcasters? More talented than the baron himself?"

Axxon swallowed nervously.

"Everything I am telling you is true," said Rew, forcing a smile onto his lips. "The spellcaster's abilities are not in doubt. The only question I have is this. What do you think he will do once he's locked the baron away somewhere safe?"

"Who is this man working for?" questioned Axxon.

"One of the three princes, of course," replied Rew. He looked between Axxon and Balzac. "I was hoping you could tell me which."

Both men stared back at him.

"How were you drawn into this conspiracy?" questioned Rew. "Who was your initial contact? An agent of the princes, I am sure, but I do not know which one. Not Prince Valchon. That's who the spellcaster claimed he was working for, and he was lying. Was it Heindaw or Calb? Who hired the thieves' guild of Falvar?"

"The—The princes?" stammered Axxon. "This is a conspiracy by the princes?"

"Yes," said Rew, continuing his slow circuit of the room. "I've always felt it best to know who you're getting into bed with, but I suppose with accommodations such as these…" He turned to Balzac. "You didn't know who you were working for, did you? Someone contacted you, though. You must have a name. Who was it?"

Balzac shook his head. "That's not the way it works, mate. You're in our guildhall. You answer our questions."

"Let the girl go. Tell me who hired you," insisted Rew. "Tell me. Then, I will answer your questions. I have nothing to hide from you, but I have something I need. Tell me who contacted you."

Licking his lips, glancing between his superior and Rew, Balzac asked, "And what's in it for us, Ranger, if we tell you what you want to know? You already threatened me with the rope, so why should I tell you who my contact was?"

Rew stopped walking, facing the man. "Because whoever hired you is the one that's going to lead the spellcaster right to your guildhall."

Balzac's lips twisted into a sinister grin, and his gaze dropped to Zaine.

"King's Sake, lass!" barked Rew.

"She's been right under your nose, Ranger." Balzac laughed. "She's our contact, and as long as she's in our care, she ain't telling that spellcaster or anyone else where we are. Fortune's dealt us the winning hand."

To her credit, Zaine looked exceptionally guilty and remorseful.

Rew stared at her, his mind churning. His ploy to frighten the thieves into immediate action wouldn't do a bit of good if their only tie to Alsayer was bound to a chair in the middle of the room. He heard Jon shifting, as if the younger ranger was realizing their time was almost up. If Jon sensed it, the thieves would as well.

Balzac turned to Axxon. "The King's Ranger doesn't have the answers we seek, but the girl does. She's the one we need to question. Axxon, he has nothing to offer us, and he says he came alone."

Before Axxon could respond, Rew reached up to his neck, and he twisted, yanking his cloak off and flinging it. The cloth, weighted in the corners, spun out flat, creating a flying wall between him and the crossbowmen. He launched himself toward Zaine and Balzac, drawing his hunting knife as he moved.

The thief's smile faded, but he didn't have time to react before Rew reached him and grabbed a handful of his tunic. Rew jerked the man around, putting him between Zaine and the crossbowmen. Then, the ranger tore his hunting knife up the back of the chair Zaine was strapped to, slicing the bindings in two. Rew kicked the back of the chair, sending Zaine sprawling, and he flung Balzac toward the crossbowmen.

The room was erupting in chaos. Several thieves advanced, but none appeared eager to engage, frightened of jumping into the line of fire for the crossbowmen. Jon drew his longsword and shuffled closer, but most of the thieves were ignoring him, focused on the action around Rew.

Balzac, regaining his balance, pulled out a wicked, curved dagger. It was the same blade he'd used to kill Arcanist Ralcrist, realized Rew. Balzac's back was to the crossbowmen, and he seemed oblivious that it was only his body in the way that prevented the men from firing upon Rew. The ranger drew his longsword and feinted at the thief, trying to freeze Balzac in place.

"Attack him!" bellowed Axxon. "Why is no one attacking him?"

Thieves closed around Rew. The attackers carried a variety of short weapons that could easily be secreted as they moved throughout the city. Rew had an advantage with his longsword, but there were a lot of the thieves, and they weren't blinded by rage like narjags were. These men were cunning survivors of a dangerous life of crime. Instead of charging directly at him, they began to encircle him, trusting to their numbers and that time was on their side.

"Get out of here!" Rew shouted to Zaine and Jon as he stepped away, moving into the center of the room to draw the thieves away from his companions.

Jon shuffled after him, as if he meant to engage the thieves, but Rew was surrounded, and the younger ranger had an opening to the doorway they'd entered through.

"That's an order, Jon. Get Zaine and get out!"

Zaine stumbled to her feet, crouched low as if to fight, but her hands were empty.

Rew rushed one side of the circle that had formed around him. The thieves wheeled back, staying well out of reach of his longsword, but he kept them moving between him and the crossbowmen.

Zaine saw the opportunity and bolted, but Axxon leapt in front of her, a long, serrated knife held low in his grip. She skidded to a halt, and Jon stepped beside her.

"I'll take him," grunted the ranger.

Rew dodged to the side, and a thief's dagger flashed past him. He smashed the pommel of his longsword down on the man's wrist, hearing it crack. He turned, tangling with another thief as the man tried to grapple with him. Rew slammed his knee up, catching the man square in the crotch. The ranger shoved the quaking thief back into his companions.

Between the shoulders of the men in front of him, Rew saw Jon advancing on Axxon. The leader of the thieves' guild, evidently not liking his chances with a dagger against a ranger with a longsword, turned and bolted down the stairs, calling for more men.

Taking a glancing blow to his arm, Rew spun and whipped his longsword across his attacker's neck. Then, he felt the tip of another dagger dragging across his hip. He whirled, whipping his longsword around him, fighting for space, realizing he couldn't defend himself for long. The thieves were being cautious, but they were quick and had a natural instinct to strike when his back was turned. These men were killers, and he couldn't fight them all.

"Run, Jon, run!" Rew shouted, lurching back and forth to distract his opponents, trying to keep their attention to give the other ranger and Zaine time to escape.

Jon stared down the stairwell, listening to the shouts of more men coming up from below.

Zaine ran toward a shuttered window. She gripped the clasp and shook it, but it was fastened shut, and her panic-slowed fingers couldn't seem to pry it open. Jon followed behind her and raised his longsword, apparently intending to bring it down and smash open the shutter.

Rew saw a blade coming at his face and leaned back, getting nicked across his chin. He snapped back and stabbed his longsword into the man who'd struck at him. A club smacked down on the ranger's back, narrowly missing his head, and he staggered forward, cursing. He grabbed a charging thief and slung him about, throwing the slender man at his companions, fouling their path.

Across the room, Balzac had taken a crossbow from one of his men, but he wasn't pointing it at Rew. He was pointing it at Zaine.

"Crossbow!" cried Rew, surging toward his companions, shrugging off another thief, parrying a strike from a short sword, and dancing through a pair of swinging long knives, trying to burst free from the group that swarmed around him.

Jon turned and raised his longsword. He stared down the bolts of the crossbows and bellowed over his shoulder to Zaine, "Get out!"

Zaine stood frozen behind the ranger, eyes wide.

Balzac shrugged and fired. Within a breath, the other two crossbowmen released as well. Jon spun his longsword, trying to knock down the quarrels. He clipped one, and it flew astray, thudding into the wall behind him. The other two smacked into his torso, burying themselves deep in his flesh.

"Run," he whimpered, wavering. His longsword fell from limp fingers and thudded onto the wood floor. Jon opened his mouth again, but this time only a trickle of blood escaped his lips.

Rew slashed wildly, racing steps ahead of the thieves, jumping onto their giant meeting table, running across it, and leaping down on the other side. Two of the crossbowmen were trying to reload. Balzac threw his weapon aside and drew his curved dagger. Jon fell to his knees, gasping in pain, his blood-slick hands fumbling at the feathered quarrels sticking from him.

He rasped, seconds before collapsing onto his face, "Run, Zaine. Run!"

Rew charged straight at the girl, slashing his longsword at anyone who tried to come in front of him. She stood, paralyzed with fear, her eyes on Jon's back where the pair of crossbow bolts had burst from his flesh like shoots of growth stabbing up from spring soil, grisly strings of blood and flesh stuck on their jagged, steel barbs.

Rew launched himself, tackling the girl and sending them both flying toward the window. He hit the shutter with his shoulder at full speed. It burst open under the combined weight of him and Zaine. His momentum carried them, and they both tumbled out the window, falling into the open air.

Chapter Twenty-Three

Wrapping Zaine tight in his arms, Rew crashed into the shutter, and it shattered from the impact. His thigh caught the bottom of the windowsill, and he flipped, falling out the third-story window. Zaine squealed, thrashing and struggling, her panicked eyes right in front of his.

Rew dropped his weapons, kicked his legs, and snapped out an arm to grab the windowsill as they fell from it. His fingers raked across rotten wood, and he tugged Zaine close with his other arm, but the ancient wood on the exterior of the brothel crumbled from the force of their fall. He felt the sill tearing away beneath his hand. They dropped.

He kicked out with his legs, trying to find purchase against the wall as they slid down. Toes dragged across wooden boards, his free hand slapped helplessly against each bump and protrusion from the wall, slowing them, but nothing could arrest their momentum, and they tumbled. Zaine flailed in his grasp, and he hugged her tight then twisted. His legs hit the ground first, and he tried to drop into a roll to displace the force of their fall, but with the thief in his arms, he ended up flopping hard onto the dirt street in front of the brothel.

He groaned, blinking up at the window above them. Flakes of

old paint from the wall and dust from where they'd scraped and scrambled against it rained down on top of them. A thief poked his head out of the window, saw them, and pointed.

Cursing, Rew scrambled to his feet, his legs almost buckling under him, an ankle throbbed with sharp pain, and his body throbbing where it'd smacked against the hard-packed street. Half a dozen lacerations where the thieves had cut him stung something awful, but his legs weren't broken, and after he tested his weight on it, he knew he could at least limp on his injured ankle.

He heard shouts and commotion inside. Fear propelled him like firepowder bursting from the back of a firework. Rew scrambled around, occasionally hopping on one foot, snatching his weapons and sliding them into their sheaths. He patted himself, realizing he'd lost his cloak, and shook his head, knowing even if they completed their escape, the cloak would be the least of his worries. The cloak—and Jon—were both lost.

"Come on," he said, reaching down to grab Zaine and haul her to her feet.

"He died because of me," she murmured.

"He did," agreed Rew.

He grabbed the back of Zaine's collar and shoved her down the street ahead of him, hurrying in a limping shuffle to get out of the dead-end street.

Behind them, he could hear thieves running out the door of the brothel, but he made it to the main avenue and turned toward the market. This way was becoming busy now, with people coming out to gossip and cheer. Their town had been attacked, but they had survived, and they would celebrate. Up and down the street, there were hundreds of people, and the thieves were not bold enough to come after him with so many witnesses. That, or perhaps, they were scared. Rew had been surrounded by twenty of them, trapped in their lair, and he'd escaped.

Zaine kept murmuring to herself and seemed to be paying no attention to what they were doing. The ranger held a tight grip on her, steering them both through the growing crowd.

"H-He could have moved…" she stammered. "He wasn't the target. I was. Balzac was shooting at me. Jon could have stepped out of the way. Why didn't he move?"

Rew let her talk, let her work it out. If she could come to terms with her actions leading to Jon's death, maybe that would make it easier to confront the truth that she'd had a part in hundreds of other deaths as well. Maybe it would shake her out of her stupor and she would finally tell him what the hell was going on.

Blessed Mother. Jon and Tate both dead, and for what?

The Investiture, swirling gently in the far-off corner of the kingdom, and two of his men had already been killed. Jon hadn't even known what the Investiture was. Tate hadn't a clue of who he'd been watching in the cell. Both men killed simply because they'd encountered three younglings in a place where they didn't belong.

Zaine, trapped in his grip, stumbled ahead of him as they approached the keep. The flags of the Fedgleys rose high, though the baron was gone and, Rew guessed, would soon be wishing he was dead. The flags of the baron, and of his children.

Raif and Cinda had been moved to their rooms to recuperate, so Rew took Zaine and Anne to a guest room in the keep and sat the thief down while Anne checked them both over. He ordered food and drink from the kitchens, but with the madness of the day, the staff could only send a loaf of two-day old bread, a sausage, and a hunk of sharp, white cheese. Luckily, they had ample supplies of ale and wine.

Rew poured himself an ale and Anne a mug of wine. He stripped off his shirt and sat on a bench, cradling his mug of ale, staring at Zaine while Anne worked behind him, poking at the various lacerations, bruises, and scrapes he'd gotten during the confrontation with the thieves, the narjags, and Alsayer's conjurings hours before.

"Save your energy," said Rew as Anne prodded a finger into a deep bruise.

"Rew," she said, "you're minced like a New Year pie."

"You've spent too much already," he argued.

"I can—" she began.

"Anne," he interrupted. "This isn't over. I'll heal, so save your strength for when I cannot. No empathy, not now."

She pinched the flesh on his shoulder where a short sword had caught him a shallow cut, and he jerked at a sudden stab of pain. She leaned close and asked, "You're sure about that, Senior Ranger? Stitches are going to sting without my empathy."

He grunted but did not reply. Instead, he turned to Zaine, and asked, "Who hired you, lass?"

She was sitting in a chair, looking down at her hands clasped in her lap. She'd been unarmed when he'd rescued her, but even if she had weapons, he didn't think she'd use them to try and escape. She was still in shock, dazed at the horrors she'd seen.

"Who hired you?" he asked again, trying to be gentle, but knowing if it came to it, they didn't have time to spare the girl's feelings. He had to get answers only she knew.

"He died for me," she said, looking up to meet the ranger's stare.

"Yes," agreed Rew, nodding to her. "He did."

"Why?" asked Zaine.

Rew sighed and sat back.

Behind him, Anne cursed and slapped him on his bare back. "Hold still or I'm going to do more damage with this needle than good."

Grunting, Rew settled down, and in between short gasps as Anne began to stitch him, he explained to Zaine, "Jon was a ranger in the king's service. Part of our role is to protect the people of the realm, even thieves. Did he put a lot of thought into it before he held his ground and took those quarrels for you? I don't know. Would he do it again, give his life to save yours? Yes, I think he would. Jon sensed something in you, lass. He sensed a goodness, despite the facts of the matter. You're a thief, and much of what happened today could be laid at your feet, but Jon wouldn't have believed all of this was your intent. Tell me, was Jon correct? Is there some good in you? What's going on, lass? Was his sacrifice worth it?"

"I've never had anyone do something like that for me," said Zaine, still lost in her own thoughts.

"Few of us have," remarked Rew. He shifted, risking Anne's wrath. The girl was young, nearly a child, but not one. He glanced at the table where they'd set their food. Should he offer her a drink? Maybe that would loosen her up, pull her out of her leaden stupor.

"Zaine," said Anne.

The girl looked up at the empath.

"Jon died for you," stated Anne. "He gave his life so that you could live. He would have wanted you to answer our questions."

Zaine looked away. "He shouldn't have traded his life for mine. If he'd moved, Balzac would have fired on me, not Jon. It's not—"

"He didn't move," said Anne, stepping around Rew and stabbing a finger at the young thief. "He died to save you. He died so that others can live. Can you make his sacrifice mean something and answer the senior ranger's questions? What you know could save the lives of countless others."

Zaine frowned then shook her head. "I-I didn't mean for any of this to happen."

"I want to believe you," said Rew. "How about you start from the beginning? Tell us how you became involved in this mess."

Zaine shifted uncomfortably in her seat. "Two years ago, I was an apprentice in the thieves' guild here. I know it's not an honorable path, but it was the only one I thought I had. My parents died, and I lived with my uncle and my aunt. They couldn't afford me any longer, and they'd decided to sell me. It's against kingdom law, but it's known Fedgley looks the other way for the brokers who line his pockets well. A girl like me? There's only one profession I'd be sold into. My uncle and aunt both knew it, but they planned it all the same. I was warned by a friend, and I ran."

Rew grimaced and drank his ale. Such things were not common in the kingdom, but they were known to happen. That Fedgley allowed it within his barony turned the ranger's stomach.

Zaine continued, "I'd rather the streets or starvation than that. And well, that's just about what I got. I had no skills that might earn me an honest living, and the inns and taverns who might've hired me refused when I couldn't provide any references. They were worried I'd bring trouble. I thought I'd found a seamstress who would take me as an apprentice 'til she caught her husband speaking to me. I scraped by for a bit, but before long, I was on the streets, picking at food behind the taverns, fighting the other urchins there. One day, the thieves scooped me up and gave me a choice. They told me I could join as one of them or work downstairs with the girls in the old brothel that used to house the guild. In the brothel, they would have offered me double until my sixteenth winter, but I told you, that's not a life I was willing to live. I don't think the thieves cared much either way, but I chose to be a thief. At least stealing... I knew it wasn't right then, and I know it's not right now, but somehow, taking from others seemed more honorable. Maybe that's just a story I tell myself, but I chose the way I did, and I won't hide from that."

Rew grimaced, and Anne moved around him to kneel beside the girl. She wrapped an arm around Zaine's shoulder. "I understand."

Zaine drew a deep breath and let it out slowly. "In the guild, the members make the decisions, and they earn the coin. The apprentices are subject to their whims. It wasn't easy for me, being a young girl. I put in a year, though, until Balzac began to gain influence. Because of his influence, the thieves weren't just slitting purses. They started bashing heads and using those cut knives on people's necks. No one from the keep, of course. They didn't want to draw the baron's eye, but out in the streets of the lower quarters, the gutters ran thick with blood. The burgher councils must have complained, but the baron was distracted, too busy with his own plotting, I suppose. I couldn't do it, couldn't put my knife into a man. Balzac laughed at me and said he'd make murder a criteria for membership. Axxon, he's not a bad sort for a thief, but everyone knew he'd lost his grip on the guild. He was scared of Balzac, just as the commoners were, just as the rest of us were. I knew with Balzac in charge, there was no future for me in Falvar, so I fled again. I went to Spinesend."

Rew glanced at Anne where she was squatting beside the young thief. Her face was etched with sorrow, and he could see the water welling in her eyes. It wasn't an unusual story, a young girl with few options fleeing all that she'd known. Half the girls in Anne's inn could tell similar. Those girls had been lucky, though, to find a caring mistress who'd put them to work ferrying ales and baking breads instead of spreading their legs. It wasn't often like that. It usually wasn't like that.

"What happened in Spinesend?" asked Rew quietly.

"I tried to join the thieves' guild there," said Zaine. "I was a good pickpocket and showed some promise as a burglar. I thought they'd take me in… But in Spinesend, it's the urchins that pick the pockets, and it's sophisticated teams that conduct the burglaries. I had to find a group leader to take me on, and I was an outsider, a refugee from Falvar. None of the captains of the teams had an interest in me, and there was no way I could prove myself without their blessing. It seemed that again, I was left with two choices—the knife or the bed."

Rew stood and began pacing the room. Anne and Zaine ignored him.

"I was at the end of my rope, hanging around the guild in Spinesend, living on odd jobs the others doled out that no one wanted, something between an urchin and an apprentice," continued Zaine. "Then, a man who came around the guild from time to time stopped me. He told me he'd heard I was from Falvar and that I had a kind face. It was not my face I ever got compliments on, you know? I knew I shouldn't, but I trusted him."

Slowing his walk, Rew waited.

"He said he needed someone who knew the thieves' guild in Falvar. He said he needed someone young and not intimidating, someone that others would trust," said Zaine. She wiped her cheek with the back of her hand, smearing a fat tear there. "He paid for new clothing, food, everything. He told me that he trusted me. After a week, he told me someone in Baron Worgon's keep was attempting to flee, and he needed my help sneaking them out and back to Falvar. Said there'd be more work for me if I was successful. He sent me here to Falvar to find Balzac and deliver a letter and a pouch full of coin. I did, and Balzac simply thanked me. He didn't jest at my expense. He didn't try to coerce me into his bed. I-I'd never had that kind of respect from the man, like from a peer. I returned to Spinesend, and my contact seemed happy. We celebrated at one of the finest restaurants in the city. The next morning, he took me to Yarrow."

"Did you know who you were to help slip from the palace?" asked Rew.

"I did," responded Zaine. "The man told me it was Baron Fedgley's children and that it was because Worgon was plotting against Falvar. It sounded plausible, and it matched with what Raif and Cinda told me after I got them out. Everything checked out, Senior Ranger. I thought this was the start of a new life, a real opportunity. They had me hooked."

"Why'd you take them to Eastwatch?" wondered Rew.

"The man told me to. He said there was an easy route through the wilderness," replied Zaine. "I didn't know. Everything else he'd said seemed the truth. The nobles thought Worgon would be looking for them on the roads, so they didn't object when I suggested it."

"That's all you were to do? Get Raif and Cinda and bring them to Falvar?" pressed Rew. He frowned, believing the girl's story but thinking it wasn't the end of it.

Zaine shook her head, tears welling in her eyes.

Rew stood and poured her half a cup of wine. "Tell us the rest, lass."

"I was told to befriend the nobles, to earn their trust and their favor," said Zaine. "I-I knew that when we got here, I was expected to help the thieves in Falvar gain entrance to the keep. The man told me that was the price into the guild, the only way Balzac would trust me. I believed that. I thought they were playing both sides, sneaking Fedgley's children from beneath Worgon's nose then taking the opportunity to get into the keep and put an extra bit of gold into their pockets. It's not unusual, in the guild, to play more than one angle. I didn't know they would kill the guards. I didn't know anything about Arcanist Ralcrist, the Dark Kind, or the baron—none of it! I overheard them talking about the arcanist's staff, and I figured the job was to steal it."

Rew refilled his ale mug, leaning against the table. "Your contact, the man you met in Spinesend, you said he was a regular around the guild. Did you know who he was?"

Zaine blanched. "I did."

"And?" asked Rew.

"He's dead," said Zaine. "His name was Fein. He was a fixer for the thieves, a man who traveled between the cities in the eastern duchy, arranging jobs that would cross the different guilds' territories. Nobles and merchants knew him. Gutter rats knew him. Fein had fingers in everywhere. It made sense he'd be involved in something like this. You have to believe me. It all made sense!"

"You're sure he's dead?" pressed Rew.

Zaine nodded. "Early in the morning before I was to sneak into Worgon's palace, Fein was killed at a gaming table in a seedy Yarrow tavern. I saw the body, but I decided I'd go ahead with the mission. I knew Balzac had the rest of the plan, and I figured that if I helped, he might not mind that Fein was dead. It'd be a bigger share for him, and he still might let me into the guild."

"So the trail ends with the death of this man Fein," growled Rew. He slammed his mug down on the table, sloshing ale over his hand. "Alsayer could have portaled anywhere in the kingdom, and that was our only lead!"

"I know who hired Fein," whispered the thief.

Rew blinked at her. "Who?"

"Sorry. You said to start from the beginning," she mumbled. "Fein was hired by Duke Eeron's arcanist. Before I agreed to do this, I followed Fein in Spinesend and saw them meeting together. I overheard them discussing the plan. It matched what Fein told me. It matched what happened up until Balzac and the others killed those guards. You have to believe me! I thought they simply meant to steal the arcanist's staff. I didn't know. None of the rest of what they said made sense at the time."

"Does it now?" asked Rew.

Zaine nodded, her eyes down on her untouched wine. "The arcanist spoke of a room for the prize, somewhere he could keep it safe. I thought it was just, I don't know, some chamber they could keep an enchanted artifact from detection, a place they'd store the staff until they sold it."

"Go on," encouraged Rew.

"The prize they spoke of had to be the baron," said Zaine. "They had to be discussing a prison for the baron. It's Duke Eeron's arcanist! He spoke of going to the chamber after meeting Fein, so it must be in Spinesend. I'm certain they're holding Baron Fedgley there!"

"Could you identify the arcanist?" asked Rew. "And are you certain he was truly in Duke Eeron's employ?

"I—Yes, I know I could," said Zaine. "I know he works for the duke. At the New Year ceremony, I was, ah, picking pockets in the crowd. I saw the arcanist on stage with the duke. I recognized him when Fein met with him later. It's the same man, and I'm certain I can identify him again. But, Senior Ranger, I think Balzac knows more than he's letting on. I believe he had contact with Alsayer."

"Why?" asked Rew.

"When I saw him today, he already knew what happened in the throne room," explained Zaine. "He must have fled right after you confronted him, so how would he know what occurred in the throne room unless he was expecting it? Alsayer must have told him. How long did it take you to reach Arcanist Ralcrist's chamber after you saw the thieves sneak in? They would have gone there right away, unless…"

"Unless they were meeting with Alsayer," growled Rew. "That's just like the spellcaster, confirming he won't be exposed before he acts. With the other five thieves dead, only Balzac knew the meeting happened."

Zaine nodded. "That was my thought as well. I went to tell Axxon about what happened, but Balzac grabbed me before I could. He seemed more worried about who else I'd been talking to than what I'd tell his boss. I think I understand now. He's not afraid of the other thieves. He's afraid of Alsayer."

Rew nodded. "He should be. If the spellcaster knows him, it's only a matter of time before Alsayer returns and ties up loose ends. Zaine, do you know of a safe house or a bolt hole the thieves may flee to?"

She frowned and shook her head. "No, they change the location of the guild and their safe houses regularly. I was able to walk the streets when we first arrived until I found someone I knew and I followed them to the brothel, but I've no clue where their safe house may be now. After what happened in the guildhall, they won't be roaming the streets."

Rew turned to look at Anne. She frowned at him, and he nodded. She crossed her arms over her chest and shook her head.

Rew leaned forward and took the wine from Zaine's grasp. "Still remembering the hangover from the morning after the miner's tower, eh? Anne can make you some tea."

"I don't—" began Anne.

"Make the tea," said Rew. "Please."

"I don't like this," said the empath, standing and collecting a hot pot of water off their table near the food. She poured a bit of steaming water into a teacup and sprinkled a pinch of herbs into it. She stood over the cup for a moment, looked at Rew in disapproval, and then turned and offered Zaine the tea. "It will soothe your nerves."

The thief took it and drank. They spoke quietly, probing her for more information about what Fein and Duke Eeron's arcanist had discussed. Fifteen minutes after her first sip of the tea, Zaine's head slumped forward. She was dead asleep.

"How long?" asked Rew.

"Twelve hours," said Anne. "I'll stay with her."

Rew nodded. "We can't let her slip away again."

"I hope you don't mean to execute her with my help," said Anne, frost in her voice. "I wouldn't be able to forgive you for that, Rew."

"The crimes she committed were not in the territory," said the ranger. He rubbed the stubble on his head, knowing it was a lousy excuse. He admitted to the empath, "That, and if we mean to pursue this, we'll need her to identify the arcanist in Spinesend. Duke Eeron has half a dozen of the old geezers, and they all look the same. Bald heads, pinched faces, and white beards. If they've got Baron Fedgley in prison at the behest of one of the princes, they'll have covered their tracks. Without Zaine's help, I'm not confident we'll ever figure out which arcanist is keeping the baron."

"You'll use her, then?" questioned Anne.

Rew shifted uncomfortably. "To save a life, if we must. You disapprove?"

Anne reached up and untied her hair. She held the binding in her hand for a moment. She admitted, "I'm not sure."

Rew nodded.

"Zaine needs something," said Anne. "There's a hurt in her that I cannot take away. This girl needs a purpose, something she can hold onto other than survival. She needs a family. If you do this, Rew, do not cast her aside. Do not use her and then leave her in Spinesend with no one around her." Anne paused, frowning, and then she added, "I will go with you, and when it's over, she can come back with me to the Oak & Ash."

"Anne, this will be too dangerous—"

"I'm going with you," said the empath.

The ranger grunted but did not respond. He stood and collected his weapons.

"Where are you going?" asked Anne.

"I need to tell Raif and Cinda that we have an idea where their father might be," he said. "I need to tell them that, and that they cannot go after him. Falvar needs them, and it's safer for them here." Rew strapped on his longsword. He added, "And once I've told them that, I'm going to go find that Balzac again."

Chapter Twenty-Four

❦

Rew walked at the head of two-score heavily armed soldiers. The men were wearing Baron Fedgley's colors, but for now, they were the ranger's men. Word had gotten out about him leading the defense of the city and battling the giant imps that Alsayer had released in the throne room. It'd earned him a certain notoriety, and Rew'd had no difficulty recruiting volunteers to run the thieves to ground.

They'd started at the brothel, and as expected, they hadn't found anyone there. Rew had found his cloak and Zaine's daggers. Jon's body was there, right where he'd slumped to the floor with the two crossbow quarrels in him. Rew left men to watch over the dead ranger until he could return. He would give Jon a proper ranger's burial, but not that night. Jon had earned it being done right, and when Rew could give the younger man his full attention, he would.

In addition to several thieves Rew had killed during his escape, they found the old guild leader's body. Axxon's throat had been slashed into a grisly red smile. Balzac's work, Rew was certain.

The thieves and their allies had fled in a panic, and it turned out it wasn't difficult to follow the trail. The locals around the brothel remembered when suddenly two-dozen scantily clad women went running through the street, hands clutching at diaphanous silk clothing, bits and pieces bouncing and flashing into view. The girls must have known too much to leave them in the brothel, and not even Balzac had the stomach to kill them all.

They followed the trail of gossiping men outside of the taverns and found the procession had rushed out the river gate toward the small settlement that sheltered at the foot of the Falvar Bridge. The settlement would be nearly empty that night, with most of its residents corralled and hiding behind the towering pale stone walls of the town. It was the perfect opportunity to confront the thieves and capture them before they slipped away.

Through the river gate, Rew led the soldiers, the stomping of their heavy feet echoing against the empty buildings ahead of them. It was two hours before midnight, and after the excitement of the day, most of Falvar was abed. As they reached the bridge settlement, Rew saw a few curtains pull back and shutters open as they marched by, but most of the windows remained dark. The citizens who had hidden out in the settlement instead of sheltering in the town stared agape at them, perhaps wondering if there was another attack, or if they would be forced from their homes into Falvar's protection.

Rew watched carefully, waiting until he saw one door open then immediately slam shut. The citizens would be watching to see what the soldiers were up to. The thieves would already know.

Rew pointed to the long, low building where he'd seen the movement, and shouted, "There!"

Behind him, the squad split into two groups, one circling around the back of the building, the other staying with Rew. He led the men to the front door of the building, which was made to look like a simple warehouse, and hammered his fist against the door. No one answered, which only confirmed his suspicion. Someone inside had peeked out the door, after all.

"Break it open," instructed Rew. "Don't rush in, though. Let me go first, and keep an eye out for traps."

A soldier stepped around him and hefted a giant maul. The man swung it back and forth a few times to build momentum and then smashed it against the door, blasting the heavy steel head of the weapon into the door handle where it'd be latched.

With a sharp crack and an explosion of wood and iron, the door burst open, and Rew jumped inside. It was dark, but he could see in the gloom that it was an open room with several hallways on the other side of it. Outside, it was made to look like a warehouse, but inside, it housed a secondary thieves' guild. In the half second he'd been in the dark room, his eyes began to adjust, and he saw several tables flipped onto their sides in the middle of the room. Behind them, a dozen thieves crouched, and the dim light gleamed on the steel heads of crossbow quarrels pointed right at the door.

"Crossbows!" shouted Rew before launching himself to the side.

He heard the crunch of metal as the armored soldiers tried to clear the doorway. Then, crossbow strings began to thump, and quarrels flew overhead. Rolling, Rew kept low and kept moving, hoping the thieves didn't have an angle on him over their tables.

Steel heads of the bolts smashed into the wall and whistled out the doorway, but he didn't hear any grunts or screams of men pierced by the flying metal and wood. The thieves had been waiting for more targets, but his warning had given the soldiers time to find cover.

Scrambling on hands and feet, Rew dodged around the room, crawling behind another table and flipping it on its side. The wood thundered as half a dozen bolts smacked into it. Splinters exploded around his face, but the quarrels stayed lodged in the table. He waited, listening to the clicks as new bolts were set and crossbows were cranked.

"They're coming in the back!" shouted a voice. "Run!"

"Where?" screamed another man. "They're already inside the front!"

Rew gripped the legs of the table he was crouched behind. Thinking it was perhaps a foolish plan, he surged off his knees, moving forward. Hefting the wooden table like a giant shield, he charged the thieves.

Another crossbow twanged, and the bolt blasted into the table, but Rew was completely hidden behind the bulky furniture, and no one had a line on him until he crashed into the thieves' own hiding spot. His table struck theirs, and he dropped it, offering a silent hope no one would be standing a few paces away from him aiming a deadly steel bolt right at his face. At such close range, he would be dead if they were. Over a constant stream of shouted curses, he heard the clatter of the soldiers rushing in behind him, and instead of firing at him, Rew found a dozen thieves were tossing their weapons down and holding up their hands.

One man, who must have recognized Rew from earlier in the day, called, "Ranger, we had nothing to do with the attack at the keep. It was Balzac. He did it all! He didn't tell none of us about it. We're innocent, honest."

Rew snorted. He thought the man might be telling the truth about Balzac keeping the attack secret, but the thief was as far from innocent and honest as one could get.

Rew demanded, "Where's Balzac now?"

"Back in the arms room," said the thief, evidently hoping his candor would earn him mercy. "Ranger, he's not going to go peacefully."

Rew nodded.

"Ranger," said one of the sergeants of the soldiers. "Shall we go root this man out?"

Rew shook his head. "I'll do it." He glanced at the thief. "Anything I should know?"

"Balzac keeps a small push dagger coated in poison up his left sleeve," said the man. "If he doesn't think he can stick you with it, he'll stick himself." The man pointed toward one of the hallways and said, "Third door on the right. There's a lotta blades in there, Ranger, and there's no way out."

Without responding, Rew started down the hallway and easily found the door the thief had referred to. He could see light bleeding out from the crack beneath the door, but over the sounds of the soldiers storming into the warehouse and capturing the thieves, he couldn't hear anything behind the barrier.

Rew reared back and smashed his boot into the door. With a crack, it burst open, and the ranger darted inside, intending to dive out of the way just like he had on entering the building, but he paused.

Standing in the center of the room, surrounded by racks of weapons, was Balzac. The thief, lit from behind by a single flickering lantern, grinned maniacally like some legendary conjuring from the demonic planes. In one hand, he held a cocked crossbow. It was pointed toward the door but not directly at Rew. In his other hand, he clutched a fist-sized glass orb that swirled with clouds trapped inside.

The thief crowed, "I was waiting on you, Ranger. I'm glad it is you who found us."

Rew frowned at the orb. "Is that…"

"It's a portal device," claimed Balzac, raising it high.

"I don't think it is," said Rew, taking a half-step back. He didn't recognize the orb, or the swirling mists contained within it, but it defied imagination that a thief in a backwater town in a backwater duchy would have access to a portal device. Rew had seen those before, and they were beyond rare. They also didn't look like a tempest in a sphere. "Where did you—"

"Your friend the spellcaster told me to use this as a last resort," snarled Balzac, gesturing with the orb and raising his crossbow menacingly. "He said it'd get me to safety no matter how many surrounded me. I suppose I should have used it already. That would have been the wiser choice, but I wanted to see your face. You ruined my plans, Ranger. I meant to rule the guild in Falvar, maybe Spinesend and the entire duchy by the time I was done. I was willing to do whatever it took, but I know that won't happen now."

Rew eyed the crossbow. "You mean to kill me and then run?"

Balzac snickered, his eyes gleaming madly. "No, Ranger, I mean for you to live. I want you to live knowing that I'm out there, coming for you and those you love. The baron's brats, the empath… I'll do them just like I did your apprentice and Axxon. Whoever else I can find, Ranger, I'm going to kill. You've ruined my plans, my life, and I will ruin yours. That's why I waited, to see the horror in your eyes, knowing there's no way you can protect them all, nothing you can do but wait for your loved ones to die."

Rew looked back at the thief, not responding. He watched the orb and saw the mists captured inside of it swirling. Finally, he advised, "That's no portal device, Thief."

"You nobles with your noble blood, thinking you know everything, treating us commoners like dirt," growled Balzac, his words snapping off like the crack of dead wood. "I can't make you all pay for what you've done to the world, but I can make you pay, Ranger."

"What are you talking about?" hissed Rew, gripping his longsword and calculating that he could reach the man before he aimed the crossbow and got off a shot, but that he couldn't stop Balzac from dropping the orb.

"I know your story, Ranger," said Balzac. "I know more than you think. The spellcaster told me all. You, him, everyone with your tainted blood, plotting and killing. It's disgusting!"

Rew cursed. Alsayer again. One day, he was going to have to do something about that man.

"Coming here to Falvar, claiming you're free of the Investiture," cried Balzac, shaking his head and laughing mirthlessly. "If you were free of it, how were you in the company of the girl and the boy? How were you the one to find us in Arcanist Ralcrist's tower? How did you confront the spellcaster in the throne room and then locate our guildhall? You're neck deep in it. I know you are. That spellcaster told me all of it, all about your foul plots! But you missed me, and you'll miss me again. How many of your friends will die because you failed your responsibilities this time, Ranger?"

The man raised the orb high, and Rew saw the tightly coiled clouds flashing orange and red, as if a storm raged within—or an inferno.

"Blessed Mother!" Rew shouted. "Do not throw that down!"

The thief swung his fist, and Rew backpedaled toward the door, shouting over his shoulder, screaming at the soldiers to flee.

"It's time for me to portal out of here!" cried the thief as he released the orb, holding the crossbow up to prevent Rew from attacking him.

Rew didn't wait for the orb to hit the floor. He sprinted out of the room, bellowing, "Run!" at the top of his lungs.

The soldiers whipped around and stared at him in shock as he barreled into the common room where they were still securing the thieves.

Rew screamed at them, "Out of the building, out of the building! Get out now!"

Perhaps it was his words, or maybe the panic in his eyes, but they turned and ran, both the baron's men and the thieves. Or, it could have been the incredible whoosh of air being drawn into the armory and the rib-rattling thump that resounded through the building as that air ignited.

Rew ran out the warehouse at full speed, soldiers and thieves racing around him in a wave. From the other side of the structure, he could hear panicked calls as soldiers fled from the other entrance. Rew hoped they were all getting out. If they weren't—

It sounded as if one of the lions of Carff was roaring behind them, a bestial, deep cry that sent a shiver down Rew's spine. A billow of flame exploded from the doorway and the windows of the warehouse, blasting wood and glass in a hail of shrapnel. The fire burst out, wrapping and consuming the wood of the structure like a hungry beast.

Rew skidded to a stop and spun to watch.

Many of the soldiers and thieves kept running, and he let them go. The soldiers would turn up later. The thieves might not, but they couldn't hold his attention right now. In moments, the entire warehouse was engulfed in brilliant, searing flame. Arms of fire snaked out the openings and curled around the outside of the structure, seeming to draw it into the belly of the blaze.

"What—What is that?" asked a soldier beside him.

"Fire elemental," mumbled Rew. "A conjuring, released from a... Released by accident by the leader of those thieves."

"Accident?" wondered the soldier, staring in awe at the raging inferno.

"The man certainly didn't expect this to happen," said Rew, holding up a hand to block the heat of the blaze from his face.

Shaking his head, he looked around and began directing some of the soldiers to guard the handful of thieves who hadn't fled, and then, he sent another contingent to circle the building and look for the other squad of men who had been covering the back. He told them the fire elemental would only consume the building it was released in but to move any flammable debris that was laying nearby. The debris wouldn't be ignited with the same frantic rage that the elemental unleashed on the building, but fire was fire, and anything that caught would burn.

By the time the fire brigade arrived from where they'd been sheltering in the town, there was little left for them to do. The warehouse was burned to the ground, but no other structures had caught fire. The soldiers had already removed loose crates and other combustibles from around the warehouse. The thieves were taken into custody, though no one knew what crime to charge them with, and in short time, Rew and the soldiers returned to the keep.

It was well after midnight when he walked out onto the battlement overlooking the town of Falvar. He could feel the pull from Mordenhold, and he could feel an even stronger desire to leave the town, to flee over the Spine and into the wilderness. He could slip away in the night and be gone from this place. In the weeks it would take him to return to Eastwatch, whatever would happen would happen, and he would be free of it. He—He would have to leave Anne behind.

He rubbed his hand over his hair, feeling the tight stubble and the slick smoothness from the ash that had landed on him from the burning warehouse. He looked down at his sooty hand. It was black in the night. Sighing, he turned to go back inside, to wash, and to sleep. It would take days to sort out the mess in Falvar, but the quicker he got started the next morning, the quicker it would be done. He would take those days to talk Anne into leaving Falvar behind them, and returning to Eastwatch where they belonged.

The next morning, an hour after dawn, Rew sat at a table in the throne room. It'd been brought in for an emergency council to meet, and he felt it rather uncomfortable, sitting in the huge open room where none of the servants and staff could miss their deliberations. They couldn't have made it more obvious that Falvar was in a panic, and the baron and his wife were both gone. Every time a servant poked their heads in, they could hear that the leaders of Falvar had no answers, no plan. No one had asked Rew, and he did not want to become even more entangled in Falvar's troubles than he already was. Soon, he would leave. As soon as he could convince Anne, he would leave.

Matters were already settling down, and experienced hands were back on the plow. Messengers had finally found Commander Broyce, and he'd traveled through the night to return to Falvar. In the hours before dawn, he'd taken control of the response in the keep and the recovery of the baron. Rew had only met the man briefly, but in that short time, he'd been impressed. Broyce was an experienced hand and loyal to the Fedgleys. He would be a good advisor to Raif and Cinda. The commander had also agreed to let Captain Gage's promotion stand and had instructed the captain to continue what he was doing out in the town. Evidently, the two men knew each other well, and both had a great deal of respect for the other. Rew took that as an excellent sign.

Rew had shared his thoughts with the men and gave what information he could. He'd made his suggestions and even acquiesced to sending a post to the king explaining what had happened, though he'd informed them the king was unlikely to respond. Unlikely to read the message, if it even made it into his hands, but they'd insisted. Rew felt that simply agreeing to their request was the easiest way to untangle himself from the affairs of Falvar and the Fedgleys.

Rew covered a yawn with a fist, half-listening to the others speak, and leaned forward to refresh his coffee. He'd woken four hours prior, well before dawn, to cart Jon's body outside of the city walls. Rew had found a quiet copse beside the river and buried the young ranger there in an unmarked grave beneath a shelter of beech trees. Jon, in his last moments, had proven himself worthy of the title of ranger. His woodcraft and skill with the blade could have used a bit of work, but when it had mattered, Jon's valor had been beyond compare. He'd committed himself and paid the ultimate price.

Sipping the steaming cup of coffee, Rew hoped Jon's sacrifice was worth it. Anne had been keeping a sharp eye on Zaine, and so far, the thief had not attempted to scuttle away, but she could be waiting for the right moment. If she helped the Fedgleys recover their father, then Rew thought Raif and Cinda would grant her leniency for her role in the conspiracy. If she didn't… Well, she would live what was left of her life as a fugitive and likely dangle from a rope when they caught her.

Rew reached to refill his coffee cup. Blessed Mother, he hoped Jon's sacrifice was worth it.

He glanced at Cinda out of the corner of his eye, around the gleaming silver pitchers that held the coffee and the piles of fruits and pastries the servants had placed around them. He was waiting for the girl to speak up, but she showed little of the fire that he'd learned to appreciate while they had been on the journey together. It seemed the shock of returning to Falvar after several years away and watching the bedrock of her life wash away beneath her was too much to bear. It was a lot, and it was tragic, but it was the Investiture. This was just the beginning.

"We must protect the town against the Dark Kind," insisted Captain Gage, drawing Rew's interest back to the conversation around the table. The captain was looking around at the other soldiers who'd joined the group. "There are still at least one hundred of them out in the grass lands, if not more."

"Aye, we need to protect the town, but I worry we're quickly going to lose the loyalty of these mercenaries Baron Fedgley brought on," said Commander Broyce, straightening his prodigious mustache and glancing at Cinda out of the corner of his eye. Evidently, he was waiting on her council as well. "If we send them out into the barrowlands to face the Dark Kind, we might lose them."

"Lose them?" questioned Gage.

"They work for coin and nothing else," reminded the commander. "They've no loyalty to Falvar. With the baron gone, I've heard rumblings that some of them are already nervous about how long we'll keep paying. Truth be told, I wonder that myself. Falvar's resources are spread thin, and these men are a significant drain on the baron's treasury. If it wasn't for the threat of the Dark Kind and the baron's situation, I'd say we don't need them. But as it is…"

Frowning, Captain Gage snatched a pastry and sat back. Rew saw him glancing surreptitiously at Cinda as well, but the girl remained quiet, letting the men discuss the future of her family's barony without her input.

A young arcanist, Ralcrist's apprentice Rew had heard, suggested, "What of a letter to Duke Eeron? If we let him know we're undermanned and that we've Dark Kind to worry about, he'll, ah… We suspect the baron is somewhere in Spinesend, did you say?"

"Of course, we send a letter to Duke Eeron!" exclaimed Captain Gage, raising his pastry in the air. "All we need to do is explain the situation, and… You don't think he knows what his arcanist is up to, do you?"

Hopeful eyes turned to Rew, and he met their looks with a scowl.

"What is it, Ranger?" asked Commander Broyce. "What do you advise?"

"There's more to this than a duke's arcanist abducting a baron," responded Rew. "I can't tell you if Duke Eeron knows what's happening or not, but either way, the duke is not who you should be concerned with."

"I don't understand," responded Captain Gage.

"Whether or not Duke Eeron is aware of his arcanist's actions, that arcanist is not the man behind the curtain. This conspiracy does not end with anyone in Spinesend," declared Rew. Around the table, the other men stared back at him in confusion. "One of the princes is behind this. I am sure of it. There's nothing we can do."

"I don't understand," said Commander Broyce. "What are you suggesting?"

"I'm suggesting that Baron Fedgley is lost, at least for now," said Rew. He glanced at Cinda apologetically. "His children and the people of Falvar should be your priority, and their safety is far from assured. Gage is right, there are still Dark Kind out in the barrowlands. I suggest you fortify the town, and then, send out patrols of loyal men to track down the surviving narjags. They should be easy enough to follow. Handle them before the next payment is due to the mercenaries. If the mercenaries don't have to risk their own necks out in the barrowlands, they'll be content to wait for that payment before they vanish. When the narjags are dealt with, that will put the townspeople at ease, and normal life can resume for a time. You'll need more guards around Cinda and her brother, of course—"

"Wait," said Cinda, suddenly snapping out of her malaise. "Are you recommending we do nothing to recover my father?"

Rew looked at her but did not respond.

"You have to do something!" insisted Cinda, standing suddenly, clenching her hands into fists at her side. She pointed a finger at the ranger. "You have to!"

"I don't have to do anything," replied Rew. "I am the King's Ranger for the eastern territory. The squabbles of nobles, the whirlpool around the Investiture, they are not my concern. I understand you want to get your father back, but what would you do? You don't have enough men to face Duke Eeron's forces, even if you convinced the mercenaries to join you and you were willing to leave Falvar undefended. You don't have the leverage to negotiate your father's release, assuming you could figure out who to negotiate with. You don't have the connections to try subterfuge or to enact a rescue mission. You are the most powerful spellcaster in Falvar, and I am sorry, lass, but I've never actually seen you cast a spell. But all of that is irrelevant because Duke Eeron is not your real enemy. It is the princes you should fear. They have your father, and I don't mean to scare you, Cinda, but they are going to come for you next!"

Cinda glared back at the ranger.

"During the Investiture, all is at risk," continued Rew. "You have to avoid it as best as you can, protect what you can. Right now, you can protect Falvar and the people who reside here. You can protect your family's seat and their legacy. You might be able to protect yourself. But if you're pulled into the maelstrom of the Investiture, all of that may be lost. Not just you, Cinda. It is not only your own life you risk. It is everyone in this room and in this town."

"What is Falvar without my father?" asked Cinda. "What are any of our lives worth if his is worth nothing?"

Rew met her eyes and shook his head. She was not ready to

see with clear vision. She didn't understand what forces were at play, how deep the machinations of the princes went. He didn't know how to convince her, to explain to her the risks.

So instead, Rew offered, "Your father was taken, not killed. Alsayer, whatever his plans, went to a great deal of trouble to keep Baron Fedgley alive. There is still hope for your father, but help must come from another quarter. For now, you must guard what you can. Look out for yourself. Look out for your people."

"My sister is in Spinesend," said Cinda. "She has connections there and can help recover my father. Or, if you are right and there's nothing she can do, then we must warn her and bring her back to Falvar."

Rew sat back and crossed his arms over his body.

"What?" demanded Cinda. "You'd have us abandon my sister as well?"

"Your sister is right under their noses," said Rew. "They have not forgotten her, Cinda. By the time you get a message to her… It's dangerous, warning her. As long as she's ignorant, no one has a reason to harm her. If she knows and tries to come here, they will."

Cinda looked away.

"Lady Cinda," said Commander Broyce, "we can begin fortifying the town today. That's common sense, no matter what else we do. We can follow the tracks of the Dark Kind on horseback and scout their location without engaging them. We can do these things today, and they will help Falvar. What we do about your father… we do not have to decide this morning. Let us begin our work around the town while we formulate a plan for the baron. In tomorrow's council, we'll know more, and we'll have better direction. I am not suggesting we ignore the peril the baron is in, but the ranger is correct. The people of Falvar are at risk as well. While we strategize, let us protect them."

"You're right, Commander Broyce," said Cinda, drawing herself up. "Let's do that. We'll begin repairs of the gate today, and… the rest of it. You men know what to do. Tomorrow, we'll make plans to free my father. And do not think to put me off, Commander Broyce. We will secure Falvar first, but I will not forget my father. All of you, understand, he is my family, and I will do whatever it takes to get him back."

"Would your brother like to be appraised of the military matters?" asked Commander Broyce. "I was told he's become quite the fighter while in Yarrow. I respect your council, Lady Cinda, but it is Raif who is the heir. While your father is gone, he should take command, and while I've no doubt he will agree with your decisions, he should be involved in arriving at them. I know he is recovering from the magical attack yesterday, but I would like to keep him informed, at least. Do you think he's well enough for visitors this morning?"

"Yes, of course…" said Cinda, looking around, brushing her hair back over her ears.

Rew frowned. It was an hour past daybreak. Not late, exactly, but there was much to do. Was Raif taking that much longer to recover from his injuries than his sister? Anne was up to her elbows in the injured from the fight at the gate the day before, but it was more important that Raif survive. If the boy was in danger, surely the empath would have said something about it.

Rew stood. "Has anyone checked on the lad this morning?"

Cinda called over a servant and instructed, "Go find my brother. Tell him he's needed in council. If he's unable to attend, I will go to him."

"Of course, m'lady," said the woman, bowing and backing away. The servant's face was clouded with worry, but she hurried to perform her task.

Cinda turned to the others and said, "He took the attack yesterday worse than I did. Both the physical strike from the spellcaster and our father's kidnapping. When the ranger told us our father had been taken to Spinesend, Raif was mad with rage. I worry he may have exacerbated his injuries from the fight yesterday."

The military men nodded. They'd seen the wreckage that

Alsayer had wrought in the throne room, and it took little to imagine the torment it would be to absorb one of his strikes.

They waited patiently, the men taking bites of the breads and meats that had been provided to break their fast, sipping their coffees. No one spoke. Cinda sat silently, staring up at the dais where her parents had held court. The chairs had been damaged from the battle the day before and carried away for repair. There were deep scores on the stone walls where Alsayer's attacks had landed. The staff had done what they could to clean the room, but the broken stone would take weeks for masons to replace. Another reason not to have the council meetings in the room, thought Rew, but things were tense enough without him questioning that decision.

"My father's greatsword," asked Cinda, "was it damaged in the fighting yesterday?"

"I don't know," responded Commander Broyce, glancing toward the dais where the greatsword normally hung beneath House Fedgley's banners. "It looks naked up there, doesn't it, without the thrones and that legendary blade. It's enchanted, you know? I would have thought it'd take more than a stray... Ah, I don't know. Perhaps high magic could damage even a weapon such as that?"

Rew stood and walked toward the dais. Behind him, he heard Cinda calling over another servant to inquire about the missing sword. Rew walked up to the dais and looked at the empty hooks. There was no scarring on the wall, nothing to imply a stray bolt of energy had struck the weapon. He looked down and saw a stool. It was high enough that a tall man—

The servant Cinda had sent for her brother returned. "He's not in his rooms, m'lady. I've asked the footmen to check outside for him."

"Check the baths as well," said Commander Broyce, gesturing with his coffee cup. "After yesterday, we could all use a good soak. The walls, too. Maybe he went to look out over the town or the barrowlands. He's the eldest Fedgley in the city, now. He'll feel responsible for those people and those lands, but for now, his time is best spent in this council. I'll talk to him."

Rew, standing in the blank space where the thrones had sat, saw Cinda. She looked confused. It wasn't in Raif's nature to shirk from a challenge or a difficult fight. The boy was a true-born warrior. Rew rubbed a hand over his head and turned back to the bare wall where the family's enchanted greatsword had hung. It was the sword Raif's ancestors had carried when they'd won the barony. They'd all been fighters, then. Raif had wanted to earn his share of greatness with the blade, to prove his worth to his father, to reclaim…

Rew glanced back at Cinda, and as their eyes met, he groaned. "Blessed Mother. The lad has left."

The sun hung low on the horizon, blazing vibrant red and orange, casting its light on the pale stone of Falvar and the jagged spires of the Spine in the distance. Lit by the falling sun, it looked like the mountains and the buildings were cast in flame—an echo of the fire and blood that had scarred Falvar the day before.

Rew, Anne, Cinda and Zaine walked from the town to the quiet settlement at the foot of the Falvar bridge. The doors of the hovels were all shut tight now, the shopkeepers who'd held out after the attack by the narjags finally fleeing to the safety of Falvar's walls when word of a fire elemental in their midst had spread. Rew wasn't sure how long it would take them to return, or how they would overcome the disruption to their lives, but he hoped they gave it time. The elemental was gone, burnt out, but the narjags still roamed the barrowlands.

It was a terrible disruption these people faced, but he wondered, perhaps it wasn't such an awful bargain. The trials and deaths of the nobles meant little to the chandler or the tanner. None from the settlement at the foot of the bridge had been killed in the attack by the narjags or the inferno that had raged through the thieves' hideout. Maybe it was only a few days that they would need to crouch behind the walls of Falvar. Then, they could return to their lives, unconcerned with the pain their leaders still faced. Rew hoped it was that way, that the impending devastation the nobles wrought in pursuit of the throne and the power that flowed from it would only strike their own. Rew offered a prayer to the Blessed Mother that it would be so, that the common people, the innocents, would hardly notice what was coming.

But he didn't think that would be the case.

Rew led the party up the steep slope of the Falvar Bridge, and they turned around, looking back over the small settlement at its foot beside the river and to the walled city beyond. Water bubbled below them, rushing through the narrow banks beside the village and heading far away from that place. The hovels and warehouses by the river were empty, the gates of the town closed, the people huddled inside to wait out the coming night. Above the keep hung the banner of the Fedgleys, but it was Commander Broyce who was running Falvar now. He would be in charge until a Fedgley was able to return.

Rew sighed. If a Fedgley was able to return. The moment they'd realized that Raif had fled, Cinda had run from the throne room, ignoring Rew, ignoring her advisors. She'd left the keep and gone straight to the makeshift hospital that was setup for the wounded soldiers. Cinda had gone to Anne, and Anne had gone to Rew.

He closed his eyes, blocking out the image of Falvar shaded in orange and red. Cinda had known he couldn't say no to Anne.

"How far to Spinesend?" asked Cinda, interrupting his grim thoughts. "A little less than a week?"

"A little less than a week," confirmed Rew.

"It doesn't feel like home," said Cinda, staring at Falvar.

"You were living in Yarrow for several years before you returned here," said Rew.

"And my family is gone," said Cinda. "Our banner is there.

Our soldiers are there, but this is no longer our place. In the ways that matter, it is no longer ours."

Rew shrugged and did not respond.

"We will find your brother," assured Anne, coming to stand beside them. "He has a head start on us, and he's young and full of spirit, but he cannot outrun the King's Ranger."

Cinda looked at him, and Rew nodded. Alone, he could run the boy down in a day or less, but the others couldn't keep his pace. They were going to slow him down, but in the time they had before Spinesend, he was confident they would find the boy. If all went to plan, they would catch him before he went too far and got himself into real trouble.

"After we find him?" asked Cinda.

"I don't know," said Rew, turning from Falvar and walking away.

Cinda looked to Zaine, who was leaning against the guardrail of the bridge. "You can identify the man that has my father?"

"I know I can," said Zaine, turning her back to the town as well and falling into Rew's footsteps. "Cinda, whatever I can do to help, I will. I know much of this is my… I will help however I can. It's the right thing to do."

"Yes, it is," agreed Cinda, her soft footfalls stalking Rew down the other side of the bridge.

"Spinesend is not safe for you, lass," he told her. "The Investiture has begun. Your father was drawn in because of his blood, and they'll want yours as well. You should drop this and find somewhere safe, and when it is done, you pick up the pieces."

Cinda laughed mirthlessly. "Somewhere safe to hide, Ranger? There is nowhere safe, nowhere to hide. You know that better than any of us, don't you?"

Rew glanced over his shoulder at the party that trailed behind him. A noblewoman and a spellcaster. An innkeeper and an empath. An orphan and a thief. The King's Ranger.

He sighed and turned back to the road. "Come on. We've a long way to go."

Thanks for reading!

K eep reading for a sneak peek of **The Ranger's Path: The King's Ranger Book 2**!

My biggest thanks to the readers! If it wasn't for you, I wouldn't be doing this. Those of you who enjoyed **The King's Ranger**, I can always use a good review, or even better, tell a friend.

My eternal gratitude to: Felix Ortiz for the breath-taking cover and social media illustrations. Shawn T King for his incredible graphic design. Kellerica for inking this world into reality. Nicole Zoltack coming back yet again as my long-suffering proofreader, joined this round by Anthony Holabird for the final polish. And of course, I'm honored to continue working with living legend Simon Vance on the audio. When you read my words, I hope it's in his voice.

Terrible 10… you know.

Thanks again, and hope to hear from you!
AC

To check out my other books (I have a lot), find larger versions of the maps, series artwork, my newsletter, and other goodies go to accobble.com.

Want more? **The Ranger's Path: The King's Ranger Book 2** is out now. I've included a sneak peek, so keep flipping!